"The adventure of THE SWORD OF LYRIC lives on in *The Restorer's Son*. The pages seemed to turn themselves as I entered a world of peril and wonder, despair and hope, doubt and fear. Sharon Hinck's masterful storytelling demonstrates why Christian fiction is such a blessing—at the same time I was thoroughly entertained, I was also inspired and challenged. Once again, I loved *The Restorer's Son* and can't wait for the next one."

—KATHRYN MACKEL, author of *Vanished*

"A triumph! In this new series, Hinck not only has blended God's might with her imagination but also gives readers insight into the power of praise and the Word of God. While turning the pages of these books night after night, I often found myself pausing to pray and repeat the songs and verses of the people of the clans, the people of the verses. On more than one occasion, I paused to consider the 'poisons' affecting my own mind. There's also enough action for all the guys and tender family moments for the moms. These are great reads for the entire family. I can't wait for the next one."

—MARILYNN GRIFFITH, author of *Turquoise*
and *If the Shoe Fits*

"Sharon Hinck has the ability to transform mere words into surprising turns of phrase and poetry, hiding nuggets of truth in unexpected places."

—HANNAH ALEXANDER, author of *Grave Risk*
and *Death Benefits*

"I loved this book! Sharon Hinck takes the meaning of being 'a sojourner in this world but not of it' to a new dimension. Our heroine returns to Lyric with one goal: finding her son. The new Restorer has one goal: avoiding his calling. Both ask honest questions that plague most Christians in their walk with an all-powerful, all-knowing God. And the answers come in unexpected ways that satisfy the reader's thirst for knowing God."

—DONITA K. PAUL, author of *DragonSpell*,
DragonQuest, *DragonKnight*, and *DragonFire*

"*The Restorer's Son* drew me in to a world so real, an adventure so exciting, a story so beautifully told that I couldn't turn the pages fast enough. I didn't want it to end! I highly recommend this book to anyone who loves energetic tales of valor and courage and Truth."

—VIRGINIA SMITH, *Murder by Mushroom*
and *Bluegrass Peril*

"I've just returned from the world of Lyric, and I'm dazzled and amazed! Sharon Hinck's powerful and inventive tale grips you from page one and doesn't let go. Her characters are made of flesh and blood and human emotion. Her writing crackles with imagination and energy, and there is a spiritual core of truth to *The Restorer's Son* that transcends the realm of fantasy. Enter the world of Lyric and see what I mean."

—JIM DENNEY, author of the TIMEBENDERS series
and *Answers to Satisfy the Soul*

"Hinck takes readers on another breath-stealing adventure, salted with humor, grace, and pathos. Her unique style blends the familiar with the fantastic to produce a riveting read that strikes to the heart of our human frailty and our potential for greatness in God. Even people who don't usually read fantasy can find a new favorite author here!"

—JILL ELIZABETH NELSON, author of the
TO CATCH A THIEF series

"*The Restorer's Son* is fantasy at its best: intriguing plot and characters that touch your heart. Even readers who prefer mom-lit or women's fiction will find this an enjoyable read."

—MEREDITH EFKEN, author of the mom-lit comedy
SAHM I Am

"Because of Sharon Hinck, I have fallen in love with a new genre. I admit, the idea of a soccer mom transporting to another world raised my eyebrows, but I had no idea I'd also be transported from my sofa to face epic battles of good and evil, discover people I fell in love with, and find a latent desire to handle a sword! Most of all, *The Restorer* and *The Restorer's Son* encouraged my own spiritual walk, and I returned from the journey a warrior, ready to sing the Verses! The Sword of Lyric series is exactly what Christian fiction should be. Bravo, bravo . . . and more, please!"

—SUSAN MAY WARREN, brand-new fantasy aficionado;
award-winning author of *Reclaiming Nick*

Also by Sharon Hinck:

THE SWORD OF LYRIC
The Restorer (NavPress)

The Secret Life of Becky Miller (Bethany House)
Renovating Becky Miller (Bethany House)

The RESTORER'S SON

THE SWORD OF LYRIC

2

SHARON HINCK

NAVPRESS®

OUR GUARANTEE TO YOU

We believe so strongly in the message of our books that we are making this quality guarantee to you. If for any reason you are disappointed with the content of this book, return the title page to us with your name and address and we will refund to you the list price of the book. To help us serve you better, please briefly describe why you were disappointed. Mail your refund request to: NavPress, P.O. Box 35002, Colorado Springs, CO 80935.

NavPress
P.O. Box 35001
Colorado Springs, Colorado 80935

NAVPRESS, BRINGING TRUTH TO LIFE, and the NAVPRESS logo are registered trademarks of NavPress. Absence of ® in connection with marks of NavPress or other parties does not indicate an absence of registration of those marks.

ISBN-13: 978-1-60006-132-5
ISBN-10: 1-60006-132-X

Cover design by Kirk DouPonce, DogEaredDesign.com
Cover images by istock
Author photo by Ritz Camera Proex Portraits

Creative Team: Jeff Gerke, Reagen Reed, Mary Johansen, Arvid Wallen, Pat Reinheimer, Kathy Guist

This novel is a work of fiction. Names, characters, places, and incidents are either the product of the author's imagination or are used fictitiously. Any resemblance to actual events, locales, organizations, or persons, living or dead, is entirely coincidental and beyond the intent of either the author or publisher.

Scripture versions used include the HOLY BIBLE: NEW INTERNATIONAL VERSION® (NIV®). Copyright © 1973, 1978, 1984 by International Bible Society. Used by permission of Zondervan Publishing House. All rights reserved.

Published in association with the literary agency of The Steve Laube Agency, LLC, 5501 N. 7th. Ave., #502, Phoenix, AZ 85013.

Hinck, Sharon.
  The restorer's son : a novel / Sharon Hinck.
    p. cm. -- (The sword of lyric ; 2)
  ISBN-13: 978-1-60006-132-5
  ISBN-10: 1-60006-132-X
  I. Title.
  PS3608.I53R48 2007
  813'.6--dc22

                              2007015672

Printed in the United States of America

1 2 3 4 5 6 7 8 9 10 / 10 09 08 07

FOR A FREE CATALOG OF NAVPRESS BOOKS & BIBLE STUDIES,
CALL 1-800-366-7788 (USA) OR 1-800-839-4769 (CANADA).

to those who wrestle with the One

"In every time of great need, a Restorer is sent to fight for the people and help the guardians. The Restorer is empowered with gifts to defeat our enemies and turn the people's hearts back to the Verses."

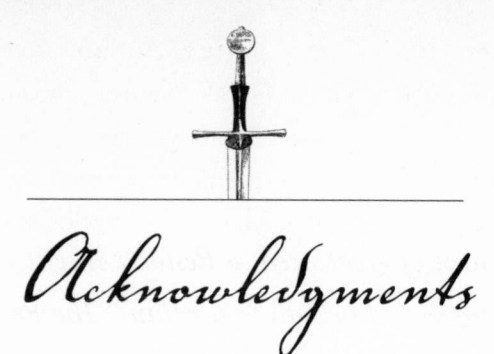

Acknowledgments

This book exists in large part because of the efforts of my "Book Buddies." Their prayers and encouragement kept me going. If you'd like to join their number, sign up for the Book Buddy monthly e-zine at www.sharonhinck.com.

The "Church Ladies" also held me up in myriad ways. Marijo, Vicki, Sue B., Becky, Marci, Sue H., Kelli, and Denise, thank you for your listening ears, warm hugs, and wisdom. And huge thanks to everyone at St. Michael's who models for me what serving Jesus is all about.

The amazing team at NavPress put muscle behind the dream, filling vital roles in the complex job of releasing a book. Special thanks to Reagen Reed, who cares about my characters as much as I do and fights with passion to make every word shine.

My agent, Steve Laube, has guided me to the high road each time the path splits. Thank you for your integrity and wisdom.

The writing community has gifted me with a wealth of dear friends. I give my deep gratitude to colleagues from Word Servants, Mount Hermon Christian Writers Conference, American Christian Fiction Writers, The Writer's View, Christian

Sci-Fi/Fantasy Blog Tour, Christian Authors Network, and Minnesota Christian Writers Guild. I've seen some of the dearest and best of the heart of Jesus amongst you. Please insert your name here and know you're written on my heart. Special thanks to Judy, Kelli, Patti, Claudia, Mary, Amy, Becky, and Jeannette for frequent talks, prayers, and encouragement.

Critique partners, Sherri Sand, Camy Tang, and Jill Nelson gave great insights to the development of this story, as did other critiquers and early readers Kristin Melendez, Nancy and Sarah Muyskens, Deb and Ian Kellogg, Vicki, Jon, and Kelly Lorton, Margaret Montreuil, Nancy Brown, Chawna Schroeder, Carol Oyanagi, and Bill and Cheryl Bader.

Flossie and Carl Marxen, thank you for your persistent faith in me.

Joel, Jennelle, Kaeti, Josh, and Jenni, you each make my heart sing.

Ted, you are the hero in all my stories. I thank God every day that we get to share life's adventures.

My deepest gratitude goes to the One who called me on this journey and has been faithful to reveal Himself as my Father—even when I shake a sword at the sky and demand answers. Through Your Son, Jesus, You have truly restored my soul.

Chapter One

KIERAN

"Hills of Hazor take you," I swore for at least the tenth time since first light. My sword hacked at thick underbrush, but when I shouldered my way forward, a twig snapped back to hit my face. I cursed the day I'd met the last Restorer. It was because of her that I was battling through this forsaken forest below Cauldron Falls. My blade deserved a more substantial enemy.

A squint-eyed badger rambled out from a thornbush and paused to sniff the air. It bristled and ducked back under cover. Wise plan. I was hungry. Stinging beetles landed on me from the low-hanging branches overhead. I swatted them away and stalked onward.

Why hadn't I convinced Tristan to leave her in Shamgar when she first turned up? A witness to his crime, and he had brought her to our refuge in the deserted city. Typical. He was a naïve idiot sometimes.

She hadn't looked very threatening that day—rain-soaked, bloody, and unconscious. If only I'd known then how much trouble she was capable of causing. What was that old saying? Don't judge a rizzid's menace until you see its teeth.

The trouble had started when a deep scrape on her face healed. Instantly. Hairs on my neck pricked as if I'd touched a misaligned magchip. I'd heard the old stories, but I'd never seen it happen. It had been years since our people had chased after a mythic Restorer, but I knew the signs.

Exactly the kind of problem we hadn't needed. We would have been in enough danger if she were just a Council spy or some other enemy. But as I had watched her wounds vanish, I knew that if she also had Restorer powers, things were going to get very complicated.

And they did. I circled the trunk of a large spice tree and stopped. My hearing had grown unnaturally keen in the past days—keen enough, I hoped, to warn me if there were any Kahlareans nearby. Cauldron Falls roared in the distance, and a few animals rustled in the damp leaves of the forest floor. Guardians from our clans patrolled the river below the falls. I should be able to hear or see some sign of them.

I frowned. Nothing.

I pulled another beetle off my arm and ground it under my heel, then pushed through a clump of bracken and caught a glimpse of the river. Water crashed from the hundred-foot falls and swirled in an angry mass at the base. Over the years the rocks had worn into a rounded bowl, earning the name Cauldron Falls. I hiked along the river's edge, picking my way over the boulders and scanning the opposite bank. The river surged, wide and rough, a natural barrier to protect our lands. Unhappily, upstream from the falls, the river narrowed and a gap cut between steep rock cliffs. The pass provided a natural pathway into our lands.

The trail to the top of the falls rose steeply. I sheathed my sword and grabbed the rocks to pull myself up. A few stones dislodged beneath my boots and crashed down behind me. I climbed faster. This was a bad spot to be caught by an enemy.

The river border used to be easy to guard, but lately our patrols were in danger from syncbeams—long-range weapons the Kahlareans used from cover on their side of the river. Tristan was worried about an invasion, so I agreed to check things out. He probably figured my trip here would follow some historic precedent because a past Restorer gave his life fighting off two hundred Kahlareans at Cauldron Falls. Tristan liked traditions.

When I reached the top of the falls, I settled on a boulder, pulled out my gourd of orberry juice, and savored the loneliness. At my feet the water rushed by, violent and unpredictable, and I knew an instant kinship with the river.

The past few days had honed my irritation to a fine edge. After Susan and Markkel disappeared, Tristan begged me to present myself to the Council and inform them that I was the Restorer. I refused. He nagged. I snarled. Then he fought dirty. He sent my sister, Kendra, to talk to me. They'd been wearing me down. When I overheard Tristan talking about his concerns for the River Borders, I jumped at the excuse to leave. I couldn't stand any more of their earnest trust in me. The look of hope in their faces. The expectations I could never fulfill. Spare me from Braide Wood's overgrown reverence for the old myths. I wasn't the Restorer they looked for. It was a cosmic joke—a worse joke than the last Restorer had been. Susan of Ridgeview Drive, she called herself. No clan I'd ever heard of.

I pushed myself back to my feet and headed upstream. With luck I'd reach the outpost before the afternoon rains. The sky pressed low in the flat gray tones of midday. The air was warmer than in Braide Wood, and my tunic soon clung to the sweat on my skin. I knelt by the river's edge to splash cold water on my face, rub dirt from the stubble on my jaw, and rake some sticks and leaves from my hair. My black hair had always marked my status as an outsider. Even as a child I'd refused to hide my Hazorite blood. Instead I made the folk of Braide Wood even more uncomfortable by cropping my hair short, like the enemy Hazorites. It would have been impossible to hide anyway. Both Kendra and I took after our mother and had the thin frames and angled cheekbones of her heritage.

I straightened up and inhaled deeply, taking in the smell of pine and the tangy bite of the golden spice trees. The non-stop roar of rushing water muted my chafing thoughts, and some of the knots in my back loosened. I rubbed the back of my neck. The cave where I slept last night had an uneven rock floor. I could have stayed in Rendor's central city but decided I'd rather take my chances with the scavengers and bears than make conversation.

I adjusted my pack, shifting the weight to a more comfortable spot on my shoulders, and scanned the opposite shoreline for any sign of movement. With a little concentration, I could see small details from miles away, one of the few advantages of being the Restorer. A red-furred rizzid sunned on the rocks of the far bank, but I didn't spot any human enemies. I made a point to study the tree line closely. Kahlarean assassins were notorious for being nearly invisible in their hooded masks and mottled gray clothes. They would be a far greater danger than an average Kahlarean soldier, even one armed with a syncbeam.

I'd fought their assassins twice now and hadn't come off well either time. I suppose simply surviving an encounter with them should be considered a success—though I'm not sure my last experience counted as surviving. They were swift and silent, and even a scratch from their venblades caused fatal paralysis. And—my stomach knotted like a three-peg weaving at the thought—the Kahlareans were obsessed with killing the Restorer. I wasn't eager for *anyone* to find out I was the new Restorer, least of all the people who still held a grudge against Mikkel, the Restorer who saved our people from Kahlarean attack a generation ago.

With a deep breath and another scan of the area, I continued upriver at a quicker pace.

The foul smell in the air was my first warning that something very bad had happened. I edged my way toward the outpost, waiting to be challenged by one of the handful of guardians assigned this patrol. Although some were young, the guardians tended to be fairly well trained and should have been watching their perimeter. A droning sound buzzed through the air as I drew closer to the clearing near the pass. Using a large tree for cover, I peered into the open area. Three men sprawled on the ground in front of the outpost's hut. The low hum was caused by swarms of insects feasting on their dead bodies.

I ran forward and crouched by one of the still forms. No need to look for signs of life. They'd been dead several days. All three showed the charred marks of syncbeam blasts. One boy hadn't even had a chance to draw his sword.

Kahlareans. How many had slipped through the pass after killing the guardians? Was this the first wave of a full-fledged invasion, or were they clearing the way for another small group of assassins to make their way toward Lyric, hunting the Restorer?

Crunching footsteps startled me. I stood and swiveled my head, but too late. Three Kahlarean soldiers entered the clearing. I took a few slow steps back, thinking fast.

"You're late," one of the men growled. Like most Kahlareans, his huge black eyes and sunken chin reminded me of a cave insect. His skin was the unnatural white of a corpse. These soldiers weren't hooded or masked, and they'd stopped long enough to talk, so they weren't assassins. So far, so good.

I shrugged. "Look's like there's been some trouble."

The soldier laughed. "No trouble at all, thanks to your syncbeams. So where is the next delivery?"

I rubbed my jaw. The Kahlareans had gotten their syncbeams from Hazor—from Hazorites with short black hair and angled features. I could work with that.

"Well, there's been a problem." I stalled, scrambling for inspiration. I could pretend to be from Hazor, but I couldn't produce a nonexistent delivery of syncbeams.

The soldier drew his sword and stepped closer. My hand tightened over my hilt, but I didn't draw.

"We don't have time for games." He kicked one of the bodies. "They could be sending reinforcements anytime."

Show no fear. Show no repulsion. I decided to try for irritation. "Don't you get any news out here? Our armies took a beating at Morsal Plains. Hundreds of our own syncbeams were destroyed. We don't have any to spare right now."

The soldier tilted his head and rolled his bulbous eyes in my direction. "Then what are you doing here?"

"Just making a friendly visit to let you know we're working on it. I can set up a new delivery time and take word back to Sidian in Hazor."

The Kahlarean shook his head. "Too risky. We're across now. Who knows how many more guardians will be sent here in a few days' time."

I shrugged. Not my problem.

The Kahlarean stepped closer and grabbed the front of my

tunic, his sword close enough to my belt to force me to suck in my stomach. It had just become my problem.

I lifted my hands away from my sword. "Relax. I'm sure we can work something out."

"I'll tell you what we'll work out," said the soldier. "You'll escort a group of us back to Corros Hills right now to collect the delivery."

I laughed but regretted it when he twisted the fistful of tunic under my neck, all but cutting off my air.

"You can't travel through the clans," I said. "You'd be spotted the first time we tried to use a transport. And if we cut cross-country, it would take half a season."

"Not us," he said. "Them." He let go of me, and I stumbled back. Three figures had melted into the clearing. They wore gray hoods, and their faces were covered with cloth masks. Assassins.

Caradung, I cursed silently.

"Them?" I said. "Why would they want to go on a trade mission?" Even a weapons trader from Hazor would know that Kahlarean assassins were an elite group. They were the villains in the tales told around glowing heat trivets on cold nights—with good reason.

The soldier grinned. "They have a few things to take care of on the way, but that doesn't need to concern you. They'll have no trouble blending in. You"—he jabbed a fat finger into my chest—"get them to Corros."

This would be a great time for some special Restorer vision to give me a plan. I wasted a few seconds waiting. Nothing. I shifted my gaze from the assassins back to the soldier.

I could draw my sword. I might have a chance against the three soldiers, but how many heartbeats would it take for an assassin's dagger to fly through the air and lodge in my chest? I'd recover, but that would be even worse. Then they'd know exactly what I was. I shrugged and willed my coiled muscles to relax.

"All right. If they can keep up. I don't have time to waste in the clan territories."

The tallest of the three assassins walked toward me on feet that didn't make a sound. His large eyes looked into mine.

I hoped that with all their other talents they couldn't read minds.

Finally, he nodded once.

I started breathing again while sweat ran down my back. "When do you want to leave?"

The two other assassins looked at each other. The tall one in front of me gestured with his arm toward the edge of the clearing. I caught a glimpse of metal strapped to his wrist when his sleeve moved. A venblade. One of a host of silent and hidden weapons I knew he carried.

I needed to get word to Tristan about the outpost attack. I needed to get as far from these assassins as I could. I needed a drink—something stronger than orberry juice.

Instead I turned and led the way into the woods, my skin crawling at the thought of the three silent figures following me.

Chapter Two

KIERAN

I tried to think like a Hazorite arms dealer. Not too difficult. I'd made enough secret trips into Hazor in the past few years to slip into the role. "We can't approach Rendor. Too many people. Too exposed." I had to glance over my shoulder to be sure the Kahlareans were still behind me; they moved liked ghosts.

Their leader simply nodded once. Not much for small talk, this bunch. Fine with me. Less interruption while I plotted how to lose them.

We cut through the forest toward a remote station where we could board a transport with a series of connections through central clans on our way to Shamgar. From there we could cross over the clay fields into Hazor. Less populated than the borders by Corros Fields and closer than the mountainous frontiers near Braide Wood.

We reached the first station at nightfall, just as the automated transport pulled in and powered down. Because the station was deserted, we set up a camp under the overhang at the side of the road. The assassins exchanged a few whispered words and divided the night watch, frustrating my plan to slip away while they slept.

I unbelted my sword and placed it close to hand, then wrapped up in my cloak and lay down, using my pack for a pillow. My fingers skimmed over the cracked leather of my baldric beside me. My second best. I'd given my good one to Susan. Resentful thoughts pulled at my mind, and as the sky turned black, I gave them free rein.

This new trouble was all because of her. Not that she would admit it. Her voice echoed in my mind: *It's not my fault. I didn't ask the One to make you the next Restorer.* Maybe. But she was way too familiar with the One. She seemed to get uncanny messages from Him. And if I didn't have her to blame, the only other place I could direct my anger was at the One.

I shot a glare toward the dark sky. I'd tried to set Him straight that first night. Even now my stomach twisted when I remembered that encounter. I'd fight off a hundred Kahlareans with venblades before I'd go through that again. A presence had drawn close to me with a power and intelligence beyond anything I could comprehend. A voice spoke to me, the words cutting deep into my heart and showing me truth I had managed to evade for decades.

No. I didn't want to risk telling Him about my anger. The less I thought about Him, the better. I pushed my frustration aside, along with a couple rocks that were digging into my back, and managed to doze.

"There's been a change in plans," a voice hissed near my ear. My eyes flew open to confront the nightmare of a masked face inches from mine. I shot upright. My hand scrambled for my boot knife before I remembered where I was.

Large eyes above the fabric mask squinted in amusement as the tall assassin waited for me to catch my breath. "We need to go to Lyric first," he said in a hoarse whisper. Behind him, only a hint of gray lit the predawn skies.

I scraped a hand over my face, trying to wake up. "Sorry. Can't do that. Too dangerous."

The hooded head moved slowly side to side. "Not for us. We have business there."

Terrific. They were probably still hunting Susan. Someone on the Council had let the word out that Susan was the Restorer, because Kahlareans came after her in Braide Wood right after the battle of Morsal Plains. Maybe I should take these three to Lyric. Markkel and Susan were safely back in their own world now. The assassins could hunt all they liked.

But too many people knew me in Lyric. How could I keep up my charade of being a Hazorite weapons dealer if we ran into anyone I knew? And if I didn't go with them, did I really want three assassins prowling Lyric on their own? "Keep your enemy within reach of your blade." It was an old saying and probably wise. Trouble was, that meant staying within reach of the enemy's blade as well.

I scrambled to my feet, hitched my cloak over my shoulders, and looked around. The second assassin waited near the transport doors. The third wasn't in sight. Maybe this would be the time to take them out.

"You'll have to make that side trip without me. I can meet up with you later." I shifted my belt and used the movement to rest my hand on my sword hilt.

"You're wrong, Hazorite," said a low voice right behind my ear.

I spun to see the third gray figure. How did they *do* that?

"You will come with us," he said.

A breathy hissing sound came from the throats of the other

two men, and their shoulders moved. They were laughing.

Never thought I'd live to hear a Kahlarean assassin laughing. Not a comforting sound.

The transport powered up, and the curved door slid upward. Oh well. It was still a day's journey to Lyric. A lot could happen on the way. I'd watch for my chance, and in the meantime maybe I could learn a few things.

"Fine." I grabbed my pack from the ground. "But you'd better show me how you stay hidden, because I don't want to be seen in Lyric." That much was true anyway.

The lead assassin didn't answer. He lifted his arm toward the transport door.

I shook my head and stepped on board. This was going to be an interesting day.

It had been a mystery to me how a team of assassins had slipped unseen into Lyric last season. The day Susan, Tristan, and I had addressed the Council, they were waiting outside and attacked us as we left the Council tower. We killed two of them, and Markkel turned one over to the Lyric guardians. The others escaped and later tracked us to Braide Wood. As before, we had no sign they were near until they chose a moment after the battle with Hazor to attack.

Today, as our transport neared more populated areas en route to Lyric, I studied the assassins' skill at being invisible. They pulled their hoods forward, shielding their faces, and kept their gaze downward. Their quiet, withdrawn demeanor made them seem like songkeepers on a pilgrimage, not elite killers. No one gave them a second look. In fact, I got more curious stares than they did. The effect was almost like the power the Rhusicans had to control people's minds. These Kahlareans seemed to convince people they simply weren't there. It would have been fun to watch if I weren't so busy trying to figure out what to do when we reached Lyric.

We switched transports several times during the day and finally found ourselves at a station between Taborn and Corros Fields. The next stop would be Lyric.

"We can't ride straight to the Lyric station," I said to the tallest of the cloaked Kahlareans. "There are Council guards everywhere. If we hike from here, we can reach Lyric by midday tomorrow and avoid the main city entrance. I know some other ways in."

The three men put their heads together and spoke almost inaudibly. If you ask me, they were carrying their silence thing a bit too far. The station was deserted, and I was supposed to be their Hazorite ally. It would have been more annoying if it weren't for the fact that I could hear every murmured word as they argued about the relative merit of speed versus secrecy.

"Give me some credit. I know the terrain around here. Let's get under cover and walk in tomorrow." Maybe if we made camp tonight, I could offer to stand watch. They could get a good night's sleep, and I'd make sure they'd never wake up. The thought made me grin.

Maybe my smile made me look trustworthy, because their leader nodded. I didn't give them time to rethink things. Shouldering my pack, I led us out across the wild prairie toward the forests between Corros Fields and Lyric. We kept a fast pace, but dark descended on us quickly, and we made camp in a small clearing. I would have preferred to find a cave, but the land around here was too level. The best we could do was to keep a tight grove of trees at our back and stay alert.

I dug out some supplies and offered the assassins bread, but they shook their heads. Maybe the rumors were true. I'd heard

Kahlarean assassins didn't need food or rest when they were hunting. I shrugged and had a solitary supper while blackness lowered around us. I thumbed the back of a small heat trivet and placed the light near one of the trees.

The One separated the day from the night. We honor Him when we release the darkness to His care. Memories of childhood Verses snagged me like waterweed. I tore them away from the grip they had on my mind. Better to break a few rules, be able to keep track of my traveling companions, and see any slimy ground-crawlers that came out at night.

My offer to stand guard met with eye-rolling amusement and more near-silent snickers. Fine. If they didn't need to eat or sleep, that was their business. I was tired. I wrapped up in my cloak and closed my eyes, listening to the sounds in the forest. There was no campsite conversation from my companions. One walked the perimeter of the clearing. I could hear the almost subliminal sound of his footsteps—but only if I paid close attention. My eyes opened a slit. The other two assassins sat near each other, backs against a tree trunk, huge bug eyes looking out into the darkness. This would be a handy time for them to talk about their plans for when we arrived in Lyric, but they didn't say a word. Letting my eyelids drop shut again, I heard the rustling of a forest scavenger. Sounded like something small. Nothing to worry about.

The rustling grew louder. A snuffling noise joined in, and a faint vibration moved through the earth beneath my ear. Something larger was rooting nearby. Very nearby.

A bear burst into the clearing with a roar.

I rolled to my feet and drew my sword.

The creature galloped right for the two seated Kahlareans. I didn't know bears could move that fast. Something about the assassins seemed to enrage the animal. He swatted one of them with a huge paw, and I used the space of one breath to weigh my options. Let the bear kill at least one? It would help my odds, but the survivors might be angry that I had sat back and ignored the massacre.

I ran forward with a yell. My sword found its target somewhere in the hard muscles of the beast's back. I jerked my weapon free before the animal's thrashing could wrench it from my hand. The bear reared up and turned full-on toward me. One Kahlarean by the tree had managed to jump to his feet. His short blade flew through the air and lodged in the dark fur. But still the animal advanced on me.

I scuffled back and swung my sword through the air between us. The monster towered over me. Blood coated its muzzle, visible in the artificial light of the heat trivet. Then the bear wavered. I dodged to the side and watched it crash forward. The venblade had worked fast. I spared a glance at the Kahlarean still sprawled on the ground. His head was bent at an odd angle, and a dark stain spread across his gray cloak. His companion crouched over him and shook his head.

I should be glad I had one fewer assassin to contend with, but as I caught my breath, my chest felt heavy and cold. The dead man had been skilled at his craft, and I respected that. He didn't deserve to have the life crushed out of him by a bear looking for a snack.

On the other hand, his crouching Kahlarean partner had his back to me and no venblade handy. I took a step forward.

The bear lurched back up onto all fours and took a swipe at me. Claws gouged my shin. I hissed, beating the huge paw back with my sword.

The leader of the assassins stepped out of the woods into

the light of the heat trivet. He pulled a rounded blade with a wooden grip from some hidden pocket, slipped up behind the bear, and efficiently slit its throat.

I blinked, impressed. My heart slowed but still beat an unsteady rhythm. If I had attacked the Kahlarean by the tree, the leader who was calmly wiping his weapon on the bear's fur would have been cleaning my blood off his blade instead.

Thank the One.

No. Thank quick thinking and luck. If the One were really with me, I wouldn't be in this ridiculous situation. Fighting bears with Kahlarean assassins, hiding what I was from the Council, posing as a Hazorite. I was losing track of whose side I was on.

The head assassin stepped closer to me. "You're injured," he said in his low, breathy voice. I looked down at the tattered strips of fabric beneath my knee and the generous amount of blood. Prickly itching signaled the skin's mending, joining, healing. I sucked in a breath, then pretended it was from pain. I could not let him see me heal.

I unwound a strip of cloth from my sleeve and quickly tied it around my leg. "It's not as bad as it looks."

The man studied me for a moment but didn't say anything. He turned to help his companion with the fallen assassin. They dragged him off into the woods.

I didn't want to know what they were doing with his body. I doubted Kahlarean assassins did anything as prosaic as a simple burial. I glared at the bear. It smelled of blood and musk and wet fur.

Maybe I should slip away into the night.

And do what? Get to Lyric first and tell the Council Guard that I had been traveling with Kahlarean assassins and they were on the way to cause some unspecified trouble in Lyric? That plan had so many drawbacks that I winced and sank down against a tree. With my sword braced across my knees, I tilted my head back and closed my eyes to wait out the night.

You are not alone.

The words were so faint that they didn't register at first. As I became aware of hearing something, my shoulders tensed.

You are not alone.

I opened my eyes and looked around. There was no one there. If I stretched my hearing, I could make out indistinct sounds from the two Kahlareans deeper in the woods. I squinted at the bear in suspicion. I'd never heard of a talking bear before, but the past few seasons I'd seen a lot of strange things.

You are not alone.

This time a hint of humor colored the quiet voice. I swallowed. The words hadn't come from the dead bear or any other apparition in the woods. I knew that voice. It was Him. The One.

Just great. Now that the guardian patrols at Cauldron Falls were dead, and assassins were on the way to Lyric, and I had nearly become bear fodder—*now* He showed up.

"I could have used a little help earlier on," I whispered. "In case you hadn't noticed, things haven't been going real well here."

This time there was no humor in the voice. Instead, warmth wrapped around me as He spoke again.

Don't be afraid.

The words tugged at me to admit that I *was* afraid. Not only about the threat to our people from Kahlarea, or my own immediate danger. I wanted to confess the fear I had of Him. Of letting the One know me, claim me, comfort me. The love in His voice was a dangerous lure.

I pulled my sword up to rest across my chest and closed my eyes again, shutting out the invisible Presence with every part of my will. "Go away." I gritted my teeth, waiting for the earth to shake or the voice to shout at me. There was only silence. And I thought I could feel sadness in the quiet.

The two Kahlareans returned to the clearing, but they ignored me. The tall leader resumed his hushed patrol of the perimeter of our campsite. They didn't bother to field dress the bear. We were traveling light and wouldn't have use for the meat anyway.

I sat awake. What were my companions planning to do in Lyric, and how could I stop it? How would I avoid being seen by any of the Council or Council Guard? And what about the regular Lyric guardians? They wouldn't call a Feast day for my return. I'd left a few battered heads behind last time I was there.

Most of all, how long could I push away the One who had saddled me with the role of Restorer? He didn't fight fair.

Chapter Three

KIERAN

After a sleepless night, we continued toward Lyric at first light. My wounds had healed, but I kept the bloody cloth tied around my leg and feigned a limp. We approached from the rolling moss-covered hills on the Hazor side.

I easily found a hidden pocket-door in one of the many curving indents in the city's wall. Any transtech worth his trade could have disabled the magnetic lock. Not that I was a transtech. It's what my father was and what I was supposed to have been. But things don't always go the way you plan.

Case in point: I had just helped two enemy assassins break into the capital city.

"Wait for us here," whispered the tall one. "We won't be long."

I pocketed my scrambler tool and turned to answer him, but they had both disappeared down a side street. Shades of Shamgar, how did they move so fast?

I raced to the gap between two tall buildings. A flicker of movement disappeared around the corner a block farther down. I tore after them, abandoning the pretended limp. I couldn't lose them.

A few blocks in from the outer walls, the streets grew crowded. People in earth-toned tunics and cloaks milled around storefronts that housed everything from grain distribution to transport construction. I concentrated on focusing my vision and scanned the streets in all directions. Two gray blurs ducked into an alley across the square.

I started running again, but when I reached the alley, they had vanished. I stretched my hearing, and pain blazed through my head from the hundreds of voices that suddenly burst into clarity. Rubbing my forehead, I took a deep breath. The assassins had headed toward the city center. That could mean any number of things—all of them bad.

"Kieran!" a high-pitched voice shouted. A hand clamped my arm.

I wrenched away.

Tagatha, Tristan's youngest sister, smiled at me. A drooling toddler straddled one of her hips as if he were a permanent fixture. "What brings you to Lyric?" she asked.

"Business. None of yours." I stalked down the street toward the city center.

She kept pace with me. "Where have you been? Have you talked to Tristan lately? Did you hear about the big battle at Morsal Plains?" Tagatha was as athletic in build as her two siblings but had a plumper, softer form. Messy brown hair hung loose around her hopelessly good-natured face. When we were children in Braide Wood, she followed Tristan and me everywhere. We called her Tagalong, but she never seemed to mind.

I walked faster, but she grabbed my arm again.

"Kieran, what happened to your leg? You should get that looked at. Why don't you come to our home for lunch? I can fix you up."

I pried her fingers off my arm. "Listen, Tag, I can't stand around chatting right now."

Her eyebrows pulled together, and her ready smile drooped. "Are you all right?"

I shifted my pack on my shoulders. "Nothing I can't handle."

She sighed and stepped back. "Well, if you have time later, stop by the house."

I nodded but was already loping away from her, aiming for the tall Council tower near the center of town.

Tristan, Talia, and Tagatha. Payton and Tara went a little overboard on choosing those names. What a mouthful it had been when Tara called them to dinner each night. Of course, "Kieran and Kendra" was a bit much too, but at our house no one ever called our names. I had sometimes wondered if our father even remembered them.

I dodged around slow-moving pedestrians and felt my annoyance grow. Cities would be so much better without all these people. In the central square, I paused to regroup. The round worship tower soared hundreds of feet above the city, with vaulted entries facing eight different directions. This was the place where people from all the clans came on the season-end Feast days to meet with the One. Some people claimed that when they gathered on the floor of the tower, a mist hovered in the vast empty space above their heads. Others said it was the place the One had decided to live. I'd been here for Feast days, of course. I usually stayed outside one of the entries, listening. The music was nice enough, I suppose, but I also watched the faces of people as they left a morning spent in the tower. They always came out changed somehow. Why would they subject themselves to that?

Across the curved street, the smaller Council tower worked to assert its presence. Several grim Council guards with heavy leather vests over their tunics and plenty of conspicuous weapons protected the main entrance. I knew a few other ways in but hoped the Kahlareans didn't. The assassins shouldn't be able to get past the doors.

My gaze swept left to the lower building that housed rooms for councilmembers and guests. Behind that was a Council office building. I turned to look at the other side of the central square and the guardian's training tower. The Lyric guardians were quartered there, but first-years from other clans came here to train as well.

So where had the Kahlareans gone? I waited for a clue. Someone screaming, "Help! Murderers!" would work.

Studying the scene for anything out of place, I noticed an odd figure near the edge of the alley alongside the Council office tower. I pulled back a few paces to remain hidden while I observed him. He was about the age of a first-year guardian, a few years shy of twenty. He wore an emblem on his short tunic, but it wasn't for any clan or nation I was familiar with—and I'd done a lot of traveling. His trousers had pouches attached all over them. A clever idea for carrying weapons and supplies, but it would get uncomfortable sleeping on the ground with all those bulges. No visible weapons, but that didn't mean anything. The Kahlarean assassins looked as harmless as songkeepers to someone who didn't know better.

What really caught my interest was how intently he scrutinized everything around him. His furtive movements triggered a flash of memory. I had moved with that same edginess the first time I made the illegal trip into Hazor as a young man. I had skulked in doorways, watching the unfamiliar people, figuring out how to avoid danger.

So he was likely a spy. But he didn't look like any Hazorite or Kahlarean I had ever seen. Were our people going to have a new enemy to worry about? When he nervously brushed his long blond hair back, two metal studs glinted near the top of one ear. I shuddered. The Hazorites did inhuman things to their slaves. But why was an escaped slave loitering in the central square of Lyric?

My eyes roamed the key buildings again, but nothing else seemed out of place. When I looked back at the youth, he was heading directly to the Council tower entrance. He tried to walk past the guards. Interesting. Of course they stopped him, but instead of backing off, he seemed to be arguing with them. One of them shoved him away, and the boy sprawled onto the stone-paved street.

He picked himself up and backed away a few steps. The boy had the gaunt look of someone in short supply of food, sleep, or safety—another state I was familiar with. A group of council-members in their rust tunics came out of the tower, followed by the inevitable entourage of assistants and sycophants. One chief councilmember stopped to talk to the youth briefly and then continued on his way. The boy moved off down a side street in a different direction.

So he was a Council spy. It figured. The Council's job was to lead and protect the people, but from all I had observed in my three and a half decades, they spent most of their time protecting themselves. I didn't trust a single one of them.

I stored the boy's face in my memory. Some people collect bits of art—woodcarvings and weavings. Some collect magchips and tech gadgets. I collect information. Small facts can lead to canny strategies. For example, I knew that King Zarek didn't actually live in Sidian most of the time. He preferred staying in a village outside the Hazor capital. I also knew he drank lehken blood.

You never knew what information might be useful one day.

My surveillance of the central square wasn't producing anything helpful. Time to explore inside a few buildings. I slipped through a side entrance of the guardian training tower and up the stairs that spiraled along the wall. From the balconies above, I searched for any sign of a disturbance. All I found were two young boys who had sneaked in to watch the sparring in one of the large rooms below. I ignored them and made my way back down to the main hall. A dozen paces from the exit, two Lyric guardians came around a corner toward me.

"You!" one of them shouted.

I looked back over my shoulder, hoping he was addressing someone behind me. No such luck.

"What are you doing here?" He reached for his sword.

I squinted in recognition. Great. Of all the Lyric guardians, I had to run into one who had tried to keep me locked up during the last Council session. I had refused to sit in a cell while the Council made their usual hash of things, so I broke out. The man glowering at me now was one of the guardians who had gotten in my way that day.

I took a few backward steps toward another doorway. I couldn't blame the man for his scowl. Being ambushed and hit over the head isn't a pleasant experience. He probably got demoted for letting me escape.

"Just passing through." I kept moving toward the door.

"Hold!" he shouted.

I ran. Heavy footfalls pounded as both guardians tore after me. I tried to lose myself in the crowd outside on the street, but when I glanced back, they were still coming. Apparently they weren't content with merely chasing me out of the building.

I'm not saying all the guardians are overgrown bullies.

Tristan is probably the only man I trust, and he's a guardian. The troops that rode out to protect Braide Wood were willing to give their lives for the clans — and many did. Let's just say some of these fellows are a little quicker to use their fists than their brains. Technically I'd been sanctioned to help Braide Wood prepare for the battle of Morsal Plains, so the Lyric guardians no longer had reason to treat me like an enemy, but I had no time for explanations.

Rounding the side of the central tower, I passed out of sight of them for a moment. I ducked into the entryway of the tower and flattened myself against the curved wall. The men lumbered past the arch and down the street.

I let my breath out in a rush and ran a hand through my hair. Then I looked around the mammoth space of the tower while I caught my breath. Light poured down from the clear windows hundreds of feet overhead. More light washed in from the high arched entries on all eight sides. The tower easily held thousands of people on Feast days, but today only one small figure knelt at the curved railing in the center of the room.

I took a few silent steps toward her. She probably wasn't a threat, but I wanted to be sure of who she was and what she had seen.

As I approached, I knew my worry was unnecessary. She wasn't aware of anything going on around her. Long blonde hair fell forward in a curtain from her bowed head, hiding her face. Her shoulders shook, but she didn't make a sound.

"Linette?" I said softly.

Her head came up and she turned to look at me, dark smudges under her eyes. She brushed a hand across her wet cheeks.

I walked the rest of the way into the center of the room, forgetting that it was my policy to avoid this tower. "What are you doing here? Why aren't you in Braide Wood?"

She had always seemed frail, but since Dylan had died last season, she looked almost transparent. Linette was a songkeeper. Not one of those pious, overbearing types who shouted Verses at people with a pointed finger. She was actually very shy. Even so, her zeal for the One was so strong that only days after learning her fiancé had been murdered at Cauldron Falls, she set aside her grief long enough to pull the Braide Wood clan together to sing the Verses at first light on the day Hazor attacked.

Not that I believed it made any difference in the battle. That was one of those old myths I didn't have time for. But it did keep the village from giving way to panic.

"Kieran." She stood with a small smile, making no apology for her obvious tears. "I didn't know you were in Lyric."

"And why are you here?"

Her smile faltered. "I needed to be closer. . . . "

The vast empty space towered over her. Seeking solace from the huge invisible One—seemed like a cold comfort to me.

"And you?" She tucked a strand of hair behind her ear.

Realization hit me. There were few people I could trust to get a message to Tristan, and one of them was standing a few paces in front of me. If I believed in miracles, this would qualify. "Technically I'm not here," I said.

She tilted her head and raised her eyebrows.

"Linette, can you get back to Braide Wood before nightfall?"

"Why?"

"I need someone to tell Tristan. The whole patrol at the Falls was wiped out. Syncbeams again. Tell him to warn Rendor and send a large force. Everyone he can spare."

Her face turned even whiter.

Guilt twisted in my gut. Giving her this news to carry was

cruel, even by my standards. "I can't go myself. I don't have time to explain. Can you do it?"

She stared at me for a moment and then nodded. "I'll leave right away. May the One guard your steps." She turned to go but then looked back at me. Her eyes narrowed. For a moment she seemed to be listening to something I couldn't hear. "And may He open your heart to receive His guidance." She didn't wait for a response but hurried toward one of the huge entries—leaving me alone in the tower.

I glanced upward, but no mist hovered overhead. I took a deep breath and realized all my muscles had knotted up. I rolled my shoulders.

At least now I knew Tristan would get word about the border being breached. Next step was to find out what my assassin friends were up to. I walked from the center of the tower, then paused.

"Thanks," I whispered to the empty space. Then I ran for an entrance before anything odd could happen.

Once again in the crowded square, I still had no clue where to look for the Kahlareans. Now that a couple of Lyric guardians were searching for me, I couldn't wait here for something to happen. Time for a new plan.

The Kahlarean leader had said they would meet me at the hidden door in the wall. I'd go back there and wait. If their mission involved assassinating some councilmembers, I didn't see what I could do to stop it at this point. Besides, they were probably just doing some reconnaissance—trying to get information about what had happened to the Restorer. They wouldn't have much success there. I was one of only a handful who knew the truth.

Unpopular streets helped me avoid the side of town where

Tag lived with her husband and children. The outer edges of the city were quieter, and by the time I reached the wall, I had walked for several blocks in solitude. As the afternoon rain began to fall, I pulled up the hood of my cloak and hunkered down by the wall.

I could probably disappear into the city. The assassins would track me, but I knew a few things about staying hidden. But then I wouldn't learn more about what they were up to. I had to discover their plans. After all, I'd let them into the city. What if they had killed someone on the Council? I shrugged deeper into my cloak, shaking some of the water off. As far as I was concerned, the Council could use some thinning. I grinned. Susan would kill me if she knew I was thinking that. After all, her husband, Markkel, was a councilmember from Rendor. Technically. But he lived in Susan's world.

I shook my head. What a mess. I still hadn't quite sorted out how Markkel, a Restorer's son, had disappeared as a youth and come back two years later forty years old and married to Susan.

And for all those years, Susan had not known who Markkel really was. I snorted. That must have been some revelation. Susan was usually too tenderhearted for her own good, but I'd seen her fight, and she could be fierce when provoked. I was surprised she forgave Markkel for all the deception. Apparently she loved him with the same blind earnestness that Kendra had for Tristan.

I shifted my back against the cold wall. That sort of commitment made no sense. Maybe companionship had some value, but there was no benefit to blind loyalty. Passion made you vulnerable. Look what it did to Tristan when Kendra was poisoned and nearly died. Or Linette. She was a hollow shell because of her grief. Much smarter never to care.

Had Linette taken the midday transport? My thoughts caught on the image of her blonde hair and slim figure in the light of the Lyric tower. The hike to Braide Wood was chancy if it was too close to nightfall. I shook off my concern. Linette looked as fragile as a blue lace fern, but she was tough. She'd be fine. I hoped Tristan was still in Braide Wood so she could get the word to him fast.

A muted sound caught my attention. By straining my hearing, I could make out the soggy footfalls of the two Kahlareans returning. They rounded a corner and came into sight.

Three of them.

Caradung! How could I have been so stupid? This was why the Kahlareans had needed to stop in Lyric. They drew closer, and I marked the instant the third man recognized me.

His eyes bulged wider. "He was with them. The night we attacked the Restorer. He fought for them."

"What? You're crazy." I sprang to my feet.

I had let assassins into the city to retrieve the one Kahlarean in existence who could connect me with the Restorer. I deserved a venblade to the heart for that bit of idiocy, but I didn't plan to make it easy for them.

I drew my sword. The door was at my back, but there was no time to release the lock.

The lead assassin was assessing me. Over the cloth mask that covered much of his face, his eyes squinted. He was smiling.

"Don't kill him," he rasped in his eerie half whisper. "We need what he knows."

Then the three of them closed in.

Chapter Four

KIERAN

The newly escaped Kahlarean hung back. They probably hadn't bothered to find his weapons when they broke him out. At least I hoped he wasn't armed.

The shorter of my two travel companions moved in fast. He pulled his sword from the folds of his cloak. His attack was quick but predictable—a hacking swing, a forceful jab. He wasn't bad, but I was better. I held him off with standard parries. Finally, I blocked upward and stepped in to envelope his blade. He was forced back and left an opening. I didn't hesitate to run him through.

Unfortunately my lunge had drawn me away from the wall.

The tall lead assassin moved in behind me. Cold metal pressed against my neck. "Drop your sword."

Right. That would be smart. Instead, I reached for my boot knife with my left hand and drove it backward.

I missed. He didn't. Of course, he had the advantage. His curved blade was resting against my throat. Even as I twisted and tried to pull away, it sliced into my skin. Now I knew the shock the bear felt last night as steel severed his arteries and his life bled away.

The leader froze for the space of a gasp as my blood poured over his hand. His desire to keep me alive gave me an edge.

I used his waver in concentration to break free and turn on him with my sword. But my movements were sluggish. Strength drained from me. How deeply had he cut me? I'd lost my dagger, so I pressed my left hand against my neck. I swung my sword toward the Kahlarean leader, but haze fell over my eyes and I missed him completely. I staggered back a few steps.

I could hold back two Kahlareans, especially with one of them unarmed. For a moment, as my vision grew fuzzy, I saw four of them. I stumbled back a few more paces and blinked them back into focus. The escapee had grabbed the sword from his downed rescuer. Make that two armed assassins.

My muscles grew heavy. If they had used a venblade, I'd be dead already. If they had intended to kill me, I'd be dead already. Even with them trying to keep me alive, I wasn't sure I'd survive. But anything was better than letting them take me.

The fog around my vision thickened. I wasn't healing fast enough. Getting dizzy. Time for another plan.

I turned and ran. One block. Two. Around the next corner I saw an old man crossing the street. His eyes widened. I tried to warn him, but my voice wasn't working. I stumbled to one knee. My legs refused to obey me. The last strength fled my muscles and I fell headlong. I caught myself with my elbow and looked up. The old man pulled out a signaler. The clear tone pierced the air.

I couldn't see the two assassins, but I heard their light feet approaching from behind me. The shorter Kahlarean ran past me toward the old man and cut him down with one brutal stroke, then ripped the signaler from his hand and ground it under foot. In the sudden silence, I heard shouts and running footsteps. My vision sparkled like a fried magchip. I collapsed against the wet street. Swirls of red swam in the puddles of rain near me. Then everything went black.

The first thing I noticed when I woke up was that the consuming weakness was gone. My first deep breath felt rich with new strength. I wasn't on the street anymore, either. I was wet and cold, and the surface beneath me was hard but not as rough as pavement. I squinted my eyes open. I was resting on a molded plastic bench against the wall of a small bare room. The light walls were dialed to a sharp glow, and excited voices projected through an open doorway.

I pushed myself up and assessed my situation: empty boot sheath, missing sword. I patted my other hidden pockets. All my weapons were gone. My clothes were a mess, and the sweet metallic scent of fresh blood was already turning sour.

A sharp-faced woman in a green healer's tunic strode into the room and glared at me. She turned and addressed the two guardians who hovered in the doorway behind her. "You pulled me away from mending a broken arm. Does he look like he's dying? Why don't you stop to get your story straight next time?"

The two guardians gaped at me as though I were one of the ghosts that are said to haunt Shamgar. I would have laughed at their expressions, but I was trying to look innocent.

The healer opened her bag and pulled out a tech gadget and a cloth. "Get me some water," she ordered. One of the guardians ran to obey her, and she started her exam. She frowned at all the blood, then fingered the thin line at my throat where my wound had already healed. "You had a small scratch at your neck, but that wouldn't have caused this. How do you feel? Any other injuries?"

"I'm fine." My voice rasped a bit, but I swallowed and tried again. "What happened?"

She narrowed her eyes and didn't respond. The guardian returned with some water, and she washed the blood away from my neck. The healer also pulled away the bloodstained bandage tied around my leg and looked at the whole skin beneath it. I kept my gaze fixed on the door behind her to avoid meeting her sharp glances. Let her draw her own conclusions. There was no explanation, anyway.

She stuffed her instruments into her bag with force and stood up. "He's fine."

"Able to be tried?" one of the guardians asked.

"I don't see why not. Now, would you please excuse me? I have some patients who really need me." She included us all in her glare and stalked out of the cell.

"I need to be going too." I stood and stretched.

One of the guardians snorted. They both turned and left, sliding the thick metal door closed behind them. Well, it was worth a try.

Low voices murmured, and I stretched my hearing.

"I don't know what strings Kieran pulled last time, but the Council will have to act now."

"They should have sent that half-breed back to Hazor years ago."

"This time there's plenty of evidence. He had a scrambler on him."

"And Case reported seeing him in the guardian training tower."

"So they'll pin the escape on him, but what about Davis's murder?"

"I don't see why not. It was his fault if he let the Kahlareans into Lyric."

I stopped listening, but the words kept repeating: "It was his fault . . . murder . . . his fault."

I've killed people when necessary. I learned early on to tune out the guilt. It's a skill like any other—sharpen your blade, cover your tracks, and ignore the nightmares that shake you out of sleep and make you relive the deaths on your head.

I stared fiercely at the blank wall across from me. The Kahlarean killed the old man. Not me. I was only doing what I've always done: try to protect my own skin. Things had gotten complicated. It wasn't my fault.

I wouldn't have been traveling with Kahlareans if they hadn't surprised me by the Falls. I wouldn't have been at the Falls if Tristan hadn't sent me there to check things out. He wouldn't have sent me there if he hadn't known I was the new Restorer. And I wouldn't be the new Restorer if . . .

It kept coming back to the One.

My teeth ground together. I knew what Tristan would say. Sometimes I envied his easy, blind faith. He'd say that the One had done exactly what He promised in the Verses. He had sent us Susan as a Restorer. And I had to admit there had been no human way for us to save Braide Wood from Hazor.

But there was a big problem with Tristan's theory: If the One was really there—and really intervening—why didn't He step in sooner? Before Bekkah was killed. Before Morsal Plains was destroyed. Before so many had to die in the battle with Hazor.

I wasn't foolish enough to think He didn't exist. I wished I could believe He didn't, but I'd seen and heard too much. So He was real. That didn't mean I would go along with Tristan and

Susan's theory that He had a benevolent interest in us.

As if in argument, images began to play through my mind. The day of the battle of Morsal Plains, Kendra, our father, and I struggled to keep the suppression field working. In spite of our efforts, the machine failed, and suddenly the Hazor syncbeams were a threat again. The long-range weapons charred our guardians, and the battle grew hopeless. Until something terrifying happened.

The sky began to fire its own syncbeams. Sounds louder than a waterfall rumbled overhead, and light seared our eyes. Susan told me later that it was a "thunderstorm" and was common on her world. My respect for her grew as I imagined the bizarre and unpredictable world that spawned her. The crackling and crashing from the sky destroyed the program chips in every Hazorite syncbeam on the field. Our odds improved from impossible to near impossible.

But if the One could reach from the sky and crush Hazor's syncbeams, why had He waited until then? And if the One had any wisdom at all, why had He chosen the wrong person to be the next Restorer?

"You make no sense," I accused the silence. Pushing myself to my feet, I paced the room. The rain was drying from my clothes, but they were sticky with blood. As I paced the limited floor space, my restlessness grew. And I was thirsty.

I paused to bang on the door. "Hey! How about something to drink?" I didn't really expect an answer. I didn't get one.

I couldn't figure out how late in the day it was—or if it was even the same day. Would the Council be in session this afternoon? Or tomorrow? Would they even ask me about what had happened?

Probably not. The Council was never efficient at anything

useful, though they were amazingly rapid at deciding on banishments.

To be thorough about my options, I checked the door. It was secure. Without my scrambler, I couldn't do a thing with the lock. Fine. I was safe from the Kahlareans for the moment—and out of the rain. Not bleeding anymore. Things could be worse. Had been worse many times.

With that comforting thought, I curled up on the bench and went to sleep.

I dozed off and on, disturbed equally by dreams and by the persistent glare of the light walls. I had lost all sense of time, when approaching footsteps echoed in the hall outside.

I pushed myself up to lounge on the bench and wait. The door slid open and the guardians entered, swords drawn and ready. My mouth twitched. Guess I had them jumpy after the last time I was here. The moment of amusement faded as the guards stepped aside and a tall man in an immaculate Council tunic walked into the cell.

Cameron was the chief councilmember of Lyric, but the power his position carried wasn't enough for him. He wasn't above using illegal alliances with enemy countries for his own advantage, and he had even tried to gain control of the entire Council last season with the help of a Rhusican mind poisoner. When Susan convinced the Council to throw out the Rhusicans and fight Hazor, his influence had taken a hit—perhaps the reason behind the new scowl lines between his eyes.

Cameron looked at me and wrinkled his nose. His dark hair was slicked back, and his tunic collar stood at attention. I was expected to leap to my feet in respect, so I slouched more deeply onto the bench. One of the guards grabbed my arm and yanked me to my feet.

"Kieran." Cameron kept his tone formal. "As chief councilmember for the people of Lyric, I will bring charges against you at the session today. My understanding is that you assisted two Kahlareans with breaking into Lyric, you diverted the guardians while they freed an assassin from the tower, and you were a party to the murder of Davis, a builder of Lyric."

Cameron's voice actually hardened when he mentioned Davis. Interesting. I'd always assumed the councilmember's only driving motive was increasing his personal power. Maybe the frequent speeches about protecting his people weren't complete lies. If I hadn't seen that bit of sincere anger, I wouldn't have bothered to answer him at all.

"The Kahlareans found me. They thought I was a Hazorite arms trader, so I played along to give me time to figure out what they were planning. If I hadn't let them into Lyric, they would have killed me and found a way in themselves. Things just went wrong."

"Your plans always do." Cameron watched me closely. "And Davis?"

Regret pricked me again, like the long thorns of a young spice tree. "The Kahlarean that escaped killed Davis. I would have stopped him if I could, but I was injured. . . ."

"Or someone was." Cameron's focus lingered on the blood staining my clothes. "The healer said you weren't damaged at all. Whose blood is it, Kieran?"

Highest hills of Hazor. I was making things worse by the word. If Cameron ever pieced things together and figured out I could heal . . . I clamped my jaw closed and shook my head.

The chief councilmember's eyes narrowed. "Leave us," he told the guards.

They puffed up with objections. However, one glance from Cameron, and their reverence for anyone wearing a Council tunic won over. They slid the door closed behind them. I sat down again, bracing one foot on the bench. Cameron wanted something from me. That gave me the first chance I'd had to maneuver since they locked me up.

"Kieran, there's no question what the Council will decide. And Tristan won't be around this time to speak for you."

Cameron couldn't say that name without sneering. I knew his reasons. His reckless son had been killed while on a training patrol under Tristan's command. He would never stop blaming Tristan. Cameron's bitterness colored all his plots. Hating Tristan was an obsession with him.

"You know they'll vote for banishment," he continued.

I kept my face impassive. This was where I was supposed to be horrified and beg for mercy. Right. I'd never fit in with the clans anyway. They'd be doing me a favor.

Cameron continued to study me. "Maybe it doesn't bother you to be separated from our people forever." It was eerie the way he seemed to read minds. "But what about Kendra?"

All the muscles along my spine tightened, but I forced myself to keep breathing evenly.

Cameron crossed his arms and leaned against the wall by the door. "What will the shame do to her? Who knows? It could be the thing that breaks her fragile mind again."

I met his eyes with a hard look of my own. Not only was that low, it wasn't true. Her mind wasn't fragile. A Rhusican had poisoned her, and we'd lost her for nearly three seasons. But Susan had brought her back. She'd been fine while I'd been in Braide Wood, at least as far as I could tell. But what *would* happen to Kendra if I were banished? And who would watch Tristan's back?

Shamgar, this guy was good. I refused to let him see the sliver of doubt wedged in my thoughts.

"I still have the power to sway the Council," Cameron went on. "I'd be willing to help you—for Kendra's sake—if you help me with something."

The poison-skinned ground-crawler was finally getting to the point. I leaned forward.

"There seems to be some confusion about what happened after the battle of Morsal Plains. We heard that Markkel rode with the two lost clans and that after the battle Susan and Markkel were both in Braide Wood."

I nodded. That was common knowledge. What information was he digging for? What could I bargain with?

"And then?" Cameron asked.

My gut tightened. And then I had died but didn't. And Susan had stopped being the Restorer. And she and Markkel had gone through a portal—which, heaven help us, Cameron had better not find out about. And I was the Restorer now. Nope. Nothing there that I could tell him.

I shrugged. "They left."

Cameron glared at me and fidgeted with one of his sleeves. "Kieran, let me explain this to you again. Tristan's made far too many mistakes for the Council to continue to forgive indefinitely. Once you've been banished, I *will* destroy him. It's only a matter of time. And when he's out of the way, maybe I'll offer my protection to Kendra."

I jumped from the bench and would have strangled him, but he lifted his hand quickly, revealing the shiny dagger he'd pulled from a hidden sheath above his wrist. A venblade. Perfect. Illegal weapons. Right up his alley.

I kept my distance, breathing hard. Maybe it would be

worth the risk to attack him anyway.

Instead I tried a desperate tactic: honesty. "Cameron, I don't know where Markkel and Susan are. But I can tell you that they won't be coming back. I talked to Susan after the battle. She believed her role was finished. They've left for good."

That information was a huge gift. It wasn't everything he wanted, but he'd be sleeping a lot better knowing Susan wasn't going to pop up again and ruin his latest plans.

He smirked and tapped on the door without taking his eyes off me. The guardians slid it open.

"Thank you for your cooperation." He gave a bureaucratic smile. "I'll be bringing the charges early in the session. I'll let the Council know that you confess to bringing enemies into the city and that you watched the Kahlareans kill an unarmed citizen of Lyric and did nothing to stop them. Your escort to the borders should be here to take you before midday. I'll be sure to give your sister my condolences personally."

Bright red seared my vision, and I threw myself at Cameron.

One of the guards grabbed me and jerked me back. Cameron shook his head with obvious distaste.

I strained against the arms holding me, my throat constricting. "Stay away from Kendra. If you do anything to hurt her or Tristan, I'll never stop hunting you."

Cameron smiled and turned away. The guard shoved me hard against the far side of the cell and left.

The door slid shut, sealing off my isolation. I slammed my fists against the wall. Then I sank down and buried my face in my freshly bloodied hands.

Chapter Five

KIERAN

I knew better. That's what made it so unforgivable. I'd told Tristan a hundred times that he had to learn to hide his feelings, that noble anger would only get him killed. But he never listened. Last season he marched in and challenged the Council to unite and defend Braide Wood—before assessing who was in power and where the vote would go.

The fact that they did what he asked was dumb luck and beside the point. It was still an idiotic plan. And now I'd been just as stupid—openly declared exactly where I stood. Tristan was a bad influence.

He was also in danger. Again.

I groaned. Cameron had revealed some of his intentions too. They weren't idle threats. With Susan gone, there was little to hold Cameron in check. The Council was loyal to the Verses and supportive of the guardians for the moment, but politicians were as fickle as a Hazorite temple priestess. Cameron knew how to wait for his moment. Without me around to steer Tristan through the murky waters of bargains and betrayal, anything could happen.

So I couldn't let the Council banish me. But what *could* I do? I prowled the small cell a few dozen times, while the lack of options made my stomach churn.

Linette had said something about the One giving me guidance. Since solutions weren't presenting themselves, I stopped, leaned my hands against one of the walls, and closed my eyes.

How did they do this? I cleared my throat. "Hey, I know we don't exactly understand each other." I aimed for a respectful tone. "But Tristan and Kendra have served you their whole lives. And they're in danger. So I need to stay around to help them. Anytime now the Council will be sending guardians to drag me to the border, and I can't let that happen. It would be helpful if you unlocked the door. I can take it from there."

I opened my eyes, walked over, and tried the door.

Locked.

Caradung. What was I expecting? Being the Restorer might have given me enhanced healing, but apparently it was also destroying my reason.

"Never mind," I growled to the empty room. "I'll handle this myself."

After that failed effort, time dragged until footsteps approached. I positioned myself to the side of the door. Four well-armed guardians swept into the room, allowing me no chance for an ambush. Two of them grabbed me and bound my wrists behind my back.

Sweat prickled my forehead. I don't like being tied.

A young guardian I hadn't met before delivered the Council's message. "Kieran of Braide Wood, you are banished from your clan and all the People of the Verses. You will be escorted to the border. You are never welcome back into our lands, and your name will be removed from the Songs of history."

I thought I was ready for the words, but they slammed into my gut like the end of a training staff.

On a dare I once swam under a thundering waterfall near our village. The force pounded me to the riverbed, knocking my arrogant confidence straight out of my lungs, convincing me that I was going to drown.

There in that tiny cell, I again struggled for air. Everything was happening too fast.

The somber guardian in front of me dropped his formal tone. "We'll give you back your gear at the border, and we've got three days' worth of supplies for you."

The pity in his voice made me scowl, and my muscles tensed.

The guardians holding me noticed, and one of them jerked my arm. "Don't give us trouble, Kieran. The Council authorized four guardians instead of two, and we're ordered to kill you if you resist."

Good to know. I had guessed they'd been ordered to kill me even if I *didn't* resist. Other people had been banished in my lifetime, and they always disappeared completely. I'd suspected they weren't being escorted to the nearest border as the Council claimed. For a long time I had wondered if the Council Guard were really an elite death squad.

As the four guardians led me out of the building through a door into the back alley, I tried to think of a smart remark, but their grave mood was contagious. I stayed silent, reeling under the barrage of unfamiliar emotions.

They led me through a side door of the city wall, avoiding the huge, crystal-lined entrance tunnel of the city. As we neared the transport station, they kept me far back from the clusters of travelers.

"Which border?" I asked quietly.

"We'll take the transport to Corros Fields and walk to the Hazorite border from there," the young guardian answered. Ironic. I had just been near Corros Fields with the Kahlareans. But I had no intention of going back. If I got on that transport, Tristan was as good as dead, and Kendra . . . Kendra was as good as Cameron's. I looked at the guard who was carrying my well-worn pack.

"Could I change my tunic before we board? I've got a spare one in my gear." I tried to sound subdued by the banishment that I was facing.

One of the men holding my arm barked an ugly laugh, but the young guardian who had pronounced the Council's sentence turned to look at me. Blood-soaked and torn clothes would be rather conspicuous on a public transport. The guardians wanted to make this go as smoothly as possible. There was something almost taboo about exiling a person from the clans, and they wouldn't want to draw attention to what was happening.

The young guard drew his sword and jerked his head toward a nearby grove of trees. "Untie him and take him over there." One of the men scowled, but there were four guardians against one unarmed prisoner, so he complied. The five of us stepped into the shelter of the trees.

A short time later, I slipped back out of the trees with my pack on my shoulders, my sword at my hip, and my dagger back in my boot sheath. No time to change my tunic. I'd have to worry about that later, before the scent of blood attracted scavengers. Right now my goal was speed. I wasn't sure how long they'd all stay unconscious. I pressed my hand against a fresh wound on my arm. The young guard had gotten in a good slice, but it was already healing. I kept an eye on the clusters of people near the road and melted into the woods on the far side of Lyric. As soon as I was out of sight of the station, I ran.

It wasn't my intention to go far. I needed to hide and make plans before I traveled much in any direction. Lyric was cupped by open rolling hills on two sides. Caradoc grazed the fields and few people inhabited those areas, but there wasn't much cover. The woods on the far side of the city were the ones I had led the Kahlareans through. If the assassins decided to go home, they'd go back that way. If. It was more likely that they would be tracking me. I'd have to be sure I wasn't followed before attempting to reach Braide Wood. The last thing I wanted to do was lead them there.

That left me these woods. They were on the Braide Wood side of Lyric but still a few days' journey from my clan if I avoided transports. I plunged deeper into the forest and climbed to a ridgeline that would give me good warning of any approach. There I set up a hiding place. At a nearby stream I scooped water into my hand, gulping while staying alert for anything out of place around me. When the area looked safe, I risked plunging my whole head under the surface to scrub away blood and grime. It was a relief to peel away my tunic and grab fresh clothes from my pack. My mood lifted more when I found a spare scrambler and some other unconventional gear untouched in a hidden inner pocket of my pack. I unearthed the food the Council guard had provided and chewed on a small bread loaf.

Did I even need food now that I was a Restorer? If every injury healed, was it possible for me to starve? Susan might know, but she was back in her own strange world. I should have asked her more questions before she left. How did she control her intense sight and hearing? When she saw strange visions, how did she know it was guidance from the One and not insanity? How did she contain the horrible anger at being chosen for something she didn't want to do?

Looking back on conversations with her, I couldn't pinpoint a lot of anger toward the One. Oh, I'd seen her mad: irate with me the day we sparred—for trying to show her that you don't pick up a sword unless you're ready to kill; furious with Tristan and me for roughing up Nolan, the Hazorite messenger; livid at the plans Hazor had for Braide Wood's children. But when she talked about the One, I didn't hear anger. Occasionally her shoulders would sag with self-doubt. Other times she would get the same faraway look in her eyes that Linette often wore, and she'd straighten and almost glow as she talked.

One night shortly before the battle with Hazor, Tristan had confided to Susan that Kahlarean assassins would be targeting her. It was one fear too many among all the dangers she faced. She looked at me with hollow eyes and reminded me that I'd predicted her death. She'd carried that comment around, letting it grate on her like sand in her boots. I didn't know how to encourage her. Tristan was the one who always knew the right thing to say to frightened first-years on the eve of battle, but he was silent. So I asked her to recite some of her Verses. She assumed I was mocking her. Maybe I was.

But when she started to quote something about faith and running a race, the transformation happened again. It was eerie. She swung from fear to hope to something beyond. I left the room, determined to keep far away from any One who could cause that much change in someone.

All these days later He still wasn't getting the point. The One was amusing Himself with a table game, but His black and white stones were real people. I didn't want to be one of the stones He moved into play. I didn't know how to convince Him to leave me alone. And I had the oddest craving to talk to Susan about it because I suspected that she might understand.

My only companions out here were the ground-crawlers and a few small scavengers. I constructed a bracken shield and positioned myself against a rock wall with an overhang, hidden from all but the most expert of trackers. I kept my sword in my hand. After the light faded to complete blackness, the air grew damp and chill. The heat of my resentment kept me warm. I sat awake, alert, and alone through the long night. First light made the indistinct line of ferns, brush, and tree limbs grow gradually visible again. The worst of night's dangers past, I let myself doze. Once the gray glow of morning was well established, I checked that my location was secure, hid some of my gear, and headed back toward Lyric.

Everything in me wanted to run straight to Braide Wood and confer with Tristan, but first I needed to draw out the Kahlareans and make sure they weren't a threat anymore. When in doubt, gather information — and I was dealing with a lot of doubt. Had the Lyric guardians found the Kahlareans? Did the Council Guard plan to hunt me? Did Cameron have the power to move against Tristan yet? Until I came up with answers, any step could be the wrong one. Lyric was the only place to find those answers.

I spent a day in the city but stayed well clear of the central square. The hood of my cloak shielded me, and I made my way along back alleys, pausing often to listen for conversations. I heard too much about people's tedious personal problems but also gleaned a few important facts. Before nightfall I slipped out of the city. Hiking toward the ridge where I'd camped, I congratulated myself on a successful day — until the rustling of footsteps sounded behind me in the woods.

My heart pumped harder. Twigs snapped and leaves crackled. It wasn't the Kahlareans. They'd never be that clumsy. Must be guardians, though it was strange for them to patrol outside Lyric so close to dark. Near my hiding place, I climbed a tree and kept watch to see who or what was approaching my campsite.

Chapter Six

SUSAN

Mark gripped my fingers with one hand and held his sword with the other, his bulk filling the tight space beneath our attic rafters. "Ready?"

A car horn sounded down the block, and the neighbor boy plucked out scales on a piano. I glanced at the attic window where the moon tossed squares of silver light through the panes. Once we stepped through the portal, we'd be back in the place without sun or moon. A world with strange creatures, foreign rules, and frightening dangers.

Jake, why did you do this? I'm not ready to face this again.

I squared my shoulders under my rough-woven Braide Wood cloak. My fingers tightened around the toy sword I'd taken through on my first journey. "Let's go."

Mark walked forward into the soft hum between the portal stones. I tried to match his confident stride, but I flinched as I waited for lightning to grab me in a fist, as it had the first time.

Susan, get a grip. You have to find Jake.

I sucked in a deep breath, closed my eyes, and stepped forward.

Other than a little vertigo, my passage through the portal felt like a simple step into another room. My ears didn't even roar from the pressure change.

Mark hadn't fared as well. My steady-as-a-rock husband looked ashen in the pale morning light outside Lyric. He wavered on the mossy ground beneath our feet, reached for one of the smooth, braided tree trunks that surrounded us in the grove, and leaned heavily against it.

I grabbed his arm. "Are you all right?"

His eyes slowly focused, and awareness washed across his face.

"I'm fine." He sheathed his sword and rubbed his temples, as if trying to press a flaring headache down to a dull throb.

I pressed my lips together and willed my pounding heartbeat to slow down. Coming back to Lyric had seemed like the obvious choice when we made it, but my stomach shifted as I looked around us. Gnarled spice trees formed grotesque sculptures of golden wood and perfumed the air with a hint of cinnamon. Beyond the grove the massive towers of Lyric glowed white as pearl in the dawn. A half mile in the distance, the rippling pattern of the wall made the entire city shimmer like a heat mirage rising from the rolling gray-green hills.

I glanced down at the sword in my hand and gasped. "Mark, look!"

He squinted, still battling pain he was trying to hide, and raked a hand through his blond hair, where hints of silver flecked the curls at his temples.

I held up my sword. The weapon in my hand was a cracked plastic toy—the sword that had once blazed with reflected lightning during the battle of Morsal Plains. The sword of the Restorer.

Mark's eyes widened. "I don't understand."

I dropped the plastic sword and wrapped my arms around him, pulling comfort from the contour of his muscles and the rough fabric of his woven sweater.

After our adventures among the People of the Verses, I longed for our normal life with its comfortable pattern of kids' soccer games, church potlucks, and family squabbles. Instead, within an hour of returning home we realized the unthinkable had occurred. Our college-aged son, Jake, had slipped through the open portal in the attic while we had been gone.

He squeezed me. "Susan, something's wrong. Maybe we shouldn't have come."

"We had to!" I pulled back to glare at him. "We couldn't leave Jake alone here. There weren't any options."

"But . . ." Mark paused.

But we hadn't bothered to ask. We hadn't stopped to pray for guidance. We had seen a problem and stepped forward to fix it.

Tension built in my neck muscles. What was so terribly wrong with taking action? "I don't care if we were supposed to come or not. We have to find Jake." I kicked the toy weapon aside and wove around the trees, searching the grove for any sign he was nearby. If I kept moving, I wouldn't have to acknowledge the dark stubbornness taking hold in my spirit.

Mark stepped in behind me. His arms encircled me and stopped my pacing. His warm breath brushed my ear. "I know," he said, his voice low and rough. "I'm worried too."

If he had hinted at disapproval for my headstrong words, I might have shoved him back through the portal and charged headlong into a rescue on my own. Instead, his acceptance and understanding melted me. I turned in his arms and let him hold me again. His chest moved unevenly under my head.

I couldn't throw away all the lessons learned in the past weeks. The People of the Verses had been watching for a promised Restorer to rise up and help them as they faced threats from surrounding nations. I was a hapless and inadequate answer to their need. Even so, the One had accomplished His purposes.

The victory was not without cost. I had seen brave guardians give their lives. I held my friend Linette when she learned her fiancé, Dylan, had been killed. I watched Mark struggle as he confronted his past and as he faced the fear that I might have to give my life. I suffered physical pain beyond description and struggled with doubt and despair that came close to crushing me when my mind was poisoned by Rhusicans.

Through all the battles I began to understand more about the One and the depth of His love for the people here—and His love for me.

No, I couldn't throw away the lessons learned now, no matter how much panic squeezed my ribs.

I drew a steadying breath. "What's the plan?"

"If the portal isn't stable, we'd better find Jake and get home. Fast."

How much time had passed here? I felt a wave of jet lag. Mark's theories about the flow of time between the two realities—our world and this other place that had birthed him—always gave me a headache. I had enough trouble figuring out daylight savings time. We had left our world in the late evening, but it was dawn over Lyric. Exhaustion muddled my brain cells. "He can't have too much of a head start. You said time moves slowly in the reality that we aren't a part of. Right?"

"I'm not sure," Mark said quietly. "Maybe he's been here for a few minutes. Maybe days. Maybe . . ."

My chest tightened, and I forced a deep breath. "Well, he's not here by the portal. Which way would he have gone?"

Mark crouched down, touching the moss-covered earth, scanning for footprints. He shook his head and straightened, brushing off his hands. "I can't spot anything useful. But I think he'd head for the city."

Mark's strong profile turned toward the distant walls, and energy seemed to fill him as he focused on solving the immediate problem. My husband was a fixer. As long as he was doing something tangible, he was happy. No matter how formidable the challenge, he was able to shut out all the dire possibilities that my less linear mind entertained.

"Makes sense. Lead on."

"We'll circle the city and come in the entry tunnel. That's what Jake would have done. He wouldn't know how to find the hidden doors in the walls or scramble the locks."

Mark's long strides left me puffing for breath behind him. We came in from the far side of the city—the Hazor side. Since this world had no visible sun to rise and set, they didn't reference compass points; but by my mental map, we were north of the city. Behind us, plains stretched out beyond the grove. Long-haired caradoc grazed on the gentle hills, looking more like unkempt sheepdogs than the sheeplike grazing animals they were.

I caught Mark's optimism. "If Jake went in the main entrance, people would have noticed him."

Mark's steps faltered. "I hope not. Any stranger is always brought to the chief councilmember of Lyric to be questioned."

I stopped dead, my heart stuttering against my ribs. "Cameron?" I knew firsthand what desperate lengths Cameron would employ to keep his position of power on the Council. If

Jake were brought to him—

"Hurry!" My jaw tightened. I reached instinctively for my sword and frowned as my hand discovered the empty space at my hip.

We ran, following the undulating wall that stretched for at least a half mile. I doubled over to catch my breath long before we rounded the corner toward the front entrance.

Mark stopped and turned. "Wait at the grove. I'll go into the city and find him."

I shook my head and straightened, still gasping for air. "We're sticking together."

"Fine." He reached for my hand with a wry grin. "I know better than to argue when you're this determined."

Determined? He hadn't begun to see determined. I'd lost the special Restorer strength that had been my gift during my last visit here. I was an out-of-shape mom with no abilities to heal, no keen vision or hearing, and no sword. But if Cameron had done anything to Jake, I would tear him apart with my bare hands.

❧

"How can it be this hard to find one teenager?" My worry over Jake's safety made me snap at the closest target: Mark.

"Lyric is a big city," he said without looking at me. A man in a rust-colored tunic emerged from a nearby building. My husband grabbed my arm and pulled me down a side street into one of the little fern-covered parks that dotted the town.

All day we'd been avoiding anyone on the Council while asking strangers near the central square if they had seen a tall, blond youth wearing strange clothes.

"Susan, we need to talk to Jorgen." Mark tugged me down

beside him on a bench. We rested a moment, hidden by a row of hedges trimmed with the same scalloped rim as the Lyric walls.

"No. Once someone on the Council knows we're back . . ." I swallowed. I had thought we were done with all this. The confusing loyalties and duties. The obligations that came as our lives entangled with those of the people of this world. A minitran scooted past our hidden alcove on the road, carrying cargo on its automated way to a nearby storefront. My eyes stung with the memory of similar machines spewing chemicals onto the fields near Braide Wood, crippling the land and the people's livelihood. I tasted the memory of ammonia fumes in the back of my throat. I didn't want to be pulled back into battles I had no strength to fight.

Two women walked past just beyond the hedges, their conversation hushed but still audible.

"You'd think they'd have announced a gathering before now. It's been over a week since Morsal Plains."

Over a week? We'd left the morning after the battle and been away less than an hour.

"Maybe they know we don't feel like celebrating. Davis's cousin was killed. And my friend from Ferntwine lost her brother."

"Every clan there lost guardians. But they protected Braide Wood. And I heard . . ."

I stretched my hearing as they walked out of range and then remembered I'd lost that skill.

Mark took my hand and absently drew circles on my palm with his finger. "Jake wouldn't know what to do, who to trust. We know he arrived before we went home through the portal, so we know he has over a week's head start on us. Maybe that's why no one remembers seeing him. There was probably a lot of chaos in Lyric around the time of the Morsal Plains battle."

"How can you stay so calm? He's been alone here for days."

He looked out at the road. "I'm relieved. It could have been years."

A hollow ache sucked my stomach toward my spine. "We could have lost him forever." We still might. This world was full of dangers. What if he'd wandered north of Lyric and into Hazor? What if he'd explored the woods and been attacked by bears or rizzids or any of the other scavengers that made travel risky?

Mark looked down and squeezed my hand as if trying to pull agreement from it. "We can trust Jorgen."

If Mark had suggested any of the others on the Council, I would have been adamant about avoiding them, but Jorgen was like a father to Mark. When Mark had been saddled with the responsibility of fulfilling a prophecy that declared he would "bring Restoration" in the steps of his martyred father, Jorgen rescued him from his ill-suited training with the guardians and sponsored him as an apprentice councilmember for Rendor. Jorgen was also the clan leader who cleared the way for me to declare myself as the Restorer to the Council.

I nodded, finding it hard to speak around the knot in my throat. Mark rested his forehead against mine for a moment, and my breathing calmed as it melded into his rhythm. I used our pause to whisper a quick prayer to the One to keep Jake safe.

Walking through the tall arches of the Council tower made my stomach clench. This grim building was the seat of power, and its imposing architecture succeeded in making me feel powerless. The ebony floors were so hard that my footprints couldn't make an imprint in them in a million years. The minds and wills of the councilmembers were equally impervious to one small woman from another world. Yet somehow, last season the One had used a chain of circumstances to sway the Council away from a dangerous mistake. And I had been part of that. I stopped watching the glossy floor and stayed close to Mark as he negotiated our way past the Council guards and back toward the Rendor outer office.

"Markkel! Susan! Our clan is honored by your presence," Jorgen boomed with his larger-than-life energy when we entered the room. He still looked like a Norse king, complete with commanding stature and long tangled hair. One glance at our faces and he stepped closer to Mark and lowered his voice. "What brings you here? The Council session is due to begin soon. Did you hear? The lost clans are rejoining the Council."

Mark's affection for his mentor warmed his face as he dipped his head in respect.

"I talked with their clan leaders about maintaining the alliance after the battle. I'm glad the Council will welcome them back." Mark lowered his voice. "Chief Councilmember, could we have one moment of your time in private?"

Jorgen's eyebrows rose and he crossed his arms. Mark's request was presumptuous and outside of protocol. It was insulting for Mark to imply that the various staff members in the room could not be trusted. And it could be perceived as threatening for Mark to request time alone with Jorgen. Councilmembers were kept well protected, and the chief councilmember of a clan was not left unguarded. But after glancing at both of our faces, he nodded and ordered everyone from the room.

"Speak quickly." Jorgen remained standing, alert for the signaler that would call all the clans into the session.

"Our son came here. Maybe about the time of the Morsal Plains battle. We aren't sure. But he isn't meant to be here, and we need to find him and take him home. We haven't found anyone in Lyric who's seen him." Mark's voice tightened.

I stepped closer to Mark, catching Jorgen's gaze. "Can you please find out if anyone from the Council has heard about him or seen him? But . . ."

"We don't want it known that we're here," Mark finished for me. "You know we have enemies, both outside and inside the clans."

Jorgen's face remained grim, but compassion sparked in his eyes. "I'll find out what I can and send word. Where will you be?"

Mark and I looked at each other. We hadn't thought that far. Our worry about Jake had made us incapable of simple decision-making.

Jorgen saw our confusion. "You're welcome to use my extra rooms again. I'll send a messenger tonight. Markkel"—he hesitated—"I advise you to remain there, out of sight, and stay on guard. The Kahlarean you captured last season escaped four days ago and apparently has allies in Lyric. They'll be hunting the Restorer." Jorgen's glance dodged over me and away.

"But I'm not—"

Mark squeezed my arm. "Thank you. Our house is grateful for your protection and aid." As he finished his formal thanks, Mark steered us out the door. Jorgen beckoned the other Rendor councilmembers and staff into the room. Some gave us curious looks. Jorgen would order them to keep our visit a secret. Still, knowing how quickly news traveled in Lyric, we wouldn't have the luxury of anonymity for long.

Mark's stride was even quicker than usual, and I scrambled to keep up with him as he led us to the nearby building that provided apartment-type housing for councilmembers and guests. When I glanced up at him, I saw a tendon along his jawline jump. I waited until we were safely behind the door of our borrowed rooms to talk to him.

"What's wrong? Why did you stop me from telling Jorgen that I'm not the Restorer anymore?"

Mark paced quickly through the kitchen and into the back bedroom, then returned to the common room. He peered out a small window before turning to answer me. "Because we need to stop and think. The less we reveal right now, the better."

I lowered myself onto the curved, wood-framed couch. "But wouldn't it be for the best? We can't hide our presence forever. If everyone knows I'm not the Restorer, I won't be a threat to anyone. I'll be unimportant. The Kahlareans will leave me alone."

Mark looked out the window again and moved to the wall to dial the light panels down a notch. "We don't know that. The Kahlareans could still come after you purely for revenge." He stopped pacing to look at me. "This time you wouldn't heal."

A cold finger traced along my backbone. I pulled my knees up and hugged my shins. "Okay. You're right. Besides, we don't know what Tristan and Kieran have done since we left. If the Council and the Kahlareans don't know that Kieran is the Restorer now, we could endanger him if we say anything."

"Now, that wouldn't keep me up nights," Mark muttered as he prowled to the kitchen.

He'd not forgiven Kieran for threatening my life. He would probably never trust him. I pushed myself from the soft cushions of the couch and joined Mark in the kitchen, where he was poking around in the empty cubbies, hoping something edible would appear. He did the same thing at home. The image of Mark's head disappearing into the refrigerator to rummage for a snack was so familiar that I felt a poignant twist of homesickness. When would our lives return to normal?

"Should I make some clavo?" I unearthed a cloth sack plump with the spicy herbs and slid the recessed lever on a heat trivet. Mark filled a bowl with water and handed it to me. My hand shook as I reached for it.

He must have noticed; once the clavo was brewing, he took a deep breath and drew me into his arms. "I'm sorry. I didn't mean to get so jumpy. Everything's going to be okay."

He was lying to me. I felt it in the tight knots in his back and heard it in the forced confidence of his voice.

"I know. We'll find him and get home, and this will all be over," I lied back to him. At the moment, it was the kindest thing to do.

Chapter Seven

KIERAN

I crouched in the elbow of a tall tree, controlling my breathing so I was inaudible as well as invisible. Beneath me a lone figure stumbled into the clear space on the ridge. He looked around and scratched his head. Something caught his eye, and he reached for the bundle of brush hiding my gear.

He'd done enough snooping. I swung down from the tree limb and knocked him to the ground. His face hit the dirt, and he grunted. I flipped him over and pressed the tip of my dagger over his heart, getting my first good look at him.

It was the fair-haired Council spy. The youth I'd seen two days ago in the square.

"How many are with you?" I whispered. He gasped and lifted his head but couldn't risk moving more than that. His wide eyes and panicked breathing didn't impress me. I increased the pressure on my dagger, and it cut through his tunic and pierced his skin. "You are two heartbeats away from dying. Answer now."

"I'm alone." His voice came out hoarse and tight.

Hard to know if he was lying. There could be a dozen

guardians right behind him. I should kill him and grab my gear and disappear deeper into the forest. First I stretched my hearing. No hint of anyone else approaching. That could mean he was telling the truth, or it could mean he was helping the Kahlareans.

"Who do you report to on the Council?"

"What?" He was breathing fast and shallow, struggling to keep his chest still so my knife wouldn't drive further between his ribs.

I grabbed a fistful of his hair and slammed his head back against the ground. "Which clan?"

He squeezed his eyes closed and groaned.

"Look at me." I waited for him to open his eyes. I wanted him to see that I would kill him in an instant. It was a glare that had always worked for me. Except the one time at the clearing when I told Susan I could slit her throat and feel nothing. With her uncanny Restorer abilities, she saw right through me.

But this youth was no Restorer.

"Please," he moaned.

I hate when they beg. He reminded me of Nolan. Both were young, scrawny, and potentially dangerous. Thinking of Nolan brought on a wave of disgust at all the things I'd been forced to do in recent years. My anger made me lean more weight onto my blade.

The boy cried out like a caradoc being slaughtered.

"Who do you work for?" I asked again.

"I don't know what you're talking about. Please. I'm just lost. I'm sorry. I didn't mean to bother you."

"Bother me?" I pulled my knife back a few inches and laughed. "You're a Council spy. You're tracking me. And you apologize for *bothering* me?"

He pressed one hand against the odd emblem on his tunic. His palm came away bloody, and he looked at it in shock. His hand shook. "I'm sorry. I just wanted to get out of the city, so I followed you. I'll go now."

I snorted and stepped back. "I don't think so. Get up."

He scrambled to his feet and stared at me with dark-ringed eyes. When had he last slept?

I covered him with my knife while I used my other hand to pull away the branches hiding my pack. When I turned to rummage for some rope, he took off running. I grinned. It was almost dark, but he was thrashing as loudly as a lehkan caught in a thicket. I grabbed my sword and followed.

He aimed roughly toward Lyric, down through the woods.

I searched for signs of an ambush but didn't see or hear anything other than his occasional gasps and stumbles. I passed him silently, using trees for cover.

He tripped over a root and fell headlong with a yelp that would attract every scavenger in earshot.

Enough games. I stepped forward and stopped with my boots inches from his face.

He lifted his chin, then groaned and buried his face in his arms. "I just want to go home." His words were muffled. "I know I wasn't supposed to go into the attic. This has got to be a nightmare. Make it stop."

A trickle of cold ran down my spine. I had heard words like that one other time. The night that a terrified woman in Shamgar had tried to explain to me that she didn't know where she was. I grabbed the boy and shook him. "What's your name?"

His unresisting body flopped like a half-filled grain sack. "Jake." His voice was strained with something beyond fear.

"Your parents. Who are they?"

"Mark and Susan Mitchell. I live on Ridgeview Drive."

I choked.

The Restorer's son. What was he doing here? I let him go, and he collapsed back onto the ground, curled into a ball, and moaned, shutting me out again.

Blood drained from my head, and I sank down to sit next to him. Markkel and Susan's son. And I had almost killed him.

"Did she send you?" I nudged him none too gently with my boot. "Jake. Did Susan send you here?"

He flinched but slowly pulled himself up to sit on the ground, hugging his knees. "No one sent me anywhere. I got home from work early and stuck my head up in the attic to see if Mom was there." When he pushed his hair back, his face stood out palely in the growing darkness. "No one was there, so I decided to look around. I saw a sketch she drew, and then I heard whispers and something grabbed me."

Just great. As if I didn't have enough problems.

I couldn't kill him, so I needed to get us both under cover. Nightfall was close. I jumped up. "On your feet."

He looked up at me, and his lower lip quivered. "I can't."

I exhaled through my teeth and lifted my sword. I wasn't going to stand around in the dark arguing.

His eyes widened. "No, I mean, I would. But I hurt my foot when I fell."

Sure he did. I'd used that trick before. I kept my sword in my hand as I knelt down to check his leg. His ankle was swelling like an overripe orberry.

I let out a string of curses that Susan would have killed me for using in front of her son. My situation had been bad enough before. Banished from the clans, Kahlarean assassins looking for me, no one I could trust except Tristan and Kendra—and they had their own problems. All I needed was another annoying other-worlder to show up. And one who couldn't travel. Perfect.

I unwound one of the strips of cloth wrapped around my tunic sleeve and used it to bind up his ankle. Then I sheathed my sword and offered him my hand.

"We have to get back to the ridge. It's not safe here." I hoisted him to his feet and let him lean on me for support. We moved with an awkward hop and hobble. His body stiffened with pain when his foot took too much weight, but he didn't make a sound during the slow trek. It was fully dark when we reached my campsite. I eased him down next to my pack under the overhang and positioned the brambles in front of him to hide him from sight.

"Who are you?" He asked so quietly that I almost couldn't hear the tremor in his voice.

Maybe I should have explained that I no longer planned to kill him. "Kieran of Braide Wood," I said automatically. Then a hard knot tightened in my throat as I realized that wasn't true anymore. "Just Kieran. I knew your mother. I won't hurt you."

I couldn't see him but heard him settle onto the earth, reassured. "I knew Mom had some weird friends in college," he murmured. The pain of injury had drained the last of his energy. Soon deep, even breathing carried from the hiding place.

I climbed up into the closest tree and wedged myself against the trunk on a well-hidden branch, prepared for another sleepless night of standing guard. I should have checked his ankle and given him something to drink, but I couldn't risk using light. Time enough to take care of things in the morning.

In spite of all my illegal travels, I'd rarely spent so many nights outdoors, away from any real shelter. It was no wonder our people honored the separation between night and day so religiously. The black sky was empty and cold. Any small sound from an insect or ground-crawler seemed magnified in the stillness. The air felt damp and heavy, as if the entire atmosphere had decided to lower down and rest against the earth. The watches of the night are a time when even the strongest man feels small. I shivered, tugged my cloak around myself, and pulled out my boot knife. I needed something to hold. Resting my head against the rough bark, I strained to hear any sounds that would signal danger in the darkness. From time to time, Jake shifted positions and moaned. From the amount of squirming around he did, he must have been in a lot of pain.

So he claimed to be the Restorer's son. I thought about her again. Susan of Ridgeview Drive. Then Susan of Braide Wood, when Tristan brought her to his family and clan. Then Susan of Rendor. I gritted my teeth at that memory.

Last season I had arrived in Lyric with an urgent agenda of my own and had come across her dueling with a councilmember. I ran in to save her — one of those misguided impulses I must learn to control — only to have her tell me that the councilmember wasn't attacking her. He was training with her. And he was her husband, a councilmember from Rendor. My world.

Cold rage had grabbed me. Not so much at her, but at myself. She had sworn to me in the past, with huge innocent eyes, that she wasn't from our world, she was stranded and alone, and she didn't work for the Council. Against my better judgment I had started to believe her. I remember swallowing my fury and working fast to come up with a new plan to get in to speak to the Council. In hindsight maybe holding a dagger to her throat and threatening to kill her wasn't the best plan I could have come up with.

I dammed up the stream of memories and set to analyzing

how to shift my plans with this added complication. It was a long night.

When I could begin to see the shape of my dagger in my hand again, I lowered myself from the tree. I yawned and rolled my shoulders to ease their stiffness, then pulled away the bracken shield from the overhang.

Jake didn't stir. He lay curled on his side, his mouth slightly open in sleep. Did he favor Markkel or Susan? His chin hinted at the same stubborn jawline as his father, but his scrawny build must have been inherited from Susan. I cleared my throat, but he still didn't move. Another thing he had in common with his mother: a complete lack of defensive reflexes.

I flicked my boot knife so that it flew in a sharp end-over-end spiral and lodged into the ground a few inches from Jake's nose.

His eyes popped open and focused on the dagger. "Oh, man," he groaned. "I'm still in the nightmare." He scrambled to sit up but ignored the knife and gave me a strained smile.

I frowned. Was everyone from his world this stupid? "You need to go back to wherever you came from." I bent to retrieve my dagger.

His smile drooped. "I don't know how."

I wiped the blade on my sleeve and paused to look at him. The strange emblem on his tunic still puzzled me. "What clan is that?" I tapped his shirt with my knife.

He sucked in his breath at the sight of the weapon so close to the wound I'd given him yesterday. I sheathed the blade, and he looked at his shirt, frowning.

"Oh, it's a band I used to like. I went to a lot of their concerts, but they've gotten so commercial I don't really like their new CDs very much. . . ."

I rubbed my temples. Hill-gods spare me, he sounded exactly like Susan, babbling nonsense. I unwrapped his ankle and tried to move it.

He gasped and stiffened. The skin around his mouth went white, and the muscles near his eyes pulled tight. I tried to be careful as I examined the injury, but his hands clawed into the ground for support.

He'd never be able to walk on the swollen joint. It looked like some bones had broken. I would have kicked him if he weren't already in so much pain. "It's a mess. What am I going to do with you?"

"I'm sorry," he said, voice tight.

I stormed away to the stream to splash my face with water and swear out of earshot. Even that did little to help my temper, but I couldn't leave him undefended for long. I walked back to the campsite and checked our perimeter.

His eyes followed my movements, but he said nothing.

When I was reasonably sure no one was approaching, I pulled out a wooden bowl and brought him some water from the stream. I split a loaf of bread with him, noticing my supplies were getting low. While he was eating, I dug up a few clumps of blue fern that were growing near the stream. I washed off their roots and brought them back. "Chew on these. It'll help with the pain."

He turned them in his hands, then took a few cautious nibbles.

"Let's sort this out," I said, determined to stay calm this time. "How do we send you back? Where did you arrive?"

"I don't know." Jake adjusted his position, his back resting at an angle against the rock wall behind him. "Something grabbed me, and then everything was dark. I kept hearing noises, so I ran."

"You mean you arrived during the night?"

"I guess so. But there was no moon or stars or anything."

He was doing it again. Using words that made no sense. In general I could understand him, but then he'd say something incomprehensible. I concentrated on his story, watching for any sign he was lying.

"When I could finally see, I was near this huge white wall. I kept walking along it until I found a tunnel and went through into the city. I tried to find a phone, but nothing looked right." He shifted again and his eyes studied me. "Where am I?"

"The city is Lyric. It's the capital."

He shook his head. "Hey, I got an A in Geography, and I've never heard of a capital called Lyric."

"Neither had your mother, but she's been here too." I watched Jake closely. "This isn't your world."

He looked at me for a moment and then at the fistful of fern roots. He shoved them back at me. "Here, I think I've had too much of this."

My mouth twitched. "Jake, your mother came here too, but she showed up in Shamgar. It's a deserted city near the border with Hazor. It turned out she was the Restorer our people had been waiting for. She . . ." I looked at Jake's hanging jaw and wondered how to explain everything that had happened last season. I gave him a short version, but judging from his glazed eyes, he wasn't absorbing much of the story.

I sprang to my feet to check the approach to the ridge again. Everything was quiet, but I knew better than to relax. The Kahlareans could be anywhere. How could I hope to trap them, or even elude them, with this crippled youth here? I should leave him and head for Braide Wood.

Kendra's face floated through my thoughts. My sister had been close to death when I'd left Braide Wood to help Tristan three seasons ago. Susan was the one who had brought her back from the Rhusican poison. I owed Susan. Markkel too. They'd both risked their lives for Braide Wood. I couldn't leave their son here unprotected. I wasn't only short on supplies; I was short on options. I slammed my palm against a tree trunk, then watched the scraped skin heal. I shook my head. Too bad Jake couldn't heal.

I glanced back at him, sprawled on the ground, and saw an odd image—almost like the forms that sometimes appear in fog, especially when you're short on sleep. I saw myself kneeling by Jake, holding his ankle. I blinked and the vision disappeared. Words from the old myth whispered in my mind: "In every time of great need, a Restorer is sent to fight for the people and help the guardians. The Restorer is empowered with gifts to defeat our enemies and turn the people's hearts back to the Verses."

Susan had discovered all kinds of strange "gifts," and they rarely worked in a predictable manner. Had she ever had this sense of being nudged in a certain direction? When the stirring wouldn't leave me alone, I walked over to Jake. He watched me warily. I don't think he had fully accepted where he was, and his pain only added to his confusion. I rested my hands on his swollen ankle and closed my eyes.

"What are you doing?"

"I don't know," I snapped. "Be quiet." I tried to remember something from the Verses to say. That's what Susan would have done. All that came to mind was the genealogy of the Blue Knoll clan, and somehow that didn't seem very helpful.

You are not alone.

"I told you to be quiet." I opened my eyes and glared at Jake.

His eyebrows pulled up. "I didn't say anything."

I closed my eyes and heard it again. *You are not alone.*

This time I knew it wasn't Jake. That was supposed to comfort me? Anger tightened my grip on Jake's ankle.

He yelped. "Hey, if you're trying to set the bone, could you give me a stick to bite down on? That hurts!"

"Sorry." Jake would think I was insane, but with everything else he had to cope with, it wouldn't matter. I relaxed my grip on his leg and spoke softly to the One. "I tried asking for Your help in Lyric. You didn't unlock the door."

You didn't ask for my help. There was a twinge of humor in the inaudible voice.

My face heated as I remembered my attempts to talk to Him in the cell. I had given Him orders. He had a point. "I guess I just don't know how this works."

Why is that?

My memory played out scene after scene of my life. A boy shutting out the evening Verses after supper. A youth avoiding the season-end prayers. A man hovering in the door of the Lyric tower refusing to go inside, jeering at Susan when she tried to talk to me about the One. I couldn't answer Him for a long moment. "All right. Fine. I admit it. It's my fault that I don't understand You. Can we deal with that later? What do You want me to do here?"

In some inexplicable way, I felt Him smile. Warmth poured through me like a fever that scalded my body but didn't linger.

"Ow! What are you doing?" Jake cried out.

My eyes popped open, and I pulled my hands away from his leg to sit back on my heels.

He leaned forward to grab his ankle, glaring at me. When he moved his hand, I saw it. Blue and purple discoloration faded, swelling withdrew. He was healing. He realized it the same moment I did and looked at me, wide-eyed. Then his face turned a shade whiter, his eyes rolled up, and he fainted.

I winced at the sound his head made when it hit the stone ledge behind him. A little light-headed myself, I stood slowly and walked to the edge of the ridge. What had just happened? Why had it worked this time? I rubbed at the several days' worth of stubble on my face and took a deep breath. Lesson one: I guess I'm not the one giving the orders.

Did Tristan and Kendra know about that? Linette surely did. Of course, it would be easier for her. She'd never been as independent as I was. And she had lots of practice talking to the One. Songkeepers did it all the time.

I looked up at the gray sky, grateful I wasn't hearing any more voices. Now I had to decide what to do with Jake. Susan hadn't known how to return to her world, but Markkel had. However, he was almost as tight-lipped as I was. He never told me how they planned to leave. So how could I find a way to send Jake back?

We couldn't simply poke around Lyric. My plans to draw out the Kahlareans would be suicidal with Jake to look after.

"Who are you, really?" Jake asked.

I spun around. He was standing several paces away from me. I hadn't been paying attention. Too many nights without sleep. I was getting sloppy. He rubbed the back of his head and stared at me with distrust.

"I told you already." I matched his irritation.

He studied me for a moment. "You pray really strange."

"What?"

"Back there. You were praying, weren't you?"

"I was talking to the One."

"Mmm hmm. Well, it wasn't like any praying I've ever heard."

I didn't need this aggravation. "It worked, didn't it?"

He rolled his foot around a few times. "All better," he agreed, still wary. "Now what?"

"I'm trying to figure that out. I think we'd better head to Braide Wood, but we'll need supplies. It's a long hike, and we can't risk the transports."

He shifted his weight. "No. I need to find a way home. Thanks for fixing my foot, but I'm going back to the city."

A cold edge of doubt slid into my thoughts. I'd seen him talking to someone on the Council. He knew I was here. And now he wanted to go back to Lyric alone. Even if he were really Susan's son, there was no way I was letting him out of my sight. On the other hand, I didn't want to keep him against his will. When we did eventually get him back to his parents, I didn't want him complaining.

It was a little late to play harmless and trustworthy, but I gave it a try. "You're going to need some help. I know this area. You'd better stick with me." I smiled and moved past him to stow my gear.

He crossed his arms and frowned. "I'm not going anywhere with you."

Yep. Markkel's stubborn jaw. "Jake, you're smart to be careful. But I'm a friend of your parents. I told you. They were here for almost a whole season. They wouldn't want you getting into trouble on your own. Lyric can be a dangerous place."

Jake's forehead wrinkled. He opened his mouth and then closed it again. Finally he worked up his nerve and confronted me directly. "You're a liar."

I was offended. I've lied often and well, but this time I had been completely truthful. "What do you mean?"

"I've seen my mom every day. She hasn't been away from

home overnight all spring. She couldn't have done all those things you said. You couldn't know her." He was tensing for a fight.

This wasn't going well. Years of keeping people at a distance gave me little skill for winning someone's trust. Guile or force had always worked for me before. "Time flows differently here. That's what Markkel said."

"Markkel?"

"Your father."

"His name is Mark."

"Right. In your world. But here he was Markkel of Rendor clan, the son of the prophecy. His father was the last Restorer."

Jake rubbed his eyes. "You're nuts. And I'm outta here." He set out through the woods.

He had nerve. I had to give him that. He walked away, setting a fast pace but not running.

I made short work of covering any signs that we'd ever been at the ridge, shouldered my pack, belted on my sword, and set out after him. When I caught up, I walked alongside him for a while. He glanced at me but kept moving.

"Jake, listen. There are some dangerous folk around here."

"Yeah, I know." His hand moved to the bloodied cut on his tunic.

"Sorry about that. I was afraid you were . . . someone else." Why was I apologizing for defending my campsite? I slowed my pace subtly, hoping he would adjust to my speed. It worked. I had precious little time to convince him to trust me before we lost the cover of the forest and approached Lyric. I hadn't made a good impression so far—jumping out of a tree at him, sticking my dagger between his ribs, having strange conversations with some invisible One. "I know this must be confusing for you, but why would I have healed your ankle if I wanted to harm you?"

He stopped and looked down at his foot and then at my face again. "How did you do that?"

"I don't know."

He rolled his eyes.

No wonder I rarely bothered with truth. Lies would have worked much better. But at least he had stopped walking. I had to keep him talking. "Look, it's been a rough couple of days. There are some people looking for me, and . . ."

His eyes lit with interest. "You mean you're a criminal?"

"No!" I objected. "Well, technically some people might look at it that way, but it was a misunderstanding." I was losing patience. We should be heading the opposite direction, and he wasn't cooperating. I was beginning to assess the merits of hitting him over the head and dragging him to Braide Wood. Time for some questions of my own.

"Jake, a few days ago, I saw you talking to a councilmember in the square." My voice hardened. "By the Council tower."

He looked puzzled. "Oh, the police station? Yeah, I thought I should go there for help, but they wouldn't let me in. And one of those guys in the funny uniforms asked me who I was and told me that if I was a visitor, I should report to the chief councilmember of Lyric. I didn't know what he was talking about, so I just agreed and left."

His eyes didn't shift. There was no fidgeting; his body betrayed no lie. He seemed completely guileless.

It made me nervous. "And what were you doing before you followed me out of the city?"

He shrugged. "Hiding, mostly. Trying to figure out what was going on. Trying to find a way back out. I lost track of how many days I was there."

For a second I glimpsed the terror he worked hard to

suppress. What would it be like to find yourself in a strange world in the middle of the night? No supplies, no weapons. If he was who he claimed, he'd done a good job surviving so far. His parents would be proud of him. But if he was lying, and I went into Lyric with him, I'd be trapped.

We studied each other in mutual suspicion. This wasn't getting us anywhere.

I sighed. "I want to get you home, but we need supplies, and we have to stay hidden. I have friends in Braide Wood who can help you. You'll like them. They're not like me."

A reluctant grin appeared at the side of Jake's mouth. "You'll really help me find a way home?"

"Jake Mitchell of Ridgeview Drive, I pledge you my protection for the sake of your parents." I offered him my right arm. He tentatively reached his hand out, and I grasped his forearm. Our eyes met, and I tightened my grip. "Don't make me regret this."

Chapter Eight

KIERAN

We slipped through a side entrance in the Lyric wall. Jake stared in fascination as I used my lock scrambler. I had the uneasy feeling Markkel and Susan wouldn't be thrilled with the things he was learning from me.

I moved quickly through side streets and was gratified that Jake followed close behind. I kept an eye on him in case he decided to bolt, but he seemed resigned to staying with me for the moment. We approached the home I was looking for, and I signaled him to stay back as I watched the street. Reassured that it was deserted, I tugged his arm and we ran for the door. I tapped lightly. When the door swung open, I didn't wait for an invitation. I lurched inside, pulling Jake behind me.

"Kieran! Are you all right?" Tag's expression blended worry and genuine warmth. She lowered her voice and looked around as if her toddlers might be Council spies. "They've had guardians searching house by house for you. What kind of trouble are you in?"

"Tagatha, this is Jake. He's the son of friends. We need some help."

She beamed at him. "Well met, Jake. You look like you could use a good meal." She threw her arms around him and drew him into the common room. He stiffened and kept his arms at his sides, looking over at me in alarm. I grinned. Tag could be a little overwhelming on first acquaintance.

"Kieran, watch Luc and Tamara while I make a meal for this poor child," Tag ordered. Now it was my turn to be alarmed. She had already pulled Jake after her and left me alone with her children. Luc gave me a drooling, toothless grin. He looked fairly harmless, sitting among a pile of carved-wood animals. He picked up one and sucked on it. Tamara was older. She waddled over to me on chubby legs and reached for the hilt of my boot knife.

"Pretty," she said with wide eyes.

I lifted her up and held her at arm's length with a scowl. "Don't touch."

She giggled.

"Bring them in here," Tag called from the back room. I tucked Tamara under one arm and scooped up Luc with the other and managed not to drop them before turning them over to Tag. She pursed her lips, clearly struggling not to laugh. Jake was already perched on a stool with a plate of fruit.

"Thanks for the meal." I eased into a chair. "We need some supplies—if you have anything to spare. I'll pay you back."

"Where are you heading?" Tag asked, pushing a plate in my direction.

Jake's head came up. "Braide—"

I kicked him. "It's better if you don't know," I told Tag, taking a moment to glare at Jake. He glared right back, but I ignored that.

She shook her head. "They've already been here asking about you."

My shoulders tensed. "What did you tell them?"

"What could I say?" She waved one hand around. "How should I know what an in-law from Braide Wood has been up to? I hardly ever hear from Tristan and his wife—why would I know anything about her brother?" She winked.

I relaxed back against the chair. "Thanks, Tag."

There was a sound at the door, and I pulled Jake off the stool and pressed us both against the wall, out of sight of the common room.

Tag settled Luc in her arms. "That will be Jameth, home for lunch." She disappeared toward the front door, Tamara toddling behind.

I risked a glance around the alcove wall.

Jameth threw the door wide. He was a burly trader with an easy smile and enough energy to keep up with his wife. Tag ran forward to greet him and grabbed him in a hug, squashing Luc and making him chortle. With a little effort I heard what she whispered in her husband's ear.

"We have guests. Kieran needs our help. He's got a boy with him who looks like he's been on the run."

"Kieran's here? Half of Lyric is hunting for him. Are you crazy?"

"Shhh. They've already been here looking."

I stepped forward. "Jameth, I don't want to cause your family trouble. I was hoping to borrow some supplies, but I'll leave if you'd rather." It wouldn't be a surprise if he tossed me out the door. Or ran to get the Council guards.

He sighed and looked me up and down. "When did you last sleep?"

I ran a hand across the rough stubble on my jaw. "A couple days, I think."

Jameth nodded. "You look it. Plan to stay here tonight. I'll get the supplies you need, and you can leave at first light."

I studied his expression, unsure that he meant it.

He saw my uncertainty. "Kieran, I may not be happy about it, but you are family. You can rest here tonight." He strode past me into the kitchen.

I followed him, stepping around Luc's toys. "No need. If you can help us restock, we'll leave before nightfall." I didn't want to put Jameth and Tag in danger. Or maybe I wasn't completely sure I could trust them.

Tag spoke up. "You are not dragging this boy out into the forest after dark. Poor thing."

Jake had settled back at the table and was busy stuffing fruit into his mouth as fast as he could. The "poor thing" looked thrilled to be offered a soft bed for the night.

Maybe they were right. Maybe we should risk a little rest. My reflexes were slow from too many nights without sleep.

Jameth saw my hesitation. "You'll both be under my protection here," he said formally.

"No one can know we've been here."

He nodded. "I wouldn't want anyone to suspect we helped you. I understand the danger."

I relaxed a little. We were a threat to each other, and that made me feel as safe as I'd been in many days. While Jameth ate, we talked over the supplies I needed, although I was careful to remain vague about my plans. Jake warmed up to Tag and began drilling her with questions about every mundane item in her kitchen, his eyes bright with curiosity. After Jameth headed back out to work, I interrupted Tag's explanation of clavo and Jake's dissertation about his favorite drinks on his world.

"Jake, enough." He had no caution. Who knew what he might let slip?

His animated gestures stopped immediately, and he seemed to pull into himself, his gaze dropping to the floor.

Tag glared at me. "I've been thinking. It might be better if Jake stayed here with us when you leave. It doesn't look like you've done a great job taking care of him." Her eyes tracked the blood on his tunic and turned back to me.

I should have jumped at the chance to get rid of the gangly adolescent nuisance. Instead, I bristled. "No. He's coming with me." He could be a hazard to me if I left him behind. I didn't bother telling Tag that. I didn't have to explain myself to her.

An expression flitted across Jake's downturned face, but I couldn't tell if it was relief or disappointment. He hid it quickly and looked at Tag. "Thanks for showing me all this stuff. And it's really nice of you to let us stay here."

Tag beamed. "My pleasure." Then she turned back to me. "So Kieran, will you take a message to Tristan for me?"

I glared at her. "You don't know where we're heading."

"Right. So will you take a message?"

"I will," Jake chimed in. "Just write him a note, and I'll take it to him."

Tag and I exchanged a bewildered look. "Do what?" she asked.

"Write a note." Jake took a swallow of water from his mug. "Words on paper? You know?" When Jake saw our confusion, his eyes widened. "You mean you don't write? How do you remember what's important? How do you send messages?"

"We have messengers," Tag said slowly.

"This just gets weirder and weirder." Jake turned back to his plate.

He had that right. And my resistance was so low from fatigue that I relented and let Tag recite a message for me to take to Tristan in Braide Wood—even while reminding her that I had no intention of heading that way.

I'd been running two steps ahead of danger for several days, so I didn't expect to sleep well that night. But apparently even Restorers need rest; exhaustion claimed me right after supper, and when I opened my eyes again, it was morning. I woke with the vague unease caused by nightmares that I couldn't completely remember. Something about being bound—struggling against ropes—and running. Lots of running. But it wasn't the Lyric guardians who had been chasing me.

I pushed aside the images along with the blanket and rubbed my neck. Past time to leave Lyric.

I offered sincere thanks to both Jameth and Tag, along with a reminder to tell no one we had been in Lyric. Then Jake and I set out through the dim, near-empty streets toward the city wall. Jake had his own pack now, and mine was restocked with enough rations to enable us to travel quickly and independently for several days. We edged our way through little-used alleys, staying pressed against buildings wherever possible. I desperately wanted to try once more to reconnoiter the Council and guardian towers for any news about the Kahlareans, but it was too risky. We'd have to set out for Braide Wood assuming the assassins were still out there and that the odds were high they would eventually pick up our trail.

When we reached the curving scallop of the white wall, I pulled out my scrambler.

"Could I try?" Jake asked.

He'd been quiet all morning, and I hadn't known what to make of his silence. I assumed he was still struggling to accept his new circumstances, and the fact was I had too much to worry about to waste time reassuring him. It was a relief to see him liven up about something—even if it was illegal lock scrambling.

I showed him how to depolarize the magnetic locking system and explained some of the uses of the tool. After a few tries, he managed to get the door open and grinned widely. I had to snatch the tool out of his hands or he would have kept playing all morning.

We jogged over several gray, moss-covered hills before reaching the shelter of the forest. Once we'd covered a couple miles, I stopped to give Jake a rest. We sat down on a fallen tree, and I pulled out a gourd of juice and tossed it to him. He drank some and his face puckered. "So you really knew my parents?" Jake asked suddenly.

I studied him without answering. He looked better today. A couple of good meals went a long way toward putting some color back into his face. Tag had replaced Jake's strange and bloodied shirt with a woven earth-toned tunic that would fit right in when we reached Braide Wood. His long hair fell across his brow, and he pushed it back, giving me another glimpse of the metal studs he wore.

"When did that happen?" I grimaced at the wounds in the upper cartilage of his ear.

He took a moment to figure out what I meant and then grinned. "My eighteenth birthday. Mom wouldn't let me get any piercings until then."

"You *chose* to have metal attached to your head?"

"Don't people here have piercings?"

"The Hazorites use them to mark the slaves they bring in from nations they've conquered. At first I figured you were an escaped slave from one of the villages on the far side of Sidian."

Jake laughed, a rich, lighthearted sound. I'd watched him in a variety of circumstances, and there was no cynicism or bitterness in him. He seemed as forthright as Tristan but without the weight of guilt and responsibility that Tristan wore like a cloak. He was a resilient young man.

I gave another grudging mental nod toward Markkel and Susan. They'd done well with him. Had they already discovered Jake was missing? What would they do? Could they return to Lyric through the portal? I didn't know enough about how it worked. If so, would they soon be roaming Lyric looking for Jake? What if the Kahlareans learned that Susan the Restorer was back and continued their quest to kill her? I scrubbed at my forehead, suddenly tired.

For a moment I almost wished for Linette's easy ability to ask the One for help. This situation was dangerously complicated, and I had a bad feeling that I could be making things worse by leaving Lyric. But waiting to be grabbed by either the Council Guard or the Kahlareans wasn't an option either.

I looped the gourd's tie around one of the straps on my pack and levered myself back to my feet, deciding to answer his earlier question. "Yes, I knew your parents. I crossed swords with your mother a few times."

His eyebrows shot up, and he eyed the sheath that rested against my hip. "Unbelievable." Then he pushed himself to his feet and fell in beside me as we continued striding through the woods. "So who won?"

A short bark of laughter burst from my chest. The first time we'd sparred was by the caves overlooking Braide Wood. She barely had the strength to swing her sword, and I left her covered with small cuts. They healed rapidly. No harm done. Still,

I didn't feel like explaining that to Jake. Then came the fight with her and Markkel in the guardians' training tower. I ended up on the floor with Markkel's foot on my chest and his sword tip under my chin. I had a fever, and it was two against one. Hardly a fair fight. I could have beaten her easily. But that was before she had fully developed her Restorer powers. The way she fought during the battle on Morsal Plains, I wouldn't have wanted to be on the wrong side of her sword that day.

"I guess we're about even." I picked up the pace so he'd be too out of breath to keep asking questions.

Late in the afternoon, when the rains had begun to ease, we arrived at a large grove of bitum trees. Clusters of these wide-leaved giants grew in almost every area of clan territories. Here they presented a challenge. Their trunks were covered with overlapping runnels of sticky black sap and grew so close together that it took effort to weave between them without touching any. This grove was also unique because it was tucked in the narrow gap between two ridgelines.

Jake walked straight toward one of the trees, his hand outstretched. "Wow! I've never seen trees like this before."

I grabbed the back collar of his tunic and jerked him away. "Don't touch it."

He coughed and straightened the shirt so it no longer cut into his neck. "Why?" He glared at me.

"Fine. Go ahead and get yourself covered with sap. But I'm not slowing down to help you."

His eyes narrowed.

I pulled my boot knife from its sheath and cut a long gouge into the trunk of the closest tree. Viscous fluid poured from the slit and pooled on the ground around the tree. Jake stood and watched me. I jerked my head. "Go on. Straight through there. I'll be right behind you."

He opened his mouth to ask me what I was doing but then shook his head and started winding his way forward between the tall trunks. His slim build helped him in the effort to slip between the trees without brushing against them. I followed, weaving side to side and cutting deeply into each trunk with my knife. The tarlike pools at the base of each tree grew and began to crawl toward each other. When we left the grove, I paused to wipe the worst of the sap off my blade and sheathed it. We picked up our pace.

"What was that all about?" Jake asked.

I ignored him and glanced at the sky. There wasn't much time left to find a defensible shelter for the night. I plowed ahead, keeping my ears attuned to the clumsy rustling sound of Jake's progress behind me but also focusing outward for the subtle hint of any skilled trackers. Another mile brought us to a natural opening halfway up the ridgeline. With scrambling we were able to climb up to it. The difficult access would give us some warning of enemies approaching, and we'd be under cover. Jake hunched over to enter the cave and collapsed onto the ground with a sigh of relief. He had lost some of the color in his face again. I suppose I should have taken into account that he'd had several rough days, but he had managed.

"Jake, do you have skills with any weapons?"

Light filtered through some branches in front of the cave entrance and scattered a strange pattern across his face. He shook his head, closing his eyes.

I nudged him with my boot. "I have to take care of something. You'll need to be able to defend yourself if anything happens before I get back."

"Okay. You can leave me your sword," he mumbled, lids still closed.

I rolled my eyes. His chest was already beginning to move in slow, deep breaths. How had Tristan ever put up with training first-year guardians all those years? I moved closer, and when Jake didn't move, I slapped him hard across the face. That worked.

"Hey!" He skittered back and rubbed his cheek, looking up at me in panic.

I pulled the knife from my boot sheath. His eyes flared with fear.

Good. A little adrenaline would help him stay awake. "Are you listening now? Stay on guard until I'm back. I should be here before it's totally dark." I tossed the dagger lightly in my hand and grasped the blade, offering it to him handle first. "Use this if you need it."

He swallowed and nodded. "And if you don't come back?"

"It means I'm dead. Follow this valley until you get to the pine forest near Braide Wood. Or go back to Lyric and ask Jameth and Tag for help." I rubbed the back of my neck. His odds of surviving were equally bad either way, but I didn't need to tell him that.

I stepped out of the cave and clambered the rest of the way up the rock face to the high ridgeline. I stretched, shoulders released from the weight of a pack, and started running. I stayed on the balls of my feet but didn't move as silently as I could have if speed were not such an issue. Twining branches reached out to grab me, and the rough terrain made my ankles buckle and recover several times as I landed on uneven roots. It didn't take long to return to the grove of bitum trees. Because I needed to circle them from the high ground, it did take some time to work my way past them and then down to the valley again. The sky was fading from gray to slate as night approached, and it was already hard to see when I approached the place where I had first begun cutting open the trees. My eyes were keen enough to spot what I was looking for and hoped not to find.

On the tar that had covered the ground throughout the pass under the bitum trees, two sets of footprints cast semi-hardened impressions. They weren't the distinctive boot prints of Council guards, either. These were the light treads of Kahlareans.

We were being tracked.

Chapter Nine

KIERAN

Night crept inexorably forward while death slipped toward our hiding place on silent Kahlarean-like feet. I could backtrack and return to the cave from the upper ridgeline, but that would take too long. Instead, I wove between the dark trees and watched the soft marks in the sap. As soon as I was clear of the grove, I ran full out. The light was so dim it was foolish to slow down to search for signs of their trail. I had to assume they were heading toward the shallow cave. Jake's only hope was for me to reach the assassins before they found him.

Without slowing, I drew my sword, expecting to stumble across the two Kahlareans at any moment. Leaves blurred past me as I ran, and my breathing settled into a steady rhythm. Sucking in air for four strides, blowing out for the next four strides as my feet pounded the earth. I looked for any sign of gray figures in the dusk. The whole world had turned gray. Tall bunches of underbrush could be sheltering an army of assassins. Slim boulders tricked the eye and resembled the cloaked figures of Kahlareans. Everything looked harmless and lethal at the same time. So I kept running.

When I reached the cliff face where Jake and I had climbed, I stopped and turned a slow, complete circle. No sign of them. I'd have to sheath my sword to climb up to the opening. First I tossed a rock upward, letting it clatter against the rocks above the cave. If Jake were still alive, he could peer out and give me a clue of how to proceed. Unless they were with him. I wanted to call out to him, but that would only attract the assassins if they hadn't already found him. There weren't many options.

I sheathed my sword and wished I hadn't left my dagger with Jake. I could have carried it in my teeth while climbing and had a weapon more readily accessible. No time for regrets now. I tossed one more rock and frowned at the loud clack as it hit solidly against the rocks over the cave. There was no sign of movement, so I started climbing.

When I hoisted myself up to the small ridge of level ground in front of the cave, I drew my sword, relieved I'd made it that far. Still no sounds and no movement. I quickly searched the area around our hiding place, nerves wound tight as I waited for a Kahlarean to spring out at me. When that didn't happen, I took a deep breath and stepped into the cave.

As expected, I found Jake's body sprawled facedown on the ground, unmoving. My skin prickled with an awareness of danger. He clutched my dagger in one hand, but there was no sheen of blood on the blade. He hadn't even managed a defense. I rummaged in my pack for a light cube and risked dialing up a small amount of light. Dark pools around his body that I had assumed were his blood were simply variations in the stone floor. I grabbed his shoulder to roll him over and look for wounds. A deep moan sounded from his chest. I jumped back a pace. I'd heard dead bodies make sounds before, but it was never a comfortable sensation. Chiding myself for my jumpiness, I stepped close again, just as Jake's eyes popped open.

We gasped in unison. His startled reaction turned to tired bewilderment. My own surprise transformed quickly to rage.

"If you're still alive, why weren't you keeping watch?" I pushed the words through clenched teeth. For a moment his face flashed annoyance at being disturbed, but then his eyes traveled to the sword in my hand and back to my face.

"What happened?" he asked muzzily. He pushed himself up to sit and looked in surprise at the dagger in his hand, as if he'd forgotten it was there.

My knuckles popped as my fingers tightened to a stranglehold on the grip of my sword. My arm shook with the effort it took to sheathe the weapon. I turned my back on Jake and left the cave. Everything in me wanted to pound his lazy, careless, annoying body to a pulp. He was putting me at extra risk by his presence and didn't have the decency to obey the simplest of instructions. Didn't he understand how much danger we were in?

No. He couldn't understand.

He wasn't in his own world. He didn't know Kahlareans were tracking us and wouldn't comprehend what that meant anyway. I heard him moving around in the cave and then his quiet footsteps coming out to join me.

"Here." He handed me my dagger, flat across his open palm. He didn't have a clue at how furious I was at him or why. I gritted my teeth harder, sliding the blade into my boot sheath quickly, before I was tempted to use it. I bundled my red-hot anger and pressed it downward into the frigid lump of stone I found easier to control. He must have been able to read the set of my shoulders, because he retreated into the cave and left me alone.

Patience.

I thought I had plenty. I could hide in a doorway for hours, motionless, assessing if it was safe for me to enter the street. It had taken years to build up my contacts in Hazor during my search for cousins lost when Shamgar fell. I could rebuild a transtech component a dozen times in a row until it worked right. I knew all about patience.

But Jake had managed to fray every rein on my temper. I should have killed him before I had found out who he was.

Much later I joined him in the cave.

"We're being followed." I kept my voice flat. Resentment continued to writhe inside me like a nest of newborn rizzids. "They usually strike at dusk when they're hunting, but they won't want to give us time to get away. My guess is that they'll attack at first light."

Jake didn't answer. He was sitting with his legs drawn up, watching me, face carefully blank.

"Are you listening? If they had moved in sooner, you'd be dead now."

In the pale glow of the light cube, his mask slipped. Honest fear skittered across his face. He swallowed. "Why? Who are they? Why would they want to kill me?" He tried to keep his voice as level as mine but couldn't hide the telltale high pitch of anxiety.

"They're after me, not you. But they aren't always particular about who they kill."

"And why do they want to kill you?"

"Actually, they want me alive. They think I know . . . something useful." I knelt down to pull some bread out of my pack. "The point is we're in danger. So when I ask you to stay on guard"— I drilled his eyes with the cold anger in my own—"I expect you to stay on guard."

His chin dropped, and he stared at his shoes.

"Understand?"

He nodded listlessly.

"Do you understand?" I bit each syllable.

His eyes flicked over my face and back down. "Yes. All right? I'm sorry."

His sullen apology made my jaw clench. I drew my sword, positioned myself near the cave entrance, and shut down the light cube. I wasn't hungry, but I gnawed on the small loaf of bread. I didn't bother to offer any to Jake. He had his own supplies if he was hungry.

I heard him position his pack to use as a pillow and try to get comfortable on the damp stone surface. I focused on the black void beyond the cave, listening, straining to see any variation in darkness or sense any movement.

Much later Jake shifted again. He tapped one finger aimlessly, as if keeping time to a song in his head. Soon he sighed and turned again.

"Now what?" I said at last.

He went very still, then cleared his throat. "Sorry. I can't sleep."

I shook my head, knowing he couldn't see me in the darkness. "Well, you didn't have that problem earlier." And suddenly it struck me as funny. A chuckle broke out of my tight throat. Then I started laughing in earnest, though I kept the volume low. We didn't want to draw the attention of anything lurking outside the cave. My free arm gripped my side as my shoulders shook. I heard Jake start to laugh too. First from nervous tension, then in genuine relief. I thought of how angry I'd felt when I discovered he wasn't lying dead in a pool of blood, and that triggered another round of laughter until I was gasping.

"You're safe for the night," I told him once I caught my breath. My voice sobered. "They aren't likely to attack until morning, and I'll stand guard."

"That's not why I can't sleep," he said quietly. "I can't figure this out."

"Figure out what?" I adjusted my position and moved my sword to my other hand for a while.

"You were really friends with my mom and dad?"

Friends? My past encounters with Susan and Markkel played through my mind. Swords, daggers, and angry confrontations seemed to be a frequent element of each memory.

"We helped each other. They fought to protect my clan. Hazor was going to destroy Braide Wood." The darkness made it easier to talk. I told him the story again. This time he was able to take more of it in. Dark watches of the night slipped past while he asked quiet questions and I wove a story that was fairly close to the truth.

"And then they left to go back to your world," I finished at length.

"But if she could do all those superhero things because she was the Restorer, does that mean you . . . ?" I could almost hear magchips sparking in Jake's mind. "How come you could heal my foot? Are you . . . ?"

What difference would it make now? He'd find out when we reached Braide Wood. Tristan or Kendra or Tara would let something slip. Not cautious enough by half.

"Yes. All right? I'm the next Restorer." Resentment sharpened my voice. "The One wants me to do something. Not sure what."

He let out a low whistle. "Wow." He nudged his pack into a new position under his head. "And you're not happy about it?"

"Happy?" So many objections raced through my thoughts that I sputtered. "No, I'm not happy."

"Humph." Jake flopped around again.

"What?"

"Nothing. Just, well . . . I'd be pretty excited if God gave me a job like that. Selling car parts at Harvey's is all right, but" — I heard the smile in his voice — "when I was a kid, I wanted to be a knight and battle dragons and fight for the helpless."

I couldn't understand half of his words. I'd had the same problem with his mother. But I followed the general idea, and my mouth twisted. "You'll get along great with Tristan." I glared out into the darkness. "But it's not like that. I'm supposed to follow the Verses, and I don't know if I believe in them. Everything keeps going wrong. Your mom was a pretty odd Restorer, but she had . . . I don't know. Faith."

"You don't?"

"I have faith that the world doesn't make sense and the One is playing some crazy game. I don't want to be a part of it, but He won't leave me alone."

Jake snickered, and some of my earlier irritation returned. "You think it's funny?"

"No, no. I remember thinking something like that once, when I was young."

As far as I was concerned, he was still young. And I didn't appreciate his condescension.

"What would you know about it?" He had two parents who cared about him. The easy way he trusted showed me he hadn't suffered enough betrayals to harden him yet. And the wistful way he spoke of doing battle for the One showed me he'd never had to cross swords with a serious enemy. He heard my disdain and was quiet for a while.

"Cancer." He said the word as if it were very significant.

"What?"

He sighed. "It's an illness. On our world. Trust me. I know a little bit about the world not making sense."

It was my turn to be quiet. "Tell me," I said at last.

He explained the battle that had shaped several years of his childhood. He told me of a sickness that poisoned the very blood in his veins and nearly took his life. He told me of the painful lengths he went to in fighting it. His voice was so low that I was grateful for my enhanced hearing so I could follow his story. I've confronted death many times, but always with strength in my arms and a sword in my hand. His descriptions chilled me.

"And after that, you still serve the One?" There was no sneer left in my voice.

"Who else would I live for? I've seen pain and evil. I know their source. It's not the One." His youthful voice deepened, and he sounded far older than his years. "He's not your enemy."

Goose bumps rose on my arms. His words were too similar to things Susan had said to me more than once. But I'd spent my life wresting my fate from the hands of the confusing and distant One, and I didn't know how to see Him as anything but one more enemy among the many that threatened me.

"So are you going to tell me?" Jake asked.

"What?"

"Why all the running and hiding? Why don't you want anyone to know where we're going? Why couldn't we ask those police guys in Lyric for help?"

I had long since concluded that Jake wasn't lying about being Susan and Markkel's son. And although he posed a danger because of his carelessness and what he knew about me,

I doubted he would willingly betray me. Yet I didn't want to answer. He would have no comprehension of what it meant to be banished from the clans . . . but I did. Putting it into words would make it that much harder for me to ignore.

"Get some sleep," I said, wishing I'd left him with Tag in Lyric.

He didn't argue with me, and soon I heard his breathing grow slow and even. As morning grew closer, my eyelids dragged down, so I pulled out my sharpening stone to help me stay alert. My boot knife needed honing after the abuse I'd given it cutting into the bitum trees. I pulled the blade smoothly across the stone, testing the edge by feel in the darkness. By the time the blade was sharp, the vague shape of trees grew visible on the ridge far across the canyon from us. I stepped outside the cave and listened.

There it was. Soft voices and an almost imperceptible brush of movement below us.

I slipped back into the cave and shook Jake. He groaned.

"Shhh. Jake, wake up. Now." I pressed my dagger into his hand and drew my sword. "They're coming."

Chapter Ten

SUSAN

After a mug of clavo and more empty reassurances, Mark left the apartment to get some food for us. The jet lag of other-reality travel rolled through me, and I curled up on the couch to nap. When you counted the day we spent traveling from Braide Wood to the portal and our own world, then the return journey and full day of searching, we'd missed a night of sleep somewhere.

Unconsciousness closed in around me like a hidden cave. My anxiety dissipated into the darkness. I was in a safe place, and I nestled down, happily unaware of time passing. Then I sensed someone else in the cave. I forced my eyes open a slit, even while part of my brain told me that I was in a dream and my real eyes couldn't be open.

A figure huddled against a rock wall. I tried to move closer, but my limbs felt filled with sand. The person turned to me.

Jake! Are you all right? I reached for him and managed to move one more nightmare-weighted step closer.

His face was strained, contorted with tight muscles. He clutched a dagger in a trembling hand.

Jake, it's me!

He looked through me toward the pale light at the cave entrance, bracing his back against the rocks.

Jake, I'm here. It's okay. We came to bring you back.

No audible words would pass my lips, and it was clear he couldn't see me. I strained to reach him but couldn't move.

"They're coming," he whispered. He hugged the dagger close, gripping it with both hands.

A crash sounded outside the cave, and both Jake and I jumped.

I bolted upright, grabbing the arm of the couch. Breathing hard, my eyes pulled open to see that Mark had banged open the door.

"I saw Jake," I gasped. Even with my death grip on the couch, I couldn't stop shaking.

Mark dropped his bundles on the common-room table and ran to hold me. "Shh. It's okay. You were dreaming."

"I was in a cave, and I saw him. He looked so afraid. Something was hunting him. Jake had a knife in his hand." I pulled back and stared into Mark's eyes. "We have to find him!"

Resolve tightened the small lines around Mark's eyes, and his forehead creases deepened. "Susan, we will. I promise."

I gave in to my fear and pain and collapsed against Mark, tears blotching the shoulder of his tunic. These were not decorous tears like those brought on by sentiment at a wedding or a sad movie. These were the wrenching cries of a parent who is no longer able to keep life safe for her child. The same kind of sobs that shook me ten years ago when the doctor told us about Jake's cancer. As he had then, Mark held me until I was wrung out and left with only damp remnants of emotion.

When a discreet knock sounded at our door, I slipped into

the back washroom and left Mark to talk with Jorgen's messenger. I splashed water on my face and then stayed bent over, curled around the physical ache I had carried in my chest since Cameron had drugged and interrogated me last season. A healer told Mark that my heart was permanently damaged—which made no sense, since at the time I was the Restorer and every other injury healed rapidly. Mark had planned to get me to a doctor in our world. One more thing we hadn't had time for before being pulled into another crisis. Murmurs of conversation carried from the outer room. I rubbed my temples in frustration as I discovered how much I had come to rely on enhanced hearing and vision that I no longer possessed. I dried my face and went to join Mark, but the messenger had already left.

Mark stood in the open doorway. By the set of his shoulders, the news wasn't good.

"Is it that bad?" I asked quietly.

Mark pivoted, as startled as when I would sneak up behind him at the computer and shout "gotcha" in his ear. Today neither of us laughed.

He took the time to slide the door closed and thumb the magnetic lock, and then he sank into a chair. He stared at the floor with more dazed intensity than I'd even seen him use on his computer screen. "Jorgen found someone who talked with Jake."

I gasped in a lungful of air but didn't say anything.

"The chief councilmember from Blue Knoll ran into him outside the Council tower a few days ago. He was asking for help, so they told him to present himself to the chief councilmember of Lyric, where all guests are supposed to report."

Black fog began crowding the edges of my vision, and I

realized I was still holding my breath. I let it out slowly, fumbling for a chair near Mark and sinking down into it.

"Jake told them he would." Mark tore his gaze away from the floor and looked at me. "Susan, he went to Cameron."

❧

"You don't need to come with me." Mark belted his sword and tugged his borrowed tunic into place. He hadn't wanted to approach a fellow councilmember without the authority of his own standing on the Rendor clan Council proclaimed across his torso. I smoothed the two stripes on his shoulder that indicated his status. When Mark faced Cameron's five stripes, his ingrained respect for any chief councilmember would flare to life and cause him to proceed with deference.

I didn't have that problem and refused Mark's offer to get me a Council tunic. I had no respect for Cameron and couldn't pretend otherwise. The complex traditions of this world didn't bind me in the same way as they did Mark. Motley travel wear suited me fine. I only wished I had my sword at my side.

During the night we did some clandestine exploration of the hidden rooms beneath the Council offices. Very few people knew they existed, and if Cameron was holding Jake, we guessed that would be where we could find him. When our search turned up nothing, we had argued long into the night about how to proceed and came to an uneasy consensus that we would have to talk to Cameron. He knew everything that happened in Lyric and was our best source of information.

"I'm coming," I said, pretending to be confident. "You'll need someone to watch your back. Cameron is a snake."

"I know." Mark opened the door and patted his pockets,

looking for car keys from force of habit—keys that he didn't have with him and wouldn't need in this world. "But don't aggravate him. We need his help."

"Help? He'd sooner poison us." I followed Mark out into the hall and matched his stride. I wished it were a longer walk to the low building that housed the Council offices.

Mark gave me a worried look. "Let me do the talking, okay?"

I sighed. "I'm not stupid."

"I didn't say you were. You just . . . you're not . . . you don't do a great job of hiding your feelings." Mark gave me a lopsided smile, begging me not to take offense. "I love you, you know."

"I love you more," I answered automatically.

"I love you more than you love pizza," he countered.

"I love you more than you love hardware stores."

"Good one!" We smiled until we reached the door outside Cameron's office.

The levity fled from my heart, and my stomach gripped and twisted. A well-armed Council guard opened the door and waved us inside, then followed us in and took up a position by the door. My skin crawled as I remembered the last time I had been in this room.

Cameron was seated behind his huge onyx desk, and he didn't get up. Mark stepped forward. "Thank you for meeting with us, Chief Councilmember." Mark held his expression carefully neutral. He had arranged for the meeting early this morning, so our presence was no surprise to Cameron.

Lyric's chief councilmember looked exactly as I remembered: hair as dark as bitum sap, tunic as flawless as his features, and eyes that followed us like a cobra's.

"I confess I'm puzzled." Cameron leaned back in his chair.

There were no other chairs in the room, so Mark and I stood like children in the principal's office. "I was told by a reliable source that you had left Lyric and didn't intend to return."

I glanced over at Mark, wondering who had been revealing our whereabouts, but Mark kept his gaze on Cameron.

"That was our plan." Mark's voice was level. "We need help with one matter before we leave. And since we know you'll be glad for that to occur, it seems we have common ground."

One of Cameron's eyebrows lifted. "An interesting notion." He shifted his weight forward, and his voice hardened. "What do you want?"

"We're looking for a visitor who came to Lyric a few days ago. He spoke to the chief councilmember of Blue Knoll and was told to present himself to you."

I watched carefully, but Cameron's face gave nothing away.

Mark continued. "He's eighteen, slender, fair-haired."

"And why are you seeking him?" This was the dangerous moment. We couldn't let Cameron learn who Jake was. Our questions would already raise his interest—and it was always dangerous to have Cameron's interest.

Mark managed a credible shrug. "I'm afraid I can't discuss it, but it's not a matter of great importance. A small thing to clear up before we leave."

Cameron turned his gaze to me, and I rubbed the sleeves of my coarse-spun sweater, suddenly cold.

"So now that you've ruined all attempts at a treaty with Hazor, you would desert the people who looked to you to be the Restorer?"

Even though I had expected it, his sneer triggered fresh rage in my core. "The Verses prevented a treaty with Hazor. I did what the One called me to do. I rode with the guardians while you hid here in Lyric."

Mark put an arm around me before I could wind up any further. "None of that is the issue today," he told Cameron. "Have you seen the young man or not?"

"Markkel, I don't think you understand what 'common ground' is all about. If you come asking me for information, courtesy demands that you have something to share with me." Cameron stood and moved around the desk. In spite of my best intentions, I took a few steps back.

Mark lifted his head, his stubborn jaw becoming prominent. "I explained. I can't tell you more about the boy we're looking for."

"Fine. But I'm sure there are other things you could tell me."

Mark glanced at me, and I shrugged. I didn't have a clue what Cameron was fishing for.

The councilmember eased himself against the front edge of his desk and crossed his arms. "All right. I'll go first. Perhaps you aren't aware that Kieran was tried by the Council several days ago and banished?"

"That's crazy! They can't do that." As soon as I blurted the words, I regretted my inability to remain stone-faced like Mark.

Cameron's smile grew slowly. "So you also didn't know that he helped Kahlarean assassins break into Lyric, liberate a prisoner, and then kill Davis, a builder of Lyric?"

I was reeling from this news, so it took me a minute to place the name. "Davis?" I turned to Mark. "I knew him. He was with me on that first trip to Braide Wood. He was a friend of Tristan and Bekkah."

My gaze snapped back to Cameron. "Kieran wouldn't have done that."

His smile broadened. "You have no idea what he's capable of."

I pressed my lips together, struggling to stay silent. I had a very good idea of his capabilities. As annoying and enigmatic as Kieran had been, he had helped me in innumerable ways when I was the Restorer—even giving his life to protect me. And he was the Restorer now. Everything was different. But I didn't dare give that information to Cameron.

When I looked up, I was relieved to see that Cameron had lost interest in me.

"You never presented a full report to the Council," he said to Mark with a frown. "And after the battle at Morsal Plains, no one seemed to know where you had gone."

"I'm happy to fill you in, if that would be helpful." How did Mark keep his tone so calm when he knew how dangerous this man was? Mark started in on a detailed report of the battle, supply acquisitions, the defeat of the Hazorite army, and the new alliance with the lost clans. After a while I decided he was trying to bore Cameron to death.

Cameron didn't blink. He studied Mark intently and waited. When Mark ran out of obscure facts to tell him, Cameron walked over to the cubby built into the side wall and poured himself a mug of water. He didn't offer us anything—which was just as well, since I wouldn't drink anything from his hands.

Cameron sauntered back around his desk and sat down. "Where have you and Susan been since the Morsal Plains battle?" He may have seen me bristling because he continued quickly. "It's my role to protect the members of any clan while they are in Lyric. I know that the assassins have been seeking you. You make my job impossible if you don't keep me informed about your movements." His voice was smooth. "Imagine my concern when I was told you both had disappeared and when Kieran confirmed that you were gone."

Kieran? He told Cameron that we were leaving the clans? That wasn't like him. Uneasy confusion stirred in my mind.

"Where were you?" Cameron thumped his mug down onto the desk. "More importantly, how did you get there?"

I shivered. Now I knew what Cameron was after. Thank the One that when he had interrogated me, I'd had no understanding of the portal that brought me to this world.

Mark stepped closer to the desk. "We were staying out of sight. As you said, we have enemies. I don't see why it interests you, but we used the transports to travel." My husband did a much better job of lying than I ever could.

It occurred to me that I shouldn't be so happy about that fact, but I put that thought aside to consider later.

"So we've told you everything we can." I forced civility into my tone. "Have you seen the visitor we described?"

Cameron turned his dark eyes in my direction. "How is your family?"

I blinked, confused by his change of subject. "What?"

"When I questioned you about where you came from, you said a great deal about an attic, and your husband building you a room"—Cameron glanced over at Mark's rigid expression — "and your children. You must have been worried about their safety while you were busy interfering with the work of the Council and stirring up ill-conceived acts of war." He leaned back in his chair, lacing his hands behind his head. "You seemed very passionate about protecting the children of Braide Wood. What about your own?"

"Our children are fine," Mark said, jaw tight.

Cameron kept looking at me. "So you were able to return to them?"

My eyes widened. I couldn't think of a single safe answer.

"I'm sorry we wasted your time," Mark cut in. "Apparently you aren't as well informed about the visitors in Lyric as we had supposed." Mark put an arm around me and steered me toward the door. The guard blocked it, unmoving, and a lump of fear congealed in my throat. Mark looked back at Cameron, who waited long enough to show us that he was in complete control of the situation before giving one staccato nod to the guard. The muscle-bound watchdog stepped aside.

I forced measured steps to carry me forward, though I really wanted to run out of the room. When the door closed behind us, I slumped against Mark.

"Not a good plan." He sighed.

"He wants to know about the portal, doesn't he? Harassing and controlling one world isn't enough for him anymore?"

"And he had no intention of helping us. I couldn't tell if he's seen Jake or not. Could you?"

I shook my head. "I'm sorry. I can't read him at all." Our steps dragged as we headed back toward our rooms. "What do we do now?"

Mark was quiet for several more strides. "Tristan promised we would always have an ally in Braide Wood," he said thoughtfully. "I think it's time to get the help of a few allies."

The churning in my stomach eased. My worry about Jake still spun in my thoughts, and I couldn't begin to sort out the horrible things Cameron had told us about Kieran. Kieran's banishment would be a matter of public record, so not everything Cameron told us could be a lie, but none of it made sense. But the thought of quiet log homes under tall spice trees, the warm welcome of Tara's table, and the firm handclasp of Tristan's sword arm gave me a rush of hope.

"You're right. Let's go to Braide Wood."

Chapter Eleven

KIERAN

The long night had provided me time to plan a strategy. My preference would have been to meet the Kahlareans alone, leaving Jake safely in the cave but the assassins would be smart enough to split up. If one got past me, Jake had no chance.

As little as I liked the idea of an untrained youth muddling up a fight, I'd have to keep him with me.

Although we had an advantage with higher ground, we couldn't wait in the cave or we'd be too easily trapped. Now that I knew they were going to make a move, I ordered Jake to stay close and led him in a quick scramble down to the canyon floor.

To wait.

And wait some more.

I stretched my hearing and tracked the nearly imperceptible sounds of their movements, but they didn't come out into the open.

Adrenaline raced through my veins like a magnetic pulse. My sword was in my hand. I was ready. I even stepped out into the open, daring them to come.

And still they held back. My coiled energy had no release. If

I couldn't cross swords with someone soon I'd go insane. They probably knew that. They were toying with me.

When half the morning had passed, I began to track them. Jake and I followed the faint sounds, trying to pinpoint their location, but they kept moving. I was in no mood for a game of cover-and-ambush like Tristan and I had played all over Braide Wood as boys.

Jake stayed close to my side, wound as tightly as I was, nervously shifting my dagger from one hand to the other. At one point I paused in my prowling to teach him an overhand grip. He had been holding the blade like a kitchen implement. Didn't they educate the young in his world? Today he didn't turn sullen at my correction. He was too worried.

When it became clear the Kahlareans wouldn't engage us, I sank onto a boulder in disgust. "They're playing with us. They want to find out where I'm going."

Jake crouched near me. "What can we do?"

I slumped back and glared into the underbrush in the direction where I'd last heard a trace sound of their movement. Then I grinned. "Can you keep up? If we travel fast?"

"Hey, I play soccer," Jake said with pride.

I had no idea what that meant. "Yes or no," I snapped. "Can you run?"

"Y-yes."

"All right. They want to play games. We'll give them games."

We grabbed our gear, and I set out straight toward the last spot I'd sensed them lurking. As expected, they faded away before we reached them, but it left the way clear. We headed directly back toward Lyric, and I started running. Jake stayed close on my heels. That should confuse them a little. From time to time I stopped to listen, wondering if we would be lucky enough to lose them. When the afternoon rains fell, we slogged through spongy marshland. After a while I doubled back, leaving clear tracks toward Blue Knoll.

Reaching a stream, I led Jake straight into the knee-deep current and changed direction again, heading upstream in the water. When we left the streambed a mile later, I paused to check on Jake. He was tiring. He stumbled along behind me, his feet making more and more missteps. Skin pale again, his pace continued to lag, yet he didn't utter a word of complaint. I appreciated the effort he was making, but my sympathy wouldn't help him get out of this alive.

I stopped and gave him a cold stare. "Jake, if you can't keep up, I swear I'll leave you here."

He stared at me, stricken.

I sneered. "I thought you said you could run."

His teeth clamped together and his jaw lifted. Anger vibrated in his tight muscles.

Good. I turned and continued to run. He followed and did a much better job of keeping up. I could feel his fury heating the trail behind me. It probably wasn't wise to turn my back on him at the moment. He did have my dagger—even if he still hadn't mastered a combat grip.

I set a hard pace until the rain stopped, and then kept going long enough for us to stay warm while the heat of our exertion partially dried our clothes. When we reached a sheltered clearing late in the day, I called a stop. Jake collapsed with an exaggerated groan and stretched out flat on the ground. He threw his arms wide as if he were soaking up strength from the dirt underneath him.

"Don't get too comfortable," I said. "I'm not sure we lost them."

He moaned. "Comfortable? My blisters have blisters. I'll

never be comfortable again."

I dropped my gear next to his sprawling form. My sword created more bulk than I wanted for reconnaissance, so I propped it against my pack and retrieved my boot knife from Jake so I could travel light and soundless through the underbrush. Then I left him to enjoy his misery while I backtracked and listened. It had been miles since I'd heard any sign that they were behind us, but I wanted to be careful.

The silence sounded promising. We'd lost them. After my erratic path, they'd have no indication of which way we were headed. If we could set a direct course now, in another day of hard travel we'd reach Braide Wood.

My mood soared as I walked back to where I'd left Jake. My plan had worked, and the long run had burned the tension from my blood. I was even feeling generous—planning to praise Jake for keeping up all day.

When I reached the clearing, my good mood vanished.

Jake was no longer sprawled on the ground. He was wielding a sword, doing a credible imitation of—well, of someone who'd never held a sword before. What *was* he doing?

I stayed in the trees and watched him flail the weapon around awkwardly.

"And once again Sir Jake drove the dragon back," he crowed.

He wound up and the sword—my sword—whistled through the air as he spun. He was playing. Playing! With *my* sword.

I stepped out from the trees.

His body swung around, pulled by the momentum of the blade. When he finished the turn and saw me, he stumbled to a stop, eyes wide.

"What. Are you. Doing?" Veins pulsed along my temples.

He dropped the sword. It bounced clumsily to the ground, forcing a growl from my throat. I strode forward.

"I was just practicing," Jake stammered. He backed away and glanced around as though looking for help. "Sorry. I was gonna ask if I could try it. I just thought . . . well, in case they came when you were gone . . ."

I snatched up my sword, rescuing it from the damp earth, and checked the long blade for any scratches.

"I didn't hurt it. I was just pretending."

"Pretending?" I choked on the word and advanced on him, sword held ready. He had reached the edge of the clearing and had a large pine tree at his back. My fingers flexed on the sword's grip, and I took a deep breath to regain control. "You know, Jake," I said conversationally, "there's an old tradition. Once you've pulled your sword in combat, you never put it away without drawing blood." I took another step toward him and watched his face.

If he so much as flinched, I'd make him sorry he'd ever even *looked* at my sword.

He held his ground, throat straining as he swallowed hard. When I stepped closer, he squeezed his eyes shut. I funneled my seething temper into a hard glare he didn't see. Slowly, the desire to murder him faded. I waited.

He squinted one eye open uncertainly.

"Don't ever touch my sword." My syllables came out clipped.

He nodded rapidly. "I won't. I'm sorry."

I lifted the sword in front of me, admiring the luster of the metal in the gray light of dusk.

Jake closed his eyes again, all his muscles knotting up.

With a sharp pull, I sliced the edge across my left palm.

Carefully wiping the blood from the blade, I turned away from Jake to restore it to its sheath. I shook my head at my own superstitions. All right. So Tristan wasn't the only one who clung to old traditions.

"I think we lost them," I said over my shoulder. "If we head out early before they can track us again, we should be able to reach Braide Wood tomorrow."

"Good." Jake's word was heartfelt. I suppose traveling with me had its difficulties. I wasn't used to being around someone so young and untrained. No one would ever accuse me of coddling him.

His eyes darted to my hand. I wiped the blood away on my pant leg, and he moved toward me, riveted by the sight of the whole, unbroken skin.

"That is so cool," he breathed.

I shoved him aside. "Unpack some food."

After we set up camp and ate, the dark closed in rapidly. Again, Jake tossed from side to side, like a lehkan fawn pressing down prairie grasses to form a bed.

"Would you teach me sometime?" His words floated through the blackness.

I didn't need to ask what he was talking about. "No. It's your father's job to teach you to use a sword. Ask him. Believe me, he knows how." Markkel had never finished guardian training, but he had an affinity for sword work that came from instinct more than drills. I was surprised he'd never taught Jake how to handle a weapon. Their world couldn't be that different from ours, could it? Didn't fathers there bear the responsibility of teaching important skills to their sons?

Thinking about fathers made me toss on the hard earth, like Jake, before settling myself. I should stand watch.

Ground-crawlers could burrow up from their holes and burn us with their toxic skin. Bears could be rummaging out in the underbrush. Rizzids preferred the light and probably wouldn't be active now, but you could never count on them to be predictable. Feral mountain cats favored the caves of the land we had passed through. And the Kahlareans might be adept at night travel, without the restrictions held by our clan culture. Still, I had hidden us as best I could, and my body screamed for rest. I couldn't muster enough fear to force myself to stay awake.

"Jake, tell me about a day in your world."

The only answer was wuffling breath-sounds of sleep.

My lips tugged upward. He was a complication I hadn't wanted to take on, but he'd done well today. Tristan had once described the strange appeal his niece and nephew held when they slept. I had mocked him for getting soft, but he only laughed. Maybe this was what he had been talking about, this feeling of protectiveness.

"Help me get Jake to Tristan," I whispered into the darkness. "Show me what I'm supposed to do." The words sprang from a part of me I barely recognized, but I didn't take them back.

A whisper in the air might have said, *I will*. More likely I had imagined it. Still, rest settled on me like a sigh, and I pulled my sword closer and slept well.

My mood was thoughtful the next morning. By my count it had been thirteen days since the battle of Morsal Plains, and nothing had gone right so far. I scouted our perimeter. No sign of pursuit. I returned to the clearing and kicked Jake awake.

"Time to move."

I led us straight for my clan. Strange how coming home had such a pull on me, even after all these years.

Jake more than compensated for his stoic courage yesterday by grumbling at every new stretch of trail. Once he worked out the stiffness in his legs and learned to ignore the pain of his blisters, he settled into a stride and stopped wasting his breath. Good thing. I was about ready to stop and grant him his request for some weapons training. Then he'd really have something to complain about.

He's untrained. He's not from this world. Markkel and Susan will kill me if I hurt him. I drilled the words into my head during the early part of the morning, holding my temper down. Good thing he had finally shut up.

The terrain became more mountainous, dense with tall pine trees and the braiding limbs of honey-colored spice trees. I stayed alert. The forests held dangers even during the day. But as we drew closer to home, something deep inside of me began to relax.

We approached the outskirts of Braide Wood just at suppertime. The central village of the clan was nestled into the dip between some high ridgelines. Hundreds of families lived in the village and surrounding forests, and the clan guardians trained on a wide plateau on the far side of the village. Tristan's family home was somewhat secluded on this edge of town, making it easier to slip in unnoticed. When I was sure there was no one in sight, I pulled Jake with me, jogged up a step to the door, and let us both in. No need to knock here. It was more home to me than my father's cottage.

Dustin and Aubrey, Tristan's nephew and niece, sat at the large common-room table, quarreling over some game they were playing with twigs. They looked up, curious. Many strange people had come and gone through this house of late. Tara bustled out of the open kitchen area and pulled up short, staring at us.

I held my breath. Had the Council already sent a messenger to tell the Braide Wood clan I was banished? What would that mean to her?

She clapped wrinkled hands to her face and smiled, tears springing to her eyes. "Thank the One." She hurried forward, her steps light for someone of her advanced years, and gave me a quick hug. "We've been so worried since we got word. What happened?" She brushed a curl of her white hair back into place and turned to look at Jake. "And who is this fine young man?"

I let my breath out with a rush of relief. Tara had cared for Kendra and me with the same firm-handed tenderness that she had given her own three children. I hadn't realized until now what it would have done to me if she had turned me away.

"This is Jake. I'll explain about him after I talk to Tristan. Is he here?"

Tara nodded. "Meeting with some clan leaders about replanting Morsal Plain. Or was that yesterday? Maybe he's training his guardians today on the plateau. But he'll be home soon for supper. Oh, you poor child." Tara had reached out to help Jake with his cloak. "You're wet clear through. And the rain was so cold today. Come on. Let me get you something dry to wear."

She shepherded Jake down a hall to the back rooms, leaving me standing in the common room.

"There's clavo on the heat trivet," she called over her shoulder.

I grinned and took off my cloak, shaking excess water from it before tossing it on a chair. I unbelted my sword and propped it against the wall. Then I noticed Dustin and Aubrey still staring at me.

"What's that?" I gestured at their bundle of sticks. I wasn't interested, but the silence was awkward.

"It's a game Susan taught us." Dustin grabbed a fistful of twigs to drop on the table.

"I miss her," said Aubrey. "And I miss Nolan, too. Where is he?"

Shamgar. How had Tara explained Nolan's disappearance? My mouth tasted sour as I remembered how I'd terrorized our prisoner, a boy who was nothing but a pawn in the war.

I'd let him escape—set up an opportunity I knew he'd take advantage of. We had fed him plenty of false information to take back to Hazor—information that bought us more time to gather reinforcements and helped us win the battle.

I hadn't wasted time wondering what happened to Nolan in Hazor after the battle was lost. I'd been busy since then. But of course Dustin and Aubrey had questions. At least when Markkel and Susan left, the two children got to say their good-byes.

I ran a hand through my damp hair and shrugged. "He had to go home." I escaped to the kitchen alcove to pour a mug of clavo. "Where are your parents?" I called, eager to change the subject.

"They went to Blue Knoll to visit friends," Aubrey chirped. "Hey, it's my turn!" She grabbed the sticks from Dustin. He threw himself across the table to reclaim them, and Aubrey shrieked. Tara came back into the room and frowned.

"Little ones, go wash up for dinner." She pried both children's hands off the collection of sticks and shooed them to the back rooms. Then she turned to me with the same frown she had used on her grandchildren. "He'd better not be another prisoner."

It took me a moment to figure out what she was talking about.

"Jake?" I laughed and dropped sideways into a chair, dangling my legs over one of its arms. "Not at all."

"How long has he been with you? Haven't you fed him? And did you see his feet? They're bleeding."

The aroma of one of Tara's rich and spicy stews drifted from the kitchen. I was warm, dry, and relatively safe for the moment, so I couldn't get annoyed at her scolding. "He'll be fine. Aubrey said Talia and Gareth aren't home?"

"Mm." Tara busied herself in the kitchen area. "They'll be back in a few days." She held on to her frown, but I knew it was taking her a lot of effort.

"Where's Kendra?" I shifted in the chair and tilted it back onto two legs.

"Oh, she's at the healers' lodge."

My chair slammed down with a thud. "Why? Is something wrong?"

Tara turned and saw my sudden panic. Her frown melted. "No. I'm sorry. I didn't mean to worry you. She's fine." She set down her bread knife and came out to sit near me. "She's been working with Linette. They've been helping with the wounded from the battle, and Linette is still trying to free some other poor souls who were poisoned."

"Kendra shouldn't be doing that so soon. She's barely recovered herself."

Tara laughed. "Have you tried telling your sister that she can't do something?"

My mouth twitched. She and Tristan were equally matched in stubbornness. And that silly urge for noble sacrifice. I yawned.

Tara's eyes softened. "Are you all right?"

I shrugged. "Why wouldn't I be? Any injury heals in an instant. Everyone's dream come true."

Tara heard the bitter edge to my voice, and her eyebrows drew down in concern. She reached forward and patted my hand. "Give it time. He has a purpose for this."

The door opened, and I pulled back, relieved by the interruption.

Tristan and Kendra entered, laughing. "No, I only told him he wouldn't be strong enough to ride this season," Kendra said, "and that I'd make sure his captain knew it." Tristan's answering laugh was rich and deep.

They both saw me at the same moment.

I stood up as Kendra threw herself at me, knocking me back a few steps. "Kieran, why haven't you sent us word? I've been crazy with worry. Tristan wanted to travel to Lyric right away to confront the Council."

I eased Kendra back from her fierce hug. In spite of her smile, there were weary lines on her face. She didn't seem to have regained any of the weight she'd lost while the Rhusican mind poison had held her. "You shouldn't be working so hard. Are you eating enough?"

She slugged my arm. She wasn't as frail as I had feared.

"I'm fine," she insisted. She and Tristan exchanged a secret smile.

I rolled my eyes. When I'd left, they were still mooning over each other like newlyweds. I hadn't been gone long enough.

Then I braced myself and met Tristan's eyes. He would be furious about the banishment and probably find a way to blame me instead of the Council.

His welcoming grin seemed genuine, so I stepped closer. He reached out to grab my forearm and slap my shoulder in welcome. His hand clamped my arm with unnecessary pressure. "You have a lot to explain."

"More than you know," I said dryly. Jake chose that moment to saunter into the room, and I broke away. "Tristan, I'd like you to meet someone. This is Jake. Markkel and Susan's son."

Everyone in the room gasped. I flopped back into my chair, enjoying the uproar I had just caused.

Chapter Twelve

KIERAN

Jake started fielding the questions, but before he could offer much explanation, Payton arrived home. The strain of the past days had deepened the grooves over his eyes, but his strong jaw and thick tousled hair still made him look too young to be Tristan's father. Never one to overreact, he raised his eyebrows when he saw his home had been invaded by unexpected guests once again, but then he welcomed us. His clothes smelled of the yellow fumes that Hazor had used to poison the farmland near the village.

"Not much progress yet," he told Tara quietly. Then he glanced at me. "Skyler is working on a way to neutralize the chemicals so we can try planting by next season."

My father was continuing to involve himself in the problems of the clan? Kendra threw me a huge grin. Good for her. She'd never stopped trying to draw him out. It was a lost cause, but I wouldn't squash her momentary triumph. I kept my face impassive.

I looked at my sister more closely. She was too pale. Was she really all right?

Kendra turned to say something to Tristan, eyes sparkling, and the question died in my throat. She was glowing. I shook off my worry. She may have been pushing herself too hard, but there were no signs of the mental poison that had held her for so long. She had never looked happier.

Tristan threw back his head to laugh. He was a different man now that Kendra was well. He tended to carry the responsibility of being the head guardian like a pack full of stones that never left his shoulders. His overgrown sense of honor and duty added to the weight and had made him almost grim in recent months. But with Kendra around, I saw my childhood friend resurrected.

Cameron's threats seemed puny in the face of Tristan's fierce energy. Even the recent Kahlarean attack no longer loomed as large. We would talk about it later. We needed to make plans. But for now I watched the few people who mattered to me gather around the table, and let myself indulge a small notion of hope.

Tara and Payton carried platters to the table, and between bites of stew and fistfuls of bread, Jake told the family about arriving near Lyric and roaming the streets alone for days. He loosened up under the warm atmosphere. It must have felt familiar to him, because I hadn't seen him relax and talk with this much animation before. When he told them about stumbling across my campsite, I interrupted.

"Give the boy a chance to eat. We've been traveling hard."

Eyes turned to me, and I picked up Jake's story while he concentrated on making up for lost meals. I glossed over what I could, but Tristan's eyes were narrow as he listened. He'd have questions for me later.

"We stopped at Tag and Jameth's house for supplies. Oh, that reminds me. Tag sent a message."

I closed my eyes for a moment to remember the exact words, then recited her greeting to the family and her updates on the toddlers. Tara kept her gaze down at the bowl in front of her, chasing a wedge of meat around with a piece of bread. Payton laid a gentle hand on her arm. She blinked several times but didn't look up.

When I finished the message, Tara pushed herself away from the table and began gathering up bowls that weren't empty yet. She had made it plain for years that she disapproved of Tag's choice to move to Lyric. I'd never understood. Sure, it was normal for large extended families to stay together within a clan, but looking around the house, I wondered where Tara thought she would have put more people. Tristan and Kendra lived here with Payton and Tara. Then there was Talia and her husband, Gareth, and their two children, Aubrey and Dustin. On top of that, there were the odd strays that this family seemed to attract—lately they had given shelter to Susan, Nolan, Markkel, and now Jake.

Payton broke the uneasy quiet. "Dustin, would you please share the Verses tonight?"

I sighed down into my chair and rested my forehead in my hand. They wouldn't be able to tell if I were asleep or just deep in thought.

Dustin stood up on legs that still hinted at youthful pudginess and managed to elbow his sister in the process. She swung a foot in his direction, but Payton rested a firm hand on her shoulder, and she subsided. Dustin cleared his throat and launched in:

> *Awesome in majesty,*
> *Is the One eternal.*
> *Perfect in His might and power,*

The only truth and only source,
He made all that is and loves all He made;
His works are beyond our understanding.

The words were too familiar for me to care about them, but I glanced from under my hand and saw Jake watching Dustin, transfixed.

In every time of great need, a Restorer is sent
To fight for the people and help the guardians.
The Restorer is empowered with gifts to defeat our
*   enemies*
And turn the people's hearts back to the Verses.

I felt Tristan's eyes on me, but I kept breathing evenly, refusing to react. He wasn't going to trap me into carrying the same rock-filled pack of obligation that he had chosen for himself.

We wait in the darkness for the One who brings light.
The Deliverer will come,
And with His coming, all darkness will be defeated.

Dustin paused to catch his breath. This was only the beginning, the standard creed. Every evening of the season had a section of the Verses to be reviewed. Before Dustin could launch into the rest, Jake spoke.

"Through him all things were made." His voice was breathy and full of wonder. "It's just like it says in John: 'Without him nothing was made that has been made. In him was life, and that life was the light of men. The light shines in the darkness, but the darkness has not understood it.' I learned that one when I was a kid!"

Tara nodded, her earlier tension dissipating. Kendra smiled warmly. Jake sat up tall, vibrating with enthusiasm for this connection he had discovered.

Riddles and nonsense.

I debated pushing my chair back and leaving, but I needed to talk with Tristan. He had sufficient reasons to be irritated with me without my stomping away from his family's table. Instead, I closed my eyes and let the conversation swirl and the Verses hum in the background while I thought about the Kahlareans and what our next step should be.

After supper I thanked Payton and Tara for the meal and grabbed my gear. Tara automatically protested and asked me to stay.

"No. It's safer for you if I stay out at the caves."

Jake groaned. "Caves again?"

My lips twitched. "You can stay here. If they'll have you."

"Of course he'll stay here!" Tara answered. She and Kendra moved close to Jake like bristling she-bears with a new cub. Jake looked at me, uncertain.

Was he actually seeking my approval? "Stay," I said. "Sleep on a soft pallet for a change."

Tara slid a closet door into the wall. "Here." She placed a spare blanket in my arms and patted it. "I know why you're worried, but you're always welcome here."

Tristan belted on his sword and took a moment to kiss Kendra. "I'll be back before dark." His eyes were soft.

"Be careful." She rested a hand against his face.

"I'll protect him." I tossed my cloak over my shoulder. "I won't let him tangle with anything bigger than a rizzid." Kendra made a face at me, and I grinned.

Tristan opened the door and checked for signs of anyone

nearby. He beckoned to me, and I grabbed my pack and followed him out. The sky was already a deep gray, so we walked fast and didn't try to talk yet. It took only a few minutes to reach my favorite refuge. On one of the ridges overlooking Braide Wood village, there were several shallow caves hollowed into the rock, with a small clearing in front of them. Because my life had necessitated secrecy in recent years, I always stayed here when passing through my clan.

I tossed my gear down and settled on the ground with a boulder at my back. I glanced again at the sky. Tristan and I would need to talk fast so he could return home before darkness fell completely.

"Linette got to you with my message?"

"Yes," he said tersely, still standing. "I was expecting you to bring me the report about the River Borders."

"Did you send troops?"

He nodded. "Twenty of my best men. We need them here. We lost too many."

"But if Kahlarea has breached the gap at the Falls . . ."

"I know." Tristan massaged his left shoulder. It tended to stiffen, ever since a skirmish with a Hazor patrol when we were youths. He glared down at me. "Well? Are you going to make me ask you?"

I rested my head back against the boulder. "So they did send a messenger here already?"

"Five days ago. We didn't want to believe it. What really happened?"

"Nothing! You know how these misunderstandings get started." I thought I was being funny, but Tristan crossed his arms and kept glaring. I closed my eyes.

"Fine. I was surrounded by Kahlareans. They thought I was

their Hazorite trader, there to arrange for more syncbeams. I played along. They sent me on my way with three assassins who were probably hunting the Restorer." I opened my eyes and saw the corner of Tristan's mouth move. At least he appreciated the irony.

Staring up at him was making my neck hurt. I stopped talking.

He took the hint and sank down onto the ground next to me, adjusting his sword out of the way. "Then?"

"I thought they wanted to go to Hazor; then they told me we were going to Lyric." I explained my decisions and sketched in how everything had gone wrong—leading up to my banishment and then my escape.

I didn't ask for or need Tristan's vindication. Still, I tensed, waiting for his response. He bent heaven and earth to try to remain loyal to the Council, and by rights he should be turning his back on me. No one was allowed to speak to or provide shelter for the banished. And Tristan took the rules seriously.

Instead he shook his head. "Why didn't you tell the Council that you're the Restorer?"

"They didn't ask."

He let out a growl of exasperation.

At least the awestruck awkwardness was gone. When he first realized I was the Restorer, he became so respectful that I feared for our friendship.

It felt wonderful to be arguing with him again. "The training of the guardians has really gone downhill," I mused. "I took out four of them without breaking a sweat."

Tristan gave me a hard shove that sent me sprawling in the dirt.

I sat up, smirking. I was about to warn him about Cameron's threats, when he cleared his throat.

"I have some news too." He picked up a twig and started peeling bark off of it. His face couldn't seem to decide whether to look serious or giddy. "Kendra said I could tell you."

"Is she all right? I thought she looked pale." I couldn't hide the edge to my voice.

"Yeah, well, she's been feeling sick a lot. Mostly in the mornings . . ." Tristan waited for my reaction, but I looked at him blankly. Blame it on the fact that I've been single and alone for so long. That and the fact that they had tried for years and resigned themselves to the belief that children weren't part of their destiny.

When I caught on, I scooted back and turned to face him, mouth gaping. "Really? When? How?"

Tristan's laughter chased away the last remnants of his disapproving reserve. "Yes. We just found out. And the rest is none of your business."

"I can't believe it." I thought my face would crack from smiling. "And can you imagine what a little tyrant he'll be if he takes after you and Kendra?"

"We want you to be around to get to know him. Which is another reason we were so upset about the banishment."

I didn't want to go back to that topic. "So what do we do about Jake? Do you know where to find the portal to send him back?"

It worked. Tristan was diverted. "No. Markkel mentioned it a few times, but I don't know where it is or how it works. Don't you think he and Susan will come back to find him?"

I lifted one shoulder. "If they can. But what do we do in the meantime?"

"He's welcome in Braide Wood. Maybe when things calm down in Lyric, I can take him back and talk to the eldest songkeeper about what to do with him."

"You should let him train with a group of first-years. He wants to learn to use a sword."

Tristan's eyebrows lifted.

"Apparently no one ever taught him." I looked up at the sky. It was almost black. We were out of time, but there was one more thing I wanted to talk to my friend about. I sprang up and paced over to a gap in the trees. From there I could look down on the rooftops of the village. Standing there conjured up memories of conversations with the last Restorer and my own struggles between caring for my clan and staying pragmatic enough to survive.

"I need help." The words twisted out of my throat with effort. Tristan came and stood beside me and waited silently. "Strange things have been happening. Voices. Visions. Give me a fair fight with my sword and nothing will stop me. But this . . . If Susan were here I'd ask her about it all. But I . . ." I didn't know what I was asking for.

"When she was here," Tristan said, "she spent most of her time training with Wade in the mornings and studying the Verses with Linette in the afternoons. Wade went with the troops to Cauldron Falls, but Linette is here. She would know the most about the things Susan experienced. They talked about everything."

It wasn't a bad idea. "I'll go see her in the morning." I turned to look at Tristan again. "You better get home. Tell Kendra to take care of herself."

He grinned and offered his arm. We clasped forearms, and I thumped his back. "Congratulations." My word was sincere.

The next morning, I slipped quietly through the woods toward the healers' lodge, careful to remain unseen by anyone stirring in the village. I planned to intercept Linette before she entered the lodge, hoping for a private conversation. Near the clearing, a small waterfall tumbled into a stream by the main building. Beyond it a narrow strip of wetlands butted up against the woods. As I drew closer, I spotted a glimmer of gold in the pale morning. The glint of Linette's hair drew my eyes to where she sat and stared out over the marsh. Her head was tilted down in concentration, and she cradled a round, stringed instrument.

I stretched my hearing and gradually made out the sound of her voice, wrapped by the bubbling of water, barely carrying over her instrument. She was composing.

I frowned. The words had nothing in common with the formal language of the songs so familiar to anyone in the clans, lofty hymns about how powerful the One was. I never understood the point. Didn't He know that already?

Linette was using conversational words, as if she were talking to a friend. And her song hinted at her own place of pain.

Nothing could make me step forward to interrupt her now. Neither could I pull myself away. I stood and absorbed the last verses of her song.

In the morning when I walk outside
To the marsh where the herons glide
I watch the fog rise up like my prayers.

When I can't face the day ahead
Can't hold on to the words You've said
I know Your hand is bigger than my cares.

I can't run, run from Your mercy
I can't hide, hide from Your love
Holy One, You are so faithful to me.

When she finished, she hugged her instrument and stared out over the water. The spell released me, and I backed silently into the trees. I let my feet carry me, not caring where I was going.

By the time I came to myself, I was in front of Tristan's home and decided it was a logical place to get some breakfast. When I opened the door, a large gourd flew past my head.

"Score!" Jake shouted. Dustin and Aubrey clapped and jumped up and down. Splattered pieces of soft rind slid down the door frame. Tara and Payton laughed from the table, where they were enjoying mugs of clavo. "I'm teaching them soccer," Jake told me with a grin.

"He needed something round," Tara said. "We gave him a couple of hollowed-out gourds."

"Right." I stepped around the mess, helped myself to a mug of clavo, and pulled up a chair. "I told Tristan to start him training with the first-years."

Tara nodded. "After he has a few days to recover from all his adventures." We watched Jake chase her grandchildren around the room.

"Mm. I can see he's on his last legs," I said. "I need to meet with Linette, but I'm trying to stay out of sight. Could I send Dustin to ask her to come here?"

Tara's eyes livened with interest. "Of course. I was planning to go out to the fields today, and I'll take the little ones so you can have some privacy." She waited for me to explain more, but I just nodded my thanks and took a long swallow from my mug. It took

Tara some effort to pull Dustin out of the game. Once she explained the mission to him, he galloped out the door cheerfully.

I had time for a second cup of clavo before Dustin returned, pulling Linette behind him.

"Kieran! I didn't know you were here. Dustin said Tara needed me."

"Well, I'm technically—"

"I know. You aren't actually here?"

I smiled. "Glad you understand. Linette, this is Jake." I turned to introduce her and found Jake's eyes riveted on Linette. She did look good today. A little more color in her cheeks. I suppose she was beautiful, if you liked delicate features and gentle eyes.

Apparently Jake did. "Wow," he breathed.

"Jake, close your mouth." I looked over at Tara for help.

She and Payton pursed their lips, fighting back laughter. "Come on, Jake. We'll show you the Morsal Plains, where your mother fought the Hazorite army," Payton offered.

Even that lure didn't have enough appeal for him. "I can stay here."

"No, you can't." I shook my head at his helpless reaction.

He ignored me and took a step closer to Linette. "Hi. I'm Jake." He held his hand out. Did he think she was a warrior? When she lifted her hand up in uncertain response, he grabbed her palm and shook it a few times. He stammered something clumsy before Payton and Tara eased him away and out the door, herding Dustin and Aubrey ahead of them. Jake kept looking back over his shoulder until I closed the door in his face.

Linette's lips curved in one of her soft smiles. "He's sweet."

"He's a little young for you," I heard myself growl. She looked at me, startled.

I shook my head. "Never mind. Sit down."

Chapter Thirteen

KIERAN

To her credit, Linette didn't laugh.

"What do you need?" Her face was tranquil. I'd never noticed before how still she was. Even her body seemed to hold a wealth of patience as she sat quietly. Nothing tapped or fidgeted or betrayed restlessness.

Frankly, I'd always found her annoying in the past. Even in her youthful shyness, she carried ridiculous levels of idealism. It didn't surprise me at all that she and Susan had forged an instant bond. Neither had a clue about the way the world really worked.

"I need information," I demanded, then realized I sounded as if I were interrogating a prisoner. Her eyebrows arched, but she waited in silence.

I rubbed my temples. "Something happened after Morsal Plains. I told Tristan and Kendra not to tell anyone." They'd seen the Restorer signs. I'd never had to talk about it—except to insist on secrecy. Trying to get the words out this first time came close to choking me.

"It seems . . . after Susan . . . " I pushed off from the chair and paced.

If Linette had pestered me to get on with it, I'd have stormed right out the door, but she simply waited. I finally stopped, grabbed the back of the chair, and glared at her. "Apparently I'm the next Restorer."

Her mouth opened, soundless. Confusion and disbelief chased across her face.

I shrugged. "I know. Makes no sense. But nothing about the One ever has."

When she remained frozen, I sighed and slipped the fine-bladed dagger from my boot, drawing it sharply across my palm like a clumsy first-year.

She gasped and sprang to her feet. "What are you—?"

I brushed away the blood and held my hand out to her so she could see the evidence. With a soft intake of breath, she stepped closer and touched the healed skin with gentle fingers. Golden hair shielded her downturned face, leaving me to try to guess her thoughts.

Her head came up, and her eyes glistened as they met mine. Lines of sympathy creased her forehead. "Oh, Kieran." She seemed as much at a loss as I was. Then she smiled, and her whole face recharged with energy. "The One has sent us more help. So soon."

I flopped into my chair and waved her into hers. "What did Susan tell you about the Restorer . . . gifts?" Once I got the first question out, the rest followed easily. I told her about the experiences that were unnerving me, all the confusion I felt. I drilled her with questions and hoarded every crumb of information.

"It unfolded gradually," she said at one point, looking at an invisible point beyond me. "Susan learned to listen and pay attention to any hint that the One was trying to direct her. We both discovered it was important to learn to recognize His voice, especially when we were fighting the Rhusican poison."

"I've certainly been hearing *something*," I said slowly. "And I think I can tell when it's the One."

"But?"

"But He hasn't told me what He wants me to do." Resentment bled into my voice.

"He didn't tell Susan, either. Not the whole plan. Did you think she knew she'd be riding with the clans into battle? Or what would happen when she did? She was confused and uncertain every day that she was here."

"Then what do I do?" I pushed myself out of the chair and prowled toward the window. This whole conversation made me itch inside my bones.

"You ask Him. And you listen. And you wait. And most of all . . ." She hesitated and focused on my face for the first time in our conversation.

I turned to face her. "What?"

"When you know what He is asking of you, you do it."

My fist flexed. My shoulders stiffened. I wanted to throw my chair across the room, but I took a few tight breaths and sat down, glaring at the floor. "Right. Anything else I should know?" I bit out the words.

"The One doesn't always do things the way we expect," she said softly.

At last I could agree with her. Then something in her tone caught me, and I looked up. She was gazing off into the distance again. She was thinking about Dylan. Linette gave her life to serving the One and could never have expected He would allow her fiancé to die. A sarcastic answer shriveled in my mouth. I swallowed.

Before I could think of something to say, she looked me

straight in the eye. "One more thing, Kieran. Susan knew she needed help, needed friends. She didn't try to face the battles by herself. You're not alone."

I froze. Those words again. *He* kept saying them. I didn't know what to do with them. They didn't make sense to me.

But I couldn't lash out at Linette no matter how frustrated I felt. "Thanks for the information," I said stiffly.

She rose and studied me for a moment. I didn't want to see what was in her face. Expectation? Disappointment? Pity? Disapproval?

Her hand rested for a minute on the knotted muscles of my shoulder. "May the One draw even closer to you, speak clearly to your heart, and give you courage for His call on your life."

No! That's just what I don't want. I don't want Him speaking anymore. And courage? What's she talking about? I have that in abundance.

Linette slipped from the house.

The voice breathed to my mind. *Courage in abundance? Yet you are afraid of Me.*

Wouldn't anyone be? I knew all about His power. Why would anyone want to let Him inside?

I'd had enough of sorting through these thoughts. This was infinitely harder than gathering secret facts about troop movements and political schemes. I grabbed some food for my lunch and stormed from the house and back to my clearing. Tristan would meet with me at midday so we could discuss what to do about the threat of a Kahlarean invasion. That was a problem I knew how to handle.

After eating my pilfered lunch, I took myself through some standard sword forms, letting my muscles uncoil and stretch with the satisfying effort of mock battle. I was sweating by the time I heard heavy footfalls scrambling up the path.

Tristan was a large man, but he didn't usually thrash this clumsily. Sword in hand, I waited to see who was approaching. Tristan's head came into view, and I sheathed my sword. When he stepped out of the darkness of the trees, I saw the hard set of his face. He stomped toward me but then stopped several paces away as if he didn't trust himself to come closer.

"What's wrong?"

He was breathing hard, and not just from the climb. "Another messenger just arrived." He waited as if that would mean something to me.

I shook my head.

His ground his teeth. "The Council is trying Jameth and Tag tomorrow. They may be banished."

"What? Why?"

Tristan wasn't appeased. "Because you stayed with them. You asked them for help. You let them shelter you. Why didn't you tell me you put them at that much risk?"

I ignored that question. I'd told him we'd gotten supplies from Jameth, but I had skimmed over the fact that we'd sheltered there when the Council Guard was hunting everywhere for me. I suppose it could be construed as a lie. I'd let Tristan think they'd helped me before it was a criminal act for them to do so.

"Come on." I reached for my pack. "We'll head to Lyric now. I'll tell the Council I threatened them and forced them to hide me."

Tristan didn't move. "You mean you want to lie to the Council." His voice rose.

I shrugged. "If it works."

"Messengers of the One, Kieran," Tristan shouted, "this isn't a game."

His rage didn't impress me. I'd known him too long. "Of course it is. You just haven't figured that out yet. Calm down. We'll handle this. Unless you have a better idea?" I hefted my pack and checked the cinch on my sword belt. When I glanced back at Tristan, he walked over to the gap in the trees that over-looked Braide Wood. He didn't speak or look at me.

"Tristan?" A chill crept under my skin. If this were a night-mare, he would turn and have the face of a monster, and I'd wake up in a cold sweat.

He didn't turn. "I want you to leave." His voice was low and raw. "Leave for Hazor. At least until you're willing to tell the Council the truth."

"Don't be stupid," I snapped. "I have to help. I'm not going to let Tag and Jameth be banished."

Tristan turned slowly. He didn't wear the face of a night-mare's monster, but he had the eyes of a stranger. Remote. Dull. "You've done enough."

"What?"

"Kieran, I told you after the battle that you needed to tell the Council you were the Restorer. None of this would have happened if you'd listened to me then."

"So you're mad that I didn't take your advice?" I tried to laugh. "Come on. I've never listened to you."

He didn't smile. "Having you here makes all of Braide Wood a target. Anyone who talks to you risks banishment."

"Tristan, I need to stay near because you *are* at risk already. I came here because you're a target. Cameron is obsessed with destroying you."

Tristan met my eyes. The muscles in his face were so tight I was surprised he managed to talk. "Don't blame your choices on our friendship. You refused banishment because you have no respect for the Council and never have. It's always been about doing things your own way."

My own anger welled up to match his, but I pushed it down for a moment. "I want to be sure you and Kendra are safe."

He stepped closer. "Protecting Kendra is my job, not yours. If you really care about her or anyone here, the best thing you can do is leave."

I felt blood drain from my face. I took a step back and watched him, waiting for him to grin and admit he was stringing me along. It took a long moment for me to believe he was dead serious.

We've been like brothers for over thirty years! The plea shouted in my brain, but I wouldn't voice it. "Why are you doing this?" I choked on the words.

"I'm not doing anything. You did it. You did it when you wouldn't take your place as the Restorer. You did it when you broke into Lyric and helped the Kahlareans. You did it when you beat up guardians who were doing their job, and then ran. When you asked Jameth and Tag for help. When you lied to me." The anger in his voice softened. "I'm sorry, Kieran."

Rage rushed through me. I could take his nagging, his frustration toward me, and his play-by-the-rules stubbornness. But not pity. I won't take pity from anyone. My hand moved to my sword hilt. Tristan's eyes caught the movement. He sighed and shook his head.

It would have been better if he'd drawn his sword. All our lives we'd settled arguments with a good fight when it was needed. When we were children, we fought with fists. We were well matched. He was bigger and stronger, but I was quicker and more creative. Even as men, we'd sometimes crossed swords in anger—but always with the care that comes from knowing you'd rather die than see the other man hurt.

Now Tristan turned away.

"Fine. I'll leave," I said to his back. "I'm sure you'll be joining me there soon, if Cameron gets his way. And you better warn Kendra when you're banished, because he has plans for her." I sneered the cruel words, hating myself as I did.

Tristan looked back at me, his eyes wide. It would have been kinder to stab him with my sword. The pain in his face would have been less.

I pushed aside my remorse. He was the one sending me away. "Thanks for the help, friend." It took tremendous effort to keep my voice cold.

"Good-bye, Kieran." He buried the flash of pain and turned aloof and hard. No better than the self-righteous, condescending councilmembers he served.

Long after his footsteps faded down the trail, I wandered to the boulder on the edge of the clearing and looked down at the homes of Braide Wood, numb.

"Good-bye," I whispered.

Chapter Fourteen

SUSAN

"Just say good-bye," I muttered. Mark was engaging in the Council tradition of protracted leave-taking, and I'd already gnawed one fingernail to the quick.

"I appreciate your help with this," Jorgen said again, grasping Mark's forearm.

"I've been in your debt for many years. I would never refuse a request from my clan's chief councilmember." Mark's fervent recommitment was making me uneasy. I understood his sense of obligation and loyalty, but we had other priorities. Still, Jorgen's nod of approval made Mark's shoulders lift. His face had the youthful pride I had seen in Jake when he bragged about the notes his favorite teacher had given him on his last research paper.

"May the One guide your steps." Jorgen walked with us to his office door.

"Amen." I hadn't meant for anyone to hear my dry exclamation, but Mark nudged an elbow into my ribs.

As soon as we were out in the hall, I gave vent to my frustration. "I thought we agreed to go to Braide Wood for help. I can't believe—"

"It makes perfect sense. Susan, think about it." Mark had the gleam again—the one that usually signaled a new home-remodeling scheme. This time the zeal in his eyes was even more dangerous.

Lord, I'll let him tear the whole house down and rebuild it when we get home. Just don't make me go though with this.

"I can't write an epic song. I can't even write a decent Christmas letter!" I started worrying another nail with my teeth.

"But it's your place. Jorgen was right. They need to call an assembly and honor the One for the victory." Mark's face couldn't have been more earnest. "Maybe this is why we were called back here. To finish it."

Anxiety birthed anger. "We came back here to find Jake. Period. End of story."

Mark grabbed my shoulders. "Do you think I've forgotten? I know more about the dangers of this world than you ever will. Do you think I'm not terrified for him?"

I bit my lip, holding back more angry words.

"What good will it do to go to Braide Wood," he said, "with Cameron's guards trailing us everywhere?" His hands tightened on my arms. Then he realized what he was doing and let go abruptly.

He was right. Nothing was going as we had planned. Before we had even reached our borrowed rooms after the useless interview with Cameron, we noticed two uniformed guards following us. They stopped at a discreet distance when we did but followed us when we continued. Finally, Mark confronted them and learned that they were assigned by the Lyric chief council-member to "protect" us. And having Cameron's thugs tailing us was only the first complication.

Jorgen had contacted us the next morning, before we could

leave for Braide Wood, to let us know there would be a special assembly to celebrate the victory at Morsal Plains. Apparently it was my job to share the song that would record the event in the oral history of the People.

"Mikkel didn't have to compose an epic poem about the battle at Cauldron Falls," I groused, incapable of letting the argument rest.

Mark's expression hardened. "That's because he was dead."

His words slammed into my heart. I had a flash of clear vision and saw every bit of my thoughtless, self-absorbed, whining nature. My breath came out in an uneven gasp.

"I'm sorry." I reached out to Mark and was relieved when he gathered me in with no hesitation. "He was a real hero," I said into his chest as I hugged him. "I know he would have happily written a song if he could have." Mark's long-buried grief over his father's death had resurfaced when he returned to this world. I couldn't believe how insensitive I'd just been.

"Nah." Mark rubbed his chin against the top of head. "He would have hated it too."

I looked up at his lopsided grin and saw not only his forgiveness for me but also another step of healing for his old grief.

I smiled. "That makes me feel better."

"It'll be only a small delay." Mark steered us onward down the hall. "Representatives will come to Lyric from each clan. Not everyone, like for the big gatherings, but odds are that Tristan will come. We can talk to him then."

I rested my head against Mark's shoulder as we walked. When we left the building, I noticed the two men from the Council Guard. They were different from the two yesterday but every bit as dogged. I was tempted to stick out my tongue at them but just frowned instead. Mark wasn't nearly as bothered by them. When we had had trouble sleeping last night, Mark told me more about his life here in Lyric before he came to our world. He had lived with bodyguards for many years. From the time enemy nations first heard the prophecy that he would bring restoration to the People of the Verses, he had been a target. A couple of official guards were no big deal to him—even if they did report to Cameron.

When we were back at our rooms, with the annoying guards hovering in the outer hallway, the work began.

It was hard enough for me to figure out how to tell the story of Morsal Plains. Factoring in the lack of written language on this world, I couldn't even piece together phrases in a notebook. Fortunately Mark had the same uncanny gift as everyone in the clans. He memorized rapidly and accurately. He carried verbatim records of the Verses in his brain. As I discarded and selected new lines for the song, he would recite back everything I had composed so far. Slowly, the account took shape.

When we finished, it was late into the evening, and we sank onto our pallet, exhausted. We clung to each other and prayed, begging God to look out for Jake and protect him. We prayed for our other children, Karen, Jon, and Anne, and hoped that time had stopped moving for them back in our own world. We prayed for all our friends in this reality. For Jorgen and his leadership of Rendor clan and the integrity he brought to the Council. For Tristan as he worked to rebuild Braide Wood and the guardians after all their losses. For Linette as she faced long seasons of grief. For Kieran, wherever he was. We still hadn't made sense of the strange bits of information we'd been able to gather and couldn't bring ourselves to believe what Cameron had told us. We took turns, and our voices grew slower and softer. Longer pauses stretched between prayers.

We were both dozing when a thought flared in my mind. "Mark, what if Jake went somewhere else?"

"Hmm?" Mark adjusted the arm he had wrapped around me and rested his cheek on my head.

"Are you awake? I just thought of something." I pulled away and waited until Mark's eyes opened to half-mast. "Do you know for sure that the portal would have led him to Lyric?"

Mark's eyelids lifted the rest of the way. "The stones were lined up correctly. They took me to the entry outside of Lyric when I came back for you. I set them the same way this time, and we both came to the same place."

"But when I first came here"—I propped up on an elbow—"I was in Shamgar. What if we can't find him because he came through to somewhere else?"

"No, no, no," Mark mumbled. "You got pulled through when the stones weren't lined up right. Besides, the Blue Knoll chief councilmember spoke to him."

"Is he sure? Maybe it was some other blond teenage boy." I sat up, holding fistfuls of the blanket. "And what if there are other worlds? What if he is in some totally different reality?"

Mark sighed and sat up, gathering me close. He smoothed the hair back from my face. "I don't know if there are other realities or not. I don't know if the portal stones could take someone to other places. But even if they can, I do believe Jake is here somewhere. We're doing everything we can."

"You're going to tell me to trust, aren't you?" I sighed and let Mark massage some of the knots out of my neck and shoulders.

"Susan, did you listen to the song you just wrote?" He edged me back down under the covers. "Listen." And in a low, rumbling baritone, he sang for me. I heard the words as if I hadn't lived through the story they told. Amazement over the miracles of the One swept through me. My eyes drifted closed, and no more panicked worries pierced the gradual quieting of my thoughts. *If He could do all of that . . .*

It was the last thought I had before sleep claimed me.

"I wish Linette were here." My fingers reached up to smooth back strands that were slipping out of my braid. "I thought they would send her."

Messengers had gone out to tell all the clans about the assembly on this fourteenth day after the battle. Anyone who could be spared had traveled to Lyric to gather in the central tower for the unusual worship time. The Feast day gatherings were held at first light, but this assembly would be after lunch to allow time for people to take transports from some of the outer clans. I'd spent the morning working with the musicians. They'd developed an accompaniment with ease. The old Welsh hymn-tune that I had chosen had a rolling melody that wasn't terribly different from some of the other worship music I'd heard on Feast day.

Mark and I stood alone on a round dais. The musicians had gathered their instruments and moved to the eight arched entry-ways around the tower. They would call the people in from all directions. The last time I was here, I had watched this dais lift and rotate, allowing the thousands of people to see the song-keepers who led the worship. I hoped I wouldn't get motion sickness.

I was turning to ask Mark for the tenth time about one of the phrases I wasn't sure of, when movement caught my eye. An elderly man was making his way slowly across the wide, light-spangled floor of the tower. He paused and lifted his face to admire the vast space overhead.

I gasped. "Lukyan!" I scrambled from the dais and ran to greet him. He turned watery blue eyes toward me, and myriad lines splayed across his temples as he smiled. I hugged him.

His hands trembled with age as they touched my back. "The clan of Braide Wood sends you their blessing," he said quietly.

"I'm so glad you're here." He leaned on my arm as we walked over to Mark. I thought of the long hike to the transport station from Braide Wood and marveled at the strength of will it would take a man of his years to make the trip.

"Mark, this is Lukyan, the eldest songkeeper of Braide Wood." I blinked back tears. "My husband, Mark."

Lukyan gave Mark a gentle nod. "Linette is working with the healers, but we knew a songkeeper from Braide Wood should be here today. May I assist you?"

Mark probably grasped the honor being given in that generous offer even better than I could. He helped Lukyan step up onto the dais. "It's a good thing you're here. I was getting worried she was going to bolt."

Lukyan's eyes sparkled as he looked at me. "Another road not of your choosing?"

"Exactly." But the sharp tang of anxiety had faded with his presence, and I smiled. "Will you help me teach the song?"

"Of course."

In the brief moments before the crowds began to gather, I taught him the words. As the musicians finished their call to worship and moved back to the area near the dais, Lukyan rested one quavering hand against my face.

"It's only right to give honor to the One."

"*Soli Deo Gloria*," I whispered.

His eyebrows lifted in question.

"To Him alone be glory."

The brightness of his answering smile, and the warmth of Mark's strong presence right behind me, enabled me to turn to the gathered clans and forget myself. I never even noticed the dais begin to move as I sang.

Hear, O nations, hear the glorious
Ways the One protects His own.
Hazor's cries of war surrounded,
In our weakness we're not alone.

Raise the Song of One who loves us,
One whose power is without peer.
Trust not in weapons, kings, or hill gods;
His deliverance is always near.

The chorus immediately repeated, and thousands of voices joined mine. Then the instruments pulled back their volume, and I began the long series of verses. Mark had helped me include each of the clan names and the role it played in bravely riding into a hopeless battle. As I sang of how the Council sought guidance from the One and how He sent a Restorer from a distant land, I felt as if I were telling the story of someone else entirely.

In a sense, I was. This wasn't my story. This wasn't even the clans' story. This was a grand, glorious celebration of the One involving Himself in the lives of the people He loves. My voice sounded breathy to my ears, but Lukyan's reedy tenor and Mark's baritone helped carry the words across the vast space of the tower.

Even the clans who refused to help Braide Wood were mentioned in the song with gentle chiding. The temptation to ignore the Verses was addressed, in addition to a reminder of the danger that comes from trusting anyone but the One.

Guardians fought, Restorer riding,
Brave my soul, march on to die.
All the heavens joined the battle;
Light and heat were thrown from the sky.

Wake, O wake and see salvation
Driving hard across the plains.
Allies, strength, and swords hold true,
Fill the valley like cleansing rain.

I looked out over the faces of the people, and even though I had no more Restorer powers, a wave of love washed through me—like the visions that once gave me glimpses through the eyes of the One. The One who had created these people yearned to heal and deliver them. Despite my impatience to search for Jake, I was grateful Mark had insisted I honor Jorgen's request. This song would be one more stitch in the weaving to bind this world into their Creator's grace.

May they remember who You are, I prayed as the chorus rang again. Then I thought of my own immediate battle and bowed my head. *Help me remember too.*

My chin came up, and I taught them the last verse.

Weep no more for the fallen warriors;
We, His children, rest in His arms.
Shout the Verses, bold with promise;
Day to day, He keeps us from harm.

Holy One, we rode to serve You;
Strong, You ride before us all.
Fix our gaze on Your great wisdom;
Fix our hearts on Your love's call.

As the last chord resonated through the room, I looked up at the skylights and so many stories overhead and realized I could no longer see the windows. A mist filled the space. Soft gasps sounded from others on the tower floor. Then all the faces turned upward in complete silence.

As if from a distance, I felt Mark's hand against my back. Some part of me noticed that the dais had stopped turning. Then everything melted away except the touch of the gentle mist lowering and brushing against my face. The spinning wheels of thoughts that I could never completely silence simply slowed to a quiet halt. Fear and anxiety dissolved in the face of a peace that was perfect and complete, telescoping to fill every cell in my body.

I don't know how long we stood. Time had no meaning. We were touching eternity. Or more accurately, eternity was touching us — with a tender hand that hovered and then slowly withdrew. As the mist lifted, I fell to my knees. I vaguely heard the sounds of voices in prayer, more music, and then the shuffle of people leaving. When I was able to lift my head again, Mark, Lukyan, and I were alone in the tower.

The men helped me to my feet. While Mark and I were left shaken and dazed by our experience, Lukyan smiled as if he had just had a chat with a familiar friend. Mark hugged me and rested his forehead against mine. The three of us walked toward one of the arches.

"Could we . . ." Mark cleared his throat and tried again.

"Could we escort you back to Braide Wood?" he asked Lukyan. "We want to talk with Tristan about something."

Lukyan nodded, his smile fading. "I would appreciate the companionship. And Tristan could use your support. He's worried about Kieran's banishment."

A wave of concern rolled past my thoughts, but it didn't create the swell of anxiety I would have expected. I still felt the weight of a calming hand in my spirit that reminded me nothing was out of the control of the One.

"Can we head straight to the transport, or is there someone you need to see before you leave?" Mark's eyes darted from side to side as we stepped through the entry and out into the central square.

"We can leave now," Lukyan said. Then he gasped. His body stiffened, and his face clenched in pain. He stumbled and fell forward. Mark and I grabbed him in time to lower him gently to the ground.

My ethereal sense of peace vanished in a microsecond. I screamed. The hilt of a silver dagger protruded from Lukyan's back.

Chapter Fifteen

SUSAN

"Susan, run!" Mark shouted over my screams. "Run to the Council tower. Hurry!"

I gaped at him. I couldn't leave Lukyan.

"I'll stay with him. Just run!" he cried again. I tried to focus on the panic in Mark's face and make sense of it, but I was thinking in slow motion. What was happening?

Then arms yanked me away. Before I could summon a coherent command to my muscles to struggle, something slammed into me. I sprawled against the stones of the courtyard and looked for Mark. A blur of movement sorted into two shapes. A Council guard brandished a sword and drove back a hooded gray figure with a short curved blade in one hand.

"Look out!" I shouted. My warning came too late. With his free hand, the assassin produced his venblade and threw it with deadly accuracy into the guard's chest. He stumbled forward a few paces then fell. I crawled toward him, desperate to do something to help.

The masked figure stepped closer, and his eyes bored into me. I didn't see hatred or rage—just remorseless intent. Then he glanced around and pulled back. He ducked around a corner and disappeared.

I looked for Mark. By now we were surrounded by Lyric guardians, Council guards, and shouting voices. I stumbled to my feet and found my husband kneeling by Lukyan.

Mark had drawn his sword but didn't appear to be injured. "Are you hurt?" His eyes searched me, love and fear commingled. When I shook my head, he turned his gaze to one of the Lyric guardians. "Get a healer. Now." The young man nodded and ran.

I sank to my knees beside Lukyan. His eyes were open. The parchment skin of his cheek rested against the pavement. His breathing was labored, but he was alive. I rested a hand gently on his forehead and began to pray. When the healer arrived, she assessed the blade in his back.

"It's high enough that it didn't damage major organs, but I'm not sure yet if it pierced the lung." She pulled out a device that looked similar to a light cube and held it near the blade, studying it with fierce intensity. She nodded and set it aside, then pressed a bundle of cloth against the entry site of the wound and slowly slid the dagger out. Lukyan moaned, and his eyes closed while the healer kept pressure on the injury. Others moved forward to help as she wrapped a bandage into place and supervised moving Lukyan to a pallet. Two men carried him to the nearby healer's office. As people moved aside, the healer hurried over to check the fallen Council guard. She hissed and drew her hand back.

"A venblade. There's nothing I can do." She glared at Mark as though it were his fault.

I shuddered. I had been stabbed with a venblade once. Creeping paralysis gradually pulled life from a body like the illumination being dimmed from a light wall. But I had been the Restorer then, and recovered. The Council guard hadn't had that gift. What thoughts had chased through his mind as he felt his life shut down? Did he have time to regret giving his life to protect us?

Mark's arm was around me in an instant, turning me toward him. "Will Lukyan be all right?" He spoke over my head.

The healer sighed. "We'll need to watch his lungs and make sure the blade didn't nick them. But I think he'll survive." She hurried away, soft-shod feet barely making a sound on the tar street.

Mark tilted my chin up to meet his gaze. "I think we still need to get to Braide Wood immediately. Lyric is too dangerous for you."

I would have rather sat by Lukyan's side or badgered Jorgen for more help in finding Jake or run back inside the worship tower and waited for mist to fall again. Incapable of making a decision in my shock, I let Mark lead me away, the faces and buildings a vague blur.

When some of the numbness lifted, I looked up to discover we had walked straight to the transport station. Mark hadn't even stopped at our rooms first.

It made sense. What did we need? He had his sword. We'd find shelter and food in Braide Wood.

In a few minutes a transport slid into the station, and we boarded. I sank onto the molded plastic seat in a daze. Mark didn't even frown when a Council guard joined us. It had been one of the bodyguards Cameron had forced on us that had saved our lives in the square.

"Thank you for your help," I said quietly.

He gave me a stony glare and didn't speak.

When the curved door slammed downward, I sank deeper into my seat beside Mark, my muscles unclenching. There were no gray-masked figures in the transport. For the moment, we were safe.

We pulled out onto the road, and I stared out the window. Moss-covered hills and then deep forest all passed in one green haze.

To "not know" is then part of the gift you offer Him. Lukyan's words from my last visit to this world whispered in my heart. *It is where your obedience is tested.*

Lord, I don't understand. Why this? Why now? What is happening? I want to trust You. Help me trust You.

I heard the murmur of voices as Mark and the Council guard talked, but I didn't pay attention. When the transport slowed, I looked up, startled to find that we were already at the Braide Wood station.

The three of us set a fast pace up the trail toward the village. The route was becoming familiar to me. The scent of pine and cinnamon began to infuse strength back into my shaky limbs. I ignored the subtle ache in my chest and refused to acknowledge my shortness of breath.

As we reached the ridgeline that overlooked the village, I longed to dash headlong toward Tara's home. We'd find the help we needed there.

"We should hike straight to the Lehkan Plateau. Tristan will probably be drilling troops this time of day." Mark's words startled me and pulled me from my trance.

"Good idea." I stared at the sky. It was the deeper gray that meant everyone would begin to finish his or her work for the day. I could get lost staring at the flat emptiness of that sky.

"Are you still with me?" Mark's eyes, full of grief and worry, searched mine.

I had to stop drifting into a daze. We weren't out of danger yet, and we still needed to find Jake. I blew my breath out. "Yes. I'm all right now. Let's go." I led the way, my feet falling into the familiar path toward the place where I had learned to ride lehkan and use a sword and lead troops into battle. It felt like a million years ago. It felt like yesterday.

My muscles strained as we clambered up a small hill that would give us a view of the whole plateau. I saw Tristan immediately. His wavy hair flew behind him as his mount charged forward. He had a group of about a dozen guardians on lehkans in formation around him. Hooves thundered against the soft earth, and another group spurred on their own mounts into an answering charge.

Normally Tristan would be shouting commands, watching his men, critiquing the riding and sword work of those he was training. But today he gave himself fully to the mock battle and rode hard, straight at one of the other guardians. Their swords rang as they clashed, and I shuddered at the power behind Tristan's blows. He wouldn't let up, and the other guardian's sword flew through the air. Tristan advanced on him, even as the man's lehkan backed away. For a moment I thought Tristan would run him through. Then he pulled up short and jerked his sword back. He shouted an order and the group dispersed, although the guardian who had been sparring with Tristan kept an uneasy eye on him as he rode toward the paddocks.

Tristan swung off his mount and handed the reins to a first-year who had been watching the training. The head guardian of Braide Wood trudged toward us, head down. Mark's shouted greeting startled him. I expected his face to light with gladness, but when he drew close, the lines of his face were weary.

He clasped Mark's arm. "Well met." The heaviness didn't leave him, but there was warmth in his voice. "We hoped you'd come for him."

"Him? Jake?" I almost didn't dare hope. "Is Jake here? Is he all right?"

"Yes. He's here with Tara."

I grabbed Mark, relief making me dizzy. "We found him? We found him!"

"Kieran brought him." Tristan turned toward me.

At first I didn't catch the tone, but as I absorbed the way he said Kieran's name, the hairs on the back of my neck stood up. "Tristan, what's been happening here?"

Mark glanced over at the Council guard who waited nearby. "Let's discuss it later."

We followed Tristan toward his home in silence.

Hurry! my feet demanded. The men's rapid strides weren't fast enough for me. I was finally going to see Jake and know that he was safe.

As we approached the house, I expected the door to fly open and Tara to run out and greet us.

And Jake. Please, Lord, where's Jake?

No one greeted us, so Tristan pulled the door open and gestured us inside.

Before we could enter, Kendra ran lightly up the path toward us. "Susan! I'm so glad you came. We didn't know if you could. Jake is a wonderful young man. You must be so proud."

"You really saw him? I've been so worried." I hugged her. "Where is he?"

"I think he went to Morsal Plains with Tara. He should be back anytime."

Patience, Susan. A few more minutes. They've all seen him. He's safe. "How is the work at the healers' lodge going? And how are you feeling?"

"I'm feeling fine." She giggled and hugged me again. "We're going to have a baby."

All the overwhelming experiences of the day fled, and I shrieked with pure joy. Kendra and I scampered into the house, our words overlapping in excitement.

After the men followed us inside, Kendra paused and looked at Tristan. She walked over to him and traced a finger over the scowl lines on his face. "What's wrong?"

Tristan closed his eyes and pulled Kendra toward him as if he were afraid she'd vanish. Mark murmured something to the Council guard and left him outside on the porch. Then he pulled the door closed.

Tristan held Kendra's shoulders and watched her face. "I got news this morning. Tag and Jameth are being tried by the Council tomorrow. It's Kieran's fault."

Her face went still. "What should we do?"

Before Tristan could say more, the door opened again, and Tara entered with a large basket over her arm, Dustin and Aubrey tugging her tunic.

"You're back!" Aubrey squealed and ran toward me. Dustin shoved past her and barreled into me as well.

Tara beamed from the doorway but quickly felt the tension in the room. "Little ones, go wait for me in your room."

The children hesitated.

"Go on." I patted Dustin's shoulder. "We'll play later."

He grinned and ran off with Aubrey in his wake.

"This is a welcome surprise." Tara was already moving toward the kitchen. "Let me get some clavo started. Jake must have been thrilled to see you."

She turned from the kitchen and saw us all frozen in silence. "Where is he?" she asked slowly.

"I thought he went to the fields with you today," Tristan said.

Tara nodded. "This morning. We all came back for lunch. Jake stayed here to rest, and the little ones and I went out to gather herbs. He must have fallen asleep."

Kendra moved first, running to the back rooms. My feet had suddenly grown roots into the wooden floor. My heart lurched, and the old pain pushed against my ribs.

When Kendra came back to the common room, her eyebrows were pulled together. She didn't look at me. "He's not here. Wait. Where's his pack?" She and Tristan rustled around the common room, banging closet doors and pulling things from cubbies. I still couldn't seem to move. Taut despair pinned me to a rack, and each moment stretched me another inch.

"His pack is gone." Tara sounded close to tears. "Would he have wandered off on his own? He said he'd stay here until I got back."

I made my feet move and shuffled toward her. "It's all right. He's got to be all right," I whispered, wrapping my arms around her.

"Shades of Shamgar," Tristan cursed. "He wouldn't have. I know he was ready to kill me, but he wouldn't—"

"What?" Kendra said. "Tristan, what's going on?"

Slowly, Tristan met her eyes, ignoring the rest of us. "After the messenger came from Lyric at midday, I went to the caves to talk to Kieran." He glanced at Tara. "Jameth and Tag are being tried by the Council. Kieran didn't bother to tell me he had stayed with them when the guardians were searching the city for him. He put them in danger." Tara stiffened in my arms, and I rubbed a hand against her back.

Tristan turned back to Kendra, his eyes pleading with her. "I . . . I said some things."

His wife took a slow, even breath. "Did you two fight?" She sounded like a mother long resigned to patching up skinned knees and refereeing squabbles.

"No." Tristan's jaw clenched. "I sent him away. I told him he was a danger to our clan right now and shouldn't come back until he's ready to take his place as the Restorer." All color dissolved from Kendra's face, and she took a step back. I expected her to rail at him, but she groped blindly for a chair and sank into it.

"But what does this have to do with Jake?" She looked up at Tristan as she said the words I'd been thinking.

"He's the one who brought Jake here. What if Kieran came back here on his way out of town and made Jake go with him?"

"He wouldn't have done that!" Tara interrupted.

"He might." Mark's voice was low. "For leverage. He might have thought he could use him somehow."

"Maybe Jake saw him leaving and decided to follow him on his own," Kendra said.

I looked around at the uncertain faces in the room, and the rack's screw twisted one turn too far. "I don't care why Jake is with Kieran," I said to Tristan. "Just tell us where Kieran was heading."

He stared at Kendra and didn't answer.

"Tristan!" I shouted.

His eyes were heavy with guilt when he pulled them upward. "He was going to Hazor."

Kendra let out a whimpering sound and wrapped her arms around herself as if the temperature had just dropped.

I pulled away from Tara and sank into a chair by the table. I couldn't cope anymore.

"Kendra, will you take care of Dustin and Aubrey tomorrow?" Tara's voice floated far away. "I'll need to go to Lyric at first light." Tara turned back to supper preparations, but she spilled the clavo herbs as she tried to pour them into a bowl. "I want to be with the toddlers in case . . ."

I should go comfort her. Her daughter was in danger. But I couldn't rise from my chair.

Jake, where are you?

We had been so close to finding him. He had been here. He'd had breakfast at this table just hours ago.

"I'm sorry." Tristan knelt in front of Kendra. "I never thought Kieran would do something like this."

"He didn't," she snapped. "Maybe Jake went for a walk somewhere in the village."

My eyes burned. The room blurred. Was there still hope that we'd find him before another night fell?

Her face twisted as she looked at her husband. "And how could you—" She bit her lip. "Just go look for him."

Tristan clearly wanted to say more to her, but after another searching look at her face, he nodded and left. Tara was talking to herself in the kitchen. Mark shifted his weight and looked from Tara to me and then to Kendra. Tears were pooling in her eyes.

"I'll go help Tristan," Mark said, already backing toward the door. There was something so sweet in his awkwardness that I gave him a brief smile, but as soon as he left, I lowered my head into my arms and let my tears fall.

A hand touched my shoulder. "Kieran would never have forced Jake to go with him to Hazor," Kendra said.

I nodded but didn't trust myself to speak. I just had to find my son. I had to know he was all right.

As if she read my thoughts, Kendra continued. "Kieran took good care of him. All he wanted was to help Jake get home. I'm sure he was angry after Tristan . . . if . . . but he . . ." She trailed off, looking helpless.

Tara joined us at the table. "When we walked down to the field this morning, Jake asked me to show him the trail to the caves. If he went to see Kieran and heard Tristan tell him to leave, he might have decided to follow. He seemed to . . ." Tara pinched the bridge of her nose. "I think he trusted Kieran." There was a bitter throb in her voice.

Kendra stood up quickly. "You know Kieran didn't mean to cause this trouble for Tag."

Tara retreated to the kitchen without answering.

When Payton arrived home, Tara took him to the back room to give him the news. They stayed there a long time. Kendra and I pulled together a supper no one would be hungry for, just because we needed something to do. Mark and Tristan returned shortly after, and I raced toward my husband.

Mark shook his head. "We looked everywhere. Kieran's gone. Jake's gone." He exchanged a look with Tristan, and I suspected that Mark was as ready to blame Kieran as Tristan was.

I wanted to sweep the wooden bowl of stew off the heat trivet to the floor and smash the water pitcher into pieces. Instead, I bit the inside of my cheek until it bled. *What was happening here? How had allies become enemies? How could a Restorer kidnap our son?*

Kendra stayed in the kitchen and kept her back toward

Tristan. He watched her for a while, then went to stare out a window.

I stalked over to him. "Tristan, I need your help."

He pulled his attention back as if from a great distance and focused on me. "I can't go to Hazor," he said quietly. "It's illegal."

"Not that. I want a sword. A sharp one."

He frowned and glanced over at Mark. I suppose it was logical for him to expect that my husband could have found one for me in Lyric.

Mark joined us. "Susan, you don't have the same skills you did before."

"My arm may not be as strong, but I'm tired of walking around unarmed. I'm not going into Hazor without weapons."

"You're not going into Hazor at all. You can stay here with Kendra. I'll see if I can track them." Mark rubbed the shadow of stubble on his jaw. It had been a long day.

"I'm not staying here. We're only a half day behind." I crossed my arms and glared at my husband. Tristan eased away and headed down the hallway.

Mark dropped his voice to a low hiss. "There are still the Kahlareans to worry about. Or did you forget what happened today?"

"No, I didn't forget. But I'm done with waiting. We've talked to Cameron. We've traded favors with councilmembers. It's not working. If Jake is heading into Hazor, then that's where I'm going."

"It's too dangerous."

"Mark, think this through. If you left me here alone, I'd be just as much a target for the Kahlareans. You'd be worrying every minute."

That stopped him. I saw him backing down and kept talking. "I don't know if Kieran dragged Jake with him or Jake saw him leave and sneaked off to follow, but either way, I think we both need to go after him. Stick together." I gave him a soft smile. "We *are* a good team, you know."

Mark raked a hand through his hair and made a frustrated sound in his throat. "Okay. You're probably right. But . . ."

Tristan strode back into the room with a leather-wrapped bundle. With an apologetic glance at Mark, he offered it to me.

I folded back the fabric and saw a long sword in a battered sheath. "Thank you." I pulled the sword out and eyed the edge. It didn't sing to me like my own blade had, but it was well balanced and sharp. I nodded to Tristan. "I'll bring it back."

Mark watched me and shook his head. "Just remember that you aren't the Restorer anymore." Then he glanced toward the kitchen to be sure Kendra couldn't hear him. His hand clenched for a moment on the hilt of his own sword. "If we find out that Kieran kidnapped Jake or hurt him in any way, I'll take care of it."

Mark walked a few steps to stare out the window with a cold resolve that made my stomach lurch. The longer we stayed in this world, the more I saw parts of him that I didn't recognize—pieces of the man he had left behind in Lyric twenty years ago. He'd threatened to kill Kieran several times, and I knew he hadn't meant it. But as I studied the strong lines of his profile, I realized there hadn't been enough time for me to learn who Mark really was now. I couldn't be sure what he would do.

Chapter Sixteen

SUSAN

Tara's innate hospitality wouldn't allow her to leave our Council watchdog alone on the porch. She invited him in to supper and then barely seemed to notice him. His aloof presence might have quenched the warm laughter that was heard around this supper table on a normal evening. Tonight it wasn't an issue. The dinner was far from normal. Kendra and Tristan weren't speaking, and Tara's red-rimmed eyes kept straying to Payton as though pleading for reassurance he couldn't give. Mark and I were lost in our own fears about Jake. Even Dustin and Aubrey felt the strain in the room and were subdued. The Council guard was the only one to do justice to the soup and bread. When the rest of us stopped pretending to eat, Aubrey pushed her bowl aside.

"My turn."

Tara focused blearily on the girl. "What?"

"My turn to say the Verses." Without waiting for prompting, she launched into the creed and then the day's Verses. I let my mind wander, expecting one of the long clan histories that were a common part of the people's records, but brought my attention back when Aubrey stumbled over a word.

"He gives us . . ." She looked at Tara for help.

"Families. He gives us families," Tara said quietly. Her hand stole across the table to rest on Payton's arm. He covered her hand with his own.

"He gives us families out of His great mercy. He knows our hearts and never leaves His people alone." Aubrey prattled forward without inflection, determined to complete her job so she could go play.

"Let love rule in your homes." The words continued. I was surprised by how similar they were to many of my own world's verses. And why not? The truth of the One didn't change from world to world. I looked around the table as Aubrey continued her recitation. Kendra's tight anger was ebbing away, and she tugged at a loose thread on her sleeve. Tristan's gaze flickered over to her, then back down to the table.

When Aubrey finished, she bounded from her chair.

"One moment." Payton's gruff voice stopped her. He turned to the stoic guard. "We are glad you could join us at our table, and I thank you for the protection you are giving Markkel and Susan. But we have some family issues to discuss. Would you please excuse us for a short while?"

"And when we're finished, you are welcome to take lodging here," Tara added, her caretaking nature reviving briefly, though without her usual warmth.

The young man gave a curt nod and went back to his watch outside the front door.

Payton looked at all of us. "Let's talk to the One," he said simply.

Tara bowed her head and spoke first. "Holy One, you know exactly where Jake is right now. We trust him to your care. Keep him safe, and help Markkel and Susan find him."

My eyes stung. She was wrestling with fears about Tag's welfare, yet she focused her prayers on Jake.

"Creator of life, and joiner of families, I ask you to take care of Tag and Jameth tonight. Be their defense tomorrow." It was Kendra's quiet voice, offering the prayers that Tara and Payton needed.

Tristan cleared his throat. "We thank You for Your promises. Thank You for the Restorers You provided to our People in the past and for providing a new one to us now. Watch over Kieran . . ." His voice trailed off.

I prayed in silence and once again felt the quieting hand that could still my anxiety with a feather-light touch. Payton began a song, and the voices in the room melded into one sound. I no longer noticed Aubrey's high-pitched chirp or Mark's resonant baritone or Kendra's wispy soprano. The music rose as one united voice.

When the last note faded, Payton leaned forward. He dismissed the children with a nod and then spoke quickly to Mark. "You'll need supplies and directions. Tristan can help." He gave Tara a steady look. "Will you pack food for Markkel and Susan and then prepare what we'll need for tomorrow?"

She nodded and moved briskly toward the kitchen. Payton went to a closet and pulled out packs and spare pallets in neat rolls.

Tristan and Mark already had their heads together. "We'll need a heat trivet, a light cube, and I'd really like to bring a scrambler," Mark was saying.

Tristan frowned. "This isn't Rendor or Lyric. Where would I find a scrambler?"

"I have one," Kendra interrupted. Both men stared at her.

"It's at Father's house. I'll go get it." She gave me a wink on her way out the door. Tristan looked dazed, and I rubbed a hand over my mouth to hide my smile.

He pulled his attention back to Mark with effort. "No one from Braide Wood has ever crossed deep into Hazor, except for Kieran. I know he's used a trail over the mountains, and he usually made trips to Sidian. It's the largest city and so an easier place to blend in. I would guess that's where he and Jake will be heading."

"Are the borders patrolled?" Mark asked.

Tristan shook his head. "Not on our side. There's a guardian at the outpost at Morsal Plains, but you can avoid that by climbing the mountains near the edge of the forest."

"Guys, we have another problem to consider." I jerked my head toward the door. "Our tail."

Tristan rubbed his temples. "Your what?"

I sighed and spoke slowly, enunciating. "The Council guard."

Mark nodded. "You're right. He won't let us cross the border."

Tara leaned into the room from the kitchen. "Don't give it another thought. I'll take care of that problem tomorrow."

Mark opened his mouth to ask her about her plan, but she had ducked back out of sight.

The next morning Tara served an early breakfast. Dustin was rubbing sleep from his eyes, and Aubrey crawled onto my lap and shared some bread with me. Tara brought out mugs of clavo for the adults and juice for the children. I glanced at Mark, wondering what we would do to get away. Now that we had made the decision to track Kieran into Hazor, I wanted to get on with it. My toes clenched and then uncurled again inside my boots. I glared across the table at the Council guard. We were so close to Jake, but each moment he could be getting further from our reach. I grabbed my mug of clavo with such force that it splashed over onto my hands.

I was blotting up the spill when I heard a thud. The Council guard's head had dropped forward and hit the table. Everyone else jumped, but Tara calmly began gathering up the dishes. "Let's be on our way. He'll have a nice nap. When he wakes up, Kendra can explain that she thinks everyone else has gone to Lyric."

Tristan's eyes stretched wide in alarm as he watched his mother traipse to the kitchen. Then he looked down at the contents of his mug and shoved it aside.

I stifled a giggle. The Braide Wood guardian was cursed with a family full of unconventional women.

Tristan shoved to his feet and confronted his mother in the alcove entrance. "How are you going to explain his little nap while everyone else disappeared?"

"The poor boy was up half the night guarding the house. He's only human. No one blames him for needing some sleep. Kendra will explain that we couldn't rouse him and couldn't wait any longer to catch the transport to Lyric."

"But what if he realizes what you did? What you used?" He rubbed his neck. "What *did* you use?"

Kendra rose and laid a reassuring hand on Tristan's arm. "It's a good plan. Stop fussing."

"Let's go." Mark brushed crumbs from his hands and stood. He and Tristan exchanged a few more words while I gave quick hugs to Kendra and Tara. Mark and I slipped out first, knowing that after Tristan said good-bye to Kendra, he and Payton and Tara would hurry to the trail to the transport station. Our path led in the opposite direction.

Mark and I slipped from the house and into the woods like wraiths. After a short walk we scrambled down the steep switchbacks through the woods toward Morsal Plains.

Hiking felt comforting and familiar. Mark and I loved to hike the woods near our home. I could almost forget we were in a strange world, pursued by danger, and facing unknown hazards. We were finally doing something useful. Each step brought us closer to Jake.

Skirting the edge of the plains, we aimed straight for the mountains that stood guard over the clans and separated the land from Hazor. Jagged black rock towered over us, daring us to climb. Two weeks earlier, I had watched the army of Hazorites crest these peaks and begin their invasion. They poured down these ridges on foot and with lehkan, blasting our armies with syncbeams. I'd felt terror that day, as well as the deep, spine-strengthening resolve to protect Braide Wood. For a moment I heard the echoes of clashing swords and the screams of the wounded.

I reached for Mark's hand, and he led me forward. As we trekked up the steep trail, I wondered what we would face on the other side of this forbidding ridge, and suddenly a children's ditty flitted into my head.

"The bear went over the mountain, the bear went over the mountain, the bear went over the mountaaaaaain, to see what he could see." I started humming and then couldn't help singing it. "And all that he could see, and all that he could see, was the other side of the mountain, the other side of the mountain, the other side of the mountaaaaaaain, was all that he could see."

Mark gave me a strange look.

"What?" I planted fists on my hips and stopped hiking. "You like *The Sound of Music* better? We could sing 'Climb Every Mountain.'"

And I started doing exactly that. Mark laughed and interrupted with "Rocky Mountain High." By the time we'd run out of mountain songs, we were breathless from clambering up the rough ledges. We were about halfway to the summit when I called for a rest.

I eased my pack off my shoulders and sank to the ground. It was getting harder for me to breathe. A knot of pain tightened beneath my sternum. I resisted the urge to rub it. If Mark noticed, it would add to his worries. He was already keeping an alert eye on the peaks above us.

"Do you miss it?" he asked, turning to me.

I looked up from retying my boots. "Home? Of course. If I could, I'd be back at our kitchen table right this second, with Jon practicing piano and Karen giggling on the phone and lasagna in the oven and—"

"No, that's not what I meant." He looked at my sword.

I squinted at him. It took me a moment to understand. "Being the Restorer?" I bit my lip and shook my head so hard my hair swung into my face. "Never."

"Are you sure?" Mark sank onto a rock near me, bracing one foot up. "The sense of purpose. The power. How can you not miss it?"

I looked down, and my words were quiet. "It wasn't like that."

Mark watched me and waited for more.

I considered how to make him understand. "How did you

feel when the Rendor songkeeper told everyone the prophecy about you? Important? Special?"

Mark shuddered. "Confused. Angry. A weight I didn't want to carry."

"Exactly." I stood up, dusting my hands off on my pants and grabbing my pack.

Mark didn't move. "But what if you could do it again?"

"Kieran is the Restorer now. My role is done." How much convincing did he need?

"But what if that was a mistake? What if Kieran stopped being the Restorer? He's not following the Verses or serving the Council. He's not even part of the clans anymore. What if the One takes that power away from him?"

Where was he going with this? This whole conversation was bizarre. I stared at Mark. His hair was growing longer, accentuating the natural waves he usually kept trimmed short. His face was leaner than it had been before all our recent adventures. I felt again that I was struggling to understand a man I barely knew. "Has that ever happened before?"

Mark shrugged. "No, but I'm just asking. What if he died and—"

"Stop it!" I picked up Mark's pack and shoved it at him with force. "Kieran is the Restorer. I'm not and never will be again. I don't know why the One has called him, and neither do you. Let's find Jake and get back to the portal and go home."

Mark pushed himself up. "I just wondered."

I couldn't read the thoughtful look on his face. He shouldered his pack and resumed climbing. I stood and watched him with a worried frown. Then I hurried to catch up.

We reached the highest peaks before midday. We hid in the cleft of two large rock formations and ate a hurried lunch. Mark went ahead to search for any sign of Hazorite patrols and came back to tell me it looked clear. He offered his hand and pulled me back to my feet to begin the hike down into Hazor. From our altitude, the land ahead looked dark and menacing. Thick forests appeared too dense to penetrate, and a marshland in the distance looked like the treacherous clay fields near Shamgar.

Mark had grown up knowing Hazor as a forbidden and frightening land. Tristan had told me a haunting story about Hazor's destruction of Shamgar. From talking with Nolan, I knew that it was a hard culture, with little compassion for the weak or small. They worshipped hill-gods, and those gods had promised them ever-expanding lands. Kieran had told the Council that Hazor believed their power came from the frequent human sacrifices in their temples. My only direct contact with Hazor had been when I had battled their armies. All I really knew was that their soldiers were skilled and ruthless.

"What will we find?" I mused aloud.

Mark met my eyes, his own reflecting a somber concern. "I don't know. But it won't be good."

I wished he would go back to telling me reassuring lies. My ability to pretend we were on a weekend camping trip dissolved. My skin prickled with cold, and I rummaged in my pack for my cloak.

Jake was ahead of us somewhere, in a very dangerous land. We were still a target for assassins from Kahlarea. Worst of all, the promised defender of the People, the new Restorer, had apparently thrown off his calling. He'd helped enemies into Lyric, been part of a murder, endangered Tristan's own family, and now, as hideous as it was to believe, he may have kidnapped Jake. How angry and desperate would he have to be to do something like that?

I shivered and pulled up the hood of my cloak. "He wouldn't."

"Hmm?" Mark adjusted a tie on his own pack and repositioned the weight on his shoulders.

"Kieran wouldn't hurt Jake, would he?"

Mark faced me squarely. "I think he'd do anything. Use anyone. Susan, he cut your throat when I wouldn't help get him into the Council session."

That wasn't exactly the way it happened, but I had to concede the point. Kieran was unpredictable and dangerous and didn't bind himself to the kind of ethics someone like Tristan lived by.

My mind followed that path. What if he had some plan that involved using Jake as a hostage? What might we have to do when we find him? I knew from experience that Restorers were hard to kill. But if Kieran had allied himself to Hazor and Kahlarea against the People of the Verses, he would have to be stopped. Mark was right. Whatever was ahead wouldn't be good.

Chapter Seventeen

KIERAN

After Tristan left the clearing, I pulled together my gear and set out. I could have used more supplies but wasn't about to ask anyone in Braide Wood for help. Furious thoughts spun around my head like a cloud of gnats, and I tried to outrun them.

I skidded down the steep trail toward Morsal Plains at a pace that would take me over the mountains and into Hazor before nightfall.

Tag had cheerfully offered help to an old friend, and now her life might be ruined.

Guilt threatened to land on me, but I batted it away. Anger was safer.

The Council was overstepping more than usual. Cameron was probably flexing his muscles, trying to stir up Tristan.

And it worked.

That thought led to the image of Tristan's cold and distant expression as he told me to leave. I rubbed sweat out of my eyes along with that picture. Better forgotten.

He was going to be a father. No wonder he was more protective of his family than ever.

And I was going to be an uncle, but I'd never see the child. I wouldn't see Kendra again. Or my clan. Those were gnats that stung. I crashed straight through heavy underbrush, ignoring the trail, letting thorns tear at me. When I reached the dark cliffs along the edge of Morsal Plains, I focused every bit of my concentration on climbing.

The rocks were sharp, and I didn't choose an easy approach up to the summit. I scraped my shin and felt it heal. I cut my hand grasping jagged handholds. It mended instantly. My muscles screamed with the pace I set for myself, and I welcomed their clamor because it shut out the other thoughts. I drove myself hard enough to leave every whisper of pain and regret behind in Braide Wood. By the time I strode down the far side of the mountain, all that remained was a cold pit of anger.

Even though I'd been traveling hard since midday, I kept walking for several miles toward Sidian. Twice I thought I heard a rustling behind me but didn't stop to check it out. If the Kahlareans had succeeded in finding me again, let them come. I would relish a battle.

Finally, I reached a barren clearing surrounded by cliffs and decided it was a defensible place to make camp for the night. A mile back I'd cut a section of a mesana vine that had snaked up a boulder, and I used my boot knife to pry back the tough fibers and scrape out the salty pith. It would taste better cooked, but I didn't want to bother.

I chewed a few bites, then tossed it aside.

Scooping up some rocks, I tested my aim by throwing them one by one at a discolored area on the granite boulder across from me.

Years back, Tristan and I had lingered by one of the clay pits near Shamgar. The thick gray-white soup blends into the surrounding land and lures creatures and humans alike to stumble forward and be sucked downward to a suffocating death. We tossed stones and watched them slowly disappear. Sometimes an air pocket would release and a small bubble would explode on the surface, as if the whole pit were boiling in a kettle over a heat trivet. But when I plunged my hand into the clay, it didn't burn. It was cold.

I sometimes wondered what happened to all the rocks the pit had swallowed. How many could it hold?

Hill-gods take me, I wasn't anywhere near Shamgar. Why were these random thoughts stirring now?

Maybe target practice with a fistful of rocks brought back that memory of tossing stones into the clay pits. Or maybe when I had stopped running, that recollection was just the first thought that was able to catch up to me. Despite my best efforts, others began to join it. The cloud of gnats became a swarm of carrion birds determined to pluck out and expose every inner organ.

When I tired of pitching stones, I couldn't settle myself enough to sleep. I grabbed one thought and examined it. Then another. And another. They all led me right where I knew they would.

Why did You do this to me?

The rage built in me, with only One place to direct it.

You called me to be a Restorer to my people, but they've banished me. I told You. I told You this was a mistake.

I rested my forehead against my fists and then laughed at my foolishness. Everyone knew the One didn't live in Hazor. He couldn't even hear me anymore.

Bleak rock faces surrounded me. I was completely alone. Just the way I liked it.

Alone except for the pain that had come flying in just a few paces behind me. I swung my hand at the space above my head. The torment of buzzing thoughts was so tangible I was half-surprised when my hand didn't connect with anything.

I laughed again. It had finally happened: The Restorer myth had broken my mind.

I sprang to my feet and stepped into the center of the clearing. The sky was close to black, and the cliffs towering over me were a deep, empty gray, disappearing into the darkness. The swarming thoughts flew thickly around me.

I had had few enough people I could trust. Now they were taken away from me. I'd never really fit in with my clan, but they were all I had. Now that one link was broken. Some part of me had been ready to learn, to follow, to make sense of the One's call to me. Hadn't I asked Tristan for help? Hadn't I listened to Linette? Hadn't I tried to understand?

Stone upon stone into the cold pit of my heart, until the wet concrete couldn't absorb any more.

I drew my sword and shook it at the sky.

"Come and tell me what You want from me!" My yell echoed back from the granite walls above. "If You're going to destroy me, at least face me! No more cover-and-ambush games. Talk to me!"

Before I could spew out more accusations and demands, a mist began to gather in the clearing.

My skin crawled, but I blamed the sensation on the chill of the night air. As I stared into the fog, a figure began to appear, moving toward me. I held my sword ready and squinted. It took a moment to see that it wasn't someone walking through the mist. Instead, the mist was curling into itself and *becoming* the figure.

The cold scraping down my spine could no longer be blamed

on climate. My hand tightened on the grip of my sword. My stomach knotted. I wanted to reach for my dagger and fling it, but I couldn't make myself move. I swallowed hard and then let anger swell up and push back my dread.

I glared at the apparition. Even in the dusk the form became vivid. He was a soldier, wearing armor unlike that of any nation I was familiar with. He drew His own sword as He stepped toward me. I heard His footsteps rasp against the grit of the hard earth.

So this was how it was to be. Fine. This was a battle I understood. I swung my sword across the space in front of me. He ignored my warning and kept coming. Now He was close enough to engage. I lunged forward with a feint and pulled back quickly, gauging His reaction. His sword flashed toward me. I blocked it easily and replied with a standard counter. He parried with skill and drove me back several paces. I increased the tempo with a flurry of strikes and circled around Him at the same time.

I had thought Him a ghost, but my arm felt the vibrations that traveled up my sword from the power of His blows. We were both holding back. Testing each other.

I swung wild, but the ploy didn't work. He blocked me but didn't move into my trap of an obvious opening. I tried a more direct attack but couldn't get past His guard. Maybe He really was a ghost. Attack and counter, thrust and parry, again and again. I couldn't touch Him. Sweat broke through my skin everywhere. After a grueling series of clashes, I shoved my blade hard against His edge with a two-handed grip and stepped back a few paces, gasping for air.

"What do You want?" I pointed the sword at Him and leaned forward to catch my breath. "Who are You?"

He stayed back, letting me recover. "You know Me."

The calm voice reignited my anger. "No!" I charged forward and propelled my sword downward. "I don't know You."

He raised His sword.

My blade crashed against pure marble. My arm shook from the shock of His unbending defense.

With a twist He deflected the edge of my sword and stepped back out of my range. "Don't lie, Kieran."

The sound of my name coming from this opponent made my heart crash against my ribs like the rapid rhythm of our sword blows. I growled deep in my chest as I ran forward again. "Fine!" I shouted as I swung.

He blocked and stepped back.

I swung again. "I know You. I've been Your pathetic game piece my entire life."

He moved around me with a crossing parry.

I spun to follow. "Did You enjoy it? You took" — our swords clashed—"everyone that ever mattered" —I slammed against His defense—"away from me."

Now He advanced, and I struggled to block His strikes. "And that wasn't enough for You." I stumbled back. "You want me to be Your Restorer."

He didn't deny it. He just let me attack again.

"Well, pick someone else!"

We fought for what felt like days. It should have become impossibly dark, but the sky seemed frozen at deep dusk. In some strange trick of the eye, it even appeared to grow lighter as we battled. I tried every ruse I knew, every unusual twist, every creative attack. He anticipated each of them. The bones in my legs went soft. My arms moved as if through mud. I fought until I had barely enough strength to stay on my feet. Still my sword didn't touch His body once. His skilled parries created plenty of openings for Him to cut me. He didn't.

I staggered back a few steps. "Enough. Stop playing these games. What do You want?"

"Yield." One relentless word.

Never! I roared incoherently and stumbled toward Him, forgetting skill, forgetting strategy. All I focused on was running Him through.

This time when He blocked me, He countered with a rapid circle around my blade. My sword flew out of my nerveless hand. He attacked with a swing that would have cut me in half had He not turned His weapon at the last moment. The flat of His blade hit my side. The force broke ribs and knocked me to my knees. I doubled over in pain. Cold steel pressed against the side of my neck.

My heart stopped. I had challenged the One of the Verses. Sneered at Him. Demanded He face me. He had let me have my say. Now it was His turn. My uneven breaths shook my whole body.

"Yield." He sounded as if He were pleading for His own life instead of demanding my surrender.

I looked up slowly, careful of the sharp edge resting against my neck.

I couldn't fight. I wouldn't yield. "Just finish it. Please." The words wrenched from me. My whole life had been some demented game, leading to this moment. He had wanted my destruction all along. My sword was gone. My strength was gone. I had nothing left to fight Him with. It was over.

"End it!"

I thought it was what I wanted, but my muscles still tensed against the final blow that would end my existence.

I closed my eyes, and stray images flashed across my mind.

Tara rolling her eyes at me with her blend of exasperation and affection. Kendra's face as she laughed up at Tristan. The way Tristan grinned when I let him beat me at a table game. Susan's earnest concern as she warned me of the dangers of my path. Linette's gentle hand on mine as she tried to ease my confusion. Further back. My mother's face, the angles softened by the roundness of pregnancy, her black hair pulled back as she peeled fruit for dessert and sang to me. The last memory I had of her before she died. If the Verses were true, maybe I'd see her now.

What was He waiting for? I didn't want to see the blade swing at me, but when nothing happened I opened my eyes.

The man hadn't moved. He held His sword as still as stone, both hands gripping the hilt—powerful arms that didn't shake with fatigue the way mine did.

I met His eyes and saw resolve. Didn't He have any mercy? Wouldn't He let me die with my pride to comfort me?

He didn't speak again, but I heard the call.

Yield.

I wanted this to be over. All of it. I had always seen myself as strong and quick-witted. Now I stared into the face of real power and true knowledge and tasted the dust of my own foolishness. I had challenged One that I couldn't even comprehend, and I deserved death at His hands. If I could have, I would have attacked Him and forced Him to strike so it could all be over, but I didn't even have strength left for that. Heaven and earth, I was grateful to be alone for this final moment of failure.

"I yield." My head fell forward. It was done. I would die without a clan, without a family, and now without even my self-respect. I felt Him lift the blade away to prepare to swing it through. I wrapped my arms tight around my center, partly to hold my throbbing ribs and partly to keep from disgracing myself by throwing my hands up to protect my neck. Then I heard the unmistakable sound of the sword being slid into a scabbard.

What was He doing? I couldn't bring myself to look.

A hand touched my shoulder. I flinched and jerked my head up.

He knelt in the dirt beside me. "Let me have a look." He pried my arm away from my wounded side. I was too dazed to protest. "Broken," He said. "We'd better wrap them. Wounds from my sword don't heal rapidly—no matter who you are." I couldn't think of anything to say. He unwound a strip of cloth from the waist of His tunic and used it to bandage my ribs. Then He walked over to my pack, pulled out a gourd, and tossed it to me.

I realized I had been thirsty for a long time and guzzled the water gratefully. Then I handed it to Him, and He drank too. I watched Him with numb confusion.

A deep shivering had taken hold of me, but He seemed perfectly at ease. He pulled my cloak out of my pack and placed it over my shoulders before sinking to the ground near me. He sat like a soldier used to relaxing on hard-packed earth and grinned at me as if we were old friends. "We have a lot to talk about."

My eyes widened. "I thought You were here to . . ."

"Kill you?" He leaned back on His elbows and looked up at the sky. "No. We need to talk."

Great. Just great. "You could have told me."

He tilted His head back further and laughed. It was a deep and confident sound—the kind of laugh that could shake down granite cliffs. I glanced nervously at the rock walls around us to be sure they hadn't moved, and He laughed again.

"Tell me what You're here to tell me." I didn't mean to sound surly. Stunned by everything that had happened, I needed sullenness to hide my fear.

He sat up and leaned forward. "Kieran, I'm here to answer your questions."

"I don't have any questions."

He tilted His head and watched me.

Then I remembered shaking my sword at the sky and demanding that He explain what He wanted of me. "All right. I may have some questions."

His smile was wide and inviting, which left me more confused than ever. By rights He should have killed me. I had given Him every reason to.

Why wasn't He furious with me for mocking Him, fighting Him, refusing Him? Why had He spared me? "Why?" I couldn't choke out more than that one word, but He understood.

"I gave you life." His eyes were warm, as if He were recalling a happy memory, but my stomach lurched as I realized again that the One with the power of all life and death was sitting only a few feet of dusty rock away from me. "And, no, it wasn't to make you a pathetic game piece."

I winced at the accusing words I had shouted at Him. I was having trouble breathing, and the tremor in my limbs wouldn't stop. How could He stand to be near me and not pulverize me into dust after the way I'd taunted Him?

"And I gave you life again when I chose you to be the Restorer. So, no, I don't want to take your life. It was My gift to you." His voice deepened, and He gave me a level look. "But understand. You belong to Me."

A ragged sob tore from me, and He rested a hand on my shoulder. His claim on me should have made me feel trapped. Instead, I felt I had a home I had never known about until now. "It's what you've really needed to hear, isn't it? You are not alone. There is One stronger than you, whom you can trust. I chose you to be the Restorer, and it was not a mistake."

Though His voice was quiet, each statement slammed into me with the power of a roaring waterfall. I couldn't answer. The sandy ground blurred beneath my gaze.

He squeezed my shoulder. "But you kept fighting Me. I know few men so persistent at finding the hardest way to do things." He released me and sat back, amused affection in His face. Then His expression grew serious. "Will you let Me help you?"

He had answered my ridiculous challenge and proven His absolute power. He had held His sword against my throat but had spared me. And now He asked my consent to give me more mercy that I didn't deserve.

"Yes. If You will." My voice was hoarse and tentative, but He laughed with joy at my words. It was His laughter that convinced me He really forgave me for all my stupidity. The fear melted away, and I suddenly had a thousand questions to ask Him. Not angry, sneering questions, but a thousand things I wanted to know His thoughts about.

We talked through long watches, but the sky never grew darker. Some of my questions received quick and clear answers. Others met only a shake of His head. But even the things He wouldn't explain loosened their hold on me somehow. After talking about the recent seasons, I found myself telling Him about my mother's death, my father's withdrawal, and the struggle of being a half-breed in the clan. I admitted that I had always assumed He wasn't near or didn't care.

He drew me out, and when I looked up at Him, I realized how twisted my understanding had been. As we talked about some of the hardest days I'd faced, He spoke with me like an old friend who had gone through each experience with me. An ache of loneliness that I hadn't realized was hiding inside me was unfolded and filled. My whole life became a different story as I looked at it with Him.

I shifted and my ribs throbbed. "But it's all gone wrong. How can I be a Restorer now that I'm in Hazor?"

He snapped off a piece of twig and flicked it in my direction. It bounced off my forehead. "Think, Kieran."

I prided myself on being a great strategist, but I couldn't see the point of this.

He smiled. "I want you to take the truth — the Verses — to the people of Hazor."

"What? That's impossible." Then it struck me that He was talking to me and we were *in* Hazor. That should have been impossible too. The One lived in the Lyric tower and spoke to songkeepers. He didn't roam the dangerous trails of the Hazor mountains and converse with the banished.

He nodded, His eyes warm. "Trust me." He sprang to His feet and offered me His hand. I reached out and He pulled me up, clasping my forearm. Warmth and strength wrapped my arm, my whole being.

I looked down.

His feet seemed to be covered by mist. No, they were dissolving into mist.

"Wait," I spoke quickly. A thousand more questions raced through my mind. "What about Linette?"

His eyes sparkled. "Yes, you'll need her help."

What did that mean?

He squeezed my arm, and His eyes grew intense. "Be sure you understand. It's going to be hard. Are you ready to follow?"

What answer could I give? I'd railed against Him nearly every day of my life but had never known Him. Now I was ready to follow Him anywhere.

"My sword is Yours." I hesitated, wishing for more to offer Him. "I pledge my life to protect Your house." The formal vow of a house protector was hardly an adequate response to His question.

He seemed to understand. "Thank you." The words were soft, and fog swirled between us.

"Can't You come with me?" I could no longer feel His arm clasping mine.

I'm always with you. You are not alone.

At last His words made sense to me. The words that Susan had passed along to me. The words He had whispered in the night air.

I stumbled through the low mist over to my pack. I reached for it, thinking I needed to head straight to Sidian. Instead, a heavy fatigue pressed me down. I couldn't fight it. I had no idea how much time had passed since I'd last slept. Somehow my head found itself against my pack, and my cloak covered me. With the mist curling around me, I felt completely safe.

Before sleep grabbed me, I forced my eyes open, worried that something was missing. Something didn't feel right. Then I realized: The cold angry pit at the core of my being was gone. I tried to probe that space, the way my tongue might prod a loose tooth, but I was too tired. I let my eyes close. In my dreams I heard warm, comforting laughter.

Chapter Eighteen

KIERAN

When I woke up, the unchanging dusky half light was gone. The sky was the pearl cast of morning. The mist had vanished, and my arm ached from sleeping on it crooked. I rolled my shoulder, but that triggered a throb in my side. I stood slowly and fingered the bandage wrapped around my chest. The wound came close to convincing me I hadn't imagined everything, but I still looked around the clearing uneasily.

My sword lay in the dust. That proved it. I had never neglected my sword before. I picked it up and tested the tip with my finger. I sucked away the drop of blood that welled up and then wiped down my sword and sheathed it. The blade should have shattered under the abuse it faced last night, but it was strong and unharmed. Old scratches had disappeared, as though clanging against the sword of the One had changed it as surely as the struggle against Him had changed me. I shook my head as I thought of the hatred I had felt for Him. He wasn't what I had expected at all.

What would Tristan think when I told him that the One was a skilled swordsman? The eager thought gave way to longing sharp as the pain in my ribs. I was filled with a hunger to see my old friend—to tell him what was happening. And I wanted—no, *needed*—to tell Kendra that I understood so much more now.

I had yielded to the One. I knew where I had to go next. Things that had infuriated me began to make sense: my heritage, my alienation, my banishment. But I ached to be with the people I cared about and let them know.

Anger and detachment, the tools that had always worked for me before, now felt out of reach. Without my wall of inner lies, I had no way to hold back the pain. My gut twisted, and I sank to my knees with a groan. This was worse than a sword against my neck.

I'd become one of the weak ones.

Now I could be driven to fear, like Tristan in his love for Kendra. I was vulnerable to being crushed as Linette had been by Dylan's death. *Shamgar*. I'd probably start making stupid, gullible choices like Susan.

I squeezed my eyes shut. What was happening to me? "Take this away." Even my voice was raw and unsteady. This was wrong. I wanted to go back. Find the person in me that I understood. "What good will I be to You like this?"

You love them. You miss them. It wounds you.

"Yes. Make it stop."

It doesn't stop. It's the price of love.

He was speaking from His own experience. It startled me like the shock from a damaged light wall. He was inviting me to be more like Him.

I nodded slowly and pushed myself to my feet. The new, frightening yearning for my family and friends didn't leave, but I shouldered my pack and began the long march to Sidian.

I had made plenty of trips along this route and knew how to avoid the patrols, but the passes that were normally well guarded were eerily vacant now. I would have expected extra soldiers to be stationed near the border of Braide Wood after the recent battle. Instead, Zarek had apparently pulled the army back to lick its wounds. Although I was grateful for the absence of Hazorite soldiers in the outlands, something dark and unseen seemed to stalk me.

The strangled howl of a mountain cat rose from one of the jagged peaks, and invisible claws scraped their way up my backbone as I walked past the stark, abandoned outcroppings.

I'd been here before and had always been alert to the human and animal dangers in Hazor, but I'd never sensed this presence of evil before. Was it because of my Restorer gifts? Or was I imagining things? I glanced at the cliffs far above me, almost expecting to see a monster crouched in wait, its eyes tracking my every movement—a mythic, house-sized rizzid with poison dripping from its fangs.

But the dull rock ledges were bare. In fact, aside from the lack of patrols, I didn't see anything out of place. Even so, I continued to feel the dark presence, and I quickened my pace.

By skirting a few outlying villages, I managed to avoid any contact with people and found an old shed in a caradoc pasture in which to take shelter. The smell of molding feed grass and wood dust settled around me. As night lowered and turned the dim interior of the shed into a black void, caradoc in the distance complained with low bleats. Insects sent up intermittent hissing and whirring from beyond the walls. The longer I listened, the more I heard whispers in the sounds.

I braced my back into the corner of the shed and tried to talk to the One, but here on the outskirts of Sidian, He seemed far away. I rested my forehead on my knees and murmured Verses into my folded arms until the whispers faded and I managed to sleep.

The next morning I hiked the final miles toward the capital city of Hazor. As I walked, I reviewed what the One had told me. Some of the conversation was already dissolving from my mind in the same way the mist had faded from the clearing, but I hadn't forgotten His goals. He wanted me to bring the Verses to Hazor. Ridiculous enough to be laughable, but I couldn't imagine laughing in the face of the Warrior who had disarmed me that night.

I needed a strategy. I was great at planning battles—anticipating every move and countermove. But the One's call didn't fit into my human logic. Despite my efforts, I couldn't develop a scheme that made a bit of sense for this. Still, I strode forward. If nothing else came to me, I could stand in the central court of Sidian and just start talking. I rubbed the sore spot on my ribs. Right. That would go over real well.

I reached tar roads well before I could see the gates of Sidian in the distance. I stayed to one side to avoid the minitrans that rolled past with greater and greater frequency. Soon I was also passing human travelers. I caught the scent of a flatbread popular in Sidian. Instead of baking on a heat trivet, it was fried in rendered animal fat. My mouth watered until I passed a group of women in the vibrant tunics of the upper class who reeked of some flowery perfume.

With my head down, I nodded an occasional vague greeting and blended in well. I looked like the majority of the population with my short black hair and worn travel clothes.

I began to stretch my hearing and eavesdrop on clusters of

people, trying to get a sense of the situation I was walking into. What I overheard startled me. The recent battle with Braide Wood was a popular topic of conversation. I expected some analysis of what went wrong in the battle and speculation about Zarek's future plans. Instead, I heard uneasy whispers about the One. More than once I heard a murmured guess that the hill-gods had found a god they couldn't conquer. Curiosity swirled about how the One could empower an insignificant clan to stand up to the might of Hazor's army.

I hid a grin. I still didn't know how I was supposed to share the Verses with the people of Hazor, but the One had certainly known when the timing was right. I'd visited Sidian frequently in past years and never noticed any interest in the provincial One of the neighboring clans before today.

A small transport glided past, so I stepped farther off to the side of the road. From this rise I could see Sidian. Hazor's capital was more than twice the size of Lyric and surrounded with dark granite walls. Jagged protrusions studded the fortification, designed to instill fear and add to the forbidding presence. This was a predatory city showing its claws.

But the bumps and outcroppings also provided handholds for a skilled climber. Sidian would have been better protected with fewer raised hackles and bared teeth, and a little more thought to practical defenses.

As I drew closer to the jagged metal gates, a mass of people poured out of the entrance. Drums pounded a somber beat, and a row of temple priestesses raised a shrill, eerie chant. It seemed unwise to fight my way upstream through the crowd and into the city. Instead, I melted into the edge of the procession to see what this group was doing.

They followed a road angling upward to a grove of trees. When

I realized where we were heading, my neck muscles tightened and my pulse battered the inside of my skull in time to the drums.

The hill-gods were too demanding and too terrifying to be invited into a major city, so the Sidian temple was set apart in this elevated forest outside of town. I'd lurked outside this shrine before. I knew more than I wanted to about how the Hazorites served their gods. I slowed, but a man a few paces behind crashed into me. The current of people continued to push forward. Pulling out now would draw attention I couldn't afford.

The temple was even more imposing than the city walls. Grotesque carvings in stone glared from every vertical surface. On my past visits I'd always found the art laughable. This time cold slithered across the back of my neck.

I'd met the One and knew firsthand that the stories about Him weren't mere myths. What if the demented hill-gods weren't myths either? Could there be some real presence behind the stone statues?

The Sidian temple's single door opened like a gaping mouth. I hated being inside a building with only one entrance, but I was swept along with the crowd.

There were no windows, so the inside was lit with vertical strips of red light walls interspersed with coarse stone. The color created an alarming effect on the faces of the gathered people. Eyes seemed to glow a feral red, and skin and hair appeared streaked with blood. A clear liquid, carrying a cloying sweet scent, poured down steadily along two sections of wall, to be circulated back up and wash downward again.

Though the hill-gods were thought to love the screams and wails of the sacrifices brought to them, apparently it was acceptable to disguise the stench of death. The strategy was only partially successful.

The priestesses who had headed the procession paced slowly up black onyx steps to a stone altar, eyes fixed on the tall pillar that boasted the most tormented carved face I'd yet seen. One young woman turned and faced the crowd, while two others lifted an ornate red robe from her shoulders. Her tunic was sleeveless. Blood didn't wash easily from long sleeves. And there would be lots of blood. There always was.

My stomach tightened, and I felt the dark presence that had crouched near during my mountain travels. I scanned the room. Not the statue. The skin-prickling feeling didn't emanate from that. The young priestesses in front stared forward vacantly, probably heavily dosed with drug patches. They were victims as much as villains in this ritual. I sensed confusion and emptiness, but not the vicious evil that spread outward like bitum sap.

Then I spotted her. An old woman hunched on an ornate stone chair in the far corner of the altar area, a hood hiding most of her face. Hazor's high priestess, Bezreth. She lifted her head slowly and scanned the crowd. Did she sense a follower of the One in the same way I sensed bottomless darkness in her? Deep creases in her skin had the texture of tree bark, as if she were so old she was only kept alive by some inhuman power.

Maybe she was. Ridiculous. Everyone knew the hill-gods were stories used by the king to control his people. Still, the hair on my arms rose as her gaze roved the temple.

I tried to ease my way out, but too many people had packed in behind me. I glanced around, trying to find a gap to slip through when, from the far left wall, several Hazorite soldiers trudged to the front, pulling something behind them. Once they reached the stairs everyone could see what the soldiers were dragging forward. Children. Five of them—a sacred number for the hill-god worshippers. They were bound together in a line with thick rope.

Bezreth lifted one hand and pointed at the first child in the line.

A soldier drew a sword and cut the little girl free. She was about Aubrey's age, and she let out a shriek at the sight of the sword flying so close to her as it cut the rope. The crowd murmured in approval. A second soldier grabbed the girl's arms and propelled her up the stone steps. The chosen priestess lifted a long twisted blade that shimmered red in the unearthly light. The child began to struggle and cry. The soldier forced her closer to the priestess. When the girl's wails rose in terror, the surrounding priestesses began to echo the sound, not to mock but to supplement her cries in order to draw further attention from the hill-gods.

The crowd began to shout and chant. The drums pounded a faster tempo. Bezreth slowly rose to her feet. She raised her hands over the priestess and the child like a perverted blessing, a toothless smile growing in her wrinkled face. I tasted bile in the back of my throat.

Holy One, make this stop!

I knew about their child sacrifices. When Hazor demanded a tribute of children from Braide Wood, I was the one who brought the truth to the Council—the truth of what they intended to do with the children, of what they had done with the children of Shamgar. But I couldn't face this.

Make them stop!

And suddenly my silent scream to the One became His compelling cry to me. It was no longer my plea. It was His command. Strength rushed through every muscle and sinew in my body, and now I had no trouble shoving my way through the mass of people. I didn't aim for the door. As people stumbled aside, I drew my sword and ran toward the altar.

Two Hazorite soldiers saw me coming and raised their weapons. With one thrust I ran the first one through and shoved him aside, spinning to slice into the second. I reached the stairs, but the priestesses were continuing their ceremony. Now that I was closer, their glazed eyes were obvious. They moved with a drug-induced detachment and paid no attention to the disturbance. The cadence of the crowd's chanting faltered — at least among the group near the stairs. The unholy wailing and driving drums continued.

I was too late.

The twisted knife cut into the girl, and her scream of pain seared into my memory. I charged up the steps and attacked the soldier holding her. He released her, and she collapsed to the floor. My vicious thrust assured he joined her on the floor in the space of a heartbeat. When I was sure he was dead, I glanced up at the priestess, who swayed in confusion and still held the bloody knife. It took her a moment to find where the girl had fallen. I didn't let her move closer but kicked the knife from her hand and shoved her back.

By now there were screams sounding throughout the room that weren't part of the ceremony. I ran toward the other children and cut their ropes. "Run. Run away." They didn't need further urging. No one tried to grab them. The crowd was pressing back, away from the commotion I had caused near the altar. I looked over their heads to where more soldiers pushed their way through the crowd. Then I crouched by the little girl. Her woven tunic was covered with blood, and her face twisted with pain. She was still alive but would never survive the gouging wound she had received.

I gathered her in my arms. "Holy One, help me!" I didn't mean to shout the words out loud. I didn't know what I was doing anymore. But I pressed her broken body against my chest and rested my forehead against hers. Heat raced through me. I sensed movement and lifted my head. The priestesses had edged away in confusion, but Bezreth was drawing closer. The old woman's pupils were huge, leaving only a thin amber ring around deep black orbs. She raised her hands again, and the full sleeves of her robe fell back, revealing her skeletal arms.

"Get back!" The words rang from me with a resonant power. "Your gods can't have her."

The ancient high priestess stopped moving forward, as if the air around me pressed her back. Her eyes widened, and she shrieked curses down on my head. She fed on death, but this life was being denied her.

The girl stirred in my arms, and I looked down. Color returned to her face. Blood stopped flowing from her wound. Her eyes opened, and she blinked in confusion. I'd seen my own wounds close and watched Jake's ankle mend; still, this sight made me catch my breath.

I glanced up. The priestesses had left the platform, and even Bezreth had disappeared somewhere. The only representative of the hill-gods that remained was the towering pillar glaring down at me. I lowered the girl to the floor and raced at the statue, hacking with my sword at the weak mortar near the base, managing to cut far enough through for the image to topple.

The screams and chaos from the floor of the temple grew, and I felt a rush of satisfaction. Then a tremendous blow cracked into the back of my head. I staggered forward. The heavy feet of soldiers pounded from all directions as I hit the ground. Someone knocked the sword from my hand. I stretched my arm, reaching for it. A fist crashed against my back. A booted foot rammed into my ribs. There was no time to gasp for breath.

I squinted through the pain to see if the little girl was fully recovered. The old priestess filled my line of sight. Bottomless eyes bored into me. She smiled.

One of the soldiers grabbed my hair and slammed my head forward into the floor. "Kill him!"

"Not here." The rasping voice of the priestess interrupted. "It will desecrate the ceremony."

I think my lip curled up at that comment. Then everything went black.

Chapter Nineteen

KIERAN

The soldiers dragged me deeper into the darkness of the prison. This was not a part of Sidian I had ever hoped to explore. My throat closed in as the hall grew narrow and the ceiling lowered. I stumbled, which gave them an excuse to swear and shove me. What did they expect? Heavy chains dragged at my ankles and ground into my wrist bones. Chains. And I had thought being bound by ropes was my worst nightmare.

We reached a gray, featureless door. One of the soldiers slid a lever, allowing the thick metal slab to grind open. Even though I anticipated the violent push that propelled me inside, I couldn't keep my balance with the tangle of metal around my ankles, and I sprawled onto the cold stone floor. By the time I got my hands under me and lifted my head, the door had closed again with a magnetic gasp.

Gaunt figures huddled around the room. Most leaned against the walls. I stayed in the center of the large cell. The porous rock walls had absorbed hundreds of years of human terror and despair. I had the strange notion that if I touched their surfaces, some of that misery would soak into my skin. I quickly scanned the other dozen or so prisoners, assessing the level of danger each might pose. A few looked strong. Soldiers, I would guess—deserters or some other breed of criminal. But the rest were hunched old men or scrawny boys.

The prisoners soon realized no one was coming for them, and the apprehension in the room sagged. Light panels lined only the upper walls and were set to a dim level, causing bizarre shadows to crawl across the floor when anyone stirred.

I kept to myself, trying to get my bearings. The soldiers in the temple must have kept beating me long after I had lost consciousness. Even with my body's ability to heal quickly, I was a battered mess. Any movement incited new pain. I rested my head on my knees and tried to stay still.

Was the little girl alive? At the moment, with every part of my body screaming, I wished I weren't. And had it made any difference? Did the other children get away? What if they had gone ahead with the sacrifices after they dragged me away?

Bleak thought. The smart approach would have been to develop a plan to undermine the hill-god worship. Or win a hearing with the powerful in government. But those things took time. Time the little girl hadn't had. A strong impulse had compelled me to stop their ceremony. I thought I was hearing the One. But if that were true, why was I in prison? I couldn't fulfill His purpose here. My physical pain was easing as each injury healed, but my doubts were just beginning to throb.

Much later, when the door grated open again, I could smell the fear in the room. Most of the men cringed closer to the walls, turning from the door, ducking their heads as if they could become invisible by squeezing their eyes shut. One boy who had a coveted corner curled tightly around himself, the bones of his spine showing through his tunic as he shivered. It didn't take a genius to understand what had caused this reaction.

Two soldiers sauntered in and gazed around the room. They grabbed one of the older men and hefted him to his feet. A low moan sounded in his chest as they dragged him toward the door. It rose to an inhuman wail as he disappeared down the hall. I was almost glad when the thick cell door slid shut and cut off the sound.

I edged closer to a man at one side of the room. "Where are they taking him?" When he didn't answer, I touched his shoulder. His head jerked around, eyes wide, and it took him a moment to focus on me. "Where are they taking him?" I asked again.

"To question him." The man's voice was hoarse, and that simple statement triggered a spell of coughing. The boy in the corner made a sound and shifted, disturbed by the noise.

"What information do they want?" I asked the old man.

His chest-rattling cough finally stilled. He lifted watery eyes to the doorway. "They don't want information. They're just bored." He turned away.

I shifted my gaze to the boy near him. "How long have you been here?" No response. I tapped his shoulder.

He started to shake. "No." His voice was a low sob. "Not again. Please."

I stiffened. I knew that voice. Moving farther to one side, I was able to see part of his face. "Nolan?"

His head jolted up, and he turned to look at me. His eyes widened as he recognized me. The blood drained from his face, making the bruises that covered him look even darker. Raw wounds on his arm hadn't been bandaged or even cleaned. I felt a wave of pity for him, then realized that to him, I was just as terrifying as his captors. I hadn't treated him much better than they had when I interrogated him after the attack on Morsal

Plains. Regret scraped me like a rusty blade.

I quickly held up my hands so he could see the shackles.

"It's all right. I won't hurt you. I'm a prisoner too."

His face was easy to read. Fear, disbelief, and then a growing hope that I wasn't a danger to him.

"What are you doing here?" I asked.

His eyes narrowed. "After I escaped, I told them Braide Wood planned to surrender their children."

I nodded. That had been the plan. Tristan and I fed him false information and let him escape. It bought us time to prepare for the invasion. "And?"

Pure hatred flared in his eyes. "I also told them you had only a hundred guardians, so King Zarek didn't call up the Gray Hills army."

"They blamed you."

He snarled. "After the battle they charged me with treason." He turned away, hunching his shoulders.

"I'm sorry," I said quietly. War called for desperate acts, but he was just a boy—fifteen or sixteen at most. Hazor's army should never have left him behind as a messenger. Anger surged through me as I thought of the way Hazor used him as a disposable messenger to our clan. Shame followed as I realized I had used him in much the same way. And now he was paying for my ruse.

I stared at the sores on his arm. His injuries, his imprisonment, were Hazor's fault. Zarek's fault. Not mine. But I couldn't tear my eyes away. Without thinking, I lifted my hands, heavy with the chains, and rested them on his arm. He winced and tried to pull away but had nowhere to go. I closed my eyes and immediately felt warmth course through me.

"Let me go." His voice was harsh but barely above a whisper. He'd been in prison long enough to know not to draw attention to himself. "Let me go."

"It's all right. I won't hurt you." I murmured the opening creed from the Verses. As I said the words about the One being awesome in majesty, I thought again of the relentless Warrior I had met a few nights ago. When I repeated the description of how He made all there is and loves all He has made, I felt again the way He had clasped my arm and promised to be with me. The words that every clan child learns were real. I almost forgot the prison cell as that realization flooded me. Then Nolan gasped.

I opened my eyes and moved my hands away. His arm was healed, and other bruises that marked his face began to fade. He stared at his arm, touched it with his other hand, and then slowly lifted his eyes to me.

His thin chest moved rapidly. "Get away from me." He wedged himself further into the corner as if he would push me away with his feet.

"Nolan, it's only—" Confronted by the terror in his face, I didn't know how to explain or calm him.

"Get away."

With a scrape of chains, I backed away and settled again near the center of the room. There was nothing more I could do for him now anyway.

The guards never brought back the older man. They must have entertained themselves too enthusiastically. I dozed off and on through the night, wondering when my turn would come to be dragged away and tortured. I tried not to think about what would happen when they saw my wounds heal.

The next morning my heart jerked into a stuttering sprint when the door slid open. There was a whole contingent of guards in the hall. I glanced around the room, confused.

"Everyone up!" one soldier shouted. He marched into the room, kicking those who didn't or couldn't move fast enough.

"King Zarek is holding court today. It's your turn." He grinned. Apparently he was anticipating the outcome of that event.

We shuffled out, some in chains, most too weak to need any. I tried to position myself near Nolan to look out for him, but he drilled a glare in my direction before dropping his gaze to the floor. I'd been hated before. By lots of people. It had never bothered me like this.

I could grab a weapon from one of the guards. I could fight with my wrists chained—some. Maybe the other prisoners would fight too. I glanced at the row of half-starved, beaten creatures around me and sighed. We'd all be dead before anyone reached the end of the hall.

One of the guards noticed me looking around and clubbed the side of my head with a meaty fist. "Eyes down!"

Old familiar rage twisted inside me, but I forced myself to look defeated and nonthreatening.

The guards led us up through a maze of underground tunnels, up crumbling stone stairs, down a windowless corridor. They directed the shuffling parade of prisoners through a door into something that looked like a pen for holding livestock. Through the metal fencing, I saw we were off to one side of an ornate room that contained a throne and dozens of soldiers in full battle dress. A polished obsidian wall filled the space behind the throne and absorbed the glow from light panels on the other walls. The center of the room was set off by a section of white stone floor bordered by a jagged-edged pattern of darker rock, like fangs waiting to close on flesh. Across from the throne, double doors marked the main entrance to the room.

I edged my way to the front of our pen, but as I drew closer to the grate, the hairs on my arms lifted. I cautiously reached one finger toward the metal bars, and my hand was thrown back by the electrical shock.

Nolan made a coughing sound and fought to hide a smirk.

I tossed him a glare as I rubbed my stinging finger, but two guards opened a side door of the pen and captured Nolan's attention. One stepped inside, grabbed the boy's arm, and pulled him out. His smirk fell away into grim resignation as they dragged him to a point in front of the throne. I moved as close as I could to the fencing.

The large doors at the far end of the room slid open silently on well-maintained tracks. A variety of courtiers and more soldiers walked in with a metered step. They took their time crossing the room and taking up positions around the throne. No one stepped on the central area of flat white stone directly in front of the throne, where Nolan huddled, flanked by soldiers twice his size.

Next, a few dozen people were ushered in to fill the space along the wall directly across from us. From the fearful and searching looks they directed toward our cage, I suspected they were friends or family of the prisoners. Finally, Zarek entered alone.

No one would doubt he was the king. He was a large man and moved with lazy power. I'd known councilmembers and head guardians who had gone soft once they had people to do their bidding. Zarek didn't strike me as a man who indulged in the luxuries of command. Muscles stretched his gilded tunic, which was emblazoned with the jagged emblem of Hazor. His head was shaved bald, but his eyebrows were black as night and slanted over eyes that didn't miss a thing.

I should have felt pure loathing for this man. It was his word that destroyed Morsal Plains and sent an army that killed many of the clan guardians. His fist grasped the throat of his own nation, while his desire for expansion threatened my people. Yet I had a grudging respect for him.

He sank into the throne and leaned back, surveying the room with an indolent stare. I knew the casual posture was feigned. He was aware of everything and everyone, and as his gaze swept the holding cell, I was careful to keep my focus down and not move.

"The court awaits the king's justice. The prisoners are present." A tall, skeletal man in a black robe intoned the opening words. "Kebron from Trezald is the first to stand before the king." One of the guards with a red emblem on his tunic stepped over and whispered something to the herald.

Beyond a brief nod, the herald didn't let a flicker of response show on his face. "The warden reports that Kebron was killed while trying to escape."

A gasp and muffled sob rose from someone in the cluster of observers across the room.

Zarek leveled a look at the warden. "Again?"

The warden's eyes darted toward his guards, and he gave a stiff bob of his head, settling his focus on the floor in front of the throne.

"Convey to the guards that I'm not pleased with the number of prisoners they have been losing." Another sharp nod.

"Nolan of Sidian is here to stand before the king. His crime is treason." The herald's face remained expressionless.

"I'm well aware of his crimes," Zarek said in a deadly quiet voice. "And I'm aware of every soldier who was lost in battle because of this boy." His volume grew, and he sat forward in the chair. "There are few criminals in all of history who have caused as much damage as this false messenger." Zarek's words rose to a roar.

Nolan swayed on his feet. The boy's face went sickly white. Black bangs fell into his eyes as he stared at the floor.

"Wait, please." A woman's voice rang through the room. She

elbowed her way through the spectators, twisted away from the reaching arms of a guard, and ran toward Nolan. Soldiers moved forward to grab her. Zarek lifted one hand, and the men froze.

"Let her speak." The king settled back and studied her with amused interest. It was no wonder he was intrigued. She stood with a sinewy grace, chin high, dozens of intricate braids falling down her back. In spite of her beauty, the ravages of a hard life showed in the strain on her face, and made it hard to guess her age. Now that she had his consent to speak, she seemed paralyzed. She turned to face Nolan, and I got a better look at her. She seemed familiar. I edged closer to the grate until the electrical field sparked and forced me back.

"Who are you?" Zarek bounced one hand lightly on the arm of his throne. He didn't have much patience. He didn't need much. No one ever kept him waiting.

"Shayla of Sidian." Even with the tension in her throat, there was a sweetness to her voice. I recognized her now. I had met her once on my first trip into Hazor. I was a clumsy youth, trying to stay hidden while searching for lost cousins. She was an adventurous girl who was attracted to the danger of helping me. Memories rushed back so vividly I almost missed her next words.

"Nolan is my son." She said it with every bit of pride and love that any mother has for a son who is a hero to his people. Her tone wasn't appreciated. Zarek's brows lowered, and there were murmurs of disapproval around the room. I wondered when she had married and if she were a widow now since there was no father to speak for the boy. I wanted to whisper advice to her because it was clear she wasn't winning Zarek's favor.

She must have felt the animosity in the room; a shiver ran through her. But she squared her shoulders and looked directly at Zarek. "I plead for mercy. He's only a boy. He carried a dangerous message to the barbarians of Braide Wood. He—"

"Enough." Zarek's single word was cold and unrelenting. His gaze shifted to Nolan. "Any son of Hazor should be willing to give his life in service to his king, not buy his life with lies that destroy his own people." Nolan seemed to shrink into himself. Zarek straightened in his chair and opened his mouth to pronounce his sentence.

"I claim the right of substitution." Shayla stepped in front of Nolan. "Take me in his place."

"No!" It was the first word Nolan had spoken. The room burst into a collision of voices. Shayla turned to Nolan and whispered something, part of which I was able to catch by stretching my hearing.

"My time is short anyway. Let me do this." She gave Nolan a gentle smile—a smile I remembered from my youth. Nolan shook his head.

Zarek ignored the chaos and waited for the noise to die away. When all eyes turned to him again, he still waited. "No one would deny that I have shown mercy when it was deserved," he said at last. "It is because of my compassion for those who were lost in battle, and for their families, that I am not content with a mere sentence of death." His eyes speared Shayla before she could interrupt.

"I deny your request for substitution. However, you will die along with him. Your execution will be swift, but Nolan will be offered to the hill-gods and kept alive as long as possible." The room had grown deathly quiet. There was a tremor of rage in Zarek's voice as he continued. "And still it is not enough to pay for his crime."

Shayla's head dropped forward, every ounce of determined hope crushed from her body.

"Wait. Let me speak," I shouted, wishing I could grab the bars in front of me. Zarek's furious eyes found me. A guard pushed his way through the other prisoners and drove his fist into my stomach. I doubled over, gasping, and lifted my shackled hands to try to block his next blow.

I caught a glimpse of the herald whispering something to the king before an uppercut slammed into my jaw and knocked me back.

"Bring him," the herald said. The guard paused with his arm raised for another punch and turned incredulous eyes toward the throne. Zarek nodded. One of the soldiers opened the cell, and suddenly two guards were hauling me out and toward the king, my chains scraping heavily along the polished floor.

Maybe they'll leave gouges. At least I'll leave some mark.

"Speak." Zarek leaned back and crossed his arms. He was curious enough to allow me a few words. If I didn't choose them carefully, I'd be the next one offered to the hill-gods.

"I'm Kieran, and I come from Braide Wood." I couldn't claim clan status anymore, but Braide Wood *was* where I had come from geographically.

Shayla gasped my name, and I was glad she remembered me.

Whispers raced around the room, but I focused on Zarek's raised eyebrows. "Nolan committed no treason. I was the one who tortured him, and he never betrayed Hazor. I was the one who gave him false information and allowed him to escape, knowing it would give us time to gather our clans." I watched Zarek's face carefully but couldn't read him.

I cleared my throat and projected to the observers. "Nolan was brave, and such a loyal servant of Hazor that all of Braide Wood was impressed by the character of your people." All right, that was an exaggeration. But Susan and Kendra were sure taken with the boy.

Zarek studied me. "Why would you speak for him? What is he to you?"

"A regret." I met the king's eyes. "One of many things I've had to do to protect my people. He doesn't deserve death."

Zarek stood up and stalked over to Nolan. "Is what he said true?" Nolan stared hard at his feet and nodded. "Look at me." The king's voice was harsh but without the blazing fury he had vented earlier.

Nolan's head stayed down, but he looked up through his dark bangs. "I was ready to give my life to serve Hazor." The boy's voice shook, but it grew in strength as he glared in my direction. "They tricked me." His chin lifted an inch, and now he faced Zarek with calm resignation. "But I brought back their lies. I deserve to die."

Zarek paced across the floor in front of us several times, watching our faces. Then he sank back into his throne and waved one hand in the general direction of the warden. "Release the boy to his mother. They are free to go."

I turned to look at Shayla. Tears ran down her face. She mouthed the words "thank you" before turning to hug Nolan. He only gave me a sullen glower of distrust, but I grinned anyway. A guard escorted them from the room, and I turned back to the king. My grin faded. Zarek was leaning forward on his throne, showing his teeth. I realized why he had been so easy to convince. He didn't much care about Nolan and Shayla. He had bigger rizzids to skewer.

Chapter Twenty

KIERAN

"You'll be executed shortly," Zarek said. "But since I did you a favor, satisfy my curiosity." His intense gaze created a space around us, as if we were the only two in the room. The soldiers, prisoners, petitioners, and attendants seemed to disappear under the strength of his ability to ignore them.

I shifted my weight, and the annoying chains rattled. "You want information on Braide Wood?" I started sorting through plausible lies.

He snorted. "I have better sources for information on your pathetic clans." He brought one fist toward his chin and tapped it thoughtfully. "Why did you stop the temple ceremony? And why did you attack the shrine?" He sounded genuinely puzzled.

I glanced around the room. Shackled. Unarmed. Outnumbered. I wasn't going to get out of here alive. No reason to keep it from him at this point. "I serve the One." A throb of something sharp and bright pulsed through me with those words. My service to Him wouldn't be long, but what did that matter? I'd known Him. He'd allowed me to glimpse others through His eyes. To speak a few words of truth. To heal a few wounds. Ignoring the menacing inlay pattern surrounding me on the floor, I stood tall, barely feeling the weight of the chains.

Zarek narrowed his eyes and waited.

I took a deep breath. "He told me to stop the murder."

"Because he's afraid of the power of the hill-gods and wants them deprived of strength?"

I laughed. I couldn't help it.

Zarek didn't react. He just watched me.

"No." I caught my breath and sobered. "Because every life is valuable to Him. Is she alive? The girl they were trying to murder?"

Zarek ignored my question. His broad forehead wrinkled; he was probably pondering creative ways to kill me. "I'm told you worked magic to reverse the girl's wound."

"No. The One healed her." The murmurs in the room reminded me of droning insects far in the distance.

After a long silence he asked, "Do you know much about the One?" The black wall loomed behind him. Guards whose faces had been etched with cruel sneers leaned forward, along with Sidian's citizens whose expressions had been carved in lines of despair.

"Enough to know a thousand hill-gods could never stand against Him." I'd broken a dozen laws, killed several soldiers, and now I was insulting their gods right to the king's face. Kendra was probably right when she accused me of being reckless.

Tension built in the room as the audience held its collective breath.

Zarek turned his head away from me. He beckoned to the herald. "Bring him to me after today's court is finished. And have him cleaned up first."

The herald's mouth puckered as if he'd bitten an unripe

mesana vine—the first visible movement on his impassive face. The guards hesitated, then pulled me away as another prisoner was dragged forward.

I twisted to look back at Zarek. His interest was already completely focused on the next case.

The use of a washroom with running water revived my energy. So did clean clothes. It was amazing how much my spirits lifted without chains weighing me down. Even better, I managed to steal a boot knife from a distracted guard and hide it under my tunic. Zarek must have gone through the rest of the morning's court with blistering speed, because it wasn't long before the guards moved me again. They had stopped shoving and punching me—uncertain about my current status—so I strolled with them into a new section of the palace, taking time to look around.

Stone carvings were prevalent. The design of the building and furniture featured jagged edges and sharp angles. Even the hall veered at random times, as if following the zigzag pattern of the Hazor emblem. It would make running a challenge. I memorized our route and watched for signs of exits.

We arrived at massive metal doors where four equally massive soldiers stood guard. Two of them held syncbeams. I was all too familiar with these focused heat weapons. I'd managed to steal one last time I was here, in order to help develop a shielding technology for our clan. We were forbidden by the Verses to use any weapons that kill from a distance, but our enemies didn't care about our Verses. Cameron's temptation to barter for weapons like these was almost forgivable. The polished black half sphere was awkward to hold and difficult to aim, but the amount of damage discharged from the angled crystals inside the sphere was brutal. The young guardians near the pass at

Cauldron Falls had learned that. Even a Restorer wouldn't last long against these weapons.

Two of the soldiers muscled the large doors open. My guards led me forward. To my right, Zarek was seated at a massive table formed from a broken slab of polished rock. He ignored our entrance, focusing on finishing a meal that was spread out before him. A seating area to my left held stark wooden chairs around a low stone bench where a few carved statues stood guard over a bowl of fruit. Woven tapestries covered the walls with images of the steep mountain peeks near Sidian. This was clearly part of the king's personal apartments but still didn't reveal any indulgences toward comfort.

A steward began clearing away the dishes on the large table where Zarek sat. Too bad. I was hungry and hoping he would decide to be hospitable while we talked. The guards escorted me straight to the table and waited.

Zarek took a swig of something from a heavy mug and handed it to another steward. He turned to look at me. "Sit down."

One of the guards pulled out a chair on the same side of the wide table as the king and steered me into it. Zarek looked at the guard and gave a staccato nod. I swiveled my head around to see what was coming next.

Both guards marched from the room, and the soldiers on watch outside pulled the heavy doors closed again. The stewards had disappeared. My muscles moved to high alert. The solitude could provide a unique opportunity.

Zarek angled his chair to face mine, leaning his left elbow on the table. "I wanted privacy for this discussion. It's a dangerous matter for conversation, even for a king."

I sat back, crossing my arms, letting one hand find the dagger hidden under my tunic.

The king studied me through narrow eyes. "I also thought you seemed more intelligent than most of the barbarians who've crossed our borders from your clans."

It took me a moment to figure out what he was talking about. The banished. Thieves, murderers, and the occasional political dissident. I could imagine the kind of impression some of them had made when they wandered into a village of Hazor.

When I didn't respond, he frowned. "Maybe I was wrong."

Stall for time to make a plan. I leaned forward, my hand palming the hilt of the dagger through the gap in the side seam of the tunic. "I'm sorry. I don't understand what you want to discuss."

That didn't help. Color rose on his skin. "Bezreth asked me to turn you over to her—to let your blood pay for disrupting her ceremony. But I wanted to talk to you first. Do you or don't you have knowledge about the One?" The banked irritation in his voice flashed with the heat of anger.

I smiled and shifted, pretending to stretch. "Oh, of course. Yes, and I was . . ."

I shot across the few paces between us, got behind him, and held the blade firmly under one ear. Major arteries. A quick death when I slit his throat. "I was sent here by the One." Vindication rushed through me. But before I could pull the blade across his neck, a fierce pain erupted inside my head. A vision flashed into my mind and froze all my muscles.

Zarek tensed. In a second he'd make a countermove and things would get messy.

I had to act now. I tightened my grip on the dagger, but like a blinding blow to the skull, the vision exploded again—a clear picture of Zarek and me talking. I shook my head and kept a tight grip on his shoulders, confused by the strong image that refused to go away.

I pressed the blade against his throat again, but my hand refused to finish the job. I groaned. "I thought I was sent to destroy you, like the hill-god shrine."

Zarek didn't breathe, didn't try to speak.

I eased the knife back. "But I think . . . I think I was sent here to talk to you." This was the opportunity to destroy the greatest threat to our clans—probably earn myself back from banishment as a hero to the People of the Verses. And now I couldn't pull the knife across his bare throat and end this. I had gone completely insane. *Holy One, let me kill him.*

Again the picture in my mind seared my brain. His answer was clear. I released my grip on Zarek and backed away without trying to hide my confusion.

Zarek sprang to his feet and glared at me. "Your One stayed your hand?"

Miserable, I nodded and backed away another step.

"Because he wants you to talk to me?"

"Yes. I think so." I pressed the heel of my hand against my temple. My head still ached from the sharpness of the vision. "It doesn't make sense."

Zarek stared at me. His knuckles rubbed the skin under his jaw absently. "All right. We'll talk. First give me the knife."

Right. I'd just tried to kill him, and he wanted me to hand over my only weapon? I took another step back. The vision stabbed me behind the eyeballs again, making me double over.

Zarek could have taken me right then, but he didn't move. He only watched me.

Straightening with effort, I walked toward him, my dagger resting across my open palm. He took it and examined it for a moment, probably figuring out which careless guard I had lifted it from.

In a blink he grabbed the front of my tunic and jabbed the point of the blade firmly under my jaw. "I could kill you ten different ways for what you just did."

I closed my eyes and listened to my heart jump to double-time.

He shoved me toward the chair and waved the dagger. "But first I think we'd better have that talk."

Collapsing into the chair, I lowered my head into my hands. The One sent me here to *talk* to Zarek? If He wanted someone who was good at conversation, why didn't He send Susan? She could have talked his ears off and enjoyed every minute.

Zarek settled across from me. "Well? Were you sent or not?"

I lifted my head and saw the intensity of Zarek's impatience. Sweat prickled my scalp. "Awesome in majesty is the One eternal," I said quietly.

The king's eyes narrowed. "Explain."

I swallowed, my mouth dry. "He . . . has always existed. He will never stop being and . . . His power is beyond all others."

"How do you know?" Zarek was toying with the dagger. If he didn't like my answer, would he decide to fling it into my heart? His ornate tunic couldn't mask the huge muscles of his upper body. He could probably impale me with one throw.

Keep your mind on the topic, Kieran. "He gave us Verses. Each clan has the Records—the truth about who He is, what He's done. The history of our people."

"I need those records," Zarek said, half to himself.

Great. I was going to be the cause of another invasion. I needed to turn the direction of this conversation. Fast. "Why do you want to know all this?"

I expected him to ignore my question, but he sat back and nodded as if he'd finally heard something intelligent. "I was there.

Morsal Plains." His face hardened, and my mind traveled again to the dagger in his hand, the guards with syncbeams outside the door, not to mention his well-equipped prison and torture rooms. "Yes, we were deceived by your tricks." His eyes flicked over me with raw hostility. "But that wasn't why we were driven back."

Now it was my turn to nod. It had been a bizarre and impossible battle.

"Electric beams flew at us from the sky. Then that she-demon rode out with the guardians and couldn't be stopped. A dozen soldiers swear they pierced her with swords and nothing worked. As I watched that battle, I decided to win the One to our side. Hazor is the strongest nation. We need to possess the strongest god."

Shamgar, he was getting this mixed up. I tried to find a tactful way to explain. "The One can't be possessed by a nation—"

"You mean He has no promised loyalties with your clans?" Zarek was looking even more hopeful.

"No. I mean, yes, He does. I mean"—I raked a hand through my hair, tugging it in frustration—"I mean He's not a weapon we possess. We serve Him."

Zarek grinned and his chest expanded. "We know how to serve the gods."

Holy One, why didn't You send Susan to do this? "No. The One doesn't want sacrifices like that. Remember? He told me to make it stop."

"But He sent you here. He must want an alliance with Hazor."

"I'm not sure what He wants. Just let me finish telling you the Verses. Please."

He waved a hand at me to continue.

I plowed forward. "Awesome in majesty is the One eternal.

Perfect in His might and power, the only truth and only source."

Zarek interrupted again. "That can't be right."

And so it went for the whole afternoon. I wasn't thrilled with his motives, but he was certainly hungry to learn everything I could tell him about the One. He dissected each Verse and raised questions that made my head throb.

There were several times I wished I had ignored the visions and slit his throat, but by the time I recited the promise of the Deliverer, I anticipated his eager questions and felt a kinship with him. I admitted there were things I didn't understand yet. "In our clans the songkeepers have the job of explaining the Verses and leading our worship of the One. I'm not a songkeeper."

"Yes, I can believe that," he said dryly. Then he tilted his head and studied me again. "So what exactly are you?"

Dangerous question. "I suppose you could say I'm . . . a messenger."

"Then let us hope you are a more accurate messenger than Nolan was."

I stiffened. "You won't change your mind, will you? You'll let him live?"

He lifted a clenched fist but then lowered it with effort. "You question my word?"

"No, no. I just don't understand how your law works."

That answer seemed to mollify him. "So what is the value of *your* word, messenger?"

"What?"

"I want you to stay here and explain more about the One. And help me find a way to introduce this to the people of Hazor. Is that what you were sent to do?"

I met his eyes. "Yes. I believe it is."

"So I don't need to keep you in prison? You'll give me your word to stay?"

My head spun. This was not how I had thought the afternoon would end. "Two things. First, I was banished by my people, so I have nowhere to go anyway." His eyes widened. Anticipating more questions, I lifted a hand. "I'll explain that later. Second, the One asked me to come here and teach the Verses to the people of Hazor. I've pledged Him my life. So if you'll allow it, that's what I'll do."

"And if I didn't allow it?" Zarek asked, one eyebrow arching toward his bald head.

I sat up taller. "I'd do it anyway. Until you stopped me."

The corner of his mouth twitched. "We understand each other."

⚜

And that was how I found myself given a suite of rooms near Zarek's own, along with free rein to explore the city. The next several days, he summoned me whenever he could arrange time to talk. He seemed to need very little sleep, and I was hard-pressed to keep thinking clearly when he drilled me with complex questions late into the night. At my insistence, the Sidian temple remained closed—although he ignored my suggestion of tearing it down.

"You still haven't answered my question about the children from the ceremony," I said one night, sitting across a game of Perish from him.

He moved one of the white stones forward, neatly winning the round. "They were small lives. Not worth your worry."

Heat burned my ears, and I leaned forward, my elbow scattering some of the game pieces. "Are they alive?"

He yawned. "Another game?" He began to reset the stones in the opening pattern.

I stared at his throat, and my hands clenched. Diplomacy was wretched work.

When I refused to counter his first move, he sighed. "Yes, they are still alive. Bezreth is pressuring me to use them in the hill-god rites. So far I've held her off—though I don't know why I bother."

"Send them back to their families."

"It's no wonder your people are so inferior. You don't understand the use of life as a commodity. Those children's lives will have meaning if they purchase us the power of the hill-gods." He locked his fingers behind his head and leaned back. "Take your move."

I fought back a snarl and captured one of his pieces in a particularly aggressive countermove, trying to remember that the One had a plan for all these conversations.

Zarek tired quickly of my nagging about protecting the lives of the young and helpless. On my side, I was constantly annoyed by his easy dismissal of my people as weak barbarians. Even so, we formed a very uneasy friendship. As I taught him the Verses, he grew to understand the role of Restorers for the clans, but I never revealed that I was one. For his part he explained to me the danger he would face by introducing the One to his people. The entire Hazorite way of life was based on serving the hill-gods. Bezreth held uncanny sway over the people of Sidian. Her support had kept Zarek's rule strong, and he was loath to cross her. We spent long hours strategizing ways to handle the opposition he was sure to face if he tried to bring change.

One morning a herald knocked urgently at my door. Having become used to being summoned by the king at all hours, I yanked my formal robe on over my tunic and followed him to the throne room. When I entered the room, I stepped around the bit of polished floor where I had stood in chains only days ago.

Zarek looked up from conferring with one of his soldiers and smiled. "Something has come up I'd like you to handle."

I nodded.

"My men captured someone from Braide Wood who crossed our borders. Go find out what sort of criminal they've sent our way now. Oh, and let me know what I should do about it."

I stammered some sort of agreement, but he had already turned away.

The herald led me back out of the room and down a hallway toward the prison.

"Was it a man or woman?" I asked. "When was he captured? Did he give a name? Are they sure he came from Braide Wood?" The Hazorites had a hard time distinguishing clans, so if someone from any clan wandered into Sidian, they would assume the person was from Braide Wood.

The herald shrugged. "I don't know. You'll find out soon enough."

Would Tristan have broken clan law and traveled here? I hoped not. It was bad enough that I'd been banished. He needed to stay out of trouble. And if Kendra had come looking for me, I'd kill her. She shouldn't be taking risks like that. No, it was probably some thief the Council had banished. We reached the steps down into the prison cells, and two guards fell in to escort me. Annoyance built inside me. I had been making some real progress here. I had Zarek's trust. Whoever had stumbled across the border was going to cause complications I didn't need.

Speculation prickled across my mind like an angry rash as we stopped before a cell door and the guards pulled the lever.

Chapter Twenty-One

SUSAN

"I'm so sorry. I should have known better." The cold stone walls of the cell tossed the words back at me.

"It's not your fault." Mark rubbed a hand over his jaw. "I thought we could trust them too."

He looked good with a few days of stubble on his chin. Rugged. Especially with the bruise on his cheek. He was less and less the corporate manager from my world, and more the Rendor clan's son who'd had years of guardian training before switching to a role in the Council.

As we had worked our way through the mountains, old skills had returned swiftly to him. I'd admired his ability to track Kieran and Jake as we ventured into Hazor.

Several times Mark found signs that we were heading in the right direction. Kieran appeared unconcerned about covering their trail, and for some reason that made Mark even angrier.

"Honey, he doesn't know we're following him." I tried to soothe him. "He's not doing this to taunt you." Mark didn't answer. He just picked up the pace.

We lost the trail in a rocky pass and wasted three long

days going in circles, trying to find clues about which direction Kieran and Jake had gone. I suggested approaching a
harmless-looking elderly couple we spotted in a remote cottage.
The woman fed us and chatted with us. She was happy to give
us directions to Sidian.

It turned out we wouldn't need them. While she was slicing
bread and serving us caradoc, her husband ran to alert Hazorite
soldiers stationed in a nearby village. The soldiers knew exactly
where Sidian was.

"Go directly to jail. Do not pass 'Go.' Do not collect two
hundred dollars," I muttered, pacing off our cell again.

Mark gave me a worried look. "Are you feeling all right?"

I sat on the floor close to him. "I'm scared."

He obligingly put an arm around me. "I love you." He
breathed the words against my face.

"I love you more."

"I love you more than you love mashed potatoes and gravy."

Why had he mentioned food? It had been too many hours
since the deceitful old woman's caradoc stew. "I love you more
than you love new computer programs." He grinned and gave
me a squeeze.

"Mark, how are we going to find Jake if we're stuck in here?
And why are they holding us?"

The soldiers hadn't answered any of our questions, and when
Mark objected to surrendering his sword, they hadn't wasted
breath arguing. They slugged him across the face and pried it
from his hand.

We stopped asking them questions.

But I had plenty for Mark. "How are we going to get out?
Do you think we broke some law? If they'd just let us talk to
someone and explain."

My husband had been patient with my nervous babbling, but now he pressed his shoulders against the cell wall and sighed. "Maybe it's a general Hazorite policy to arrest all strangers."

"Which means the way the Council banishes people is even crueler than they realize. They shove people across the border and leave it to Hazor to imprison them or . . . Anyway, it's wrong. Someone should do something."

"I'll be sure to discuss banishment policies with the Council next time I'm in Lyric. And I'll lodge a complaint with the Sidian tourism bureau while I'm at it."

"You don't have to be snide. I was just saying."

Mark reached for my hand and rubbed it between both of his. "Hey, we've been in worse spots than this. Remember when our van blew a gasket on the Lake Street bridge during rush hour? Or what about the time a hailstorm hit when I was reroofing the house?"

"This is supposed to cheer me up?"

He laughed. "At least we're together." We heard a sound from outside the cell, and his face sobered. He jumped to his feet, helped me up, and positioned himself in front of me. He was poised for a fight, and my muscles tensed.

The heavy door slid open with a grinding sound, revealing a familiar slouching figure.

Kieran looked at us from the hall, his surprise evident. "What in heaven's name are you doing in Hazor?" He stepped forward with two guards flanking him and gave Mark a wry grin. "I knew she was crazy, but I would have expected more sense from you."

Mark lunged forward and grabbed Kieran by the throat, jamming him against the door frame. "Where is he? What did you do with him?"

Mark's rage was so fierce, I stumbled back a step and stared at him, paralyzed. The guards rushed forward. They yanked Mark away from Kieran and held him.

I tugged at one of the soldier's arms but couldn't pry him off Mark. "Let him go." I whirled to glare at Kieran. "So it's true? You've become an enemy to the clans?" I took in the ornate formal robe and his clean-cut appearance. He looked almost civilized. I wondered whom he'd had to betray to win that kind of status here.

Kieran's eyes narrowed as he gave me a cold look. He rubbed his neck and turned back to Mark. "I asked you a question. What are you doing in Hazor?"

"Kieran, please." I stepped in front of Mark, who was still struggling against the guards. "I don't know why you're doing this. I don't care. Just tell us where he is, and we'll go."

"What?" A flash of confusion crossed Kieran's face before it became a mask once more.

"We know you took him," Mark shouted. "Where is he?" He bucked and almost broke out of the grip of the two guards, but they jerked him back.

Kieran shoved me aside and stepped closer to Mark. "You know," he said in a measured tone, "for the Council ambassador who formed a treaty with the lost clans, you have a lot to learn about negotiations."

"Don't play your games with us. You've done enough damage. Where. Is. He?" Tendons on Mark's neck stood out in bas-relief.

Real anger flared in Kieran's eyes, but after several volatile seconds, he took a step back and shrugged. "Fine. If you can't be civil, I'll talk to *her*." He still didn't look at me but tilted his head in my direction. "Bring her." One of the guards switched his grip to a chokehold on Mark while the other grabbed my arm and propelled me out of the cell.

Mark swore and ground out threats that I knew wouldn't win us Kieran's help.

I twisted to call back to him. "I'll be all right. Don't worry."

"Don't do this—" Mark's yell was cut short by a choked gasp.

I was dragged farther down the hall. The soldier hurried me around a corner and ushered me into another room, empty except for a table and a few spartan chairs. A perfect set for a *Law & Order* interrogation scene. I hoped he had plenty of questions, because I was good and ready to give him a piece of my mind.

In a few minutes Kieran and the second guard joined us there.

"Leave," Kieran said. Both soldiers left the room, and the door closed behind them.

Traitor. Any hopes I held on to about Kieran's loyalties left with the guards. He was clearly giving the orders.

Kieran sprawled into one of the chairs. "Sorry about all that. Is Markkel always that irrational?"

I had been wading through oceans of disbelief and disillusionment during our hunt for Jake, knowing that Kieran might have taken him. Now I felt a riptide of pure anger. "How would you act if your son was in danger?" I flexed my hands and took a step closer, considering picking up where Mark left off in his attempt to strangle Kieran.

Kieran must have read my face, because he pinned me with a warning glare. "Sit down."

Oh, for a sword or even a boot knife. But they'd taken our weapons, and I wasn't going to get anywhere attacking him anyway. I lowered myself onto the edge of a chair across the table from him. Whatever alliances he had made, he had the power here. An icy current of fear wound through my other emotions.

"Now, what is this about?" he asked.

Why would he taunt me about something so important? I had known him as a dangerous and complex man, but he had never been malicious. "Kieran, please. Tristan told us you brought Jake to Braide Wood."

He sprawled back in his chair and nodded. "Right. And did Tristan also mention that he told me to leave?"

"Yes, and I understand you must have been upset . . ." He snorted but didn't say anything, so I kept talking. "Look, we couldn't figure out if Jake decided to follow you, or if you"— I looked down at my hands, twisting in my lap—"made him come with you. But I don't blame you. Really. Just tell us where he is." I looked up.

Did I imagine it, or had his eyes widened in surprise? "You went to Braide Wood? You talked to Tristan?"

"Yes, I told you." Impatience made my voice rise in pitch.

"And Tristan told you I left?"

"Yes. And I can understand you were upset—"

"And Jake was gone? And all of you think . . . ?"

I was ready to scream at him for being so dull-witted. How many times did I have to go over this? "I told you. It's all right. I understand. Just tell me where he is."

Another hint of anger or something else flickered in his eyes. He leaned forward, resting his elbows on the table. "I'm impressed you could be so 'understanding.'" Hard angles on his face were as tight and stiff as his words. "Considering you think I kidnapped your son and dragged him into an enemy country.

I don't think I'd be nearly that gracious." He took a slow breath and looked almost bleak for a second. "I thought you knew me better than that."

I said nothing, unsure how to talk to him when he wasn't mocking or cynical.

He shook his head. "Susan, I'm sorry. Jake's not here."

"No. You're lying!" I jumped to my feet. Jake had to be here. We'd come so far. Before I could form more angry words, my breath caught mid-gasp. A crashing pain grabbed my chest, and black sparkles flooded my vision from all sides. My body sank. I tried to find the chair but missed it. The cold of the floor felt soothing under my face. It reminded me of my mom's hand when I had a childhood fever.

I heard Kieran open the door. "Get her husband. Hurry." Then he was kneeling beside me. "What's wrong?" His words were rough and uncertain.

I tried to tell him about the heart problems but couldn't get enough breath to talk.

There was a commotion in the doorway as a guard wrestled Mark back from lunging at Kieran. "What did you do to her?" Mark's voice was thick with fear and rage.

Kieran stood up and confronted him. "Markkel, don't waste time. I didn't touch her. If you can't stay calm, I'll lock you up again."

I squeezed my eyes shut and gasped as another fist of pain slammed into me.

They must have come to some sort of understanding, because a few seconds later Mark gathered me into his arms. "Susan, I'm here. It's all right. Keep breathing."

I loved the sound of his voice, but he could just as well have been telling me to stand on my head and whistle "Dixie."

Drawing breath was impossible, and the black sparkles were winning their invasion of my vision.

"Do you have a healer? It's her heart. The old injury." More voices, more movement . . . it all began to seem very far away.

"Too late . . ."

"Do something!" Mark sounded so upset.

I tried to pat his hand. I wanted to comfort him, but I couldn't find him. I wasn't there anymore.

Chapter Twenty-Two

KIERAN

Susan's skin turned as white as Lyric's walls while Markkel wasted precious moments blasting me with violent accusations. He finally explained she'd still been having problems with her heart. So why had they stupidly ventured into Hazor without a plan and predictably gotten themselves captured? I didn't bother to ask.

I sent one of the guards to the palace. Hazor didn't have healers like the clans did, but Zarek had a practitioner who seemed to have some skill with injuries and illnesses. I had the uneasy feeling that his craft was tied in to some sort of hill-god worship, but I didn't have time to worry about that. Susan needed help fast.

Her lips were turning blue. I pressed my hand against her neck. I couldn't feel any blood thrumming past.

"Don't touch her." Markkel wrapped his arms further around her.

And to think that when the cell door had first opened to reveal the two of them, I'd had a moment of hope that this might be the One's answer to my pleas for help. Susan would know how to teach Hazor about the One. That optimistic thought had lasted until Markkel grabbed my throat. I'd have lost the respect of the Hazorite soldiers if I had let him get away with that, so I separated them. Markkel's panic had been obvious when I ordered the guards to take Susan out, and I let him jump to every wrong conclusion he could. He deserved to worry. Of course, his animosity now was understandable.

Markkel stopped glowering and focused all his attention on his wife.

I tried again to find a hint of pulse along her neck. I focused my hearing. I could hear Markkel's heartbeat crashing through his veins, but there wasn't a hint of breath or life from Susan. "We can't wait for the practitioner," I said. "Her heart stopped. It'll be too late."

"Do something!"

Was Markkel's anguished cry directed toward me or the One? I took one of Susan's cold hands in mine and thought about the One as I had met Him in a rock-strewn canyon in the mist. "I know You're here. She needs You. Tell me what to do." I whispered the words and tried to ignore how lifeless she felt without blood pulsing under the skin of her throat and without warmth to her hand. I blocked out the waves of distrust radiating from Markkel. I shut out my own rising fear.

When I closed my eyes, I saw the holy mist again. Among the fog, three figures appeared. In the vision, Markkel sat on the floor, cradling Susan's limp body. My form knelt beside them, one hand searching for signs of life along the arteries of her neck. Then I saw Him. The Warrior I had met in the flesh. He crouched beside her with a tender smile and rested a hand against her forehead. His mouth moved, but I couldn't hear the words. Then the picture floated away.

I dared to open my eyes. A hint of color bloomed across the skin at Susan's throat and spread, tinting the pallor of her face. Warmth returned to her hand, and the glow of circulation moved up her arm. Just as I made out the steady rhythm of her heart again, she stirred.

Markkel noticed the change and gasped, gathering her closer and murmuring to her. Susan's eyes opened, and she smiled up at him.

I let go and sank back, suddenly aware that all the strength had left my bones. A tight pressure squeezed my chest and made it a struggle to breathe. I dropped my head forward and concentrated on taking deep, shuddering swallows of air. The pain eased slowly.

When I looked up, Markkel and Susan were staring at me. The mix of expressions was enough to make me want to laugh, but I didn't have the energy for that yet.

"A Restorer gift?" Susan asked, pulling herself up, still wrapped in Markkel's arms.

I nodded. I felt queasy and hoped they weren't going to start yelling at me again.

"So you're still the Restorer?"

Markkel's question startled me. "That's why I'm here. The One told me to bring the Verses to Hazor." I managed both sentences with only a few pauses to breathe.

Comprehension bloomed across Susan's face like the new color in her complexion. "Kieran, I'm so sorry. We thought . . ."

"I know what you thought."

Markkel frowned. "But what about Jake?"

I shook my head. "I brought him to Tristan. That's all I know."

Some of the anguish returned to their eyes. I staggered to my feet. I didn't want the guards to come back, find me sprawled on the floor, and think they needed to kill these two prisoners. "Are you all right now?" I asked Susan.

She took a deep breath. "Yes." She sprang up with more energy than I felt.

"Then could we please sit down and talk?" I glared at Markkel, who stood with a protective arm around Susan again. "And can I point out that it is not a good idea to attack the king's advisor if you want to get out of here alive?"

The guards returned at that moment, and I stepped out of the room to tell them everything was under control and to thank the practitioner for his time, though he was no longer needed. The soldiers gave each other uneasy glances before closing the door to resume their post. Great. They'd be spreading rumors about how I nearly killed a prisoner after only a few moments of interrogation. Oh, well. In Hazor that was a good reputation to have.

I slumped into a chair across from Markkel and Susan.

He still looked shaken. "You saved her? You can do that?"

"Sometimes the One gives me a vision and . . . things happen." It was too hard to explain.

Susan leaned forward, her eyes as bright as Jake's when he watched me use my lock scrambler. "And do you hear His voice sometimes?"

I nodded, but before we could start comparing experiences, Markkel interrupted. "You saved her. Again."

I had wondered whether he'd forgotten I'd defended her against Kahlareans after the battle with Hazor.

"I owe you." His words were strained but sincere.

About time he realized it. Of course, when he rode into battle with the lost clans he had done more than any single person to save Braide Wood, but I didn't bring that up. Better to have him in my debt.

"So where is Jake?" Susan asked. "Could he have followed you?"

"Why would he do that?"

"Tara said he admired you and trusted you. She thought he might have seen you leave and decided to go with you."

It was a kinder theory than thinking I'd kidnapped him, but it still didn't make sense. "I traveled fast. He's not an experienced tracker. And if he had been close, I would have heard him."

"You mean he might be lost somewhere in Hazor?" Susan didn't seem aware of the way she was tapping her fist against the table.

"Are you sure he wasn't still somewhere in Braide Wood?"

Markkel nodded. "Tristan and I looked everywhere."

Not good news. "All right. Don't panic. Tell me everything you've done since you came to the clans. Everywhere you've searched."

They looked at each other and communicated with one of those significant silences I've seen Tristan and Kendra exchange. Then Susan nodded and they started their story. They interrupted each other enough to make my head start aching. I was tempted to roll my eyes at some of the clumsy things they'd done, but I forced myself to listen closely. When they finished, I asked them to tell me all of it again.

Arriving in Lyric, approaching Jorgen for help, learning that Jake had been seen, asking Cameron for information, being shadowed by Council guards, sharing the new Song at the assembly, the attack by Kahlareans, the decision to get Tristan's help, the arrival in Braide Wood.

I was beginning to form some guesses. By the time they

ended their second narrative of their search for Jake, answers grew obvious to me. "You really don't see?"

They looked back at me blankly.

I didn't disguise my irritation. "Think! Who would benefit the most from having Jake?"

Susan winced. "Well, we thought you maybe . . ."

"Yeah. We've been over that. You figured I'd, what, use him as a hostage to bargain my way back into the clans?" I shook my head. "Stupid theory, and now you know it's not true. Who else?"

Markkel squeezed the bridge of his nose. "The Kahlareans?"

"That's a better guess, but I don't think so. They had opportunities before Jake and I reached Braide Wood and didn't take him. And it doesn't fit their pattern."

Susan's spine stiffened and she gasped. "Cameron."

I nodded. "He has people reporting to him in every clan. As soon as you left his office, he wouldn't only have assigned guards to watch you—he would have sent out word to watch for a strange, fair-haired youth to turn up in one of the clans. He probably guessed Jake was yours, but even if he didn't, Cameron would know he was significant to you. That would be enough for him to want him."

Susan jumped to her feet. "We've got to get back to Lyric."

Sometimes she tended to ignore obvious obstacles. Markkel reached for her hand. He looked at me and raised his eyebrows in question.

I shrugged. "I'll talk to Zarek, but I don't know if he will let you leave."

Susan sank back down, finally remembering they were prisoners.

"I was hoping you'd help me teach the people of Hazor

about the One," I said, looking at her.

She met my eyes. "I'm sorry, Kieran. For a lot of things. And I'm especially sorry I can't help. But we have to find Jake and get home." The softness left her voice. "And if you can't get us out of here, we'll find our own way."

Terrific. She'd get them both killed. And she'd ruin the fragile alliance I was building with Zarek.

I leaned forward. "Give me your word that you won't do anything. Both of you."

They exchanged another one of those significant looks.

"Susan, you don't understand how things work. At the moment we may have some options. If you do something crazy, you could ruin any hope."

A visible tremor ran through her. "I can't sit here knowing that Cameron might have Jake."

Markkel took her hand. "If Cameron thinks Jake will be useful to him, he won't hurt him."

"That's what you thought about me. You didn't believe Cameron would hurt me." There was a bitter edge to Susan's voice.

"But Jake isn't the Restorer. He wouldn't have a bad reaction to Cameron's drugs." Markkel's attempts to reassure her were making things worse.

Susan looked ready to bolt from the room and take on the soldiers bare-handed. As a child I'd seen Tara plunge through a swarm of stinging beetles to rescue Tag from a tree she'd climbed. Mothers did irrational things out of fear for their children. And Susan didn't seem to remember she no longer had Restorer gifts. The impatient, zealous gleam in her eyes guaranteed trouble.

"Enough." I pushed my chair back and stood up. "I'm willing to do what I can, but it's clear you don't trust me."

Susan looked up at me. "It's not that we don't trust you. But we can't wait while—"

"You don't have a choice." I walked to the door and hit the lever to slide it open. "Take him back to the cell."

The guard led Markkel out. He gave me a worried look but didn't resist. He understood the way things worked in this world, even if Susan didn't.

Susan started to follow, but I grabbed her arm. "Wait, I need to talk to you."

She turned uncertain eyes on me.

I wished I could reason with her, reassure her, persuade her to be patient. But it would take too long and probably wouldn't do any good. Right now I just needed to keep her out of trouble. The Hazorite prison guards weren't like Lyric guardians. They didn't wait for excuses to hurt people. "I'm having you moved to a different part of the prison."

She jerked her arm away and opened her mouth to argue.

I kept talking. "The prison warden will report to me. If you do anything—try to escape, insult a guard, anything—Markkel will be the one to suffer."

She recoiled as if I'd slapped her.

I fought the urge to apologize or explain. I could see her mind working—grasping for wild solutions, then reluctantly realizing she had no options. As anger settled in her face, I knew I was also killing my hopes for a helpful conversation with a past Restorer. She wouldn't easily forgive me for this. But maybe with luck, she'd survive and eventually get out of Hazor.

I stepped out of the room and spoke to the guards. I explained she was in protective custody of the king and was to be treated well. When they escorted her away, she scorched me with her glare, but behind her rage I saw the hurt of disillusionment.

What did she expect me to do? Maybe she'd be a little more grateful for my help and advice after she stewed for a while.

I trudged back to the palace, trying to figure out the best way to approach Zarek. When I reached my rooms, I asked a herald to request an audience with the king when he was available.

Before I opened the door to my rooms, another herald came running down the hall. "Excuse me. There is someone at the palace gate who's been asking to speak with you. He's very insistent. Should we send him away?"

Now what? I wanted peace and quiet. And lunch. I rolled my tight shoulders. "No, bring him here."

I entered my rooms, leaving the door open behind me. Drained from the events of the morning, I poured myself some water and sank into a chair. When I looked up a short time later, the herald had returned with my visitor. The mug almost dropped from my hand, and I fumbled to set it down.

What was *he* doing here?

Chapter Twenty-Three

KIERAN

"Come in," I said, working to cover my shock at the sight of the young man in the doorway.

Nolan wavered in the entry, eyes darting around the room. He looked as haggard as when I'd last seen him. And almost as terrified. I didn't blame him. If I were him, I wouldn't have wanted to set foot in Zarek's palace again either. I dismissed the herald, who hurried away. Nolan still didn't move.

I pushed myself to my feet and walked over to him, guided him a few paces forward, and closed the door. I went back to my chair, but he stayed frozen, looking everywhere but at me. "Do you want to sit down?"

His eyes came up and he shook his head.

Fine. Stand there shuffling your feet all day. "Was there some reason for this visit?" I didn't mean to sound quite so sarcastic, but it had been a rough morning.

Resentment flared on his face.

I kneaded the back of my neck. I'd had just about all the hostility and fear directed toward me that I could take for one day.

"I heard—" His voice cracked and he cleared his throat. "I

heard that you can do magic."

I rubbed a hand over my face. "What?"

"Is that what you did to my arm? And at the temple. They say you fixed a girl who was dying."

"Well, that's not exactly—"

"Can you do that?"

"Nolan, it's not me. I serve the One. The One healed that girl."

His eyes grew large. "The One that Tara and Susan told me about? The One in the Verses?"

I smiled. I'd forgotten the days he had spent in Tara's home. "Yes."

Anger flared again. "*You* serve the One?"

He had every reason for his disdain. I'd lied to him, terrorized him, hurt him. "I do now," I said quietly. "Nolan, what do you need?" I tried to put some warmth into my voice.

He looked over his shoulder at the door. Then he glared at me again. "Would you come and see my mother?" He took a deep breath and braced himself. "She's sick, and it's getting worse."

When she was trying to take his place at the trial, she had said something about her time being short. I jumped up. "Of course I'll come."

Nolan flinched but stood his ground.

Tossing aside my formal robe, I grabbed my sword. "We were friends years ago. She helped me once." I looked up from adjusting the belt and saw my attempts at genial conversation weren't helping.

His scowl made it clear he considered this the best of bad choices, and only desperation would have driven him to my door.

This day just kept getting better. "Let's go."

We followed the zigzagging halls to the building's outer gate. Some of the tightly wound tension in Nolan's shoulders eased as we stepped outside the palace walls. He moved with the darting speed typical of young messengers, and I was tempted to ask him if he were trying to leave me behind on purpose. Instead, I saved my breath and wove through crowds and into winding alleys, barely registering the activity around us. No time to gawk if I wanted to keep up. Besides, I'd explored plenty of dismal Sidian streets in prior visits. Cities were cities. All alike. A concentration of people spawned unpredictability, which in turn equaled higher danger levels. The neighborhood Nolan led me to wasn't familiar and looked especially bedraggled.

I paused to loosen the strap around my boot knife. He pulled up short outside a tiny building wedged between two taller structures. The hovel looked like an afterthought. Not much more than a roof attached over the diagonal alley created by the small gap.

He reached for the door lever but stopped to look at me. "Maybe this wasn't a good idea." His hand dropped back to his side, his face revealing his inner struggle. In his mind, he was bringing a monster from an enemy nation to see his mother. It was clear that my "magical powers" suddenly weren't enough of a trade-off.

"Did you tell her you were coming to get me?" I was careful to hide my exasperation and impatience. He was as skittish as an unbroken lehkan, and I didn't want to set him off.

He nodded but still stayed between the door and me.

"Nolan, if she wants to see me, then it's all right. If I didn't want to help, I wouldn't have come."

He gave me another uncertain look but pulled the door

lever. The door slid about halfway open and stuck. He stepped into the gap and pushed it the rest of the way with the ease of habit.

I paused to glance at the track as I stepped over the threshold. Old transtech training flared; my fingers itched to dive into a good electrical repair. But when I looked up to see Shayla, I lost interest in the broken door.

In the dim glow of the light walls, she looked so much like my memories from all those years ago that I grinned as I stepped toward her.

She smiled but didn't try to rise from her chair. Tight lines of pain compressed around her temples. Her eyes were too bright.

I took her hand and felt the heat of feverish skin. Her loose sleeve slipped back, revealing a drug patch on her arm.

"They aren't helping much anymore," she said, following my gaze. "It's Rammelite fever."

My eyes widened. "How did you manage to stand up in Zarek's court?"

Her smile was soft. "I used every chemical the practitioners would give me. It worked. For a little while." She pulled her hand away and made a small movement. "Please sit down."

I grabbed the only other chair and slid it closer to hers.

She looked over my shoulder at Nolan. "Could you please run down to Abet's? He was too busy to drop off our order today."

Nolan glowered and made a wide detour around me to come and stand by her. "I'll do it later."

She shook her head, and her eyes roamed his face with the hunger and love of someone struggling to let go. "Now," she said quietly. "It's all right."

Nolan chewed on his lower lip. Then he glared at me. "Make her better. She deserves it as much as that girl in the temple did." He stormed out without waiting for an answer.

Shayla watched him leave, then looked at me and suddenly giggled. "You look the same as you did the first time I saw you in the square all those years ago."

I laughed and let her steer the conversation to a little reminiscing. She asked about my life with the clans, my travels, and my status in Hazor at the moment. Though she kept her words playful and causal, she seemed to be studying me. Curiosity pulled my body forward. "I know why Nolan asked me to come, but why did you want to see me?"

"Still good at reading people, aren't you?" She shifted in her chair, and her face tightened in pain. She hid the grimace with another smile. "It was such an impossible coincidence seeing you in the king's court after all these years. I never expected to see you again after you went back to the clans."

Although I had made other trips into Hazor in later years, I'd never tried to find her again. She was a short, bright, but very closed season from my youth. "It's good to see you, too," I said, still not sure of her purpose.

Her laughter was light and sweet. "Oh, Kieran. You never were good at small talk, were you? All right. I wanted to see if you were the man I remembered." I must have passed her test, because she was smiling. "Fate brought you here because there is something I need to do before I go." Her smile faded, and her forehead creased as she studied my face again. "After you left Sidian seventeen years ago, I found out I was going to have a baby." She reached out one hand, and I took it in both of mine. "Nolan is your son."

Shock ran through my body, every synapse freezing in

overload. I was vaguely aware of the gentleness of her tone. No recriminations, no anger.

"I'm sorry," I stammered. "I mean, I'm sorry you were alone. I never thought . . ."

"I know." She squeezed my hand. "It's all right. He's the joy of my life. But I've been so worried about leaving him. After you spoke for him in Zarek's court, I decided to tell you." She took a slow breath. "Will you look out for him when I'm gone?"

I realized I was breathing hard. Panic and remorse danced around my brain. I hadn't even known. All this time. I couldn't be a father. I didn't know how. Another thought hit. "Have you told Nolan?"

She shook her head. "I wanted to talk to you first. If you want to walk away, he'll never have to know."

Nolan already hated me, with good reason. What would he feel when he learned the truth? Holy One of the universe, this was beyond any mess I'd ever faced before.

I was squeezing her hand too hard and let go. "I don't know what to say. Of course I'll do what I can for him. But he . . . he doesn't like me."

"I want him to know the truth before I die."

"But you don't have to die. I can heal you," I blurted, relieved at this easier solution. I took her hand again and closed my eyes. I talked quietly to the One, waiting for a vision of mist, or a warm power to surge through my hands, or a clear voice to speak into my heart. Time passed, but I didn't move. I kept remembering the Warrior who had batted my sword aside like a toy and called me to yield.

The door ground aside when Nolan returned. Head bowed, I kept mouthing words, begging the One to remove the fever. Nolan was right. Shayla deserved life as much as the little girl from the temple. As much as Susan. As much as me. I'd seen Him heal. It's what He had to do now. More time passed. But there was only the one awful word: *Yield*.

I finally opened my eyes.

Shayla had slumped lower into her chair. If anything, she looked worse. Pale, haggard, tired. Nolan knelt near her.

My eyes drank in every detail of his face. I had a son. The truth blindsided me again. I couldn't pull my gaze away. I memorized the line of his frame, the shape of his dark hair. What had he looked like when he was a baby?

He turned to glare at me.

I forced myself to meet his accusing stare. "I'm sorry. I tried." The words were so cruel and empty.

Shayla took a deep breath and met my eyes. "May I tell him?"

I nodded, helpless. "After I leave." I couldn't stay here to see his face when she told him. "Is there anything I can do for you?"

Her smile brought a faint glimmer in the fading light of her eyes. "No. It's been wonderful to see you again. I feel so much better."

Not physically, she didn't. My efforts had failed. Nolan and I got her settled on a pallet in their small back room.

I rested a hand on the boy's shoulder. "I'll tell the palace herald to let you in any time of day or night." He wouldn't look at me, but he was listening. "If you need anything . . . if she . . . just come for me. I mean that."

He shrugged out from under my hand and turned away.

What could I offer him? I hadn't given him the one thing he had asked me for.

As I made my way back to the palace, emotions jostled me

like the crowds of people in the square. If Susan weren't so angry with me, I could ask her why the One hadn't healed this time. But the thought of facing her justified fury was too much to stomach at the moment.

My solitary quarters held no appeal. Instead, I went to one of the training facilities within the palace. No one questioned me when I appropriated an empty room. I drew my sword and forced myself to focus as I went through deliberate, systematic patterns. Then I gave the intense confusion that battered my thoughts a free rein and lost myself in pure, reckless sword work. I drove myself until my muscles ached and my breath came in gasps. I beat back the shock and pain I had felt at Shayla's revelation. I lashed out against the worried thoughts that pummeled me. Sweat ran into my eyes, and I finally stopped to wipe my face.

"I was told I'd find you down here." Zarek stood just inside the threshold. He crossed his arms and watched me in amusement.

He would want my report about my visit to the prison. I still needed to figure out the best angle to use to get Markkel and Susan freed.

Before I could speak, he stepped into the room and drew his own sword. "I've been needing some exercise."

Spar with the most powerful man in Hazor? The man who could order me executed with a word? The man who had a city full of soldiers who would do it for him? Not a good plan.

I shook my head and stepped back. "I'm sure you have others to train with, more worthy of your skill."

He frowned, not impressed with my attempt at flattery. "Don't tell me the One doesn't allow you to fight. I know better." He advanced on me. "Are you ignoring a request from your king?"

I decided not to point out I'd sworn no allegiance to him as my king. Fine. I just needed to let him have his fun and be sure not to hurt him.

I raised my sword, and he attacked. At first I parried his advances and made polite, ineffectual countermoves. He wasn't content with that. I should have known he wouldn't be. He circled me, and his strikes became more aggressive, forcing me to answer in turn. I was so busy guessing the penalty for accidentally wounding the king that he slipped around my guard and slid his blade along my arm.

He stepped back and grinned, flourishing his sword. "Sorry."

Blood soaked into my tunic sleeve. Time to start paying attention.

You learn a lot about a man when you spar with him. His sword work confirmed what I'd already seen. He was straightforward but not predictable. He was strong but didn't rely on sheer power. His strokes were carefully calculated, and his strategies were creative. In short, he was a daunting opponent. I wouldn't want to face him in a true battle.

"Are kings here chosen by tournament?" I said, breathlessly trying to keep up with his flurry of moves. The royal line was carried through heredity, but after fighting him, I wouldn't have been surprised if he'd won a contest for best swordsman in Hazor.

His laughter was boyish and free of the normal weight of his role. "Not exactly." He swung again. "But I've found it doesn't hurt to have a few skills."

We continued to spar, and his stamina showed no signs of giving out. Thankfully, he finally grew bored of the bone-jarring play and disengaged with a step back and a wave of his hand.

"Thank you." He wiped down his blade, looking pleased with himself.

I nodded. He had been assessing me throughout our sparring, just as I had studied him.

He sheathed his sword and straightened suddenly. "What did you learn about the new captive from the clans?"

I turned aside to wrap a strip of cloth around my arm over the already-healed gash and knot it with my teeth. "Two people. A husband and wife wandered too far searching for a son who was lost in the mountains near Braide Wood. Nothing to worry about. You could have them escorted back to the borders."

"Anyone you knew?" he asked. "They are from your clan?"

Sweat trickled down the center of my back. I looked at him.

His face was bland. I'd once seen a mountain cat staring at a lehkan with that same expression, waiting for the best moment to attack. The predator looked completely relaxed until the hairbreadth moment when it sprang.

"They knew me," I said carefully. His soldiers would have told him Markkel's reaction on seeing me. "They assumed I'd betrayed the clans by advising you."

His eyes narrowed, and he waited for me to say more.

"I really think you should send them back home."

He paused and rested a hand on the pommel of his sword. "I see." Was that distrust or disappointment in his voice? "I'll think about your suggestion. We can talk again tomorrow. I'll send for you." Then he was gone.

I sank onto a bench at the side of the room, completely spent. That could have gone better. But it could have gone a lot worse. I raked my damp hair back from my face. Shower. Supper. Sleep. That's what I needed. With that decided, I headed back along the jagged corridors to my rooms.

I cleaned up and ate, ruthlessly shutting out every thought that tried to nag me. I didn't allow myself to think about Markkel and Susan and their hunt for Jake, or Tristan and Kendra, or Shayla. Most of all, I didn't let myself think about Nolan. Collapsing into my uncomfortably soft pallet, I replayed my sparring match with Zarek and analyzed each blow—an effective way to soothe my mind into sleep.

Sometime deep into the second watch of the night, a movement whispered in the outer room.

I lurched into wakefulness in a heartbeat and waited, unmoving. Long moments dragged by. Then I heard another sound. A footfall. I stretched my hearing and could make out the rasp of someone breathing. Someone who wasn't me. There was a soft scrape as the intruder moved something from a table in the outer room. Whoever it was had amazing patience, creeping forward in very slow increments.

I reached for my dagger and adjusted my position. The intruder stopped advancing. I kept my breathing deep and even, and eventually he continued forward, passing the threshold into the back room where I waited. There was a small glow from a light panel in the common room. Enough to silhouette the shape in the doorway.

I shifted the grip of my dagger, wondering whether to throw it or wait for a chance to fight at close quarters. If I missed now, I'd lose precious moments scrambling for my sword.

Too late. The figure threw himself across the room. The blade in his hand flickered darkly as it thrust down toward me.

Chapter Twenty-four

KIERAN

I rolled and launched into the attacker, hitting him low and knocking him to the floor. My forearm slammed down on his wrist. His knife clattered as it fell. I grabbed a fistful of his tunic in one hand and pulled him to his feet, my dagger wedged against his side as I dragged him toward the doorway. I hit the light panel and banged him into the wall while I waited for illumination to fade up.

Shamgar. I shoved him away and stepped back. It was Nolan.

As the room brightened, I could see his eyes were red and manic. He threw himself at me again, a writhing bundle of fists, flailing feet, and teeth. Didn't he realize that I had a weapon and he didn't? That I was a whole lot stronger than he was?

I struggled to fend him off without hurting him. Exasperated, I threw my dagger across the room so he wouldn't accidentally impale himself. I flung him against the wall again. "Nolan, what are you doing?"

"You were supposed to heal her." I could barely understand his strangled cries. He charged into me again, knocking me back a few steps. "You said your magic words and killed her. You killed her!"

Killed her? Shayla was dead? I froze.

He swung hard and connected with my jaw. Then he ran past me to scramble for his weapon.

I snapped out of my paralysis and blocked his attempt to stab me. Twisting the knife from his hand, I grabbed his upper arms and shook him. "Stop it!" I held him at arm's length. "Are you saying she . . . that she already . . . ?"

"She died, and it's your fault!" he screamed, wrenching free from my grip.

"No. It was the fever. I tried to help her."

He wouldn't be reasoned with. He ran toward me again, jamming his shoulder into my chest. I stumbled back. He connected with one more blow to my stomach before I caught his flailing arm and twisted it behind his back. From behind him I wrapped my other arm around him, trying to hold him still. He continued to thrash against me, so I wrenched his arm up until he screeched in pain.

The sound sickened me. I released him abruptly and stepped back. He whirled to face me again.

I lifted my hands. "Don't. I don't want to hurt you."

"Why not? You didn't mind killing her." His eyes were wild, and his chest heaved in anguish. He threw himself at me again.

This time I wrapped my arms around him and held him. "You know that's not true. Nolan, think." He battered me with his fists but couldn't get leverage to do much damage. I waited until his rage shifted into wrenching sobs. Even when I no longer had to keep him from attacking me, instinct made me hold him, wanting to shut out all the grief that was ripping him apart. "I'm sorry. I'm so sorry I couldn't save her," I said against the top of his head. My own eyes stung, and his raw pain made my stomach twist.

When his sobs subsided, I eased back and looked at him. "Did she tell you?"

His eyes met mine with renewed helpless fury. "I didn't believe her."

I let him go and sank down to sit on the edge of my pallet. "It was a surprise to me, too."

His eyes were swollen and his mouth twisted with frustration. "She made it up. She just wanted to know someone would look after me." His fists clenched as though he dared me to disagree.

"Sit down. We need to talk." When he didn't move, I rubbed my sore jaw. "Please."

His gaze shifted to the door and scanned the floor for his knife. How much more fight did he have in him? "You aren't my father." He backed up a few paces.

"It doesn't matter."

His eyes widened. "I'm glad we agree." He turned and walked toward the door.

"It's what Shayla wanted that matters." My words stopped him, his left hand on the door frame, shoulders hunched in pain. I talked faster. "She was never a liar. If she says I'm your father, I believe her. But it wouldn't matter if I didn't. I promised her I'd look out for you when she couldn't anymore."

He pivoted. The misery in his face forced me to look away. "I don't want you to." He ground out the words.

"I know."

"I can take care of myself."

"I'm sure you can. Although you aren't making a very good start. Attacking a king's advisor with a . . ." I glanced around the floor and saw the weapon he had lifted from the outer room. It was a table knife. *A table knife?* He tried to murder me in my sleep with a common table knife? This boy needed a father. I stood up.

He edged back across the threshold. If he ran now, he'd disappear into the streets of Sidian.

"All right." I tried to keep my voice gentle — not something I'd had practice with. "I know you've never had a father and you don't want one now. But please stay. For her sake. It's what she wanted." I tried another cautious step toward him.

He backed further into the outer room.

"You don't have to decide right now. Just stay here for the night. I don't want you roaming through the city." Hazor didn't honor the night in the same way the People of the Verses did. They used large light panels in the streets, so people continued with their business long after daylight faded from the sky. Even so, the city wasn't a safe place for a shattered boy to wander alone. "We can talk about what you want to do in the morning." I managed one step closer to him without him pulling back. "Please?"

His eyes were wary. "Just until tomorrow?" he asked, voice hoarse.

"For now." I nodded. "Give me your word that you'll stay until we can figure out what to do tomorrow."

Or what? I'd tie him up or beat him to force him to stay? I hoped Nolan didn't realize it, but I was completely out of options. He held all the power right now. In this wing of the palace, there weren't any guards to stop him if he ran. And I'd told the herald to give him entrance any time of day or night, so they wouldn't hold him at the main palace doors.

No matter what I had promised Shayla, I wouldn't keep

him against his will. But I would use all my skills at manipulation to keep him here. "If you want, in the morning I'll show you the right way to hold a dagger."

There was a brief flare of interest in his eyes before he gave a tired shrug. "Just tonight."

I nodded and gathered up a few things. "You can stay in here. The pallet's too soft for me anyway. I'll sleep out there."

He took a few uncertain steps into the room again.

I retrieved my dagger and the knife, then quickly scanned the room for any other potential weapons. Giving him a wide berth, I moved past him. "Get some sleep." I paused in the doorway to look back at him. "It's going to be all right." *Shamgar*, it was a sure sign that I was falling apart if I was spouting empty clichés.

He gave my comment the silence it deserved.

I retreated to the common room, pulled a pallet from the couch, threw it down in front of the main door, and collapsed.

I heard him stirring and settling down. The sounds reminded me of traveling with Jake. Same constant alertness to another's presence. Same feeling of responsibility. Same odd blend of annoyance and tenderness warring inside. And now it was my son in that other room. I had a son. The realization flooded through me again. Tristan and Kendra had been hoping for a child for years. What would they think when they found out?

Kendra would be furious with me. People of the Verses didn't treat physical intimacy like a game. Neither did I. Not really. I had been young when I met Shayla, and not sure if I believed anything the Verses had to say. Once I traveled outside the clans, the old rules didn't seem to apply. I drifted away from the understanding our people had of the bonds of marriage and commitment. Then over the years I began to drift back. I found myself avoiding entanglements at any level—even physical. Maybe something stirred my conscience. Or maybe I just gave up casual dalliances as I had given up so many other comforts. Sleeping alone in caves was safer.

I certainly never lost sleep looking back, but I was losing sleep now. Memories of my time with Shayla played out in my mind, and I let myself grieve for her in my own way. I had let her go seventeen years ago, yet she had become briefly and vividly alive to me again. I had tried to heal her, and now she was gone. The confusion over that failure shook me—kept me awake through the night wrestling with what to do next.

❦

Nolan emerged in the morning looking wary. I had already spoken to one of the palace servants and had plenty of food on the table to catch his interest before he could slip away. While he ate, I gave him the promised lesson on the correct way to use a dagger. The heavy weight of his loss never fully left him, but I was able to distract him. Maybe he even forgot to hate me for a while.

"I came up with an idea," I said when we finished breakfast. "There's someone that I think you'd like to see. And I need her advice too." I slipped my boot knife back into its sheath and headed toward the door. Nolan followed me, too listless to argue. As we walked down the hall, I barely resisted an impulse to put an arm around his shoulder.

"Where are we going?" He pulled the question out of his lethargy with effort.

"To the prison." I planned to throw myself on Susan's mercy. She wouldn't stay angry. She had a soft spot for Nolan and would be the best person to comfort him. And I really needed to ask her about why the Restorer powers hadn't worked. I was three paces farther down the hall before I realized Nolan had stopped.

I glanced back. The expression on his face made my stomach lurch.

He had gone white. All the muscles in his thin frame had knotted up. He stared at me in horror, and I realized how far I still had to go to earn his trust. He had completely misunderstood. He thought I was going to throw him into prison, let Bezreth and her hill-gods have him as Zarek had threatened. And why wouldn't he? Why wouldn't he believe I'd leave him in that miserable place? His young life as a conscripted messenger had been full of abuse and lies—including from his encounters with me.

He stood frozen now, too battered by grief and shock to have fight enough to run.

I cursed my stupidity as I hurried back to him. "No, I just wanted you to see someone. Never mind. We won't go. I wasn't thinking. I'm sorry."

I couldn't tell if my words were sinking in, but I realized in that moment I would do anything to change the paranoid, frightening place his life had become. This time I did put an arm around him and guided him back down the hall to my rooms. I kept talking, but even when I settled him on the couch, it was clear I had lost him. He sat where I told him to because he was terrified of what I'd do if he didn't obey. He seemed even more frightened than he had been when I had interrogated and broken him last season in Braide Wood. He sat very still, his eyes unfocused.

I felt physically sick at the damage I'd done, then and now.

I went back into the hall and pressed a wall-mounted sig-naler to request a messenger. Sending for Susan was a risk, but she wouldn't try to escape while I had Markkel locked up. She didn't have any reason to doubt my threats. Even though she was obsessed with getting away to find Jake, she wouldn't leave without Markkel; and she wouldn't do something crazy if she thought he would be hurt because of it. I hoped.

I still had to convince Zarek that the two captured foreign-ers were of no interest to him. Their outburst when I met with them hadn't helped them keep a low profile. Bringing her here could make things worse. I glanced back at Nolan, huddled on the edge of the couch. Linette was the one who told me not to do everything alone. To ask for help. If this made things worse, I'd have a few things to say to her.

Chapter Twenty-five

SUSAN

How could he do this? I prowled the small confines of my cell until I felt dizzy. If Kieran were a normal, caring human being, my guess would have been that he was suffering from hurt feelings, but that was impossible. He had claimed to me once that he didn't have a heart anymore. I didn't believe it then, but I was beginning to now.

All right, he might have been offended when we had accused him of kidnapping Jake. But he was blackmailing me by threatening Mark. He knew very well that Mark and I needed to find a way out of this prison, out of Sidian, and out of Hazor.

If Cameron had Jake . . .

My fears spun the combination on a steel vault deep in my soul. Cameron's impassive face as I screamed in pain. Medea's even more lethal torture as she infected my mind with her lies. Waiting for rescue that came too late. Crushing pain. Blood.

My son might be strapped to a chair in Cameron's inner office. Like the dream I'd had of Jake's terror in the cave, the images pushed adrenaline through my nerves.

If Kieran had let us be, we could have found a way to escape.

He didn't even need to help us if he was so worried about his alliance with Zarek.

I brushed a strand of hair out of my face and then sat down to unfasten my braid. I combed my fingers through it and began to braid it again, yanking each strand tightly into place.

Kieran seemed convinced that the One wanted him to bring the Verses to Hazor. My hands slowed. An amazing thought. So unexpected it rang true. Kieran's unique past and unusual . . . skills . . . had positioned him to be in the perfect place for this specific season in their people's history. What an incredible difference it would make if Hazor stopped following the hill-gods and offering their hideous sacrifices. Guilt nudged me. I should be praying for Kieran and his efforts instead of pondering how much I'd like to tear him apart piece by arrogant piece.

The memory of his face rose to mind—the bleak look, the strange play of emotions I had seen there yesterday. He'd never been easy to read. He could mask deadly intent with sneering humor and hide rare moments of nobility behind slouching nonchalance. How could I know what was real? If the vulnerability I saw yesterday was an act or evidence that Kieran had changed?

I took a deep breath and realized the persistent pain in my chest hadn't come back. No matter how furiously I paced the space in this cell, the shortness of breath that had plagued me since Cameron drugged me never returned. After I collapsed to the floor yesterday, I felt myself . . . disappearing. The world shrank away, ever smaller and darker until something called me back.

Kieran had healed me. I still couldn't take it in. When I was the Restorer, my own body had repaired quickly and I'd been able to help people recover from Rhusican poison. But I'd never physically healed someone else. I huffed in frustration. How could I stay aggravated at Kieran when he'd saved my life? Again.

Not only did I have gratitude to contend with, I also worried about him—cut off from his clan, estranged from Tristan, alone in a strange nation, and so new in his faith. He really had looked hurt when I told him we thought he had taken Jake. But he covered that vulnerability quickly with condescension—ordering us to tell him about our search so far and looking scornful when we couldn't follow his twisted train of thought. The maddening thing was he was probably right. He did understand how things worked on this world a lot better than I ever would. If he thought Cameron had taken Jake, then that's where we needed to look next.

That thought started me pacing again. Suddenly, heavy boot steps sounded in the hallway. I tensed, ready to attack whoever opened the door. Then I thought of Kieran's threats and took a deep breath. *Stay calm. Don't do anything that might get Mark hurt.* When a guard ordered me out of the cell, I didn't argue. I did plan to ask him where we were going but was distracted by the sound of an inhuman wail farther down the hall. Hairs lifted on the back of my neck. My mouth went dry, and I no longer felt like striking up a conversation.

When the guard led me down the hall, I thought Kieran had relented and was sending me back to Mark. As we emerged from the prison, I hoped he'd arranged our release. But Mark was nowhere in sight.

Led into an imposing building and down a series of diagonal corridors, I quickly lost all sense of direction. We stopped beside a door guarded by an attendant who tapped on the sculpted metal surface and thrust his head inside.

Kieran appeared in the hallway and waved away both the guard and the attendant. He grabbed my arm and pulled me a few feet away from the door. I opened my mouth to demand that he get Mark and me out of Hazor.

He spoke first. "Susan, don't start. I know you're angry. I don't have time to explain my reasons to you again."

He wasn't doing a great job winning my sympathy. I twisted my arm in his grasp and glared up into his face. Then I faltered.

He looked awful. His eyes were bloodshot, and his short hair looked as if he'd been pulling at it in frustration. The muscles around his eyes were tense with worry. "I need help."

I didn't need Restorer insights to see that. In spite of my best efforts, I softened. "I know I'm going to regret this, but go ahead and tell me. What happened?"

He didn't give me the expected wry grin. He also didn't seem to remember he was gripping my arm. "I found out I have a son. Nolan. He's mine." He ignored my gasp and plowed on. "I never knew about him. I mean, I didn't know he was my son. And his mother died last night. I tried to heal her and couldn't. He blames me. I need to ask you about that. But first I want you to talk to him. Would you? He . . . he's so afraid." Kieran's voice trailed off, anguish in his face.

I shook my head, trying to take this all in. Rarely had I heard that many sentences in a row from this man. Certainly none that sounded so raw with pain.

He frowned. "She asked me to look after him."

So he was feeling trapped by those human entanglements he made it a point to avoid? I bristled. "And you don't want to?"

"Of course I will." He sounded appalled that I'd even question it. "But he hates me. And right now he's scared. I don't know what to do."

I would have placed bets on never hearing those words from him.

It took me a moment to sort out this information. Once,

in Jorgen's rooms in Lyric, I had seen Kieran unconscious from a clay-field fever. The hard planes of his face softened in sleep, and dark bangs fell against his flushed skin. He had reminded me of Nolan. Now that I knew the truth, I could see even more resemblance.

I had also watched Kieran question Nolan, backhand him, and drag him away. I groaned. "The poor boy. Where is he?"

"In there." Kieran pushed me toward the door.

I stopped. "You're coming too."

"Maybe it would be better if you talked to him alone," he said, misery written across his face.

I shook my head. "Kieran, you gave me lessons in sword fighting and battle strategies. This is my turf. I've been a parent for eighteen years. If you want my help, don't argue. You're coming with me. And pay attention."

No snide comment followed, though he trailed after me.

I gave him a worried look. He really was a wreck.

As soon as I saw Nolan, I forgot about Kieran's problems. The boy looked like he'd been trampled by the whole Hazorite cavalry. Yet his face came to life when he saw me.

I ran to hug him. "It's so good to see you. I've worried about what happened to you." I smoothed the dark hair back from his face.

His eyes were black pools of pain.

Tears welled up in my own. "I'm so sorry about your mother."

His jaw tightened and he nodded once.

I hugged him again and felt some of the stiffness ease from his spine. "Will you tell me about her? She must have been a wonderful woman."

His few hesitant words led to longer sentences. As I listened and nodded, his sentences stretched into stories, telling me about the person she had been. Some of the shock eased from the tense lines of his face as he talked.

Kieran stood near the door, stiff and grim.

I made a small gesture to urge him closer. I'd seen him rush into hand-to-hand combat with a Kahlarean assassin with more enthusiasm, but he slowly eased himself near.

When he settled onto the floor by us, Nolan barely gave him a glance. "And she found the funny side to everything," Nolan was saying. A wistful smile flitted across his face.

Kieran nodded and spoke up. "She hid me in the pallet shop behind her family's house once. . . ."

Nolan darted a look in his direction.

Kieran squeezed the bridge of his nose. "After the soldiers gave up searching the neighborhood, she came to find me. I was covered with white caradoc wool. She laughed so hard she crashed into a shelf loaded with more stuffing. Head-to-toe fluff, both of us."

Nolan studied him, uncertain.

Kieran seemed not to notice, lost in thought. "And she was incredibly brave," he continued, looking at me. "She stood up in front of the king and offered her own life to free Nolan." The admiration is his voice was genuine. Nolan sat up taller in response.

"What happened then?" I asked Nolan, reaching for his hand. I didn't know the whole story, but it wasn't simple curiosity that made me ask. He needed to process the things that had been happening to him.

Remembered terror played across his face. "Zarek said he'd kill us both."

I gasped, not bothering to hide my shock at the cruelty of this insane culture. "What did you do?"

Nolan shifted. His eyes darted toward Kieran and away again. "*He* told the king that it was his fault, and Zarek let us go." Before I could comment, Nolan went on. "But then I asked him to heal her, and he didn't." Resentment and distrust edged his voice.

"I'm so sorry," I said.

Nolan lifted his head to answer me, but I wasn't talking to him.

I put a hand on Kieran's shoulder and continued. "I know you cared about her. It must have torn you apart when she wasn't healed." Out of the corner of my eye, I saw Nolan's jaw gape.

Kieran met my eyes with his own confusion and resentment, his face suddenly very much like his son's. "Why didn't the One answer? I waited. I talked to Him. Nothing worked." He was no longer thinking about his goal to ease Nolan's hatred and fear, but his own genuine pain was exactly what Nolan needed to see.

"Did you ask Him?"

One shoulder lifted and dropped. "All He said was, 'Yield.'"

"Surrender," I said.

"What?"

"It's what He told me. After Cameron tortured me and I found out Mark wasn't who I thought, I wanted answers from Him. I wanted Him to explain what it meant to be a Restorer and what His plans were." My face warmed at the memory of the One drawing so tangibly close to me. "He wouldn't explain it all to me. He just asked me to surrender . . . to let Him take care of me." I was aware of Nolan listening intently.

I leaned forward, my hand still on Kieran's shoulder. "I know it's not easy. I want Him to explain every detail, and sometimes all He shows me is the next step to take. But I do know that He loves you, and the things He's asked you to do are because of that love."

To my surprise Kieran nodded. "I met Him. One evening traveling here. I know I can trust Him. I just wish I could understand Him better."

I stared at him. That was a story I definitely wanted to hear.

He held up a hand. "I know I'm supposed to bring the Verses to Hazor. I've been trying to do that." He looked down. "But I don't know why He didn't heal Shayla, and I don't know how to help you find Jake."

"He'll show us what we need to know. Our job is to follow." I tried to believe the words as I said them, my worry about Jake spinning again. Then I put an arm around Nolan and smiled at him. "I'm glad He's given you such a great person to look out for you. A man who has met the One and would risk his own life to defend you."

Nolan blinked at me as if that were the last way he would describe Kieran, but I hoped I had planted a seed.

Kieran looked embarrassed and pulled away.

All right. I'd done what he asked. Nolan was no longer frozen in a limbo of fear and rage. He had started voicing his grief and could even tolerate having Kieran nearby.

I straightened. "I want to see Mark."

Kieran's jaw came up, and he speared me with his eyes. "Will you give me your word not to try to escape? I'll find a way to get you both out as soon as I can. But this isn't Lyric." The rare glimpse of gentleness was completely erased. His tone was hard-edged again. "These guards would like nothing better than an excuse to kill you."

"Yes, it's been somewhat of a problem," said a voice from the doorway.

Kieran and Nolan both scrambled to their feet, but it didn't take their sudden tension to alert me that the man leaning against the doorjamb was someone important. His skin was darker than that of other Hazorites I'd seen, and he had the rare, perfect bone structure that enabled his shaved head to look handsome. The arms crossed in front of him showed the swells of defined muscles, even in his relaxed posture. His tunic was woven with silver threads, and his embroidered robe swung back, revealing a jeweled scabbard at his side. He gave me a disarming smile, but his eyes scanned me like an airport security gate. The metal detector must have beeped, because he stepped forward, frowning. "Have I seen you before?"

Kieran stepped between us. "This is one of the new captives you asked me to question. The ones who got lost." He had assumed his usual slouching stance, but a vein along his temple throbbed.

"The ones you want escorted back to their borders." The man's voice was smooth. The corner of his mouth moved as he looked at Kieran. "You can leave. Take the boy with you. I want to speak with her."

I began to appreciate the dangerous line Kieran had been walking when he turned toward me. Pure fear flashed in his eyes, and I knew it was for me—a warning I didn't need. My pulse was already bouncing to a demented rhythm.

"Susan, this is the king. Zarek of Hazor."

I stood up and nodded. My mom always said manners counted. "I'm honored to meet you," I said quietly.

The king's smile grew. Then he glanced at Kieran, as if surprised he was still there. Kieran hesitated, giving me another worried look. Short of attacking the king, he didn't have a lot of choices. He put a hand on Nolan's shoulder as they left the room, and Nolan didn't pull away.

I had a second to feel gratified that in their shared anxiety, they forgot to be awkward with each other. Then I looked back at the king.

"I interrupted an interesting discussion." His teeth gleamed.

He didn't apologize for the interruption. I'd never met a king before, but I suspected they didn't often apologize for anything. I struggled for something harmless to say. "Would you like to sit down? Can I get you something to drink?" I looked around the room, realizing I didn't know where anything was kept.

He pulled up a large chair across from the couch, amused by my attempt to play hostess. The heavy wood creaked as he sank into it. "Sit."

My pulse didn't slow as I lowered myself onto the edge of the couch.

"Kieran didn't mention your clan. But it's Braide Wood, is it not?"

"Y-yes." That much was true. They had adopted me.

"I heard what you said." He leaned back, crossing his arms again.

My mind scrambled to remember what we had been talking about. "About Kieran taking care of Nolan? His mother died of a fever. It's great that he'll have Kieran to look out for him after all he's gone through . . ." My voice trailed off. Much of what Nolan had suffered had been brought about by this man's orders.

Zarek waved one hand. "Unimportant. We'll use him in another battle or two." His eyes squinted in a brief flash of anger. "He wasn't a bad messenger before Morsal Plains. But he's scrawny, so I doubt Kieran will have to worry about him for long."

My antagonism flared at the mention of Morsal Plains, and the king's easy dismissal of Nolan's human worth.

Zarek yawned. "No, I was referring to what you said about the One. You were explaining that He doesn't reveal all His plans to those who serve Him."

I eyed him, uncertain whether his interest was sincere. "I'm sure Kieran's told you that the One has love for all His people, and that—"

"Why are you sure?"

"That the One loves you?"

"No." He shifted impatiently. "That Kieran has told me."

"Well, because . . . if he . . . that is . . ." Creases were deepening on Zarek's forehead, and I forced myself to come up with a coherent answer. "Because if the One asked Kieran to do something, he would. What better way to bring the truth of the Verses to Hazor than to share them with the king?"

"And do all servants of the One have the power to heal?"

"No. I never . . ." I swallowed, disoriented by the swerving directions of this conversation. "I don't know of anyone else."

He sighed. "He would be a good ally." His voice was colored by a tinge of regret, and he stared off into space.

"You sound like that won't be possible," I said slowly. My heartbeat had stopped pounding in my own ears, but now the fine hairs on my arms prickled.

Zarek's eyes stopped tracing thoughts in the room at large and zeroed in on me. "I've explained to Kieran that I want to bring the One to Hazor. The hill-gods demand a high price and haven't always brought us success. Of course, the commanders of my armies prefer the old ways." He shrugged. "In time I may have been able to change their thinking. But what I haven't yet told Kieran is that Bezreth, the high priestess, has spoken to my commanders."

I wished that Kieran were here. I never followed the

intricacies of political intrigue, and a power struggle within an enemy's military was not something I felt skilled at understanding. Maybe it wasn't so different from my stint in the Parent Teacher League—like the time the school library committee tried to take over the teacher's lounge—but I still felt out of my element.

"History tells us it was the One who was able to hold us back from Shamgar for many years." Zarek was looking off into space again. "I saw Him protect Braide Wood with my own eyes. Bezreth has convinced the commanders that the best course of action is to destroy the One so that we can expand into the clans."

I boggled. "You can't destroy Him."

"Her plan is logical. She's learned where He lives. In the central tower of Lyric. Our army will destroy His home. Perhaps then He'll ally Himself with Hazor. Perhaps He'll simply leave. Either way, we'll be free to move ahead with our plans."

"You can't believe that! That wasn't why the One sent Kieran to you."

The king looked at me again, his face somber. "I may be the most powerful man in Hazor, but I hold that power because I recognize dangers. Our people just lost a major battle. If I don't lead them into a victory soon, my control will slip. This is not the time for me to introduce his crazy notions, no matter how much I would like to believe them. How long have you known Kieran?"

He was doing it again—veering onto a new course and leaving me dizzy.

"Why?" I stalled.

"Will he wait until the dust settles?"

I wasn't sure what he was asking.

His fingers tapped a random riff on the arm of his chair. "I'd like to keep him around. He could explain about the One later . . . if I'm not forced to kill him. What do you think? Will he wait?"

"You mean will he cooperate with you while you send children to the hill-gods and armies against Lyric?" My own horror at the future that Zarek was describing made my voice shrill.

He grimaced. "I thought not. Such a waste." His eyes perused me slowly. He shook his head with another look of regret.

"Why are you telling me this? Aren't you afraid I'll tell Kieran or warn Lyric?" My voice trailed off. I was every bit as naïve and stupid as Kieran had accused me of being. Zarek had no intention of letting me go. And he probably planned to move against Kieran before I ever had a chance to see him again. The king assessed me as realization dawned. Mark always told me my face was easy to read.

Zarek's smile was placid. "You chose a bad time to stumble into Hazor."

"Is there ever a good time?" My tone was dry.

"I'll have the guards take you back to your husband." He leaned forward. "Kieran was worried about keeping you alive. I'm not. I'll leave that choice to you. Cause any trouble and you'll die." He sat back and opened his arm in a magnanimous gesture. "But after we take Lyric and things calm down, I'll consider letting you continue your search." It was clear he expected thanks for his generosity.

I wasn't feeling particularly grateful. "Zarek, er, King, um . . ." Apparently he wasn't as worried about protocol as the councilmembers in Lyric. He didn't bother correcting my form of address. "Why don't you talk to Kieran about what your commanders want? About Bezreth's control over them? He could help you come up with a new plan. You could avoid a war. And most of all, you could bring the One to your people."

He stood up, indifferent.

I sprang to my feet as well. "The One loves you." My voice throbbed with emotion. "He doesn't only live in the Lyric tower. That's a special place He chose to meet with the clans, but He lives everywhere. If you kill Kieran and attack Lyric, how will you ever learn to know Him? Please, you've got to—"

"I'm sure I've seen you before." He spared a thoughtful look in my direction, ignoring my pleas.

I dropped my gaze. He'd supervised the attack on Morsal Plains from far up the mountain and couldn't have seen my face. But what would he do if he realized I was the Restorer who had ridden against his armies? Maybe he'd pay more attention to my arguments if he knew. Or maybe he'd run me through on the spot. I struggled to think of the best plan.

But he had already lost interest. He strode to the door and said a few words to the guards waiting outside. Then he left without looking back.

The two guards who surged into the room and grabbed me were a far cry from the polite escort I'd received coming here. I needed to warn Kieran but couldn't think of anything to do as I was rushed back to the prison. My answers had convinced the king that Kieran was more of a liability than a tool. Despair gripped me with the same force as the guards' rough hands. We were trapped far from Jake and the portal. If Hazor attacked Lyric, the portal might be destroyed by the time we got out of this prison. And the one ally we had—and the Restorer of the clans—was about to be killed because of me.

KIERAN

I hurried down the hall with Nolan in tow. No sense trying to hover nearby with several of the king's elite guards glowering in the doorway of my apartment.

"Where are we going? Aren't you going to help her?" Nolan's voice rose over the sounds of our footsteps as we turned a corner.

"Quiet." I nudged him forward with my hand against his back.

Around another sharp angle of the hall, I found the door we needed — to the room that housed one of the king's attendants. If my past reconnaissance was accurate, it backed up against mine. I grabbed my son's shoulder. "Nolan, I'll need your help." His eyes grew round, but he nodded. I released him and told him what to do, then I walked farther down the hall and hid around the next bend.

His fist struck a firm beat against the door, covering his nervousness. Someone opened the door. "The king requests your presence in his court. A matter of urgency." Nolan slipped easily into the bored tone of a messenger. The attendant asked no questions but hurried past Nolan and down the hall.

I ran forward and glided through the door before it closed, pulling Nolan with me. It took a moment to orient myself and decide which wall was closest to where Zarek sat talking with Susan. I signaled to Nolan to stay silent, closed my eyes, and focused my hearing. At first I heard indistinct murmurs. Soon I could make out bits of their discussion—Zarek's voice was as powerful as his sword arm.

He was telling her the plans his commanders had developed. Not a good sign. He was testing the waters about something. Then he asked her about me.

Keep your mouth shut, Susan. Don't say anything.

But of course she was affronted by Zarek's plans and made it clear that I'd never go along with them. My fists clenched. I wanted to swear but had to stay quiet so I could hear the rest of it. She made an impassioned plea, which went over as well as I would have expected. Spare me from innocent idealists.

Zarek told Susan he would send her back to Markkel. He might have been lying to keep her calm. Or perhaps he really would send her back to him. It would be his idea of a generous gesture before having them both killed.

I opened my eyes and turned to Nolan, who was watching me with alarm.

"She's in trouble. So am I." I raced to the door and gave the hallway a quick scan, then glanced back over my shoulder.

Nolan stood in the center of the room, shifting his weight from side to side.

I cursed under my breath. Accustomed to working alone, I wasn't used to having to explain myself. But he didn't know what I had heard. "Zarek is sending Susan back to Markkel in the prison. He won't let them live long. We have to move fast."

Still Nolan hesitated.

A huff of impatience escaped my lungs. "I've got to help them. Are you coming?"

He bit his lip, ducked his head, and then gave a small nod.

I felt a rush of something that could have been gladness, though it was probably just adrenaline.

We raced through the halls, slowing only when we passed other people. Maintaining the façade of my role as trusted advisor would be possible only a short while, but I'd take advantage of each moment.

With a nod we strode past the guards at the main palace doors and crossed a courtyard. Tunnels led directly from the prison to the palace court, but the main entrance of the prison faced a street. When we arrived at the dark doorways, Nolan lifted a grim face to the entry.

"Wait here." I pulled out my boot knife and tucked it into my belt. "If I'm not back soon, disappear into the city." He nodded, and I clapped him on the shoulder before marching through the doors.

The prison captain didn't show surprise at seeing me.

"I need to interview the two Braide Wood prisoners again." My shoulders tightened, but I forced myself to relax and look bored.

"Yeah, they just brought her back. End of hall two," the captain said with a yawn. Even better, instead of ordering his men to grab me, he just assigned two guards as an escort.

Keep moving. Word would spread soon that my status had changed again and Zarek wanted me dead.

My first hitch came when the cell door opened. Susan was all set to blurt out everything the king had said. "Kieran, thank goodness. I have to tell you —"

"Quiet," I snapped.

"But you don't understand—"

I pulled my dagger from my belt and advanced on her. "I told you to be quiet."

She stumbled back.

One of the guards smirked and moved in closer. I waited until he reached to grab her. The pommel of my small weapon made a satisfying crunch as it hit his forehead square center. I didn't wait to watch him fall but whirled toward the second guard. Thankfully, Markkel had caught on and jumped him from behind. Two blows of my fists to the face, and the second guard was down.

I shook my stinging knuckles and stuck my head out of the cell door. "It's clear."

"What are you doing?" Susan stood frozen in shock.

I rolled my eyes. "Want to explain it to her?" I asked Markkel.

"We're getting out." He reached for her hand. "Time to go find Jake." That worked. She sprang to life and let Markkel lead her out into the hall.

We made it past several doors, although Susan jerked to a stop when a scream rang out from farther down the wing.

I shoved her forward and toward the entry. "No. We can't help them all."

At the main doors I gave a curt nod to the prison captain. "The king wants to see these two."

He frowned. "Hold on. Where are the guards?"

"Some problem in another cell," I shrugged. We kept moving and reached the street, although I could hear the captain call for someone as we hurried out.

Nolan's face lit with relief when we emerged. "This way." He took off at a run, darting down a narrow alley. We all struggled to keep his lithe body in view.

When we were a safe distance from the prison, I caught up to him and pulled him to a stop. "Best way to the city gate?" Nolan knew the maze of angular streets better than I did.

He leaned forward to rest his hands on his thighs, breathing hard. "Too many guards."

"Don't argue. We need to get out of the city now."

He frowned at my abrupt orders but headed out in a new direction. When we got close enough to see the gates, I realized our chance to bluff our way out had passed. Soldiers jogged toward the entry from several directions. New orders were being issued. It was clear they had moved to high alert. We pulled back. Nolan gave me a "told you so" smirk.

"All right. Change of plans. Get us to the far side. And we'll need to pick up some rope along the way."

"Kieran, I need to tell you what Zarek's planning," Susan said.

"I heard."

She blinked. "Oh. Well, why don't we try talking to Zarek again? He really seems open to truth. Maybe if you talked to him again you could convince him to stand up to his commanders."

I let out a low snarl that made Susan and Nolan both startle. Markkel gave me a sympathetic grin. "Nolan," he said, "would you please lead us out?" He put an arm around Susan. "We can't fix everything. Kieran's right. We need to get out of Sidian now."

"Remind me never to plan an escape by committee," I muttered, as Nolan scurried back up the street we had just come down. I waved Markkel and Susan ahead and took up the rear, glancing back for any sign of pursuit.

Nolan managed to find us some rope on one of his detours along the way, along with a canteen of water and a pack of quickly procured supplies. We arrived at a deserted street along the Sidian wall in good time. This dirty, neglected neighborhood was far from any city entrance and was the last place Zarek's soldiers would search for us since there were no doors in this wall.

I didn't need a door. Several days ago, roaming the city and indulging my habit of cataloging exits, I had found this forgotten niche of Sidian and noted a perfect place to snag an abutment. The brickwork was uneven enough for me to scale unaided, but my companions needed extra help, so I grabbed the rope from Nolan.

A knotted loop, a quick toss, and a sharp tug secured the cord. Markkel and Susan started climbing. Heading down the outer side, there would be easy hand and foot holds in the jagged protrusions in the wall. When the two of them reached the top, I turned to help Nolan start the climb, but he stepped back, uncertainty in his nervous movements.

"Sidian won't be safe for you anymore." I tested the rope with a tug.

He narrowed his eyes and watched me.

All right, so he didn't feel particularly safe with me, either. His thin shoulders rose and fell. With a burst of clarity, I knew that I wanted him to come with me. And it wasn't only because of an obligation to protect him.

"I can hide. I have friends here." His voice was low. He fidgeted but didn't back away.

"Nolan, I know you aren't sure if you can trust me." I edged a step closer to him, sliding my dagger from my belt. His eyes caught the movement, and I grabbed his arm before he could run. I held the weapon out to him, hilt first. "If you really believe I made Shayla die, then kill me now. Otherwise we need to get out of here."

His hand closed around the grip.

I was gratified to see he remembered the right way to hold it. I'm not sure what he would have done, but Susan called to him from the top of the wall.

"Hurry!" She waved and disappeared from sight as she began the climb down.

Nolan gave me a searching look, then tucked my dagger into his own belt and walked past me to grab the rope. I indulged a paternal grin of admiration. He was keeping all his options open for the moment.

Because so many guards were focusing on Sidian's main gates, we managed to climb the wall along this decrepit corner of the city without being seen. Creeping down the outside was possible because of all the architectural embellishments jutting out at odd angles. Still, it wasn't an easy climb, and we were all scraped and winded by the time we reached the ground.

We ran hard across the open hills, heading roughly in the direction of Corros Hills. We had a few bad moments when a lehkan cavalry troop rode out, circling the city. We were far enough away to take cover in an outcropping of rocks. Good thing. There were few places to hide any closer to the city. As soon as they passed, we ran again.

The farther we ran from the city, the more pressure lifted from my lungs. It was as if the hill-god spirits covered the whole town like water-soaked blankets. Even my mind had been subtly weighted with a layer of darkness, making it hard to hear the voice of the One.

Thank You for getting us out of there. Show us what to do next.

Give me courage to protect Your house.

In spite of all the abuse he'd suffered in recent days, Nolan settled into an easy lope and had no trouble keeping up. His years of training as a messenger had given him speed and stamina, even though he looked frail. The healing I'd been able to give him in the prison had cleared away the physical signs of torture, but his eyes were still shadowed, and he was far too thin.

Markkel kept asking Susan if she was all right, but her heart seemed to be completely healed. She still wasn't very fast. When it was clear she couldn't run much longer, we stopped to rest. She took a long drink from the canteen and passed it to Nolan.

"I thought Braide Wood was over those mountains." Markkel waved his arm past the imposing fortress of Sidian.

"We're heading to Corros Hills," I said.

Nolan choked on his swallow of water. "Are you crazy? Zarek keeps his second army there!"

"Wouldn't it be smarter to go to Braide Wood and get help from Tristan and the guardians?" Markkel reached for the canteen.

I glared at the lot of them. I'd bet my last magchip that Tristan never had to put up with people questioning his orders. Tristan was a natural-born leader. He could do anything, from whipping a bunch of quarreling clans into a unified army to calming a nervous first-year on the eve of battle. He understood people.

How could I ask Markkel to trust my plans when he didn't trust me? How could I ask Susan to pay attention and follow orders when I knew she wouldn't? And Nolan. How could I ask anything of Nolan? I'd never wanted or needed to explain myself to anyone before now, but somehow I had to get us all to Lyric; their arguments would only slow us down.

"We're going through Corros Hills *because* of Zarek's army.

I want to find out the number of those troops, because it will be those soldiers that he sends against Lyric. It's also the shortest way to Lyric." I grabbed the canteen back in frustration.

Surprisingly it was Susan who came to my defense. "Well, you got us out of prison and out of Sidian. Looks like we all owe you our lives. The least we can do is take your advice." She smiled and pushed herself to her feet.

My *advice*? I was giving an order, not advice. But I was grateful to her for the show of support, so I didn't bother clarifying.

Our group settled into a trudging pace, slogging through open prairie during the afternoon rain.

Markkel and Susan fell behind, but I could still make out snatches of their quiet conversation.

"Didn't you get tired of it raining every single day when you were growing up?" Susan asked him.

He laughed. "It was one of the things that scared me when I first came to your world. I was sure the plants would shrivel up and die. Day after day of no rain and burning sunlight. You can't imagine how strange it was to see the sun and the moon."

"You have to tell me how you managed and how you ended up at Ridge Valley College."

"I promise. After we find Jake and get home, we'll build a fire in the fireplace, make some popcorn, and I'll tell you the whole story."

Much of their conversation was incomprehensible, but my admiration for Markkel grew a notch. It would take strength to adapt to a completely different world. I glanced to the side. Nolan kept his eyes down, watching his footing. His hand strayed to the dagger in his belt occasionally as if he were checking to be sure it was still there.

"We'll be fine when we get to Lyric. Don't worry," I said.

He stumbled and looked over at me. "I'm not." Fear, resentment, and some other expression played across his face before he ducked his head.

I let him fall back. The next time I looked over my shoulder, Markkel was chatting with him. Nolan's face was animated as he explained something, hands tracing a story in the air. Markkel threw his head back and laughed. Nolan gave him a shy smile.

I stormed ahead faster, not understanding the sharp jealousy that slipped under my guard. Even though Markkel hadn't taught his son Jake how to use a sword, he was undoubtedly a great father. Pain twisted like a blade behind my ribs, and I ground my teeth.

Dark closed in while we were still many miles from Corros Hills. We set up a rough camp, and I took the first watch. We couldn't risk any light that would attract the attention of patrols or even caradoc herders that might be in the area. All I could do was stay alert to the noises around us in the dark. The others settled down quickly into deep breathing. I stretched my hearing to take in sounds around our perimeter but didn't notice anything alarming. After some time had passed, someone sighed and stirred. Then tentative footfalls approached until someone bumped against me.

"Sorry," Susan whispered. "I can't see."

Remarkable grasp of the obvious. She settled near me on the ground.

"Will you tell me about when you met the One?" she asked quietly.

"It's hard to explain." Then again, if there were anyone in this world who would understand, it would be her.

First I told her about the things that had happened after she left: the murdered guardians at Cauldron Falls, captivity in Lyric, Cameron's threats, my escape. She made an occasional soft sound in her throat but didn't interrupt until I told her about meeting Jake. Then she peppered me with questions. I reassured her that he had been fine. She didn't need to know I'd nearly killed him. When she was convinced I'd told her everything I could about him, she let me continue.

I took a moment to gather my thoughts, grateful for the darkness. The next part of the story was hard to put into words. A Warrior made of mist, a sword fight that seemed to go on for days, a final yielding to One I had fought all my life. It was impossible to describe it all well, but as she listened, her hand found my shoulder and rested lightly on it.

"You should get some sleep," I said when there was nothing left to tell her.

She shifted. "I tried. I'm too worried about Jake. And our other kids, too. We aren't sure how much time will have passed when we go back through the portal. We think they won't even know we've been gone, but . . . I'm worried."

"Yeah, nothing like worrying about a child to keep you awake nights," I said with a sigh.

She paused. "Kieran, he'll be all right."

"Maybe. But will I?" My attempt to laugh stuck in my throat.

"You never really told me what happened when you dragged him out to the clearing in Braide Wood. You only told me you'd scared him and set things up so he could escape. Would it help to talk about it?"

I shuddered. "No."

"Okay. But have you talked to Nolan about it? Has he had a chance to tell you how he feels?"

"He tried to stick a knife in me. Does that count?"

Her elbow hit my ribs. "I'm serious."

"He was pretty serious too."

She didn't respond.

I sighed again. "What good will it do to talk about it? It's done. I regret it. I can't change what happened."

"Did it help you to tell me about everything you've gone through in the past days?"

Consign her to the deepest clay pits of Shamgar, she's right. But I couldn't force those words from my mouth.

After a long pause she spoke again, voice gentle with understanding. "Just try to talk to him. Maybe not about what happened in Braide Wood—although I think you'll need to eventually. Keep trying. He needs his father right now."

"It's not what I'm good at."

She laughed. "That's exactly what I told the One when I found out what He wanted from me. Kieran, it doesn't come naturally to you to listen to the One, to have the ability to heal people, or to be a father and restore the spirit of one boy. But it didn't come naturally to me to confront the Council, or swing a sword, or ride into battle either." The direction of her voice changed, and I realized she was leaning back on her elbows, looking up into the empty night sky. "'And my God will meet all your needs. . . .' It's from the verses of my world. The One will supply you." She yawned.

"Get some sleep," I said. She murmured an agreement, and I listened to the scuffing sounds as she felt her way back toward the others. Markkel stirred, and she settled in by him with a murmured reassurance.

I leaned back on my elbows and looked at the unending darkness stretching in all directions.

I've pledged to protect Your house. I'll be Your Restorer. But I need Your help.

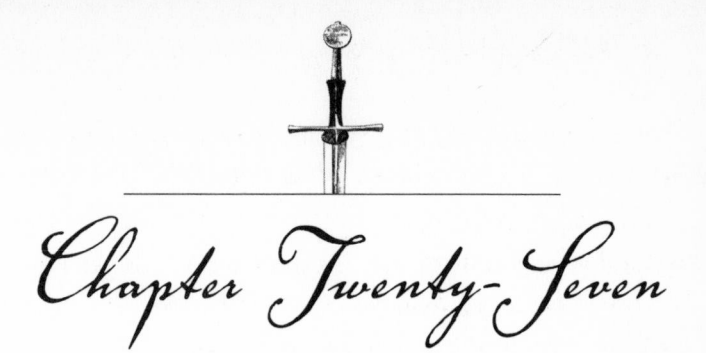

Chapter Twenty-Seven

KIERAN

Markkel took the second watch while I got some sleep. In the morning we all stumbled to our feet and continued hiking with empty stomachs. Nolan hadn't had time to grab much in our race through Sidian, and our small stash of food was depleted last night. Perhaps we'd manage to steal something when we reached Corros Hills.

Susan and Nolan lagged behind. Taking care of Nolan seemed to be the one thing that could distract her from worrying about Jake.

Markkel settled into stride alongside me. "Have you decided how you're going to get the Council's help?" he asked.

I kicked a stone and sent it skidding along the flat earth of the plateau we were crossing.

When I didn't answer, he kept talking. "You know, if you had just told them right away that you were the Restorer—"

My warning glare cut him off. "*If* we aren't grabbed by the soldiers from Sidian that will be tracking us, and *if* we reach Lyric before Zarek's armies, I'll worry about it then." My feet moved faster.

Markkel kept pace easily. "Susan told me that Nolan is your son."

Of course she did. Now what? Was he about to subject me to his own parenting advice? I hunched my shoulders and tugged my tunic collar up.

Markkel glanced back over his shoulder. "He looks a lot like you. He's a fine young man."

I slowed my steps and stared at Markkel. He was totally sincere. I glanced back at Nolan. I didn't see the resemblance, but another of those strange twinges of parental pride moved through me.

"By the way," Markkel added, "thank you for taking care of Jake when you found him. Getting him safely to Braide Wood was a great plan."

"It's all I could think of at the time. If I had known Cameron would find out about him, I would have warned Tristan."

"That was our fault. You couldn't have known." We trudged several more paces, Markkel silent, seeming lost in thought. "Cameron wouldn't dare hurt him, would he?"

I could be more honest with Markkel than with Susan, but I still thought it kinder to lie. "Probably not. He'd just question him and hold him somewhere."

"But Jake doesn't know anything useful to Cameron. . . ."

"Except that I'm the Restorer and that there is a portal to your world somewhere outside Lyric."

"So what would Cameron do with that information? He arranged your banishment. Will he want to let anyone know who you are?"

"That's what I'm trying to figure out." It had been quite a while since Tristan and I sat around his table planning battles. Markkel and I were far from friends, but I enjoyed talking strategy with him. He understood the politics of Lyric, having been on the Council himself. "You were in Lyric before the battle at Morsal Plains."

He nodded.

"How did the Council Guard handle the banishment of all the Rhusicans?"

"They moved fast." He sidestepped a cluster of rocks. "The guards went to any clan where Rhusicans had been allowed and escorted them to the border. Why?"

"Cameron was way too sure of himself when I saw him. It didn't seem right at the time." I hadn't tried to analyze it, since I was a little preoccupied with his threats and my own banishment.

"You're right. And he backed down so quickly when the Rhusicans were thrown out. That's not like him either. Do you think he's still in touch with them?"

"It wouldn't surprise me. From things Zarek told me, I know Cameron was in secret negotiations with Hazor."

"Yoo-hoo," Susan called from behind us. "Are we planning a break anytime soon?"

Markkel abandoned his interest in our discussion and walked back toward where Susan and Nolan had dropped to rest on a few boulders.

Nolan rummaged in his pack and pulled out something to show Susan. It looked like an old rag, but her eyes brightened with tears.

"What's that?" I asked as I drew closer.

Nolan pulled his hand back, but Susan stopped him with a light touch to his arm. "It's a weaving his mother made," she said.

I leaned over to look at it.

Nolan glared at me and stuffed the cloth into his bag.

He must have stopped at his home on one of his detours as we darted through the city. Crouching down beside the boulder, I looked up at him. "I'm glad you were able to bring something of hers."

Nolan turned away, but Susan gave me an encouraging nod.

After our rest I pulled Nolan aside. "Do you know the way to Lyric from here?"

He hunched his shoulders. "No. I've always been a messenger in Sidian. Never been this far before." A shadow crossed his face.

Was he remembering my interrogation of him?

"Nolan, which part of Hazor are you from? Come on. This is an easy one. Where were you born?"

He looked away and named a small village far from Sidian.

"Don't lie to me again."

I could hear again the sharp crack as I backhanded him across the face.

I shook myself out of the memory and called Markkel over. "Do you know how to get to Lyric from here?"

He looked offended. "Of course not. No one crosses the borders except . . ."

"Criminals. Yes, I know." I gave him some quick instructions and told him to lead the others on ahead. "I have something to take care of. I plan to catch up, but if I don't, head across Corros Fields. You'll see the Gray Hills ahead in the distance. That's when you'll know to turn. Lyric won't be far."

Markkel gave me a searching look.

"Hey, wait a minute," Susan said. "I don't think it's a good idea to split up. What's so—"

Mark put an arm around her, and she snapped her lips shut

to glare at him. He gave a small shake of his head, then turned back to me.

I untied the canteen from my belt and handed it to Markkel. "Go. I'll see you soon."

He nodded and squinted toward the hills before them. The terrain changed up ahead. Hard, level ground began to undulate in sweeping knolls. He led Susan and Nolan forward. I veered off to hike straight up one of the first hills in the chain near Corros.

Corros Hills was a Hazorite stronghold. It was also the easiest place to cross the border. The Gray Hills by Shamgar were hazardous with clay pits. The mountains between Morsal Plains and Sidian were rugged and dangerous. But it was a simple hike from Corros Fields in the clans across the border into Hazor's Corros Hills. I knew this area even better than Sidian.

I also had one particular place to visit before aiming for Lyric, and I couldn't risk bringing the others with me.

As I climbed the hill, the occasional scattered underbrush gave way to more frequent trees. Near the crest I had to weave my way through a thick ring of forest. The foliage grew so dense that I heard a few ground-crawlers slither in the detritus, even though they rarely came out of the earth during the day. Low whispers teased at the edge of my hearing. The creeping impression of evil returned, but I ignored it. My shoulders bowed under an invisible weight, but I forced my legs to keep moving.

The building at the top of this hill was exactly as I had remembered it. Not as ornate as the one in Sidian, made of wood instead of stone, but with the same carved faces on the walls. This was the shrine where the children taken from Shamgar so many years ago had all been sacrificed. People of the Verses. My cousins. Children cherished by the One.

I stomped through the entry. No one was around this early in the day, but I knew the local priestesses would be back soon. Sacrifices weren't the only way the hill-gods were served. Smells of musky perfume, sweat, and stale copper clung to the walls. Overseeing it all was the leering face of a hill-god statue. Loathing tightened in the pit of my stomach. Faintly, I thought I heard the screams of the children who had been terrorized here, and cold shaved across my skin. Bloodstains on the altar floor cried out for justice.

This was tactically a foolish thing to do. Like poking a stick into a tree trunk full of stinging beetles. But I knew. I knew in my marrow that I couldn't let this shrine stand another day.

I ran to the altar and shoved at the primary statue with my bare hands, rocking it until it toppled.

Darkness seemed to fly at me from the broken pieces. It drove me back until I stumbled on the steps and fell. Although no human sound was audible in the shrine except my ragged breathing, shrieks of protest exploded in my head. Pain built inside my skull. I drew my sword and staggered to my feet.

My muscles bunched with the effort it took to merely stand, and sweat broke out on my face. "He does not forget us in the night when scavengers howl." I grated out the words from a Song I'd learned in childhood. "His arms hold us up, and we are not alone."

The gibbering shrieks retreated from my head. The dark pressure of evil pulled back slightly, as though I were a light cube slowly burgeoning into brightness. A pure and holy rage infused me. Not thin human anger corrupted by selfishness, but the powerful, pure love of the One, and His wrath at any who hurt His children.

With a roar I ran forward again and swung my sword. I

struck every image, every decoration. Implements used in the temple worship scattered and broke. I even stabbed at the light walls until no more red glow stained the building.

Words of another old Song rang through my mind. With everything in my reach destroyed, I stopped and shouted them to the empty shrine.

> *Awesome in majesty, perfect in power,*
> *One to deliver us, He is our tower.*
> *Enemies circle us, darkness descending;*
> *He is the Morning Light, love without ending.*

I glared at the destruction around me. My arms shook from exertion. The fury slowly ebbed away, and my body sagged, barely able to stand.

We have to find a way to bring them truth. Holy One, show me how.

I realized my plea was an echo of His yearning for these people. The last line of the hymn sang through me again. Love without ending. It was still a mystery to me. I understood His power. I understood His light. But His love bewildered me. Why would He make Himself weak? Yet I couldn't close my heart to what He showed me as I stood in the rubble of the shrine. He loved the People of the Verses. He loved the people of Hazor. He planned to come to them in His love. How He would do that was beyond me.

Right now I needed to catch up to the others. We had to warn Lyric.

The menacing presence I'd felt here was gone. My lungs expanded freely. I sheathed my sword, ran from the building, and thrashed my way down the far side of the hill. I climbed the next ridge, where I could see the encampments of the Gray Hills army. In preparation for the battle of Morsal Plains, Zarek had pulled them into Corros, drawing them away from the desolation of Shamgar. He'd chosen not to call them onward toward Sidian and the attack on Braide Wood, so they waited here—close to Lyric. I counted each division of troops, dread growing as I discovered the army had nearly doubled since my last reconnaissance in this area.

I skirted the main city and was able to knock out a guard and slip into a paddock on the far edge of the encampment. I borrowed four lehkan and tied them together. It wasn't easy riding out with a group of these nervous animals, but we'd never reach Lyric in time if we continued on foot. Zarek's cavalry was probably almost to Corros by now.

I picked up Markkel, Susan, and Nolan's trail, somewhat obscured by the afternoon rain that had begun while I circled Corros. I was happy to see they had taken cover in some trees. Nolan had my dagger, but they didn't have any other weapons. At least they had the sense to hide when they heard hoofbeats approaching.

They looked bedraggled and weary when they stepped out to meet me.

Susan beamed at the sight of the lehkan. She loved the temperamental creatures. Markkel gave a resigned nod. "Good plan," he said. "Not that I ever thought I'd be glad to ride again." He had ridden in the charge of the lost clans but had never developed the kind of affinity that a guardian has for his mount.

"Can you ride?" I asked Nolan.

He shook his head. "I'm sorry."

Somewhere buried in his mix of feelings about me, I sensed his desire to win my respect. That knowledge sent a pulse of warmth through me. I slapped his back. "Don't worry. You'll learn." I helped him up and gave him some hurried instructions. I also kept his mount's reins so his lehkan trailed closely behind my own.

As soon as we were clear of the small strand of woods, I led us into a canter.

Not a moment too soon. Looking back, I saw something rippling along the upper edges of a hill. Cavalry from Sidian.

"Hang on!" I urged my lehkan to the pace of a full military charge, keeping a careful eye on Nolan. He dug his hands into the long fur along his mount's neck and hunkered down, managing to keep his seat—barely. Susan flew along behind us. Markkel took up the rear, swaying precariously, but with fierce determination on his face.

Soon we were out of the hills. Our lehkan stretched out into a wild gallop toward Corros Fields. The soldiers behind us were gaining. They were close enough now to count. Five sets of five. Fully armored. We passed the border into the clan lands and kept riding hard. I heard them break off before I glanced back to see what they were doing. When I dared to look over my shoulder, they had stopped, lined up along the Hazor border. We kept cantering, but eventually our mounts were spent, and we slowed to a walk.

"Why didn't they keep coming?" Markkel asked.

I shook my head. "Orders? They must not have Zarek's consent to cross into our lands yet."

"He'll wait until all the armies are massed together," Nolan said darkly. He knew more than any boy should about the workings of Hazor's army.

I nudged my lehkan closer and tossed him his reins. "Great riding. You're a natural."

His eyes met mine, startled. Then he managed a ghost of a smile and gave a brief nod of thanks.

We rode at as fast a gait as our exhausted lehkan could handle and saw the white wall surrounding Lyric grow larger as it turned gray in the fading light. We were approaching from the back side, but I no longer had a scrambler, so we circled the city and advanced toward the huge entry tunnel.

When Markkel saw me continue forward, he rode past and cut me off.

"You can't bring a lehkan into the city." The shock on his face was almost comical.

I had just started to believe it might be possible to get along with him, but there were times he was the epitome of a councilmember. "That's not in the Verses. It's just a tradition. I'm in a hurry. Catch up to me later."

Susan and Nolan had already dismounted.

"Keep Nolan with you, all right?" I called.

Markkel nodded and moved aside.

I nudged my heels into my lehkan and charged through the tunnel, right past the Lyric guardians. I knew exactly where I needed to go first.

Chapter Twenty-Eight

KIERAN

Shouts and general chaos followed in my wake as I rode straight into the central square of Lyric. The lehkan's hooves clattered and skidded on the stone pavement. I leapt from its back before it came to a full stop, and charged through the doorway into the building that housed the Council offices. After spending some time in the prisons of Hazor, the Council guards looked smaller than I had remembered them. I got past most of them through sheer speed and determination. No one even tried to stop me until I reached Cameron's office.

I threw a series of punches at the guard by the door before he could draw a weapon, then hauled his unconscious body into the room and dropped him on the floor. I slammed the door behind us and turned.

Cameron had heard the commotion and was on his feet behind his large desk. I pulled my sword and advanced. "Chief Councilmember Cameron of Lyric." I managed the official title with only a small sneer. "You are going to help me."

He didn't blink, although his eyes darted to the guard's body. "And what possible reason would I have to do that? You don't even exist here anymore."

I pointed my sword at his chest. "Because if you don't, when your friend Zarek razes Lyric you'll die along with everyone else."

Cameron's hand reached for something below his desk.

I vaulted across and shoved him back against the wall, bracing my sword against his throat. A small blade dropped from his hand.

"You don't want to do that," I said in a level voice.

His eyes remained cold. "No, from what I understand, it wouldn't do much good anyway." His tone was bitter and almost resigned.

"So you do have Jake."

He smiled. A ground-crawler with teeth.

I took a deep breath to keep from pressing the blade into his neck.

"I'd be happy to discuss it with you," he said, "if you want to be civil."

"No discussion. You're going to send out word now."

There was noise in the corridor outside. I dragged Cameron to his office door and shifted my sword so he could feel it pressing into his ribs while I stood behind him. "Tell the Council Guard to stand down."

He grimaced and opened the door just as three burly guards were about to rush it. "Stand down. Just a misunderstanding. He has an appointment." He slammed the door in their startled faces and turned back to me, raising his eyebrows with a "now what" look.

"Call the Council into session for tomorrow at first light. You're also going to have Jake brought here, unharmed." It bothered me that I was breathing hard. Even with my blade threatening him, Cameron wasn't sweating.

"Is that all?" His sarcasm grated on me.

"No. But that's first."

"All right." He was agreeing too quickly, but there was little time to analyze his response. I let him go and sheathed my sword. He smoothed his tunic and then crossed his arms. "It will be difficult to send word when my guard is out cold."

"So wake him up." I grabbed a mug of water from Cameron's desk and handed it to him. He walked around his desk and flung the water into the guard's face. The man moaned and opened his eyes.

"Get up," Cameron snapped in disgust. As the guard stumbled to his feet, he reached for his sword, but Cameron shook his head. He gave terse instructions, and the man left to begin the process of sending messengers to each chief councilmember. There would be just enough time before dark. Cameron also told the guard to get Jake and bring him to this office. So far, so good.

"Zarek has decided to attack?" Cameron asked.

I lounged against the edge of his desk. "I'll inform the Council of everything tomorrow. You'll find out the details then. What happened to Jameth and Tagatha?"

He gave an exaggerated sigh and walked back around his desk. I watched him warily, but he pulled his chair back into place and sat down. "We had an 'invasion' from Braide Wood. Tristan and his family set up such a clamor that the Council chose not to banish them as they should have." He smoothed back his glossy black hair with one hand. "Order has been decaying recently."

"I've noticed. I had an interesting visit to Sidian. Imagine learning that a chief councilmember has been forging illegal alliances—again."

He raised his eyebrows. "I've been protecting the clans. The rest of the councilmembers are stumbling along like a herd of caradoc, ignoring the danger. And I hardly think the associate of Kahlarean assassins should be lecturing me."

Before I could answer, the door crashed open.

Susan raced in first. "Where is Jake?" She looked ready to dive across the desk and throttle Cameron, and she didn't even have a weapon. I shook my head. No finesse at all.

Then again I really wasn't in a position to criticize. I held out an arm to stop her. "He's having Jake brought here right now."

She paused and looked at me. "Really?"

I nodded.

Markkel stepped up beside her and put an arm around her shoulders. She burrowed into him, her shoulders shaking. Nolan hovered in the doorway, looking lost.

I walked over to him and nodded at the dagger in his belt. "I'm glad you're here. Will you keep an eye on Cameron for me?" I lowered my voice. "Be careful. He's dangerous." Surprise lit his eyes, followed by eager determination. He drew the knife and marched to one side of the desk, planting himself and glaring down at Cameron. The chief councilmember rolled his eyes.

Markkel looked at me over the top of Susan's head. "What's the plan?"

"Cameron is calling an emergency session for tomorrow morning. He'll bring me in, and I'll address the Council then."

Cameron propped his elbows on the desk to lean forward, frowning. Nolan adjusted his grip on the dagger and stepped closer.

I rubbed my mouth to hide a grin. My son was taking his assignment seriously.

"I'll let you speak to the Council," Cameron said, "because I've been concerned about Hazor's growing aggression, and we need to know what you've learned. But I won't endorse your claims if you try to take over as the Restorer."

"But I will." Susan's head came up, and she speared Cameron with her eyes. "I doubt they will care much what you have to say." She looked as though she would have said more, but there was a sound at the door.

Jake sauntered in, looking totally at home. He had filled out since I'd seen him last. Apparently Cameron hadn't starved him. His face was bruised, but otherwise he didn't seem injured.

Susan ran toward him and hugged him, tears spilling out. Even given a young man's discomfort with blatant mothering, his response seemed odd. He showed no warmth. She pulled back and touched his face. "What did he do to you?"

Jake jerked away. "Mom, cut it out. I just got banged up in training yesterday."

"Did I mention he's staying at the guardians' tower? He's been training with the first-years." Cameron's smug words added to the crawling itch under my skin. Something wasn't right. But I had other things to do before dark and couldn't stay to sort it out now.

"Will you be staying at the same place?" I asked Markkel.

He nodded and then turned to join Susan in a family hug.

"I'll meet you there later," I said, although I don't think they were listening. "Nolan, stay with them, all right?" He nodded, not taking his eyes off of Cameron.

Jake eased out of his parents' arms and looked at me. "Why are you here?" No smile. Flat, cold eyes. When I hesitated, he added, "Cameron told me the truth about you."

That could account for the disdain I read in his face, but it still didn't explain his aloofness with his parents. I shrugged. It was a problem I could solve later. "Nice to see you again, too." I walked toward the door. When I glanced back, Markkel's eyes glistened as he tousled Jake's hair, and Susan beamed, oblivious to the stiffness in Jake's manner. And Cameron? Cameron leaned back in his chair and smirked.

When I reached the central worship tower, I was still worrying about why Lyric's chief councilmember was acting so confident. I stopped under one of the arches and took a moment to compare the way this building felt after having been in Hazorite shrines recently. The vast open space here felt full of a bright presence—an inviting presence. These stones weren't stained with blood. These walls never absorbed the screams of victims.

Instead, the crystal-lined walls held echoes of hundreds of years of voices raised in song. There was a group of songkeepers in the center of the tower, wrapping up a rehearsal time. I held back, not wanting to interrupt, letting their music wash over me. It stirred vivid memories of the Warrior I had met in the mountains as well as the quiet voice I had heard so often of late. When the last notes faded, the musicians rustled around packing away instruments and I saw a flash of white-gold hair.

My pulse sped up, but I hung back. I shouldn't let anyone see me until after tomorrow. But when Linette headed toward one of the arches, I slipped toward that entrance and caught her arm as she passed by.

She started, and I put a finger over my lips and pulled her aside. She called a good-bye to her friends and then turned worried eyes to me. I suddenly realized that under all my travel grime, I was wearing the tunic of a Hazorite advisor, but she didn't seem to care.

"Let me guess. Technically you aren't here?" she said, holding back a smile.

I shook my head. "Not until tomorrow. But I needed . . ." I stopped, remembering her words when I found her alone in the tower so many days ago. I glanced up to the clear windows far overhead. "I needed to be closer." Her eyes widened, but she didn't burst into a slew of questions. It was what I admired about her: inner quiet and patience.

"I'll let you be with Him, then." She turned toward the entry.

"Wait." I grabbed for her hand.

She looked back at me, confused.

I dropped her hand. *Shamgar*, I was as awkward as Jake. "I need to talk to you about something . . . after I talk to Him. Will you stay?"

"All right." We walked slowly toward the dais in the center of the empty tower. With each step I felt a growing weight — an awareness of coming closer to the One that I hungered to know. I forgot all about Linette and dropped to my knees at the railing.

I wasn't surprised to feel a mist settling on me. My senses were so attuned, I could almost feel each molecule of moisture against my skin. But even if He hadn't come in a visible way, I would have known He was there.

At first I reached out to Him with a tumble of words. "Show me how to protect Lyric. Tell me what You want me to do. Please find a way to bring the truth to Hazor. And if You could let me survive to take care of Nolan, I would be so glad. But if not, keep him safe. . . ."

Eventually my words trailed off, and I felt love tug at me. I no longer wanted to close off any part of me from His touch, His knowing, and His light. As I caught a small glimpse of His tenderness, I stopped feeling the need to beg or convince Him to help. Instead, when my words ended, I rested in a place outside of time, knowing with each breath I took that He was in control. Living or dying, I would be all right.

Visions came again. Some were fragments and puzzles—hints about the promised Deliverer that would come soon. Other pictures formed in my mind with clear direction and purpose. Slowly understanding formed. Clear direction was a gift, but as He revealed His plan, I didn't know if I had the courage to carry it out.

A wave of reassurance passed over me again. Even if I failed, everything was in His hands. The wonder of it was too much to bear, and I crumbled under the weight. Time must have passed, but I lost awareness of it.

"Kieran." A soft voice called me back. "It's getting dark." A hand touched my back.

I looked up.

Linette's eyelashes were wet with tears.

"Did you see Him too?" I asked.

She nodded. "So you've gotten to know Him a bit better since we talked last?"

"A bit."

Her smile was soft but glowing. Then she glanced up at the darkening sky beyond the windows. "I need to go."

"Wait. One thing. If I can get the Council to approve it, do you think any of the songkeepers would be willing to go to Hazor to teach the Verses to the people there?"

She bit her lip and wrinkled her forehead.

"It's not my idea," I hurried to explain.

"No, I wouldn't think it was." Her mouth curved at the edges. "And yes, if it's something the One is asking for and if the Council approves it, I'm sure there will be at least one songkeeper willing to travel to Hazor."

Then she turned and slipped out of the building on light feet, leaving me to wonder what exactly she had meant by that. I strolled outside, thoughtful, then realized it was almost night and broke into a run to Markkel's borrowed rooms.

I made it without trouble. No Kahlarean assassins burst out of an alley. No Council guards appeared to drag me off to a cell. No old friends happened by to put themselves in danger by associating with me. But when I entered Markkel's common room, I knew something had gone wrong.

Susan and Markkel were standing in the middle of the room, as if so engaged in conversation they had forgotten to sit down. Nolan was on the corner of the couch, his legs curled under him.

"Where's Jake?" I asked, scanning the room.

Susan gave me a tight smile. "He insisted on going back to stay at the guardian tower." She blinked several times and turned away. Markkel reached a hand toward her but then held back. She was so brittle that it seemed a touch would shatter her.

"We told him he could stay until tomorrow." Markkel spoke to me, but his worried eyes never left his wife. "Susan wants to be there to tell the Council she's no longer the Restorer, but we'll leave right after that."

Susan suddenly fled the room. We soon heard bowls being banged around in the kitchen. Markkel turned toward me. "Jake said . . . he said he wants to stay here."

"What?"

"Of course he can't. We have to take him back to our world. But just the fact that he said that . . ." The clattering in the kitchen had stopped, and I heard sniffling. Markkel waved a hand in my general direction. "Make yourself at home." Then he hurried to the kitchen. I heard their murmured voices and their footsteps as they went to the back room. A door shut, and I shook my head.

"They're upset," Nolan said.

"I can see why." I looked at him more closely. "Hungry?"

The worry dissolved from his face. He nodded.

"Let's see what we can find." We managed a rather odd meal scrounged from the few staples in the cubbies. Nolan relaxed enough to laugh a few times. That plus the lingering warmth of my time in the tower kindled a sense of well-being that eased my concern for Markkel and Susan and the things I'd be facing the next day.

The thought of the coming battles reminded me I still had some ground to cover tonight—not tactical, but personal. When we finished eating, Nolan and I left the food out in case Susan and Markkel wanted anything. Then we settled on the couch in the common room.

"Nolan, I'm not sure what's going to happen in the next few days. . . ."

He frowned at me. "Because Hazor is going to attack?"

"Yes, and because I'm a Restorer. 'In every time of great need, a Restorer is sent to fight for the people and help the guardians. The Restorer is empowered with gifts to defeat our enemies and turn the people's hearts back to the Verses.'" As I quoted the promise of the Restorer, the power of the words flared through me like an electric current.

He nodded solemnly. "Tara taught me that."

I smiled at him. "Good. So I thought we should talk now in case . . ." I cleared my throat. "Well . . . because it might get busy in the next few days."

"In case you die." His voice was tight.

I blew out my breath through pursed lips. "Yes."

His eyes darkened. He watched me without answering.

I got up to pace the room. I didn't know how to broach this—but Susan was right. Nolan and I needed to talk. Gathering my determination, I pulled up a chair across from Nolan's corner of the couch and sat down.

His eyes widened in alarm.

I found it easier to look at my hands and then wished I had something to do with them. I couldn't sharpen my dagger. That was still firmly tucked in Nolan's belt. I took a deep breath. "I'm sorry for hurting you." I couldn't look at him, so I hurried on. "I mean in Braide Wood. When Tristan and I questioned you. And then when I—"

He made a strangled sound and cut me off. "Yes, I know when." He sprang from the couch and ran into the kitchen.

I buried my face in my hands and listened to Nolan rummage around for a while, pour some water. Then there was a long silence. I wasn't sure what to do, so I just waited.

Eventually he came back out, but he didn't sit down. "I'm tired. Where can I sleep?" Retreat and diversion. Good tactics.

"Please sit down." I kept my voice deliberately gentle but firm.

He groaned and settled back onto the couch.

"You understand that I was just doing what I could to save Braide Wood?"

"It was war." He shrugged. "I expected Tristan to kill me as soon as I delivered Zarek's message. When he didn't, I . . ." He swallowed. "I begged Susan to kill me because I knew . . ." He pulled his knees up and wrapped his arms around them.

I mentally cursed Zarek for sending a young boy to deliver his ultimatum, and I cursed myself for using Nolan as a strategic advantage. He was right. It hadn't been anything personal. It was war. But it was personal now. "It wasn't Tristan or one of his men who . . . questioned you. It was me. And I need you to know I'm sorry."

"Stop it. I don't want to talk about it." He stared fiercely at the floor.

Maybe it was too soon. Maybe I should let this drop. I studied his bowed head. The One had showed me a path today that would certainly have a fatal outcome. I may not have another chance. I scooted my chair forward and reached a hand out to touch his shoulder.

Quick as a rizzid's strike, the blade flashed in his hand. He pressed back against the couch, holding the knife in a shaking hand. "Don't touch me."

I backed off.

The dagger gave him confidence, and he let his rage show. "You think I hate you because you beat me up?" He gave a short bark of laughter. "You don't understand, do you? I failed." The words choked him, and he fought back tears. "I knew what was going to happen, and I still broke." Shame blended with the fury in his voice.

I understood for the first time the real damage I had done to him. He could forgive that I had threatened him, beaten him, and used him as a pawn in battle. But he couldn't forgive me for seeing him broken and begging. And he couldn't forgive himself for crumbling. That would have been bad enough to endure if he had never seen me again. But here I was—a constant reminder.

My stomach felt like it was filled with cold Shamgar clay. I begged the One for wisdom. I had once healed Nolan's body. I longed to help heal his soul before I left him for battle. "How long were you in the prison in Sidian?"

He gave me a suspicious glare at the sudden change in subject. "Too long."

I nodded. *Stay with me here.* "And how many of the men that the guards dragged off to question do you think managed to keep from screaming?"

His eyebrows pulled together, and he didn't answer.

"When you were in Braide Wood, you were braver and stronger than any man has a right to be."

He wasn't buying it. The eyes looking out under his bangs still held a glower, and his hand still held my dagger pointed firmly in my direction.

I pushed my chair back in frustration and paced to the door and back. The room felt too small. "I always thought I was strong." I sank onto the couch near him.

He tensed.

"I was so confident in myself that I challenged the One Himself to come and face me." He was paying attention now. "I was angry. I'd been banished from the clans, and my closest friend even told me to leave. I told myself it didn't matter. I wouldn't let anything hurt me. But to tell you the truth, the thought of never seeing my sister again . . ." I shifted. "It was hard to ignore. Kendra and I were always close."

"Kendra?"

She had fussed over Nolan as much as Tara had, but that was before I arrived in Braide Wood. He had never made the connection. I smiled. "I just realized that she's your aunt. She's going to be . . . surprised."

Nolan looked a bit dazed.

I hurried on with my story. "I was miserable but couldn't admit it. So I demanded that the One come and have it out with me."

My son lowered the dagger a few inches and stared at me, mouth open. "Did He come?"

"Oh, yes. I learned real fast that I wasn't strong or brave. I ended up on my knees begging Him to kill me."

"Why didn't He?" Nolan was leaning forward now.

I swallowed. "He loved me. Stubborn, independent, angry as I was. He . . ." I cleared my throat. "The point is you showed more courage than I did. I'm proud to know you're my son. And I need to ask you to do one more brave thing."

He lifted wary eyes to my face. "What's that?"

I wanted to close my eyes, but I made myself look at him squarely. "Please forgive me for hurting you."

He rubbed a knuckle against an eye and turned away, a gesture that made him seem much younger than his sixteen years. I risked touching his shoulder. This time he didn't raise the knife. "All right," he whispered.

I wrapped an arm around him and rested my chin against the top of his head. "Thank you."

Chapter Twenty-Nine

KIERAN

A good night's sleep should have bolstered my determination. Instead, I woke up with dread clutching at my throat and twisting my innards. The feeling of forgiveness that had warmed me as I collapsed onto my pallet last night dissipated like wisps of a happy dream that I couldn't quite remember. The resolution and strength that had been born in my heart yesterday in the tower had dissolved as well. I sat up and rested my forehead against my knees.

Holy One, could we just skip the Council? I could face anything but them. Self-important, treacherous, power-hungry representatives of the people. Why did He involve them in His plans? Uneasy, I opened these rebellious thoughts to His gaze. My muscles tightened as I waited for rebuke or disappointment from Him. Instead, I sensed a gentle hand rest on my shoulder. He didn't speak, but I felt His compassion. He wouldn't release me from this path, but He understood my struggle. My muscles relaxed. It was enough.

Ever the practical one, Markkel had rounded up clean, non-Hazorite clothes for all of us. He and Susan would wear official

Council tunics and sit with the Rendor Council since that was his clan. Markkel had procured a rust-colored tunic for me as well, but I refused to touch it. Even with Cameron's sponsorship to get me into the session, I wasn't sanctioned by any clan and wouldn't pretend to a rank in the Council. Markkel insisted that as the new Restorer it was my right, but I wore a comfortable brown tunic with no emblem and strapped on my sword. I noticed the leather of the belt needed oiling. It had gotten stiff after a few days of hiking through rainy afternoons.

Susan made a bowl of clavo and ladled it into mugs for each of us. The scent of spices seemed sharper than usual. The curved mug fit the hollow of my palm, and I marveled at the skill of the potter who formed it.

I recognized this heightened awareness . . . noticing details of every kind. It often happened on the eve of battle. Life became precious when you knew the time might be short. Like the last flare of light that blazed in a heat trivet just before the magchip burned out. I stared at Nolan, noticing the way his head tilted as he listened intently, even while he appeared to be looking somewhere else. There were suddenly hundreds of things I wanted to learn about him.

He was pensive this morning and had eyed me warily when I first shook him awake. Once he realized I wasn't going to bring up our conversation of the night before, he relaxed and entered into a brief conversation with Susan, though she was quieter than usual today.

Markkel looked around our subdued group as we finished breakfast. "Let's talk to the One." Susan gave him a grateful nod and bowed her head. I closed my eyes and felt the power of the words as he spoke.

"Father, You are the strong tower. You stand unmoved by

those who would harm us. Thank You for bringing us this far, for keeping Jake safe, and for providing a Restorer to the people."

Then Susan piped in, her voice quiet at first but soon resonating with strength. "'And the God of all grace, who called you to his eternal glory in Christ, after you have suffered a little while, will himself restore you and make you strong, firm and steadfast.' Holy One, I thank You for that promise. Give Kieran the strength he needs, and help the Council accept him. Thank You that even when You call us to bring healing or protection or justice through some special role, it is actually You who are the Restorer. Even though the People of the Verses have suffered from the attacks of enemies, we know You will restore them. Even though there are things we don't understand . . ." Her voice broke and she took a shaky breath before continuing. "We know that You are in control."

Then she sang a short common Song. I was startled to hear Nolan join her in a sweet, clear tenor. He must have learned the Song from Tara and Kendra.

> *Lord of the Verses that teach us Your way,*
> *Guardian of seasons and Chief of each day,*
> *Looking with mercy on each need we bring,*
> *You give us strength through the Songs as we sing.*

I wanted to sing with them, but my throat constricted with emotion and I couldn't produce a sound. Markkel and Susan's prayers were like a parent's tuck-in blessing—something I hadn't experienced since I was four years old.

We sat in silence for a little while, letting the strengthening words take hold. Then I looked at Nolan. "You'll go with

Markkel and Susan today. You'll be able to wait in the Rendor outer office during the session."

He chewed on his lower lip but finally nodded. He wouldn't be allowed into the central room of the Council tower, but I wouldn't have wanted him there anyway, in case things got ugly. I gave a quick look at Markkel and Susan. They nodded. Whatever happened, they'd make sure Nolan was all right.

※

When I arrived at the Council tower, Cameron stood outside talking to a Council guard. I stretched my hearing and caught the last part of his orders. "Bring them after the session begins." The guard nodded and strode away. Cameron saw me approaching, and his eyes flicked over me with scorn. "You insist on going through with this? You could just give me the information you've gathered. I'll pass it along to them."

That actually made me laugh. "How considerate of you." Then my hand rested on my sword. I gave him a level stare. "Let's go."

He sighed and shook his head as if I were an annoying child who didn't respect protocol—which was half true. He led me into the building, through the imposing entryway, and past the guards at the inner passage. This corridor circled the outer rim of the tower with doors leading into each clan's office. The inner chamber could be entered only through one of the outer offices, and only after the Council was officially called into session. The halls were nearly deserted. Our footsteps echoed on the polished granite. Most councilmembers were already in their rooms, waiting. My chest tightened as Cameron nodded to the guard posted outside the Lyric office. The man eyed me with suspicion but slid the door aside. Cameron strode inside, and I followed, alert to any betrayal. But there was no one else in the room.

Each clan cast one vote in the Council, and the number of councilmembers was left to the discretion of the clan. Some had up to twenty other members sit in on sessions and advise their chief councilmember. Interesting that Cameron didn't make a pretense of including other representation for Lyric. Before I could comment on it, the chimes sounded — a low, doleful bell that rang out twelve times to symbolize each of the clans. When the last note faded, Cameron slid the door aside. We stepped through.

I'd been in the Council chamber once before. Today I felt a wave of vertigo when I looked down from the Lyric balcony. Men and women were settling into chairs in their segments of the room. Twelve low balconies, partitioned with wooden railings, surrounded the middle of the tower. Right now, Jorgen from Rendor was marching down a ramp toward the center. I was grateful that Jorgen was today's leader. In my mind he was one of the least objectionable councilmembers. Susan gave me an encouraging nod from the front row of the Rendor balcony.

Jorgen wasted no time. "Rendor is present and represented by Chief Councilmember Jorgen." His voice boomed through the large room. He went on to name each person in his section and affirm his sponsorship of them. Then he turned to the next clan.

Landon of Corros Fields stood and announced his members. He was a short, round man who I knew was a firm ally of Cameron. He had benefited for many years from the illicit trading that Cameron had initiated between Hazor's Corros Hills and the clan of Corros Fields.

The roll call continued around the room. I watched with interest as the two lost clans spoke, announcing their place in the Council after decades of absence. One more good thing to come out of the battle of Morsal Plains.

Cameron stood and declared himself but didn't declare official sponsorship of me. Neglecting to introduce me was a serious breach, but Jorgen ignored it, probably suspecting there would be more treacherous clay pits ahead and waiting to choose his battles. As soon as each clan's chief councilmember had spoken, Jorgen nodded to Cameron.

Cameron strolled down the ramp and took a moment to turn, looking at each balcony.

"Honored councilmembers, I called this emergency session because our clans are facing a potential threat. I have learned that Hazor has regrouped from the battle at Morsal Plains. They are planning—"

"I ask to be recognized." I directed my interruption toward Jorgen.

Cameron glared in my direction, and annoyed murmurs sounded in several balconies. I wasn't about to let Cameron take over the session and distort the truth.

"Who sponsors you?" Jorgen asked, turning his gaze to Cameron. It was clear to everyone that I was in the Lyric balcony.

Cameron waved a hand. "I brought him because he has information. However, I'm uncertain of protocol, given the fact that he does not exist."

There were gasps throughout the room, and he barely hid a smile. "I know." Concern dripped from his words. "It offends me as well to bring an exile into our holy chamber. But regrettably, he refused to give me all the information, and it is critical to the safety of our people."

Someone shouted an objection, and a raging debate started

over the audacity of bringing a banished criminal to the Council.

I rubbed my temples where a throbbing pain was rising. This could go on half the day. I glanced across the room toward the Rendor balcony. Susan was watching the proceedings with a look of exasperation. Finally, she rose to her feet.

Jorgen saw her. "The Council recognizes the Restorer, Susan of Rendor." His loud voice brought instant silence to the room. All eyes turned to Susan.

"Esteemed councilmembers," she said, "I have something to share that will help you with your current dilemma." I'd never heard her use such a winsome voice before. She smiled at them with what looked like genuine affection. The mood softened throughout the room. "The One granted me the privilege of serving the People of the Verses in a small way." Smart. She was gently reminding them of how she'd saved them from the destruction of Braide Wood. "Now my time as the Restorer has ended, and I'll be leaving the clans." Dismayed whispers fizzed around the room like static. She held up a hand. "But the One has promised that in every time of great need He will provide a Restorer. I am honored to introduce to you the new Restorer who was chosen by the One: Kieran of Braide Wood."

The room exploded. I assessed the tide of emotion swelling around the tower. My knuckles turned white as I gripped the railing in front of me.

"Do you endorse him?" Jorgen asked Cameron. The Lyric chief councilmember didn't have to reject me openly. He simply refused to answer. We had anticipated this. Susan had faced similar opposition.

I left the balcony and walked down the ramp to the center of the tower, where I asked Jorgen for his boot knife since Nolan still had mine. I rolled up the sleeve of my tunic and ran the blade deeply along the skin of my inner arm. Blood dripped to the glossy black floor. I had a sudden flash of memory from the Sidian temple in Hazor. Good thing they couldn't read minds. The Council wouldn't appreciate the mental comparison.

The skin began to tingle with the now-familiar sensation of rapid healing. Jorgen handed me a cloth. His face was grave and noncommittal, but one eye closed in an approving wink. Markkel had prepared him for this.

I wiped off the blood and held my arm up so everyone could see it. "The One has called me to be the Restorer. Will you allow me to speak?" I no longer had to force respect into my voice. My irritation for the Council had faded. Their danger was too near for me to antagonize them.

Jorgen spoke quickly. "We will hear you."

I don't know if he had the right to make that proclamation, but no one argued, so I began. "I've just arrived from Sidian and Corros. The One called me to bring the Verses to Hazor, but Zarek faces too much pressure from his commanders and the followers of the hill-gods. He has massed an army to ride against Lyric. He plans to destroy this city and tear down the central tower because he thinks the One will then no longer be able to protect the People of the Verses."

Their skepticism gave way to panic. Chief councilmembers jumped to their feet, waving their arms and shouting to be heard. Whatever they thought of me personally, they wanted any help they could get.

"How long do we have to gather the guardians?"

"How does he plan to breach the walls?"

"How big is the Corros army?"

Questions flew across the room.

Before I could continue, Cameron stepped forward. "Yes, it sounds dire," he said in a soothing voice. "Thankfully, I've seen this coming and made arrangements for the support we'll need to hold back Hazor's army." He had every eye focused on him, including mine. What was he up to now? He gestured to a Council guard, who opened the door to the Lyric outer office.

Two hooded and masked figures drifted inside.

"Kahlarea has generously offered their alliance and their considerable weapons."

Shock rippled through the tower room.

Cameron didn't look at me. "All they ask is that we turn over the new Restorer to them. After all, it's the Restorer's role to die for the People of the Verses. It's why they are sent."

So this was what he'd been working toward all along. I looked at the two assassins. Hard to tell with their faces masked, but I knew I'd seen those eyes before. The taller one gave a brief nod in my direction, and his eyes squinted. He was grinning. That fact made my stomach hurt. "No." I was glad my voice stayed calm. "If this was what the One had called me to do, I would go happily. But He has another plan."

Cameron's sneer was broad. "So the One confides in you now? A criminal? An outcast? You aren't worthy to be a Restorer."

"Of course I'm not." Cameron's words had the opposite effect than he'd intended. Gratitude welled up inside me and gave me strength. I looked up at the balconies and the faces of the Council that I'd always distrusted and despised. "None of us is worthy of His attention. But He's chosen to love us. And I believe He'll save us from Hazor. But even if He doesn't choose to spare Lyric, I'd rather die in His will than ignore the Verses and put my trust in other alliances."

"Yes!" That was Jorgen's deep shout.

"We follow the Restorer," came another voice.

"We can't betray a promised Restorer to our enemies."

Soon the entire room was clamoring.

Cameron gestured broadly and reclaimed their attention. "Since Kieran hid the fact that he was a Restorer, I made what plans I could for our people. But if you believe you can trust him" — he shrugged — "so be it."

I gave him a sharp glance. Again he was backing down too easily. Whatever his schemes were, it hardly mattered now. Nevertheless, cold fingers crawled across my skin as I looked at the two silent assassins. They never took their eyes off of me.

Cameron signaled to his men, and they led the Kahlareans back out through the Lyric office. I'd leave with a different clan when the session was over. Preferably a large contingent. With lots of swords. After the door closed, Cameron returned to the Lyric balcony and sat down, divorcing himself from the proceedings.

I hated turning my back on him, but I addressed the room as a whole. "We need to move quickly. Zarek's Gray Hills army was already in Corros, and I counted about five hundred there. He also brought some of his Sidian army to join them — maybe all of them. Send word to your guardians to come to Lyric."

"That will take too long," whined the chief councilmember from Braide Wood.

"Yes, I know." I pivoted to face him. "But it's a backup plan. We also need to send Lyric guardians out on patrol to watch the Hazor border."

All eyes turned to Cameron, since the Lyric guardians were part of his clan. He pretended to join the swell of planning with good grace. "Send orders to the head guardian at the tower," he said to one of the Council guards. The man nodded and left the room.

I looked back at the Braide Wood chief councilmember. "Will you send for Skyler and tell him to bring the equipment for the syncbeam suppression field?" He nodded and immediately signaled one of the Council apprentices to leave and send a messenger.

This was going better than I'd expected.

Suddenly, there was a disturbance at the door of the Lyric balcony. It slid open, and a flushed and agitated messenger whispered something to Cameron, arms waving.

Cameron stepped forward calmly. "I ask you to reconsider the generous offer of the Kahlareans. I've just received word that Hazor's army is approaching. Hundreds of soldiers are already crossing Corros Fields. We may get a few messengers out of Lyric before we're surrounded, but the guardians from the other clans will never arrive in time. Kieran came too late."

There was a moment of stunned silence.

"Not too late." I was able to speak quietly and still be heard. "The One showed me what He wants me to do."

Chapter Thirty

KIERAN

"The Verses forbid us from making military alliances." I lifted my chin toward the balconies. Cameron stepped forward to protest, so I continued quickly. "And it would be too late to ask for Kahlarea's help now, even if it weren't forbidden." Apparently Cameron didn't have hundreds of Kahlarean soldiers and assassins hidden in the basement of the Council offices, because he raised his hands and backed down. "But the Verses don't say it's wrong to forge a friendship with a surrounding nation."

Puzzled faces ringed the room, but they weren't shouting me down. That was promising.

"There is one thing that Hazor wants. They have come to recognize the power of the One, and they want Him. Let me offer them the One. I could even bring them one of the Records so they can hear the original Verses for themselves. We can send them songkeepers to teach their people." No one heard the last part because they'd all started yelling in protest. I stepped back and let them storm until they were out of breath.

"And this is your great plan?" Cameron's teeth were showing.

I turned away from his balcony and faced the other clans around the circle. "Not all of it."

And then I told them the rest.

The session wrapped up very quickly after that. The primary plan the One had shown me had shocked them into rare silence, followed by somber agreement. There weren't many options open to them. As I'd expected, they wouldn't agree to giving one of the Records to Hazor. But they wouldn't stand in my way for the rest of it. When Jorgen adjourned the session, the councilmembers hurried away, not meeting my eyes.

Markkel and Susan waited for me, and we walked out of the chamber and into the Rendor office together. Relieved to be past this hurdle, when I saw Nolan I hugged him without embarrassment. I can't say the same for him. He squirmed and pulled back as soon as I let go.

"The Council accepted him as the Restorer," Susan told Nolan with a soft smile. I noticed she didn't tell him the rest.

"When?" Markkel asked me.

"As soon as possible."

He didn't argue or turn away like the other councilmembers. "What can we do to help?"

"You need to take Jake and get home," I reminded him.

"If Hazor is approaching, we've missed our chance to leave the city and get to the portal." So the portal wasn't in the city. I was tempted to ask more, but this wasn't the time for it.

As we walked out into the hallway, I drew my sword, still uneasy about the assassins who had been in the building with Cameron's full approval. We made our way along the curved corridor to the main entry.

"Expecting trouble?" a gruff voice asked from the side of the arching door.

I whirled, sword ready.

Tristan laughed and stepped forward.

My mouth gaped in a moment of surprise. "What are you doing here?" Then worry washed through me. Another friend to die if Lyric fell.

Kendra stepped out from behind him and smiled. "Put your sword away so I can give you a proper hug."

I glared at them both. "You've got to get out of here right away. Hazor is attacking. Tristan, there might still be time to get her back to Braide Wood."

He shook his head. "I know about the invasion. While you were in session, I was meeting with the head guardian of Lyric. It's too late to leave. Besides, you need someone to watch your back."

"How close are they?"

"Close. What's the plan?"

I filled Tristan in and ignored Kendra's dismay. Tristan's face grew even more grim than usual, but he didn't argue. Instead, we discussed alternatives—options for whether my plan succeeded or failed. Then I noticed Nolan, hovering behind me. Susan had been trying to distract him with conversation, but the pale cast of his skin showed that he'd overheard too much.

I put an arm around him and nudged him forward toward Tristan and Kendra. "I learned something else while I was in Hazor: Nolan is my son."

Their shock was total. They looked at Susan and Markkel for confirmation. Did they think I'd make up something like that?

"I should have known." Tristan broke the awkward silence. "He was every bit as bold and stubborn as you." We laughed more than the joke deserved, but Nolan only watched me, somber.

I shifted my weight and turned back to Tristan. "Markkel and Susan need to take Jake back to their home as soon as they can. But if . . . if Nolan needs someone to care for him . . ."

Tristan interrupted and held out his sword arm to me. "He'll always have a home with us." I clasped his forearm, my throat too tight to speak. Then he released me and held his arm out to Nolan. Nolan looked at me, and I nodded. He offered his right arm.

Tristan grasped it. "I pledge you the protection of my house."

Nolan swallowed and pulled away as soon as Tristan let him go.

A messenger raced past our group, bumping Markkel in his hurry to carry news to the city. Time to move. Yet my feet didn't want to obey my orders.

Word had gone out to the other clans, and more guardians would arrive at Lyric in a few days. Skyler would soon be on his way with the suppression technology. Messengers had been sent throughout the streets. Lyric guardians raced from their tower, getting into place to set up a defense along the walls. Everything was as ready as we could make it, be it for siege or outright attack. But if my plan didn't work, the city would probably be a pile of dust by nightfall.

I rubbed the back of my neck. "It's time. I have to leave."

Tristan nodded calmly. "We'll walk across the city with you."

"No. You should meet with the other head guardians. Kendra, take Nolan to someplace safe."

My sister slugged my arm. "Stop being stupid." She fell into step, along with Markkel and Susan. No one ever listened to me. As we passed the central tower, Linette rose from a bench and joined us. She had been sitting outside, watching as people left the Council session. Perhaps she overheard the conversations of councilmembers as they left, because she asked no questions. I wondered what she thought of the plan but couldn't bring myself to ask.

We walked through the city in silence, under a sky that was as dark as early evening instead of midday. Maybe it was my imagination, but the air even felt cold.

When we reached the small hidden door on the Corros side of the city, I looked at the faces I loved. Kendra's cheeks already showed a new roundness from her pregnancy. She tried to frown fiercely at me, even while a few tears escaped her eyes.

I couldn't help but smile. It reminded me of all the worried lectures she'd given me whenever I used to leave Braide Wood.

Tristan was grave. Lines of guilt and responsibility carved his forehead. I was grateful for this chance to see him again. Neither of us said anything about the last time we had spoken. But his presence here now told me all I needed to know. And my willingness to entrust Nolan to him answered him in kind.

Linette wore her gentle smile, as if she were hearing a voice the rest of us couldn't. I marveled again at how so much strength could burn inside her lithe frame.

Markkel stood back, providing quiet support. He was a man who had once had valid reasons to distrust me but had still offered me friendship.

Susan looked at me with somber eyes. She was the only living person who fully knew the road I had been walking.

Nolan stepped forward. "Go with the One," he said softly. Then he held out my dagger, resting it on his palm. "You might need this."

"Thank you." The words could barely get past the choking

knot in my throat. I slipped the blade into my boot sheath, grateful for the excuse to avoid my friends' eyes. In my mind I heard the echo of the voice and those early words He had whispered to me so often: *You are not alone.*

He had always been beside me. And so had these friends. Friends who had nagged me, argued with me, lectured me, taken risks for me . . . forgiven me.

I didn't dare linger another moment, or I'd lose my resolve. Markkel worked the lock and slid the door open. Tristan stuck his head out and pulled back. "They're out there."

I nodded. Messengers of the One, I hoped that Zarek was true to form and riding with his troops. I treated myself to one last look at the faces of family and friends. Then I turned and stepped through the door.

In the Lyric tower the evening before, the One had shown me my path. I knew what to do next. But He hadn't shown me what the result would be. I stood still for a moment as possible outcomes played through my mind, each more dire than the last. *No.* If He called me to this road, whatever happened next was in His hands. I forced every thought but that one from my mind and walked forward.

Somehow I expected everything to look strange and different beyond the walls. But the wide, rolling hills were amazingly normal. I could be strolling toward the grove of trees for a picnic lunch instead of marching out to meet the huge army stretched across the distance. I saw the tall standard of the commanders of the Sidian troops and aimed for that. The armies were still being readied for the attack. Lehkan cavalries were shifting position. Commanders were shouting orders. I ignored the activity and walked toward the front line, resisting the temptation to look back at the white wall of Lyric.

The sight of one lone man walking out onto a battlefield was so disorienting that even after some soldiers spotted me, they didn't react immediately. But as I drew closer, a shout went up. A foot soldier lifted his hand and fired a syncbeam in my direction. Scorched sod flew up near my feet. I kept walking, hoping I could get close enough to hail them before they figured out how to aim the awkward weapon. His next attempt hit somewhere behind me. The grass hissed as it fried. I kept my pace steady.

Then he zeroed in on me. The beam sliced across my chest from shoulder to lower ribs. For the space of a heartbeat I didn't feel anything but surprise. Then the pain caught up with me and I staggered. The smell of burnt flesh made me gag.

I tried to catch myself with my hands, but my seared shoulder buckled and I fell awkwardly to one side. My nerve endings screamed so loudly that for a few moments I forgot there was an army ahead of me and a city behind me. I forgot my purpose. I forgot who I was. Then the deep inner damage began to mend. I found the strength to push myself back to my feet, although I swayed. I stared at the ground, determined to keep moving forward, and managed a few more steps. When I dared to look up, the syncbeam was aimed directly at me again.

"Hold. Let him approach." A voice boomed. Hooves pounded toward me.

I lifted my eyes.

Astride the largest lehkan I had ever seen, its antlers honed to deadly points, was Zarek, king of Hazor. He stared down at me, expression unreadable.

My knees could barely support me yet, but I tried to stand up straight.

He waited for me to speak, his fingers tapping against his

mount's rein in a familiar sign that he was growing impatient.

"I come with an offer from the People of the Verses and the clan of Lyric." It was a struggle to make my voice carry the distance to where his lehkan posed on the rise of the hill.

He threw his head back and laughed. "They offer to rip down the walls themselves and save us the trouble?"

My chest was still burning from the injury scored across my flesh, and I found it hard to appreciate his sense of humor. "Something better." I met his eyes. "I know what you're seeking." His commanders sought something simple: the destruction of Lyric and its tower. Zarek's motives were more complex.

"You want to destroy the Lyric tower because it is a place where the One physically visits His people. But there is another way the One has chosen to be embodied among His people: The Restorer."

Zarek's eyes lit. "You'll turn her over to us?"

"The woman you faced in battle at Morsal Plains is no longer the Restorer."

The lehkan shifted, as impatient as its rider.

Holy One, give me the words. This is treacherous ground.

"So you waste my time?" His eyes flared, warning me to get to the point.

I shook my head and dared to take another step forward. "The One can't be wrested from our people, but He can be given. He has called a new Restorer to the People of the Verses. And yes, we will surrender him to you."

Sounds of disbelief and shock came from some of the commanders behind Zarek, but the king showed no reaction. "How will I know it isn't a trick?"

"When I served in your court, I taught you about the Restorer. What is one of the signs?" My voice was growing hoarse from shouting across the distance. I wished he'd let me approach and just talk to him. But this was his stage. He needed an audience for this confrontation. It was part of why this could work.

"Wounds that heal rapidly." He grinned. "Where is he?"

I took a deep breath and lifted my arms a few inches from my sides. "Right here."

Zarek's eyes narrowed, anger in the set of his jaw. I had lived in his palace and even sparred with him, and he hadn't known. He wasn't used to surprises. "Then you won't mind if we test that sign, will you?" It was a rhetorical question. He had already signaled one of his men, who drew a short sword and walked toward me, alert for any reaction. Getting back on my feet after being hit by a syncbeam should have been enough proof, but they probably thought I'd only been grazed.

I held my ground and kept my hand away from my sword.

The young soldier paused a few paces from me. He met my eyes in question, and I read his hesitation. Running someone through in the heat of battle was one thing, but killing a man who didn't lift a sword in defense was another.

"Now," Zarek said. The man stepped forward, the full weight of his lunge adding to the thrust. His sword drove hard into my stomach, under the ribs. Then he pulled it free.

My lungs spasmed with the effort to draw in a breath as I gasped in pain. I collapsed to my knees. I meant to keep my hands clear of the wound so they could see there was no trick, but my arms wrapped around my stomach in reflex, and I doubled over. Sweat beaded on my skin. I fought to stay conscious long enough for the healing to take hold. *Shamgar*, couldn't he have just cut a small slit on my arm?

I couldn't move and couldn't hurry the healing. Yet even within the dark cave of incredible agony, I was aware of the world outside this place of pain. A lehkan stamped its hoof and the tack jingled. Gray-green moss stretched like a pallet across the ground beneath me. When I could breathe again, I even caught the scent of the honey-colored trees in the grove nearby.

I wanted to bound to my feet, prove my claim, and get on with this attempt to convince Zarek that killing me would be of more worth to him than tearing down a tower. But the previous injury had weakened me. This wound was slow to mend.

I managed to lift my head a few inches, and terror grabbed me. Zarek was turning away, already losing interest. I braced one foot underneath me and managed to lever myself back to my feet.

"Wait." I coughed and tried again. Time to challenge his ego. "Have your hill-gods ever healed a mortal wound?" My voice was stronger now.

Zarek turned to glare at me. I moved my arms, pushing the torn tunic up and wiping away the blood so he could see the restored flesh. The soldiers close enough to see gasped and looked at each other. Then their eyes turned to their king.

I had his attention again.

He studied me for a long moment. "As the Restorer, you represent the One," Zarek said.

I nodded, still struggling to stay upright as damage deep inside my body slowly repaired.

"As king, I represent the hill-gods of Hazor," he shouted.

I squinted up at him, unsure where he was going with this.

"Accepting your surrender would certainly prove our greater power. But battle will provide more convincing proof." He gave me a genuine, enthusiastic smile.

I fought not to moan in frustration. Battle was exactly what I was trying to prevent.

His voice grew louder. "Imagine the representative of the hill-gods defeating the representative of the One in individual combat!"

His men roared with approval, and he leapt from his mount. My jaw hung open. He knew how to play to his audience. I had to give him that. But this wasn't part of my plan.

He was supposed to be appeased by the gift of the One's own Restorer, save enough face with his commanders that he would withdraw from the attack, and take me back to kill me when it suited him. I was still struggling to catch up with this development when he crossed the space between us. His eyes raked over me appraisingly, the way they had when we had sparred. He didn't look worried, and I couldn't blame him. Well, if this would satisfy his need to prove something, I'd give them a good show. I tried to take a deep breath, but the pain still caught me in the side.

Zarek grinned at me. "Draw your sword."

Chapter Thirty-One

KIERAN

"Why are you doing this?" I said in a low voice, taking a step back.

Zarek pulled his heavy sword free of the steel scabbard, unhooked the scabbard from his belt, and tossed it aside. An aide ran forward to grab it and moved back into the ranks.

"I offered my life freely. You don't have to do this." We were far enough from his men to avoid being overheard. "This will get you what you need. Just kill me, declare your victory, and go back to Hazor."

"Where's the fun in that?" He sliced his blade several times through the air to loosen his arm.

"Zarek, you know the One has more power than your hill-gods. Just accept His gift."

"He has more power? Maybe." As I had seen it do before, his face took on the bland, ready expression of a mountain cat. "You represent Him. Prove it." He prowled closer.

My hand moved by reflex to the hilt resting against my left hip. I drew my sword with a familiar whisper of sound. "No." I backed away. The One had asked me to offer myself to Zarek. I didn't know what game the king was playing, but it had taken all my inner strength to resign myself to die. I wanted to get it over with.

"All right. Refuse to fight. Die—however long it takes to kill one of your kind. And then I promise you"—his voice hardened—"I will order my armies to tear down each stone of Lyric, kill every man and woman in the city, and carry the children back to Sidian."

Adrenaline surged through me, erasing the pain of the recent wound. Rage poured into my veins. I raised my sword without even realizing I had.

Zarek gave me a lazy smile. When he moved, the first strike was so fast I never saw his muscles prepare and barely got my blade between his sword and my neck.

I blocked and shoved his edge away and answered with a thrust of my own. He countered easily and picked up the pace.

Our swords rang with jarring clashes and scrapes. My own labored breathing sounded loud in my ears. I heard the occasional grunt of effort behind Zarek's powerful swings. Everything else disappeared. Lunge. Pull back. Block. Attack.

Zarek landed a few cuts. He remembered my patterns from our sparring in Sidian and anticipated my responses. With his next attack, I dodged aside and countered with a crossing move, shifting our positions. Now I could see Lyric rising up in the distance but closed it out. I forced Zarek to slightly lower ground on the slope and managed to get past his guard once, with a glancing blow. He barely seemed to notice. He drove me back, and our positions shifted again.

He feinted high then spun past me and slipped in a low gash across my sword arm. A roar went up from Zarek's men. I shut them out. Blood poured down over my hand, making my grip slippery. I brought my other hand forward in a two-handed clasp. The move gave more power to my swings but also exposed a wider target as I was forced to face him head-on. We continued to circle, exchanging blow after blow. I shifted my weight and angled my body as I switched back to a one-handed grip. For a while that helped as I attacked and danced back out of range over and over.

I saw the flare in his eyes when he decided to finish this. Suddenly the tempo of his strikes increased. Nothing I tried held him off. He kept coming, driving me back. I stumbled, and he ignored my sword and swung at my arm. This time the strike went deep. My mind willed to hold on, but my weapon dropped from my deadened hand. I watched the sword fall.

He cut across my chest with an almost leisurely swing.

I fell back to the ground.

Bare, gray sky filled my vision, and the cool moss beneath me seemed to draw the last of my strength and suck it into the ground.

Zarek's head appeared in my frame of view. He stepped forward and studied me, assessing his angle. Now that I was down, he took his time. Then he lifted his sword.

My hand closed around the dagger in my boot. I flung it straight into the shoulder joint of Zarek's sword arm. His eyes widened, and he glanced down in shock.

I don't know how he managed to keep a grip on his sword, but I didn't stop to watch. I rolled to the side, found my sword again, and came up in a crouch.

He pulled the knife from his shoulder as if he were plucking a stray thistle off his clothes and turned to face me. This time he didn't smile as he moved in.

We returned to the exhausting rhythm of strikes and

parries. Drizzling rain began to fall—my only indicator of how much time had passed. I wondered if I'd still be on my feet when the afternoon rains ended.

I watched his eyes, watched his feet, and watched the tell-tale flickers in his muscles before he moved. Sweat stung my eyes. My feet skidded as the ground grew wet. Every breath burned in my lungs.

Then something changed. He frowned and pulled back. It took me a moment to realize what he was reacting to. There was a sound carrying over the hills. Drums.

"What is this? Treachery? Do you have armies approaching?" He was breathing hard too, but his voice was still strong with anger.

I looked back at Lyric in shock. "No. This wasn't a trick." Then I realized what the sound was, and a smile grew on my face. "It's the songkeepers."

"What?"

I lowered my sword. Zarek was interested enough to stop swinging at me, and I was desperate for a break. "The Verses tell our people that whenever they are attacked, they should sing to the One who delivers them." Then I narrowed my eyes. "The people of Braide Wood sang the day you invaded Morsal Plains."

He looked back at Lyric. For the first time, I saw a flicker of alarm in Zarek's face. I followed his gaze. Over the tall central tower, where I knew the songkeepers and citizens of Lyric had gathered, a thick mist had formed. The fog surrounded the tower like a cradling hand.

With the sight of that mist and the hint of melody floating across the air, I could suddenly breathe again. The One would preserve His people. My role was actually very small. I turned back to Zarek, still smiling. He sniffed in a breath like a lehkan bull about to charge. I readied my sword.

This time, after I parried his first strike, I plunged right back in. I caught the first hint of uncertainty as Zarek responded. He slipped into standard forms while his mind struggled to regroup. We fought on, evenly matched, equally resolute. Suddenly a memory played across my vision. A memory of crossing swords with a Warrior far stronger than Zarek. As the king swung at me the next time, I countered with a rapid circle around his blade. It was the move the Warrior had used on me. Zarek's sword flew free. I quickly swung the flat of my blade into his side, knocking him to his knees.

As I held my sword against his neck, he looked at me without blinking. There was no fear, no anger. Only resignation and maybe even respect.

"Nothing has changed, Zarek." I waited for my chest to stop heaving for air. I raised my voice so his commanders would hear me. "The One has sent me to the people of Hazor." I tossed my sword away and reached out my hand to Zarek. "You can accept my life or my service." All the soldiers within earshot held their breath. Zarek lifted his hand, and I clasped his forearm, helping him to his feet.

"You're a worthy opponent." He turned so that his voice carried easily to his men. "We accept the gift of your service and offer our service to the One who is proven strongest in battle." The soldiers, who had also seen the uncommon mist over Lyric, had no desire to argue Zarek's decision. The king dropped my arm and called to his commanders: "Ready the troops to return."

I stood in the rain, suddenly empty and confused. It was over. The armies would leave. No one in Lyric would die. And I was still alive.

Zarek glanced back at me. "You seem surprised."

I squinted at him and pushed wet hair back from my face. The gash in my arm, which still hadn't completely healed, protested, and I winced. "I didn't know how this would end."

"And still you go where the One sends you." Zarek studied me. "He must deserve your trust." He snapped some orders, and an aide came running to wrap the wound at his shoulder. He shouted something at one of his commanders and then turned back to me.

"We can start by having you teach the Verses at the largest shrines in Hazor. Or would it be better to use a different place? You'll have to decide. And . . ."

Where did he get his energy? I looked back at Lyric with longing.

Zarek stopped talking and watched me. The edge of his mouth moved. "Go. Say your good-byes. Join me in Corros in two days."

The One had called me to help Hazor's people, and for His sake, I'd do it with all my strength; but in that moment Zarek earned my genuine friendship. "If I can convince the Council to send some songkeepers, would you give them your complete protection?" I was uneasy at the thought of taking others into the very dark world of Hazor, but I would need help. "Will you let them come and go? Can you guarantee their safety?"

"After today I can guarantee anything," he said. "Bring any help you need."

"What about my son? If I bring him, will he be safe?"

He nodded, then drilled me with his eyes. "And do I have your word? Corros in two days?"

"We will be there."

Zarek, true to form, instantly shifted his attention to the next thing he wanted to do.

I was left to turn toward Lyric. Looking up, I let the rain sheet across my face. I grabbed my sword and sheathed it. The walk back seemed to go on for miles. My whole body was heavy with a fatigue that pulled with such persuasion, I almost sank to the ground. But I stumbled forward, at long last reaching the wall.

The door slid open, and the arms of my friends reached out to gather me in. No one seemed to notice the blood on my clothes as they held me, and no one seemed troubled by the shudders that ran through me as I gradually accepted that the crisis had passed.

After a moment Tristan stepped back. "So the army is really leaving? Just like that?"

I tried to smile. "Just like that."

"What about your plan?" Susan asked.

"I've promised to meet Zarek in two days." They started to protest, but I continued. "Not to give my life. To give my service. And he'll guarantee the safety of anyone who comes with me." I looked at Nolan. "Is that all right? Will you mind going back to Hazor with me?"

He lit up for a moment, but then worry chased across his face.

I reached out to tousle his hair. "You'd be too busy helping me. You wouldn't have to serve as a messenger anymore."

He ducked his head, but not before I saw his wide smile.

Kendra brushed tears from her face and wouldn't look at me.

I punched her arm lightly. "I'm sure Zarek will let me come back to visit once in a while. I'll need to meet my new nephew."

"Or niece." Kendra met my eyes and tried to frown. "And see that you visit soon."

"We watched from the wall," Markkel said. "Except for Linette. She went back to the tower when everyone gathered to sing. You had us worried."

"How many times have I warned you?" Tristan said. "You always leave an opening on the outside when you're tired."

I rolled my eyes. "Could we just go back to the tower and let them know it's over?"

Markkel laughed. "I don't think you need to worry about that. Word spreads fast in Lyric."

Of course. The guardian watch on the wall would have already sent word back that Hazor's army was retreating. Even so, I needed to be in the tower. Put my feet on that sacred ground. Feel the mist settle over me.

We walked slowly through the empty streets. My legs were unsteady, but most of my injuries had stopped bleeding. The music grew louder.

I paused and looked at Markkel and Susan. "After the gathering in the tower, I'll come with you to talk to Jake." Susan answered me with a grateful smile. They had set aside their worry to support me at the Council session and stand with me as I faced Zarek and his army. But something odd was going on with their son, and I planned to help them figure it out and get Jake safely home before I left for Corros.

We rounded a corner and saw the tower. As we moved under an arched entry, I caught a glimpse of Linette on the dais with some of the other songkeepers. Faith radiated from her uplifted face. I gave myself a moment to enjoy the sight.

"You'll tell her soon, won't you?" Kendra whispered close to my ear.

I started and looked at her. "Tell her?"

"How you feel."

I wanted to deny whatever it was she was implying. Instead, I gave her a rueful smile. "Maybe. One day."

"Good." She nodded and stepped forward to join the singing.

How had she known? Was I so easy to read? I watched Kendra smile at Tristan. She might be my younger sister, but she had a head start on some things. Then I looked at Nolan, whose neck was going to snap if he kept tipping it back so far, staring in awe at the mist high above us. Warmth poured through me like a swallow of hot clavo. I had a start on a few things too. I closed my eyes and let the mist touch my face.

Chapter Thirty-Two

SUSAN

The music in the tower washed over me. Awe left my emotions ricocheting in strange directions. It occurred to me that Kieran would need to compose a Song to record the events of the day, and I stifled a giggle at the thought. Maybe I'd point that out to him after the gathering.

My laughter slipped away as I thought back to the heart-breaking picture of Kieran's wiry figure walking out to face the entire army of Hazor. Alone. I knew very well that the One sometimes called His Restorers to sacrifice, but I had wanted Him to find another way. Kieran often triggered a maternal mix of compassion and worry in me, although I could well imagine the mockery on his face if I ever admitted that to him.

When Mark and I had followed Tristan and Kendra up a stone stair to the walkway on the top of Lyric's outer wall, I hadn't wanted to watch but couldn't turn away. I felt the searing burn of the syncbeam and the merciless thrust of the sword that nearly killed Kieran. Kendra swayed but gripped the low marble battlement and shrugged off Tristan's efforts to pull her away. Nolan felt each blow as well. I kept my arm around his shoulders. I didn't want him to see this, but nothing would persuade him to leave. All through the long duel, as Zarek and Kieran fought, we watched. We prayed.

When Kieran had his sword to Zarek's neck, I squeezed my eyes shut. It was Mark's gasp that snapped them open again.

"What's he doing?" I asked Mark when Kieran tossed his sword away.

"He's offering himself again. If he killed Zarek, the armies would ride forward in revenge." When the king had given Kieran his hand, I had let tears run down my face, unashamed.

Now I joined in the next hymn as the songkeepers led worship, letting relief rest on me along with the mist that filled the lofty space in the tower. Then in another swerve of emotion, I grinned again. Kieran was going to teach the Verses. That would be interesting. Hazor would never be the same.

When the hymn ended, my gratitude ebbed and I was forced back to earth—to the problem that consumed my thoughts. I had been able to push it aside when we were all facing death. But we had survived. Now we had to figure out what was wrong with Jake.

Yesterday in Cameron's office, I had been so thrilled at the first glimpse of my son I hadn't even noticed his strange aloofness. After Kieran left, Jake pulled away from Mark and me to stand near Cameron.

"Are you all right?" I had asked him, noticing how small he looked in the guardian tunic and trousers and how much he needed a haircut. "We got to Braide Wood, but you'd disappeared. We've been so worried."

Jake shrugged. "Cameron sent someone to bring me here. He's been great."

I had stared at Cameron in shock, but he ignored me and

smiled at Jake. "We've had some wonderful discussions. He's told me a great deal about your world. He'll make a fine guardian."

Jake's chest swelled with pride. Mark and I exchanged a worried look. "Jake, you can tell us all about it later," Mark said. "Let's go home now."

Our son simply shook his head. "I'm not going."

That's when the growing lump of cold congealed in my stomach.

He turned his attention to Cameron. "I have to get back to the guardian tower." Cameron nodded and Jake hurried out, ignoring us. It happened so quickly we didn't have time to react. When we realized his intent, Mark and I ran out into the hall. "Jake, wait!"

He was already at the end of the corridor. His steps slowed for a fraction of a second, but then he strode ahead and bounded down the stairs out of sight. He never looked back. With all the terrible possibilities I had tried to prepare myself for, nothing in my imagination had come close to the sight of him walking away.

One of the elder songkeepers recited some Verses in benediction. My hand found Mark's, and he gave me a reassuring squeeze. Then he put his mouth close enough to my ear to tickle. "Did you wish you were up there singing?" he asked.

I jabbed my elbow into his ribs. He chuckled, and I turned to look at his face. We'd had several rough days. Yet Mark had a sparkle in his eyes that was brighter than I had seen in a long time. Part of him was thriving from being with his people again.

I shifted uneasily and tightened my grip on his hand. "I

wonder if Jon and Anne are still having fun at my mom's."

It took him a moment to jump thought trains with me. "I'm sure they've had time for only one more hand of Go Fish."

"Poker."

"What?"

"She was teaching them poker. She told me when I called them. They got bored with Go Fish," I said. "And what about Karen? Do you think she's still at Amanda's? What if the whole night has gone by and she comes home and can't find us?"

Mark studied me. "What's bringing this on?"

"I just didn't want you to forget about them."

He dropped my hands and stepped back. "What?"

"Well, you've hardly talked about them; and you don't seem very upset about Jake; and you seem to be enjoying yourself here. . . ." My voice rose in volume as the noise of people leaving grew around us.

Mark's eyes widened. Then he grabbed my arm and pulled me toward the closest archway. Once we were outside, he tugged me over to an empty spot near the tower wall. "Susan, I don't know what you've got spinning around in that brain of yours, but just because I don't talk about our kids constantly doesn't mean I've forgotten them." He let go of me and ran a hand through his hair. "We've been a little busy, you know."

I looked down, chewing my lower lip, but didn't answer.

"And I'm worried sick about Jake. But what did you expect me to do? Grab a sword and kill Cameron?"

"No." I shook my head. "I just get the feeling that maybe . . ."

"What?" He growled his frustration.

My fears surged forward and found words. "That you want to stay here too."

He stumbled a step closer to the marble wall and put his hand against it as if he needed support. He closed his eyes, and his lips moved silently. I realized he was counting to ten. He took a deep shuddering breath. "When . . . Why . . . What made you start worrying about that?"

"I don't know." I floundered to remember the little signals that had made me uneasy, but his unusual level of aggravation distracted me. Mark always took things in stride. He was always so calm it drove me crazy. Not today.

"You can't accuse me of something like that and not explain why." The tendon along his jaw jumped.

"All right. You were so happy to see Jorgen . . ." I said.

"He was like a father to me. Of course I——"

". . . and then when we went off to Hazor, you acted like it was some fun adventure . . ."

"You were the one who was singing hiking songs!"

". . . and you asked me if I wanted to be the Restorer again, and that's when I thought you wished we could stay, and . . . and after Jake . . . when he said he wouldn't go back, we went back to your rooms, and you didn't do anything . . . and I . . ." Tears ran down my face, and I couldn't string any more words together. Mark looked blurry through my flooded eyes, but I saw the struggle of competing emotions on his face.

Exasperation seemed to be winning, but he pulled me into a tight hug anyway. "Susan, I made my choice a long time ago. When we get home, I'll tell you about the exact moment I knew I wouldn't come back to the clans."

"Popcorn by the fireplace?" I sniffed.

"Yes." His chest vibrated under my cheek. "The whole story." Then he held me back enough to look down at my face.

"I belong with you and the children. And Jake belongs with us. For now."

I stiffened, and Mark hurried to continue. "He starts college this fall, and he'll be out on his own soon. We're going to need to let go of him."

"But not to Cameron and the guardians!"

"You're right. I don't think he's supposed to be here." Mark rubbed his hands along my shoulders. "So let's go get him, all right?"

I gave him a watery smile and nodded.

He stepped closer. As his lips found mine, my whole body sighed with reassurance. He wasn't wishing he had stayed here.

His hands dug into my hair as his kiss deepened. He wasn't sorry he had married me.

My arms went around his waist. Everything was going to be all right. My skin glowed with the same warmth it did after a day basking on a beach.

Then someone cleared his throat.

Mark and I pulled apart.

"Are you ready to go talk to Jake?" Kieran's tone was carefully bland. "I could come back later."

Mark grinned and threw an arm around my shoulder. "Let's go."

We crossed the large square and approached the guardian training tower. As we neared the door, Kieran hesitated. "Maybe it would be best if you talked to the guards and brought Jake out." He jabbed his boot against a crack in the pavement. "Some of the Lyric guardians might not be happy to see me."

"For crying out loud," I said. "You just saved the whole city."

He shrugged and led us through the entrance, but his hand strayed to his sword.

The tower was almost empty, as most of the guardians were still stationed on high alert around the city. The head guardian was out with his men, but we found the captain of the first-years. Because of the invasion threat, training had been cancelled for the day. Most of the first-years had been at the gathering in the worship tower and were now enjoying their afternoon off. The captain told us Jake had stayed behind and directed us to a practice hall.

We stood in the door for a moment, watching him step through complex patterns with a blunt training sword. I had no idea how to approach him. Our son looked like a stranger.

"You've improved," Kieran said, striding into the room.

Jake turned and glared at him. "What do you want?" The sullen tone was so unlike Jake that even Kieran seemed startled, and he barely knew our son. Then Jake noticed Mark and me standing in the doorway. His face took on harder edges. He moved a step back, lifting his sword in an unconscious defense.

Kieran watched him closely. "I came to see how you are." Kieran smiled and tried to be disarming. Standing in torn, burnt clothes, his hands still stained with blood, I didn't think he was doing a great job.

I stepped forward, but Mark held my arm. "Give him a minute," Mark whispered. "He's the Restorer."

"I'm fine." Jake's voice was cold. "You can go now." He turned away and went back to his pattern.

Kieran watched him through a series of movements. "Wait. Keep your swing lower on that cross."

"He's giving him lessons?" I hissed to Mark. "How's that going to help?"

"Shh. Give him a chance." He pulled me further toward the corner of the room, where we could watch but be less noticeable to Jake. "Something is really strange."

He didn't need to tell me that.

"Here, I'll show you." Kieran stepped closer and pantomimed the stroke through the air. Jake swung his sword again. "That's better, but keep the edge forward, and it's still a little too high." Jake tried it several more times, and some of his bristling animosity eased.

"So you weren't worried about the attack from Hazor?" Kieran slipped the question in between his coaching comments.

Jake stretched. "Nah. Cameron told me he had a plan and everything would be fine."

Kieran stiffened for a second, probably remembering Cameron's plan had involved turning the Restorer over to the Kahlareans. Then he eased back into casual conversation.

"Not bad. Try that same pass from the left. Good." He gradually moved until he was directly in front of Jake, still watching him intently.

Jake tested a pattern of sword movements again, but Kieran studied his eyes.

Suddenly Kieran swayed on his feet.

"Something's wrong," I said.

Mark ran forward with me close behind. Kieran's face paled, and he stumbled back a few steps. Mark reached him in time to put an arm around him and brace him. Jake turned away, ignoring them both and resuming some slow-motion drills.

Mark helped Kieran stagger over to the door and sink onto a bench.

"Sorry." Kieran seemed to be struggling to breathe.

"Is it your injuries? Are you not healing?" I asked.

He shook his head and took another few breaths. "I'm fine. I saw something. I don't know what it is, but I felt like I recognized it." He closed his eyes. Then he shot up and looked at us. "It was Kendra. It was like the thing that had her. I didn't know what it was back then when she was trapped."

"Rhusican poison?" A wave of horror left me light-headed. "The Rhusicans were all banished."

Kieran cocked an eyebrow. "Right. And no one uses ven-blades because they're illegal, and the Council would never consider an alliance with the Kahlareans, and Cameron has the best interests of Lyric in mind."

I didn't appreciate his sarcasm, but this wasn't the time to get into an argument. "So heal him. Hurry."

"I don't know how." He met my gaze with pain and weariness. "Whatever that was . . . it hit me hard."

Frustration throbbed through my temples. He'd face a whole army but balk at helping Jake? "You have to. When I was the Restorer . . ."

Mark rested a hand on my arm. "Kieran's gifts are different," he said quietly.

Kieran shot Mark a grateful look. "You have to get him home, fast. The poison . . . the control . . . it goes deep. I don't think I can do anything." His focus traveled to me. "I'm sorry."

"You've got to try. How are we supposed to get him to the portal?"

From his seat on the bench, Kieran gave a heavy nod. "Jake," he called. "Could you come here?"

Jake turned and gave us a wary look, but he sauntered toward Kieran anyway, probably hoping for more sword-fighting tips.

Kieran met his eyes and spoke firmly. "We wait in the darkness for the One who brings light. The Deliverer will come, and with His coming all darkness will be defeated."

Jake lowered his sword, confused.

Kieran's face tensed in concentration or pain. "In him was life, and that life was the light of men." He was struggling to force the words out. I suddenly recognized them. They were from our world. Our verses. When had he learned them? "Jake, what comes next?" Kieran leaned forward, compelling him. "Remember? You told us that verse at Payton and Tara's house."

"The light shines in the darkness, but the darkness has not understood it." Jake's voice was quiet, and his eyes were unfocused, but for a split second his face was familiar to me again. He was still there. Then his eyes went blank.

Kieran collapsed against the wall. "That's all I can do right now. You've got to get him home."

Jake as a pliable zombie wasn't much better than Jake the adamant fan of Cameron. "Wait. He's not—"

"Hurry." Kieran's rough command propelled us into action.

Mark put an arm around Jake. "Come on, son. This way." We walked slowly, not wanting to jar him from the trance-like state he was in.

I glanced back at Kieran.

He gave us a quick nod, still recovering from something that had shaken him even worse than his encounter with Zarek. "Go with the One." He glanced at Jake. "Once he's home, use your verses."

"Thank you," I said.

But he had closed his eyes, and I wasn't sure he heard me.

Concerned about the long walk through the city with so many people milling around today, Mark guided Jake to the main entry facing south. I started breathing easier when we were outside the walls. The walk along the eastern wall to the north side seemed to take forever, but there was something soothing in the squish of wet moss and the even scallops of the wall as we passed one after another of the curved sections of white marble.

When the grove was in sight, my pulse started racing.

"Almost there," Mark said quietly. Jake stared ahead, still moving wherever Mark guided him. I thought I heard something and turned to look behind us. A shape moved into an indent of the wall. I was about to call out to Mark when I realized it was just an illusion. My eyes must be tired from the effect of the ripples in the wall. My head began to ache. I rubbed my temples and forgot what I was looking for behind us. We reached the safety of the trees. Gazing off into the distance, I no longer saw any sign that Hazor's vast army had stretched out across the plains just hours ago.

Mark led us into the grove. We had to slip between two narrow trees to reach the place the portal was hidden. The three stones on this side had been buried in position, but Mark had never forgotten the one central place that the Lyric eldest songkeeper had led him to when he was eighteen and fleeing for his life. Tiny hairs on my arms lifted as I felt a tingling electrical pull. Mark was about to coax Jake to the right spot, when our son stiffened. He looked at us both in confusion and pulled away from Mark, stumbling out of our reach. We ran after him and stopped him several yards away.

"It's okay," I crooned. We both wrapped our arms around him and held him. "We're almost home." Then I looked back toward the portal. Something moved in the trees, and I suddenly remembered that I had seen shapes following us. Or had I? My head throbbed in confusion.

"Mark . . ." I forgot what I needed to tell him. He was still soothing Jake, and I battled the cloud in my mind. Focus. One important goal. We need to get Jake home.

I squinted into the trees.

A woman stepped out, no longer bothering to stay hidden. She had auburn curls and vivid green eyes that seemed to twirl.

"Medea!" The name choked out of me.

"What?" Mark pulled his gaze from Jake's face to look at me. I lifted a shaking hand and pointed at the Rhusican who had once poisoned my mind to its deepest core.

There was intense satisfaction in her face—the same look she had worn when she thrust a dagger into my heart. Terror paralyzed me, but the nightmare moved forward. Now Cameron walked out from between the narrow trees to stand beside her. His lip curled in a smirk.

Mark saw them and sprang forward with a shout of rage. Medea lifted one hand, and Jake shrieked. He grabbed his head and doubled over, stumbling farther from me. Mark jolted to a stop and looked back at us.

"No!" I screamed.

Medea and Cameron turned and stepped through the portal. I heard a crackling hum, and they vanished.

Jake collapsed to his knees, his body limp, as if the strings holding him up had been snipped. Mark bounded back to us and scooped up our son as if he were four years old again.

"Hurry!" he said.

I ran toward the portal but pulled to a stop when I felt the skin-prickling buzz of energy.

"Go!" Mark shouted.

I looked at him in panic. What if they were waiting for us as we stepped through? What if they moved the stones on the other side? What would that mean? Where would we find ourselves?

He read my fear. "We have to get home," he said, catching up to me. So with Mark beside me, and Jake in his arms, I stepped through.

Chapter Thirty-Three

SUSAN

The familiar rafters of the attic appeared over and around me. Stale summer air trapped in the dusty space smelled sweet to me. Relief swirled through my lungs at the sensation of being in my own world. My joy at being home lasted for only the space of one breath.

Mark's legs buckled and he fell to the floor. Jake rolled from his arms, unconscious. Sweaty blond hair framed my son's face as he splayed against the backdrop of the rough plywood floor.

I dropped to my knees. "Jake, are you all right? We're home. Jake, wake up."

He was breathing, but I couldn't get him to open his eyes.

I pivoted to my left, where Mark had landed on his side. He had lost all color, and every muscle in his face spasmed with pain. I'd seen Mark take twenty-five stitches from a table saw accident without wincing. Right now he groaned in agony. Then he sucked in a sharp breath and went limp.

God help me.

I didn't know what to do. My first impulse was to scramble down the ladder and call 911. But would a paramedic know how to treat the Rhusican poison that had invaded Jake? Did the local hospital have a trauma center for folks who'd had a rough passage through an interdimensional portal?

Susan, think! I pressed the heel of my hand against my forehead in frustration.

I felt for Mark's pulse and held my ear near his mouth. While Jake seemed to be in a deep sleep, Mark was completely lifeless. A cry tore from my chest. "No! You aren't leaving like this. We're home. You're safe now."

I grabbed Mark's shoulders and shook him. "Come back. Please. Come back!"

Both men lay unmoving, and a terrible fear warned me that I was losing them.

Use your verses.

Kieran's last words to me sounded in my mind like an echo through the portal.

I drew a shuddering breath. My panicked mind couldn't pull a single verse from my memory, but my Bible was still next to my journal on the small table. I reached for it. The book fell to the floor in a splash of pages. I rifled through the chapters with frantic, shaking hands. A bookmark held a section my moms' group was studying. I squinted in the glare of the bare lightbulb overhead and read the words aloud.

"We are hard pressed on every side, but not crushed; perplexed, but not in despair; persecuted, but not abandoned; struck down, but not destroyed." Jake exhaled with an almost imperceptible moan, and I scooted closer to him on the floor. "We always carry around in our body the death of Jesus" — a sob caught in my throat — "so that the life of Jesus may also be revealed in our body."

I stopped to rest a hand on Jake's forehead. "Jake, can

you hear me? Come back." I looked back down at the pages and chose another section on the same page. "It is written: 'I believed; therefore I have spoken.' With that same spirit of faith we also believe and therefore speak." I looked over at Mark. His chest still wasn't moving. I dropped the Bible and threw myself across him, crying. Draped over him, I willed my life to somehow pour into him.

Father, help us!

I stifled my sobs so I could listen for his heartbeat, pressing my ear against his chest. I thought I heard a soft whoosh of air and pressed my face harder against him, straining my hearing.

Mark groaned. "Your chin is digging into my ribs."

I sprang back and stared at his face.

His eyes opened a slit, and the corner of his mouth twitched. He reached an arm toward me. "That wasn't a complaint. Come back here."

I gave him a fierce hug, blotting my tears onto his tunic. It took a minute to calm the shaking in my limbs so I could help him sit up. "What happened to you?"

He started to shake his head, then grimaced in pain and rubbed his temples. "I don't know. It was ten times worse than when I came through the portal last time. How's Jake?"

I shifted my position so he could see our son, sprawled near dented boxes of tax records. Fear squeezed more tears from my eyes. "I was trying to call him back. Kieran said to use our verses. Can you help me?"

"I'll try." He shifted his position gingerly and reached for Jake's hand. "What were you reading?"

I grabbed my Bible again. "Therefore we do not lose heart."

"Jake, don't lose heart," Mark said. "You aren't lost in there."

"Though outwardly we are wasting away, yet inwardly we

are being renewed day by day." I stopped to brush away tears.

"I know they hurt you." Mark's voice turned gravelly with emotion, but he focused intently on Jake's face. Every ounce of inner strength seemed to gather in him as he spoke. "His Spirit is inside of you. He's renewing you. Let Him fight the darkness they planted in your mind."

I pulled my eyes away from watching Mark and Jake to keep reading. "For our light and momentary troubles are achieving for us an eternal glory that far outweighs them all. So we fix our eyes not on what is seen . . ."

Mark gasped.

Jake's gray-blue eyes, so much like his father's, had opened. He still seemed far away, focused on some place beyond the eaves.

Mark glanced over at me. "Go on. Read more."

"So we fix our eyes not on what is seen, but on what is unseen. For what is seen is temporary, but what is unseen is eternal."

I looked at Jake again. Silent tears pooled and spilled over from his eyes. He still hadn't moved. Was he paralyzed? I remembered what it had felt like when I had been battling Rhusican poison. I had been near a deep black abyss, gripped by voices that overwhelmed every other thought. The memory of those hideous voices triggered another inspiration. I flipped pages frantically, looking for a psalm that our congregation had recited last Sunday.

"Here it is. Jake, listen: 'The voice of the Lord is over the waters; the God of glory thunders, the Lord thunders over the mighty waters. The voice of the Lord is powerful; the voice of the Lord is majestic. The voice of the Lord breaks the cedars.' Jake, say it with me: 'The Lord gives strength to his people; the Lord blesses his people with peace.'"

Mark joined with me. "The Lord gives strength to his people."

Had Jake's lips moved? Mark and I both held our breath.

"The Lord blesses his people with peace." Jake's voice was unsteady, but his eyes were clear.

"Say it again." Mark rubbed Jake's hand.

Together they repeated the verses several times.

Jake managed a crooked smile. "Yeah, I remember that one. Our youth group wrote a song from that psalm." He stirred, and Mark helped him sit up. Jake looked down at the guardian uniform he wore and blinked several times. "It wasn't a dream?" He stared at Mark's Council tunic and my coarse-woven travel cloak.

"What do you remember?" I wanted to grab him and never let go but didn't want to risk him pulling away from me like he had in Lyric. Instead, I reached out to brush his hair out of his face. He really needed a haircut.

He studied the floor, gnawing his lower lip. "I was lost. There was a big city with a white wall. And a guy with a sword. I remember lots of hiking and running and caves, and Braide Wood." His face brightened as he pieced together memories. "Tara makes really good stew, and I taught some kids how to play soccer. And then . . ." He frowned. "Some guys came to take me to Lyric and . . . everything gets fuzzy." He looked at us again. "But you found me?"

My tears splashed onto the pages of the Bible in my lap. "Yes," I whispered. "We found you. Everything is all right now."

"Well, not everything." Mark stood up and helped us both to our feet. "Wait here. I'll go see if they're in the house."

I'd been so focused on Mark's rough passage through the portal and the poison pulling life from Jake that I'd almost forgotten about Cameron and Medea.

"Why did they want to come here?" I asked Mark.

"I don't know." Mark turned to Jake, his voice gentle. "Do you remember what you told Cameron about our world? He said you had a lot of discussions about it. Do you know what he was interested in?"

Jake shook his head. "I don't know." He sounded lost and afraid.

I gave Mark a worried look. "It doesn't matter. We'll sort it out later."

Mark nodded and drew his sword. He listened at the open trapdoor for a few seconds, then climbed down the treads. A few minutes later he called for us. Jake and I both followed him through the hallway and into the living room.

The colors of the room seemed too bright, and the air smelled like lemon furniture polish instead of cinnamon and cloves. The overhead lights hurt my eyes. I missed the mild glow of light walls. But it was home. Jon's Legos were scattered all over the coffee table, and Anne's library books spilled from the couch.

As my eyes traveled the room, I realized a lamp had been knocked on its side. We walked through to the dining room and saw a chair had been smashed into the glass-fronted cabinet where I kept a collection of teacups. Numb and confused by the destruction, I stepped around broken shards and looked into the kitchen. Cupboard doors hung open, and canisters had been spilled everywhere. The kitchen door was wide open, and I heard a buzzing sound. A june bug had gotten inside and was crashing against a light. I glanced at the digital clock near the toaster. If it was accurate, only about an hour had passed since we went through the portal to rescue Jake.

"Whoa." Jake peered over my shoulder at the kitchen.

"Should we call the police?"

Mark shook his head. "I don't think that's a good idea. Besides, they're gone now."

"What were they doing?" I picked up the bread box from the floor and set it back onto the counter.

"Probably just grabbing some supplies," Mark said. "And making a point. I should try to track them." In the harsh kitchen light he looked drawn and pale. I was worried about our enemies lurking outside but much more concerned that Mark and Jake had barely survived our homecoming.

"Honey, I think you need to rest. And we should stick together. We can make a plan tomorrow."

Mark looked around at the mess. Sheathing his sword, he picked up an overturned kitchen stool and sank onto it. "You're right. The important thing is that we made it home. And Jake is all right." We both smiled at our son.

He stepped over a broken jar of molasses. "It's *really* good to be home," Jake said with some of his normal sparkle. "So we should celebrate. Could we order a pizza?"

"What?" I tried to frown. He thought every occasion was a great excuse for fast food. "We have a perfectly good spinach salad and leftover rice casserole in the fridge. Unless they took that, too."

Mark and Jake groaned in unison.

"Fine," I said. "If you help me get this mess cleaned up, we can order a pizza." Both my men grinned, and I let warmth flood through me. Sometimes keeping them happy was easy. Keeping them safe was another story. I stepped closer to where Mark sat and rested my cheek against the top of his head. Jake stuck his head in the refrigerator and popped back out, beaming.

"Hey, they didn't take the Dr Pepper." He tossed us each a

can and raised his own in a salute. "To all who serve the One."

I smiled at him and thought of Tristan riding with the guardians on the plateau near Braide Wood, and Tara making pepper soup for weary travelers, and Linette writing new songs to encourage the people of her clan, and Kieran standing alone against an army. I lifted my can. "And to the One."

We all took a drink, and then Jake set his can on the counter. "Dad?" He seemed older than his eighteen years for a moment. Noble. A young man who had faced difficult journeys.

Mark looked at him and noticed it too. He sat up taller and answered him gravely. "Yes?"

"Tomorrow, would you start teaching me how to use a sword? In case I ever need to?"

I shook my head, but Mark had already answered. "Sure." They exchanged a very male look of camaraderie, and I knew that even though Mark might never survive another trip through the portal, another of the Mitchell men was ready to answer the call if help were ever needed. I sighed. If we were going to keep Medea and Cameron from causing trouble, it made sense to keep our swords ready. I squeezed my pop can too hard. It made a loud crinkling noise.

Jake shook off the serious mood and pulled out the garbage can.

"Come on. I'm starving. Let's get this cleaned up. I vote we throw away anything with whole grains or lentils."

I grabbed a dish towel and swatted at him. His laughter rang through the kitchen. Mark stood up, closed the screen door, and started chasing down the bugs that had come in.

Jake reached to pick up the broken jar on the floor. "Ow!" He dropped one of the pieces and shook his hand. Blood welled up on his palm.

"Jake, be careful. Here, let me see." I hurried over and gently blotted the cut with the dish towel. "I'll go find a Band-Aid. I think I saw the first-aid kit in Anne's room. She was using it on her Barbies." I started to leave.

Jake stopped me. "Um, Mom?" His voice sounded strained.

Mark and I both turned to look at him.

He swallowed hard and held up his hand, looking dazed. "Never mind the Band-Aid."

Mark stepped closer and put his arm around me. I was grateful for the support. My fingers trembled as they reached out to touch Jake's palm.

The cut had completely disappeared.

etc.

bonus content includes:

Reader's Guide

1. Kieran responds to the One's call with a variety of reactions—from confusion to resentment to stubborn rebellion. Have you ever felt as if God were calling you to a deeper walk with Him or to some special task? Can you relate to any of Kieran's feelings?

2. In the first book, Susan dreamed of being like Deborah in the book of Judges. Gideon is another leader from Judges, and he answered God's call by saying, "If the LORD is with us, why has all this happened to us?" (6:13). What similarities do you see between Gideon's story in chapter 6 of Judges and Kieran's path?

3. Kieran's spiritual journey also contains some parallels to the accounts of Jacob (see Genesis 32), Jonah (see Jonah), and other biblical heroes who had tempestuous encounters with God. How have you wrestled with God at difficult times in your life?

4. Many characters in this story struggle with conflicting priorities. What did you see as driving goals for Mark and Susan, Kieran, Zarek, Tristan, Nolan, and other characters in the story? Do you have clashing priorities in your life? What are some of the forces that are

pushing you in two opposing directions? How do you resolve that tension? What ways do you find guidance through difficult decisions?

5. Although His plan isn't always obvious at first, the One is working out a design rich with love and grace throughout the story. Which plot thread resonated the most with you in regard to how the One's intentions were revealed and developed? (Kieran? Hazor's people? Nolan? Mark? Susan? Jake? Linette?)

6. The Old Testament is full of "Christ-types"—prophets and leaders who provide a symbol or foreshadowing of the true Messiah that is to come. Do you see ways that the Restorers are foreshadowing an ultimate Deliverer for the People of the Verses? What qualities in the Restorers (Mikkel, Susan, Kieran) reflect hints of a Christ-type figure, and what qualities clearly show that they are *not* the ultimate Deliverer?

7. Did you spot the three Restorers' sons in this story? Markkel is the son of a Restorer. He was expected to bring restoration but brought it in an unforeseeable way. Nolan is the son of the current Restorer and begins a road toward healing. Jake is the son of Susan the Restorer and may have his own calling to face in the future. Which of the three sons in the story do you think had the most challenging path? Why?

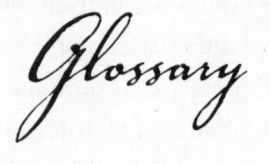

Glossary

blue lace fern: Rich blue-green color and delicate foliage, the roots have medicinal qualities and are used to treat inflammation and pain. Grows along edges of forest areas and near rivers.

boot knife: A small dagger, carried in a sheath strapped to the ankle. Versatile, used as a tool as well as a weapon.

cover-and-ambush: A child's game, similar to hide-and-seek.

first-years: Men and women in the first year of guardian training. Usually about eighteen years old.

ground-crawlers: Ten times the size of a North American earthworm, these burrowers only come out at night. Their skin is toxic to anything they touch, causing acidic burns to animals and humans.

house protector: Someone who takes a formal vow to defend to the death another person and his or her family (household).

mesana vine: Dark maroon parasitic plant that grows in harsh terrain. The pith is fibrous, salty, and edible, though far from tasty.

Perish: A table game of strategy, played with two sets of small stones, one black and one white.

pocket doors: Doors designed to slide into the wall. In the curving walls of Lyric, there are several hidden pocket doors that allow access through the sides of the city in addition to the main entry tunnel.

Rammelite fever: Progressive, fatal illness that causes joint pain and ongoing bouts of high fever; thought to be caused by a small parasite found on plants in low-lying swamplands.

scrambler: A device used to deactivate magnetic locks.

Sidian: The capital city of Hazor. A center of commerce and home to Zarek's palace, the prisons, and the primary hill-god shrine.

stinging beetles: Nonpoisonous but prone to inflict uncomfortable stings, these flying scarabs are common along the River Borders near Rendor. They are the size of large dragonflies, and the yellow and orange beetles are more likely to attack humans than the blue and green varieties.

suppression field: Technology developed to project a dampening field on the magnetic programming of focused, synchronized weapons and render them useless. Skyler, Kieran, and Kendra created this in preparation for the battle with Hazor at Morsal Plains.

waterweed: A dangerous plant found along riverbanks, its tendrils entangle moving creatures and can cause drowning.

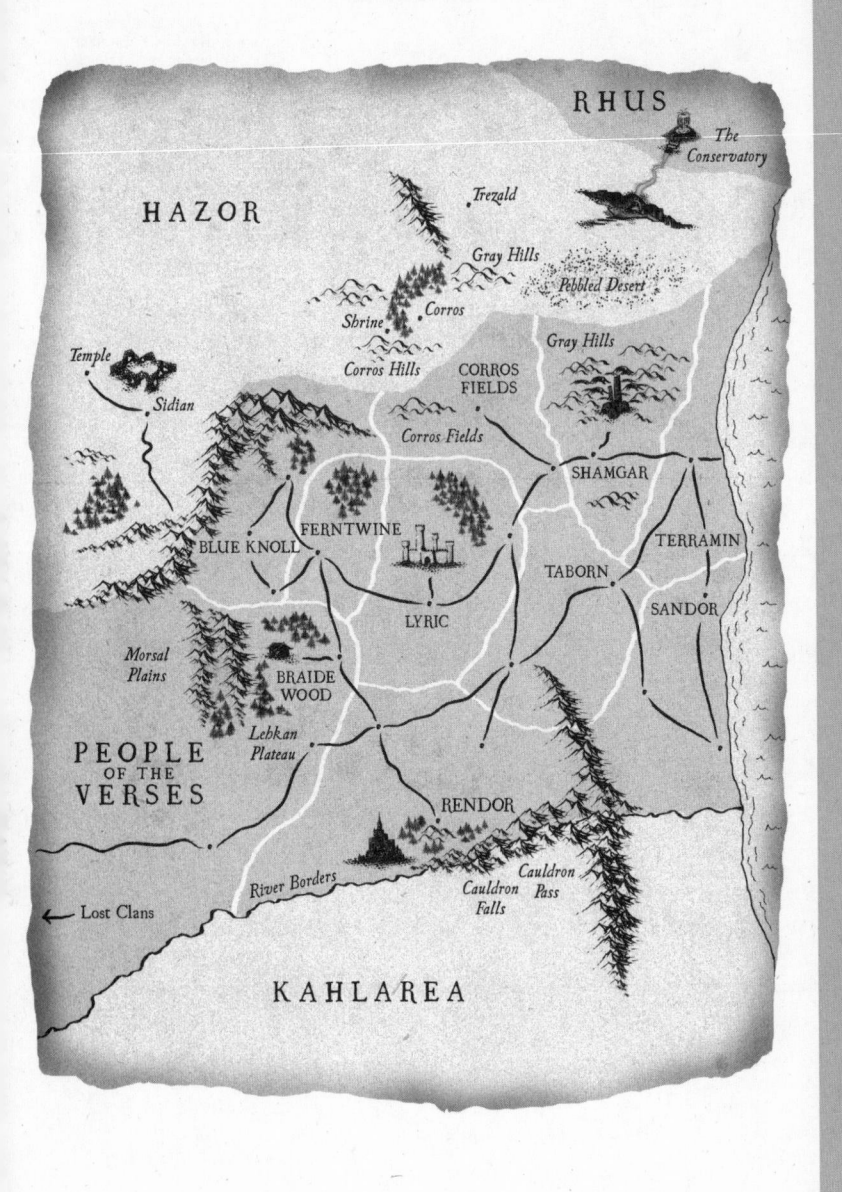

Hear, O Nations

Words by Sharon Hinck
Tune by Rowland H. Prichard
Arranged by Joel Hinck

1. Hear, O na - tions, hear the glo - rious ways the One pro - tects His own. Ha - zor's
2. Guar - dians fought, Re - sto - rer ri - ding, brave my soul, march on to die. All the
3. Weep no more for the fal - len war - riors; we, His child - ren, rest in His arms. Shout the

cries of war sur - round - ed, in our weak - ness we're not a - lone.
hea - vens joined the bat - tle; light and heat were thrown from the sky.
Ver - ses, bold with pro - mise; day to day, He keeps us from harm.

21

Raise the song of One who loves us, One whose po-wer is with-out
Wake, O wake and see sal - va - tion driv - ing hard_ a - cross the
Ho - ly One, we rode to serve You; strong, You ride_ be - fore_ us

28

peer. Trust not in weap - ons, kings,_ or
plains. Al - lies, strength, and swords_ hold
all. Fix_ our gaze_ on Your_ great

32

hill_ gods; His de - liv-'rance is al - ways near.
true,_ fill the val - ley like cleans - ing rain.
wis - dom, fix our hearts_ on Your love's call.

Coming Soon

The Restorer's Journey

Chapter One

JAKE

Mom was freaking out.

She stared out the dining room window like major-league monsters were hiding in the darkness beyond the glass. Give me a break. Our neighborhood was as boring as they come. Ridgeview Drive's square lawns and generic houses held nothing more menacing than basketball hoops and tire swings. Still, Mom's back was tight and tense, and in the shadowed reflection on the pane, I could see her biting her lip. I didn't know what to say to make her feel better.

I ducked back into the kitchen and used a wet rag to wipe off the counters. Clumps of flour turned to paste and smeared in gunky white arcs across the surface. I shook the rag over the garbage can, the mess raining down on the other debris we'd swept up. Broken jars of pasta and rice filled the bag. Our dented toaster lay on top of the mess, looking like it had been drop-kicked across the room. I stomped it down, twist-tied the bag, and jogged it out to the trash can by the garage. Usually I hated the chore of taking out the trash. Not tonight. Maybe if I erased the signs of our intruders, Mom would relax a little.

So Cameron and Medea dropped a few things when they were looking for supplies. No biggie. Why did my folks have such a problem with those two anyway? They'd been great to me. I trudged back into the house, rubbing my forehead. Wait . . . that wasn't right. A shiver snaked through my spine. Never mind. They were probably long gone by now.

"Kitchen's done." I carried the broom into the dining room, hoping Mom had finished in there. But she was still hugging her arms and staring out the window.

She turned and looked at the china cabinet, then squeezed her eyes shut as if they were hurting. "Why?" she whispered.

One cabinet door had glass shards jutting from it, and the other hung crooked with wood splinters poking out. Broken china covered the floor. Mom and Dad had been collecting those goofy teacups ever since they got married.

I pushed the broom against the edge of the fragments, but the chinking sound made her wince, so I stopped. Dad strode past with an empty garbage bag from the hall closet and stopped to give my mom a squeeze. He nodded toward me. "Honey, Jake's alive. Nothing else matters. We all got back safe." He leaned his head against hers, and I edged toward the kitchen in case they started kissing. For an old married couple, they were a little too free with their public displays of affection. No guy wants to watch his parents act mushy.

But my mom didn't look like she was in a kissing mood—not with her lips pressed together like that. I had a sneaking suspicion she was more freaked out about what had happened to my hand than to our house. Like when I had cancer as a kid. She'd gotten really stressed about the details of a church fund-raiser and cranky about everything that went wrong — stuff that wasn't even important. It gave her a place to be angry when she was trying to be brave about a bigger problem.

"It's only a piece of furniture." Dad was doing his sooth-ing voice. When would he catch on that it only made things worse?

"Only a piece of furniture we bought as a wedding gift to each other." She swiped at some wet spots on her face. "Only twenty years' worth of poking around garage sales and thrift stores together. Don't tell me what it's only, okay?"

"Okay." Dad backed away from her prickles.

I made another ineffectual push with the broom. My folks didn't argue much, but when they did, it grated like a clutch struggling to find third gear. Typical over-responsible firstborn, I wanted to fix it, but I didn't know how.

Mom picked up a Delft saucer — what was left of it — and laid the pieces gently into the garbage bag. Dad folded his arms and leaned against the high back of one of the chairs. "I can fix the cabinet. That splintered door will need to be replaced, but the other one just needs new hinges. I can put in new glass." His eyes always lit up when he talked about a woodworking project. The man loved his tools.

Mom smiled at him. Her tension faded, and she got all moony-eyed, so I ducked into the kitchen just as the doorbell rang. Thank heaven. "Pizza's here!" I yelled.

Dad paid the delivery guy, and I carried the cartons into the living room. Flopping onto one end of the couch, I pried open a lid. "Hey, who ordered green peppers? Mom, you've gotta quit ruining good pizza with veggies."

That made her laugh. "We'd better save a few pieces for the other kids." She cleared the Legos off the coffee table and handed me a napkin.

I gladly surrendered the top pizza box, along with its green pepper funk, and dove into the pepperoni below. "Where is everyone?"

"Karen's spending the night at Amanda's — trying out her new driver's license. Jon and Anne are at Grandma's. But if they see the pizza boxes when they get home tomorrow . . ."

I nodded. "Yep. Pure outrage. I can hear it now: 'It's not fair. Jake always gets to have extra fun.'" I did a pretty good impression of the rug rats. What would the kids think if they found out what else they had missed? This had been the strangest Saturday the Mitchell family had ever seen.

I popped open a can of Dr Pepper. My third. Hey, I'd earned some extra caffeine. "So what do we tell the kids?"

Mom smiled and looked me up and down, probably thinking I was one of the kids. When would it sink in that I was an adult now? I guzzled a third of my pop and set it down with a thump. "We could tell them there was a burglar, but then they'd want to help the police solve the case, and they'd never stop asking questions."

"Good point." Mom licked sauce from her finger. "Jon and Anne would break out the detective kit you gave them for Christmas."

Dad tore a piece of crust from his slice of pepperoni. "If we finish cleaning everything, I don't think they'll pay much attention. The cabinet is the only obvious damage. If they ask, we'll just say it got bumped and fell."

Dad wanted us to lie? So not like him. Then again, when

Kieran told me Dad wasn't originally from our world, I real-ized there were a lot of things he'd not been honest about. Now I was part of the family secret too.

He rested his piece of pizza on the cardboard box and looked at Mom. "Do we need to warn them?"

"Warn them?" she mumbled around a mouthful of melted cheese.

"In case Cameron and Medea come back." His voice was calm, but I suddenly had a hard time swallowing. Something cold twisted in me when he said their names. The same cold that had numbed my bones when I'd woken up in the attic. Why? They'd taken care of me. No . . . they'd threatened me. Confusing images warred inside my brain.

"You think they'll come back?" My baritone went up in pitch, and I quickly took another sip of pop.

Dad didn't answer for a moment. "It depends on why they came. If they plan to stay in our world, we need to find them—stop them. But my guess is that Cameron wants to return to Lyric with something from our world that he can use there. That means they'll be back to go through the portal."

Mom sank deeper into the couch and looked out the living room windows. At the curb, our family van shimmered beneath a streetlight.

They might be out there too. They could be watching us right this second.

"Maybe we should call the police." Mom's voice sounded thin. I'd suggested that earlier. After all, someone had broken in—well, broken out.

Dad snorted. "And tell them what?"

He had a point, but it's not like there's a rule book for

dealing with visitors from other universes. Unless you attended Star Trek conventions.

"So what's your plan?" I asked.

"I'll get extra locks tomorrow. Maybe look into an alarm system." Dad believed every problem could be solved with his Home Depot credit card.

"And shades." Mom chewed the edge of a fingernail.

"What?"

"We need some window shades."

He nodded, then turned to me. "Can you remember more about your conversations with Cameron? What did he ask you about? What did he seem interested in?"

A shudder moved through me, and pain began pulsing behind my eyes.

Mom gave Dad a worried glance, then rested a hand on my arm. "It's okay, honey. We don't have to talk about it right now." She smoothed my hair back from my face.

"No problem." I brushed her hand away, sprawled back on the couch, and studied the ceiling. "It just seems like it was all a dream."

"What's the last thing you remember clearly?" Dad pulled his chair closer and watched me.

"Braide Wood." I closed my eyes and smiled. "It reminded me of summer camp. And I was so tired of running and hiding in caves. I finally felt safe. Tara fussed over me, and I taught Dustin and Aubrey how to play soccer. It felt like home."

I struggled to remember the rest. For some reason my memories were tangled up, like the time I had a major fever and took too much NyQuil. Mom and Dad waited.

"I went to see Morsal Plains with Tara. Brutal. The grain was all black, and it smelled weird. Tara told me about the attack—how Hazor poisoned it on purpose and how Susan the Restorer led the army to protect Braide Wood." I squinted my eyes open and looked sideways at my mom. They'd told me she had ridden into battle with a sword. "Unbelievable."

Even though she was watching me with a worried pinch to her eyes, she smiled. "I know. I lived it, and it's hard for me to believe."

"Anyway, I hiked back to Tara's house, and some guys came to take me to Cameron. He made a big fuss over me. Said it was his job to welcome guests to the clans. Said I'd run into bad company but he'd make it up to me. He gave me something to drink, and there was this lady. She was amazing." No matter how fuzzy my memories were, Medea was easy to remember: the long curly hair, the sparkling green eyes, the dress that clung to all the right places. My cheeks heated. "I can't remember everything we talked about. She made me feel important, like I wasn't just some teenage kid. It was . . ." I sat taller and angled away from my parents, my jaw tightening. "She helped me realize that no one else had ever really understood me. I wanted to become a guardian. I had an important job to do."

"Jake." Dad's voice was sharp, and I flinched. "The woman you met was a Rhusican. They poison minds. Don't trust everything you're feeling right now."

A pulsing ache grabbed the base of my neck. I pressed the heels of my hands against my eyes. Mom's hand settled on my shoulder, and I stiffened. Weird static was messing with my head.

"Jake, they used you to find the portal. She doesn't really understand you." Mom's voice was quiet and sounded far away. I felt as if I were falling away inside myself. She squeezed my shoulder. "Remember my favorite psalm?"

I managed a tight smile. "How could I forget? You made us learn the whole thing one summer: 'O Lord, you have searched me and you know me,' blah, blah, blah."

Despite my smart-aleck tone, the words took hold, and some of the static in my brain quieted.

"What's the rest?" Dad pressed me.

What was he trying to prove? That I couldn't think straight? I could have told him that. I struggled to form the words.

"You know when I sit and when I rise; you perceive my thoughts from afar. You discern my going out and my lying down; you are familiar with all my ways." Once I got started, I rattled off the verses by rote. In some strange way, the words actually stopped the sensation of falling away inside myself.

"Sounds like there's someone who understands you a lot better than Cameron and Medea. Remember that." Dad stood up and tousled my hair. Then he yawned. "Let's get some sleep."

Mom didn't move. She was still watching me. "How's the hand?"

I rubbed my palm. "Still fine. Weird, huh?" I held it out.

A scar, faint as a white thread, marked the skin where broken glass had cut a deep gash an hour earlier. My heart gave a weird double-thump. What did it mean?

Dad shook his head. "Come on. Bedtime."

Mom hesitated but then stood and gave me a quick kiss on the forehead. "Good night, Jake. We'll talk more tomorrow."

Oh, great. She sure loved talking. I looked at Dad. His

mouth twitched. "I'll get us signed up for some practice space at the fencing club."

Good—he hadn't forgotten his promise. I couldn't make sense of my trip through the portal or the sudden-healing thing, but I knew I wanted to learn to use a sword.

My parents gathered up the pizza stuff and carried it to the kitchen—out of sight but not out of earshot.

"If we hide the portal stones, Cameron and Medea won't be able to go back," Dad said over the crinkling of aluminum foil.

Someone slammed the fridge door shut hard enough to make the salad dressing bottles rattle. "We don't want them running around our world. They don't belong here." Mom sounded tense.

"I know. We have to send them back. But on our terms. Without anything that would hurt the People of the Verses. And what about Jake?"

Silence crackled, and I leaned forward from my spot on the couch.

When Mom refused to answer, Dad spoke again, so quietly that I almost couldn't hear. "We need to keep the portal available in case he's needed there. But how will we know?"

Needed there? Did he really think . . . ?

I waited for them to head back to their bedroom, then slipped down the steps from the kitchen to the basement. Most of the basement was still unfinished—except for my corner bedroom and Dad's workbench.

I hurried into my room and shut out the world behind me. Tonight everything looked different—the movie posters, the bookshelves, the soccer trophy. Smaller, foreign, unfamiliar.

I pulled a thumbtack from my bulletin board and scratched it across my thumb. A line of blood appeared, but in a microsecond the tiny scrape healed completely. I had assumed the healing power was some heebie-jeebie thing that Medea had given me or that had transferred over from my interactions with Kieran.

But now that my head had stopped throbbing, I could put the pieces together. Excitement stronger than caffeine zipped around my nerve endings. My folks thought this was more than a weird effect left over from my travels through the portal. They thought I might be the next Restorer.

About the Author

SHARON HINCK is a wife and mother who has had many adventures on her road with God, though none has involved an alternate universe (thus far). She earned an MA in communication from Regent University in 1986 and spent ten years as the artistic director of a Christian performing arts group, CrossCurrent. That ministry included three short-term mission trips to Hong Kong. At various times she has been a church youth worker, a choreographer and ballet teacher, a homeschool mom, a church organist, and a conference speaker. She is the author of *The Restorer* (NavPress, 2007), *The Secret Life of Becky Miller* (Bethany House, 2006), and *Renovating Becky Miller* (Bethany House, 2007), as well as numerous nonfiction articles, devotions, and essays. In 2007 she was named Writer of the Year at Mount Hermon Christian Writers Conference. She loves to hear from readers, so send a message through the portal into her writing attic on the Contact Sharon page of her website: www.sharonhinck.com.

CHECK OUT THESE OTHER GREAT TITLES FROM THE NAVPRESS FICTION LINE!

The Restorer
Sharon Hinck
ISBN-13: 978-1-60006-131-8
ISBN-10: 1-60006-131-1

Meet Susan, a housewife and soccer mom whose dreams stretch far beyond her ordinary world. While studying the book of Judges, Susan longs to be a modern-day Deborah, a prophet and leader who God used to deliver the ancient nation of Israel from destruction. Susan gets her wish for adventure when she stumbles through a portal into an alternate universe and encounters a nation locked in a fierce struggle for its survival.

The Reluctant Journey of David Connors
Don Locke
ISBN-13: 978-1-60006-152-3
ISBN-10: 1-60006-152-4

Family man David Connors is standing on the brink of suicide. In his darkest moment, he finds an old and mysterious carpetbag buried under a snowy ledge. Soon, what seems like coincidence draws him closer to understanding and healing. As David reaches his journey's conclusion, he gains freedom from a devastating childhood event.

A Crooked Path
Annette Smith
ISBN-13: 978-1-57683-996-6
ISBN-10: 1-57683-996-6

Manny Ortega works at the Eden Plain cattle ranch for cranky, prejudiced Owen Green. Over time Owen and Manny forge a close friendship, but the arrival of Owen's daughter, Chaney, strains their relationship as she and Manny fall in love. Owen's deeply hidden issues involving race and class are revealed, while a tragic accident threatens to shatter any hope of reconciliation.

To order copies, visit your local Christian bookstore, call NavPress at
1-800-366-7788, or log on to www.navpress.com.
To locate a Christian bookstore near you, call 1-800-991-7747.

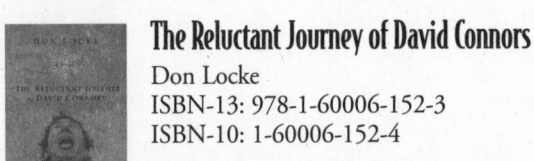

NAVPRESS®